ABRAHAM LINCOLN: VAMPIRE HUNTER

THE NATIONAL BESTSELLER

New York Times
Washington Post
USA Today

Los Angeles Times
Wall Street Journal
Publishers Weekly

**One of the Best Books of the Year by *Kirkus Reviews*
Translated into 15 languages**

"Grahame-Smith is a lively, fluent writer with a sharp sense of tone and pace. And as in *Pride and Prejudice and Zombies*, the mash-up is not as arbitrary as it first seems." —*TIME*

"Thanks to *Pride and Prejudice and Zombies*, a delicious mutant book craze was born. But then opportunists infested the territory...It's nice to see plucky Grahame-Smith retake his turf." —*Entertainment Weekly*

"The setup works brilliantly...Grahame-Smith's ability to serve up moments of real poignancy within a B-horror movie context just might make him something of a Joss Whedon for the niche literary set." —*Los Angeles Times*

"Grahame-Smith's breezy narrative style makes this a quick and easy read guaranteed to tickle the funny bone." —*Booklist*

"The difficult part was creating a believable narrative that wouldn't send readers howling with laughter and tossing the book aside, and darned if Grahame-Smith didn't do it."
—*Chicago Sun-Times*

"Fun to read…Lincoln would have fun with it…I enjoyed it thoroughly."
—Doris Kearns Goodwin, NPR's *On Point*

"A glibly entertaining and engrossing slice of historical revisionism…Grahame-Smith is good at such gruesome, breathless prose, and that's what gives VAMPIRE HUNTER its feverish energy. He's also clever at subverting actual events and rewriting them."
—*Fort Worth Star-Telegram*

"Sure to become a classic."
—*BookPage*

"The book's grotesque joviality should be fun for those looking for it…Not to be missed are Lincoln's trusty companions in his crusade against the undead."
—*Kirkus Reviews*

"Entertaining…[This book] walks a fine line but it walks it well."
—*Las Vegas Review-Journal*

"Superb…Grahame-Smith masterfully weaves fact with fiction…dark, graphic fun."
—HeraldPublications.com

"There's a rich ending worth sinking your teeth into."
—*Los Angeles* magazine

Abraham Lincoln

VAMPIRE HUNTER

SETH GRAHAME-SMITH

GRAND CENTRAL
PUBLISHING

NEW YORK   BOSTON

Copyright © 2010 by Seth Grahame-Smith
Excerpt from *Unholy Night* © 2012 by Seth Grahame-Smith
Cover Art © 2012 Twentieth Century Fox Film Corporation. All rights reserved.

Grand Central Publishing
Hachette Book Group
237 Park Avenue
New York, NY 10017
www.HachetteBookGroup.com

Grand Central Publishing is a division of Hachette Book Group, Inc.
The Grand Central Publishing name and logo is a trademark of Hachette Book Group, Inc.

The Hachette Speakers Bureau provides a wide range of authors for speaking events. To find out more, go to www.hachettespeakers bureau.com or call (866) 376-6591.

The publisher is not responsible for websites (or their content) that are not owned by the publisher.

Printed in the United States of America

Originally published in hardcover by Hachette Book Group
First media tie-in mass market edition: April 2012

10 9 8 7 6 5 4 3 2 1
OPM

ATTENTION CORPORATIONS AND ORGANIZATIONS:
Most HACHETTE BOOK GROUP books are available at quantity discounts with bulk purchase for educational, business, or sales promotional use. For information, please call or write:

Special Markets Department, Hachette Book Group
237 Park Avenue, New York, NY 10017
Telephone: 1-800-222-6747 Fax: 1-800-477-5925

For Erin and Joshua.

CONTENTS

The boundaries which divide
Life from Death are at best shadowy
and vague. Who shall say where the
one ends, and where the other begins?

—*Edgar Allan Poe*

FACTS

1. For over 250 years, between 1607 and 1865, vampires thrived in the shadows of America. Few humans believed in them.

2. Abraham Lincoln was one of the gifted vampire hunters of his day, and kept a secret journal about his lifelong war against them.

3. Rumors of the journal's existence have long been a favorite topic among historians and Lincoln biographers. Most dismiss it as myth.

Introduction

I cannot speak of the things I have seen, nor seek comfort for the pain I feel. If I did, this nation would descend into a deeper kind of madness, or think its president mad. The truth, I am afraid, must live as paper and ink. Hidden and forgotten until every man named here has passed to dust.

—Abraham Lincoln, in a journal entry
December 3rd, 1863

I

I was still bleeding... my hands shaking. As far as I knew, he was still here—watching me. Somewhere, across a vast gulf of space, a television was on. A man was speaking about unity.

None of it mattered.

The books laid out in front of me were the only things now. The ten leather-bound books of varying size—each one a different shade of black or brown. Some merely old and worn. Others barely held together by their cracked covers, with pages that seemed like they'd crumble if turned by anything stronger than a breath. Beside them

was a bundle of letters held tightly by a red rubber band.
Some with burnt edges. Others as yellowed as the cigarette filters scattered on the basement floor below. The
only standout from these antiques was a single sheet of
gleaming white paper. On one side, the names of eleven
people I didn't know. No phone numbers. No e-mail. Just
the addresses of nine men and two women, and a message
scrawled at the bottom of the page:

Expecting you.

Somewhere that man was still speaking. Colonists...
hope... Selma.

The book in my hands was the smallest of the ten, and
easily the most fragile. Its faded brown cover had been
scraped and stained and worn away. The brass buckle that
once kept its secrets safe had long since broken off. Inside,
every square inch of paper was covered with ink—some
of it as dark as the day it dried; some of it so faded that I
could barely make it out. In all, there were 118 double-
sided, handwritten pages clinging to its spine. They were
filled with private longings; theories; strategies; crude
drawings of men with strange faces. They were filled with
secondhand histories and detailed lists. As I read them,
I saw the author's penmanship evolve from the overcau-
tious script of a child to the tightly packed scribbling of a
young man.

I finished reading the last page, looked over my shoulder to make sure I was still alone, and turned back to
the first. I had to read it again. Right now, before reason
turned its dogs on the dangerous beliefs that were beginning to march through my mind.

The little book began with these seven absurd, fascinating words:

This is the Journal of Abraham Lincoln.

———————

Rhinebeck is one of those upstate towns that time forgot. A town where family-owned shops and familiar faces line the streets, and the oldest inn in America (where, as any townie will proudly tell you, General Washington himself once laid his wigless head) still offers its comforts at reasonable prices. It's a town where people give each other homemade quilts and use woodstoves to heat their homes; and where I have witnessed, on more than one occasion, an apple pie cooling on a windowsill. The place belongs in a snow globe.

Like most of Rhinebeck, the five-and-dime on East Market Street is a living piece of a dying past. Since 1946, the locals have depended on it for everything from egg timers to hem tape to pencils to Christmas toys. *If we don't sell it, you don't need it*, boasts the sun-beaten sign in the front window. *And if you need it anyway, we'll order it*. Inside, between checkered linoleum and unflattering fluorescents, you'll find all the sundries of earth bursting, organized by bin. Prices written in grease pencil. Debit cards begrudgingly accepted. This was my home, from eight-thirty in the morning to five-thirty at night. Six days a week. Every week.

I'd always known I'd end up in the store after graduation, just like I had every summer since I was fifteen. I wasn't family in the strictest sense, but Jan and Al had always treated me like one of their kids—giving me a job when I needed it most; throwing me a little pocket money while I was away at school. The way I saw it, I owed them six solid months, June through Christmas. That was the plan. Six months of working in the store by day, and working on my novel nights and weekends. Plenty of time to finish the first draft and give it a good polish. Manhattan was only an hour and a half by train, and that's where I'd go when I was done, with four or five pounds of unsolicited, proofread opportunity under my arm. Goodbye, Hudson Valley. Hello, lecture circuit.

Nine years later I was still in the store.

Somewhere in the middle of getting married, surviving a car accident, having a baby, abandoning my novel, starting and abandoning half a dozen others, having another baby, and trying to stay on top of the bills, something wholly unexpected and depressingly typical happened: I stopped caring about my writing, and started caring about everything else: The kids. The marriage. The mortgage. The store. I seethed at the sight of locals shopping at the CVS down the street. I bought a computer to help track inventory. Mostly, I looked for new ways to bring people through the door. When the used bookstore in Red Hook closed, I bought some of their stock and put a lending shelf in the back. Raffles. Clearance sales. Wi-Fi. Anything to get them through that door. Every year I tried something new. And every year, we barely scraped by.

Henry* had been coming for a year or so before we got around to talking. We'd exchanged the expected pleas-

---

*Not the name he went by at the time. For the sake of consistency, I refer to him by his *actual* name throughout the book, including here.

antries; nothing more. "Have a good one." "See you next time." I only knew his name because I'd heard it through the Market Street grapevine. The story was he'd bought one of the bigger places off of Route 9G, and had an army of local handymen sprucing it up. He was a little younger than me—maybe twenty-seven or so, with messy dark hair, a year-round tan, and a different pair of sunglasses for every occasion. I could tell he was money. His clothes screamed it: vintage T-shirts, wool blazers, jeans that cost more than my car. But he wasn't like the other money that came in. The asshole weekenders who liked to gush about our "cute" little town and our "adorable" little store, walking right past our *No Food or Drink Please* sign with their oversize cups of hazelnut coffee, and never spending a dime. Henry was courteous. Quiet. Best of all, he never left without dropping less than fifty bucks—most of it on the throwbacks you can only pick up in specialty stores these days—bars of Lifebuoy, tins of Angelus Shoe Wax. He came in, paid cash, and left. *Have a good one. See you next time.* And then, one day in the fall of 2007, I looked up from my spiral notebook and there he was. Standing on the other side of the counter—staring at me like I'd just said something revolting.

"Why did you abandon it?"

"I…I'm sorry?"

Henry motioned to the notebook in front of me. I always kept one by the register, in the event that any brilliant ideas or observations popped in (they never did, but semper fi, you know?). Over the last four hours, I'd jotted half a page of one-line story ideas, none of which warranted a second line. The bottom half of the page had descended into a doodle of a tiny man giving the middle finger to a giant, angry eagle with razor-sharp talons. Beneath it, the caption: *To Mock a Killing Bird*. Sadly, this was the best idea I'd had in weeks.

"Your writing. I was curious as to why you abandoned it."

Now it was me staring at him. For whatever reason, I was suddenly struck by the thought of a man carrying a flashlight—rifling through the cobwebbed shelves of a dark warehouse. It wasn't a pleasant thought.

"Sorry, but I don't—"

"Understand, no. No, I apologize. It was rude of me to interrupt you."

Jesus...now I felt compelled to apologize for his apology.

"Not at all. It's just...what gave you—"

"You seemed like someone who writes."

He pointed to the lending shelf in the back.

"You obviously have an appreciation for books. I see you writing here from time to time...I assumed it was a passion. I was just curious as to why you hadn't pursued it."

Reasonable. A little pompous (what, just because I'm working in a five-and-dime, I'm not pursuing my passion?), but reasonable enough to let some of the air back into the room. I gave him the honest, depressingly typical answer, which amounted to "life is what happens while you're busy making other plans." That led to a discussion about John Lennon, which led to a discussion about The Beatles, which led to a discussion about Yoko Ono, which led nowhere. We talked. I asked him how he liked the area. How his house was coming. What kind of work he did. He gave me satisfactory answers to all of these. But even as he did—even as we stood there chatting politely, just a couple of young guys shooting the breeze—I couldn't avoid the feeling that there was another conversation going on. A conversation that I wasn't participating in. I could feel Henry's questions becoming increasingly personal. I could feel my answers doing the same. He asked about my wife. My kids. My writing. He asked about my parents. My regrets. I answered them all. I knew it was strange. I didn't care. I wanted to tell him. This young, rich guy with messy hair and overpriced jeans and dark glasses. This guy whose eyes I'd never seen. Whom I hardly knew. I wanted to tell him everything. It just came out, like he'd dislodged a stone that had been stuck in my mouth for years—a stone that kept all of my secrets held back in a reservoir. Losing my mom when I was a kid. The problems with my dad. Running away. My writing. My doubts. The annoying certainty that there was more than this. Our struggles with money. My struggles with depression. The times I thought about running away. The times I thought about killing myself.

I hardly remember saying half of it. Maybe I didn't.

At some point, I asked Henry to read my unfinished novel. I was appalled by the thought of him or anyone reading it. I was even appalled by the idea of reading it myself. But I asked him anyway.

"No need," he answered.

It was (to that point) the strangest conversation of my life. By the time Henry excused himself and left, I felt like I'd covered ten miles in a flat-out sprint.

It was never that way again. The next time he came in, we exchanged the expected pleasantries; nothing more. *Have a good one. See you next time.* He bought his soap and shoe polish. He paid cash. This went on. He came in less and less.

When Henry came in for the last time, in January of

2008, he carried a small package—wrapped in brown paper and tied up with twine. Without a word, he set it next to the register. His gray sweater and crimson scarf were lightly dusted with snow, and his sunglasses speckled with tiny water droplets. He didn't bother taking them off. This didn't surprise me. There was a white envelope on top of the package with my name written on it—some of the ink had mixed with melting snow and begun to bleed.

I reached under the counter and killed the volume on the little TV I kept there for Yankees games. Today it was tuned to the news. It was the morning of the Iowa primary, and Barack Obama was running neck and neck with Hillary Clinton. Anything to pass the time.

"I would like you to have this."

For a moment, I looked at him like he'd said that in Norwegian.

"Wait, this is for me? What's the—"

"I'm sorry, but I have a car waiting. Read the note first. I'll be in touch."

And that was it. I watched him walk out the door and into the cold, wondering if he ever let *anyone* finish a sentence, or if it was just me.

II

The package sat under the counter for the rest of the day. I was dying to open the damned thing, but since I had no idea who this guy really was, I wasn't about to risk unwrapping a blow-up doll or kilo of black tar heroin at the same moment some Girl Scout decided to walk in. I let my curiosity burn until the streets turned dark and Mrs. Kallop finally settled on the darker of the green yarns (after an excruciating ninety minutes of debate), then locked the doors a few minutes early. To hell with the stragglers tonight. Christmas was over, and it was deadly slow anyway. Besides, everybody was home watching the Obama-Hillary drama play out in Iowa. I decided to sneak a cigarette in the basement before heading home to catch the results. I picked up Henry's gift, killed the fluorescents, and cranked up the TV's speaker. If there was any election news, I'd hear it echoing down the staircase.

There wasn't much to the basement. Other than a few boxes of overflow inventory against the walls, it was a mostly empty room with a filthy concrete floor and a single hanging forty-watt bulb. There was an old metal "tanker" desk against one wall with the inventory computer on it, a two-drawer file cabinet where we kept some records, and a couple of folding chairs. A water heater. A fuse panel. Two small windows that peeked into the alley above. More than anything, it was where I smoked during the cold winter months. I pulled a folding chair up to the desk, lit one, and began to untie the twine at the top of the neatly wrapped—

The letter.

The thought just popped in there, like one of those brilliant ideas or observations I kept the notebook around for. I was supposed to read the letter first. I found the Swiss Army key chain in my pants pocket ($7.20 plus tax—cheaper than you'll find anywhere else in Dutchess County, guaranteed) and opened the envelope with a flick of the wrist. Inside was a single folded piece of gleaming

white paper with a list of names and addresses typed out
on one side. On the other, a handwritten note:

> There are some conditions I must ask you to
> agree to before opening this package:
> First, understand that it is not a gift, but a loan.
> I will, at a time of my choosing, ask you to return
> these items. On that point, I need your solemn
> promise that you will protect them at <u>all</u> <u>cost</u>, and
> treat them with the same care and respect you
> would afford any item of tremendous value.
> Second, the contents of this package are of an
> extremely sensitive nature. I must ask that you
> not share or discuss them with <u>anyone</u> other than
> myself and the eleven individuals listed opposite
> until you have received my permission to do so.
> Third, these items are being lent to you with
> the expectation that you will write a manuscript
> about them, of, let us say, substantial length,
> and subject to my approval. You may take as
> much time as you wish. Upon the satisfactory
> completion of this manuscript, you will be fairly
> compensated.
> If you cannot meet <u>any</u> of these conditions for
> <u>any</u> reason, please stop and wait to be contacted
> by me. However, if you agree, then you may
> proceed.
> I believe it is your purpose to do so.
> —H

Well, shit . . . there was no way I wasn't opening it *now*.
I tore the paper off, uncovering a bundle of letters held

tightly by a red rubber band, and ten leather-bound books. I opened the book at the top of the pile. As I did, a lock of blonde hair fell onto the desk. I picked it up, studied it, and twirled it in my fingers as I read a random sliver from the pages it'd been pressed between:

> …wish I could but vanish from this earth, for there is no love left in it. She has been taken from me, and with her, all hope of a…

I skimmed through the rest of the first book, spellbound. Somewhere upstairs, a woman was listing off the names of counties. Pages and pages—every inch filled with tightly packed handwriting. With dates like November 6th, 1835; June 3rd, 1841. With drawings and lists. With names like Speed, Berry, and Salem. With a word that kept showing up, over and over:

Vampire.

The other books were the same. Only the dates and penmanship changed. I skimmed them all.

> …there that I saw, for the first time, men and children sold as…precautions, for we knew that Baltimore was teeming with…was a sin I could not forgive. I was forced to demote the…

Two things were obvious: they were all written by the same person, and they were all very, very old. Beyond that, I had no idea what they were, or what would've compelled Henry to lend them to me. And then I came across the first page of the first book, and those seven absurd words: *This is the Journal of Abraham Lincoln*. I laughed out loud.

It all made sense. I was amazed. Completely, kicked-in-the-teeth amazed. Not because I was holding the Great Emancipator's long-lost journal in my hands, but because I had so thoroughly misjudged a man. I'd taken Henry's quietness to mean he was reclusive. I'd taken his fleeting interest in my life to mean he was outgoing. But now it was obvious. The dude was clearly out of his mind. Either that, or messing with mine. Playing some kind of hoax—the kind that rich guys with too much time on their hands play. But then, it couldn't be a hoax, could it? Who would go through this much trouble? Or was it—was this Henry's *own* abandoned novel? An elaborately packaged writing project? Now I felt terrible. Yes. Yes, of *course* that's what it was. I looked through the books again, expecting to see little hints of the twenty-first century. Little cracks in the armor. There weren't any—at least as far as I could tell on first glance. Besides, something kept nagging at me: if this was a pet writing project, why the eleven names and addresses? Why had Henry asked me to write *about* the books, instead of asking me to *rewrite* them? The needle began to lean toward "crazy" again. Was it possible? Did he really believe that these ten little books were the—no, he couldn't possibly believe that. Right?

I couldn't wait to tell my wife. Couldn't wait to share the sheer insanity of this with someone else. In a long line of small town psychos, this guy took the cake. I stood, gathered the books and letters, crushed the cigarette under my heel, and turned to—

Something was standing six inches from me.

I staggered backward and tripped over the folding

chair, falling and banging the back of my head against the corner of the old tanker desk. My eyes were thrown out of focus. I could already feel the warmth of the blood running through my hair. Something leaned over me. Its eyes were a pair of black marbles. Its skin a translucent collage of pulsing blue veins. And its mouth—its mouth could barely contain its wet, glassy fangs.

It was Henry.

"I'm not going to hurt you," he said. "I just need you to understand."

He lifted me off the ground by my collar. I could feel the blood running down the back of my neck.

I fainted.

Have a good one. See you next time.

III

I've been instructed not to get into the specifics of where Henry took me that night, or what he showed me. Suffice it to say it made me physically ill. Not from any horrors I may have witnessed, but from the guilt that I'd been a party to them, willing or not.

I was with him for less than an hour. In that short time, my understanding of the world was torn down to its foundation. The way I thought about death, and space, and God...all irrevocably changed. In that short time, I came to believe—in no uncertain terms—something that would've sounded insane only an hour before:

Vampires exist.

I didn't sleep for a week—first from terror, then excitement. I stayed late at the store every night, poring over

Abraham Lincoln's books and letters. Checking their incredible claims against the hard "facts" of heralded Lincoln biographies. I papered the basement walls with printouts of old photographs. Time lines. Family trees. I wrote into the early morning hours.

For the first two months, my wife was concerned. For the second two she was suspicious. By the sixth month we'd separated. I feared for my safety. My children's safety. My sanity. I had so many questions, but Henry was nowhere to be found. Eventually I worked up the courage to interview the eleven "individuals" on his list. Some were merely reluctant. Others hostile. But with their help (begrudging as it was), I slowly began to stitch together the hidden history of vampires in America. Their role in the birth, growth, and near death of our nation. And the one man who saved that nation from their tyranny.

For some seventeen months, I sacrificed everything for those ten leather-bound books. That bundle of letters held tightly by a red rubber band. In some ways they were the best months of my life. Every morning, I woke up on that inflatable mattress in the store basement with a purpose. With the knowledge that I was doing something truly important, even if I was doing it completely, desperately alone. Even if I'd lost my mind.

Vampires exist. And Abraham Lincoln was one of the greatest vampire hunters of his age. His journal— beginning in his twelfth year and continuing to the day of his assassination—is an altogether astonishing, heart-breaking, and revolutionary document. One that casts new light on many of the seminal events in American history and adds immeasurable complexity to a man already thought to be unusually complex.

There are more than 15,000 books about Lincoln. His childhood. His mental health. His sexuality. His views on race, religion, and litigation. Most of them contain a great deal of truth. Some have even hinted at the existence of a "secret diary" and an "obsession with the occult." Yet not *one* of them contains a single word concerning the central struggle of his life. A struggle that eventually spilled onto the battlefields of the Civil War.

It turns out that the towering myth of Honest Abe, the one ingrained in our earliest grade school memories, is inherently dishonest. Nothing more than a patchwork of half-truths and omissions.

What follows nearly ruined my life.

What follows, at last, is the truth.

> —*Seth Grahame-Smith*
> *Rhinebeck, New York*
> *January 2010*

— Part I —

BOY

One

Exceptional Child

In this sad world of ours, sorrow comes to all;
and, to the young, it comes with bitterest agony,
because it takes them unawares.

—*Abraham Lincoln, in a letter to Fanny McCullogh*
December 23rd, 1862

I

The boy had been crouched so long that his legs had
fallen asleep beneath him—but he dared not move now.
For here, in a small clearing in the frostbitten forest, were
the creatures he had waited so long to see. The creatures
he'd been sent to kill. He bit down on his lip to keep his
teeth from chattering, and aimed his father's flintlock rifle
exactly as he'd been taught. *The body*, he remembered.
The body, not the neck. Quietly, carefully he pulled the
hammer back and pointed the barrel at his target, a large
male who'd fallen behind the others. Decades later, the
boy would recall what happened next.

> I hesitated. Not out of a conflict of conscience,
> but for the fear that my rifle had gotten too wet,
> and thus wouldn't fire. However, this fear proved
> unfounded, for when I pulled the trigger, the
> stock hit my shoulder with such force as to knock
> me clean onto my back.

Turkeys scattered in every direction as Abraham Lincoln, seven years old, picked himself off the snow-covered ground. Rising to his feet, he brought his fingers to the strange warmth he felt on his chin. "I'd bitten my lip clean through," he wrote. "But I hardly gave a holler. I was desperate to know if I had hit the poor devil or not."

He had. The large male flapped its wings wildly, pushing itself through the snow in small circles. Abe watched from a distance, "afraid it might somehow rise up and tear me to pieces." The flapping of wings; the dragging of feathers through snow. These were the only sounds in the world. They were joined by the crunching beneath Abe's feet as he found his nerve and approached. The wings beat less forcefully now.

It was dying.

He had shot it clean through the neck. The head hung at an unnatural angle—dragged across the ground as the bird continued to thrash. *The body, not the neck.* With every beat of its heart, blood poured from the wound and onto the snow, where it mixed with the dark droplets from Abe's bleeding lip and the tears that had already begun to fall down his face.

> It gasped for breath, but could draw none,
> and its eyes wore a kind of fear I had never seen.

I stood over the miserable bird for what seemed
a twelvemonth, pleading with God to make its
wings fall silent. Begging His forgiveness for so
injuring a creature that had shown me no malice;
presented no threat to my person or prosperity.
Finally it was still, and, plucking up my courage,
I dragged it through a mile of forest and laid it
at my mother's feet—my head hung low so as to
hide my tears.

Abraham Lincoln would never take another life. And
yet he would become one of the greatest killers of the
nineteenth century.

The grieving boy didn't sleep a wink that night. "I
could think only of the injustice I had done another living
thing, and the fear I had seen in its eyes as the promise of
life slipped away." Abe refused to eat any part of his kill,
and lived on little more than bread as his mother, father,
and older sister picked the carcass clean over the next two
weeks. There is no record of their reaction to this hunger
strike, but it must have been seen as eccentric. After all,
to willingly go without food, as a matter of principle, was
a remarkable choice for anyone in those days—particularly a boy who had been born and raised on America's
frontier.

But then, Abe Lincoln had always been different.

America was still in its infancy when the future president was born on February 12th, 1809—a mere thirty-three
years after the signing of the Declaration of Independence.
Many of the giants of the American Revolution—Robert
Treat Paine, Benjamin Rush, and Samuel Chase—were
still alive. John Adams and Thomas Jefferson wouldn't

resume their tumultuous friendship for another three years, and wouldn't die for another seventeen—incredibly, on the same day. The Fourth of July.

Those first American decades were ones of seemingly limitless growth and opportunity. By the time Abe Lincoln was born, residents of Boston and Philadelphia had seen their cities double in size in less than twenty years. New York's population had tripled in the same amount of time. The cities were becoming livelier, more prosperous. "For every farmer, there are two haberdashers; for every blacksmith, an opera house," joked Washington Irving in his New York periodical, *Salmagundi*.

But as the cities became more crowded, they became more dangerous. Like their counterparts in London, Paris, and Rome, America's city dwellers had come to expect a certain amount of crime. Theft was by far the most common offense. With no fingerprints on file or cameras to fear, thieves were limited only by their conscience and cunning. Muggings hardly warranted a mention in the local papers, unless the victim was a person of note.

There's a story of an elderly widow named Agnes Pendel Brown, who lived with her longtime butler (nearly as old as she, and deaf as a stone) in a three-story brick mansion on Amsterdam Avenue. On December 2nd, 1799, Agnes and her butler turned in for the night—he on the first floor, she on the third. When they awoke the next morning, every piece of furniture, every work of art, every gown, serving dish, and candlestick holder (candles included) was gone. The only things the light-footed burglars left were the beds in which Agnes and her butler slept.

There was also the occasional murder. Before the

Revolutionary War, homicides had been exceedingly rare in America's cities (it's impossible to provide exact numbers, but a review of three Boston newspapers between 1775 and 1780 yields mention of only eleven cases, ten of which were promptly solved). Most of these were so-called honor killings, such as duels or family squabbles. In most cases, no charges were brought. The laws of the early nineteenth century were vague and, with no regular police force to speak of, loosely enforced. It's worth noting that killing a slave was not considered murder, no matter the circumstances. It was merely "destruction of property."

Immediately after America won its independence, something strange began to happen. The murder rate in its cities started to rise dramatically, almost overnight. Unlike the honor killings of years past, these murders seemed random; senseless. Between 1802 and 1807, there were an incredible 204 unsolved homicides in New York City alone. Homicides with no witnesses, no motive, and often no discernible cause of death. Because the investigators (most of whom were untrained volunteers) kept no records, the only surviving clues come from a handful of faded newspaper articles. One in particular, from the *New York Spectator*, captures the panic that had enveloped the city by July of 1806.

A Mr. Stokes, of 210 Tenth Street, happen'd upon the poor Victim, a mulatto Woman, whilst on his morning constitutional. The Gentleman remark'd that her eyes were wide open, and her body quite stiff, as if dry'd in the sun. A Constable by name of McLeay

inform'd me that no blood was found near
the unfortunate soul, nor on her garments,
and that her only wound was a small score
on the wrist. She is the forty-second to meet
such an end this year. The Honorable Dewitt
Clinton, Mayor, respectfully advizes the good
citizenry to prolong their vigilance until the
answerable scoundrel is captur'd. Women and
Children are urg'd to walk with a Gentleman
companion, and Gentlemen are urg'd to walk
in pairs after dark.

The scene was eerily similar to a dozen others reported
that summer. No trauma. No blood. Open eyes and rigid
body. The face a mask of terror. A pattern emerged among
the victims: they were free blacks, vagrants, prostitutes,
travelers, and the mentally impaired—people with little
or no connection to the city, no family, and whose murders were unlikely to incite angry mobs seeking justice.
And New York was hardly alone in its troubles. Similar
articles filled the papers of Boston and Philadelphia that
summer, and similar rumors filled the mouths of their
panicked populations. There was talk of shadowy mad-
men. Of foreign spies.

There was even talk of vampires.

II

Sinking Springs Farm was about as far from New York
City as one could get in early nineteenth-century America. Despite its name, the 300-acre "farm" was mostly
heavily wooded land—and its rocky eastern Kentucky

soil made the prospects of bumper crops unlikely at best. Thomas Lincoln, thirty-one years old, had acquired it for a $200 promissory note in the months before Abe was born. A carpenter by trade, Thomas hastily built a one-room cabin on his new land. It measured all of eighteen by twenty feet, with a hard dirt floor that was cold to the touch year-round. When it rained, water leaked through the roof in bucketfuls. When the wind howled, drafts forced their way through countless cracks in the walls. It was in these humble circumstances, on an unseasonably mild Sunday morning, that the sixteenth president of the United States came into the world. It's said that he didn't cry when he was born, but that he merely stared at his mother, quizzically, and then smiled at her.

Abe would have no memory of Sinking Springs. When he was two, a dispute arose over the deed to the land, so Thomas moved his family ten miles north, to the smaller, more fertile Knob Creek Farm. Despite the much-improved soil, Thomas—who could have made a comfortable living selling corn and grain to nearby settlers—plowed less than an acre of land.

> He was an illiterate, indolent man who could not so much as sign his name until instructed by my mother. He had not a scrap of ambition in him…not the slightest interest in bettering his circumstances, or in providing for his family beyond the barest necessities. He never planted a single row more than was needed to keep our bellies from aching, or sought a single penny more than was needed to keep the simplest clothes on our backs.

It was an unduly harsh assessment, written by a forty-one-year-old Abe on the day of his father's funeral (which he had chosen not to attend, and perhaps felt a pang of guilt over). While no one would ever accuse Thomas Lincoln of being "driven," he seems to have been a reliable, if not bountiful, provider. That he never abandoned his family in times of desperate hardship and grief, or abandoned the frontier for the comforts of city life (as many of his contemporaries did), speaks to his character. And while he didn't always understand or approve of his son's pursuits, he always permitted them (eventually). However, Abe would never be able to forgive him for the tragedy that would transform both of their lives.

Typical of the times, Thomas Lincoln's life had been one of continual struggle and frequent tragedy. Born in 1778, he moved from Virginia to Kentucky with his father, Abraham, and mother, Bathsheba, while still a child. When he was eight, Thomas saw his father murdered before his eyes. It was spring, and Abraham Sr. was busy clearing land to be planted, "when he was waylaid by a party of Shawnee savages." Thomas watched, helpless, as his father was bludgeoned to death—his throat cut and scalp taken. What (if anything) provoked the attack, or why his own life was spared, he couldn't say. Whatever the reasons, life was never the same for Thomas Lincoln. With no inheritance, he was left to wander from town to town, toiling in an endless series of odd jobs. He apprenticed with a carpenter, served as a prison guard, and rode flatboats on the Mississippi and Sangamon Rivers. He felled trees, plowed fields, and attended church when he could. There is no evidence that he ever set foot in a schoolhouse.

This wholly unremarkable life would have surely escaped the notice of history had Thomas not ventured into Elizabethtown one day when he was twenty-eight and, by chance, laid eyes on the young daughter of a Kentucky farmer. Their marriage, on June 12th, 1806, would change the shape of history in ways neither could have dreamed.

By all accounts, Nancy Hanks was a bright, gentle, and handsome woman who had a "remarkable" way with words (but seldom spoke among new acquaintances on account of painful shyness). She was literate, having enjoyed the formal education that her son never would. Nancy was a resourceful woman, and though books were hard to come by in the Kentucky wilderness, she always managed to have at least one borrowed or begged tome around for those rare moments when all the work of the day was done. Beginning when he was barely more than an infant, she would read Abe anything she could get her hands on: Voltaire's *Candide*, Defoe's *Robinson Crusoe*, the poetry of Keats and Byron. But it was the Bible that young Abraham loved above all others. The attentive toddler would sit on her lap, thrilling to the larger-than-life stories of the Old Testament: David and Goliath, Noah's ark, the plagues of Egypt. He was especially fascinated by the tale of Job, the righteous man who had everything taken from him, every curse, sorrow, and betrayal leveled at him, yet continued to love and praise God. "He might have been a priest," a childhood friend would write years later in an election pamphlet, "if life had been kinder to him."

Knob Creek Farm was about as tough a place to live as one could find in the early 1800s. In the spring, frequent thunderstorms flooded the creek and turned crops into fields of waist-deep mud. In the winter, all color drained from the frozen landscape, and the trees became twisted fingers rattling against each other in the wind. It was here that Abe would experience many of his earliest memories: chasing his older sister, Sarah, through acres of blue ash and shagbark hickory; clinging to the back of a pony for a gentle summer ride; splitting kindling with a small ax beside his father. It was also here that he would experience the first of many devastating losses in his life.

When Abe was three, Nancy Lincoln gave birth to a boy christened Thomas, like his father. Sons were a double blessing to frontier families, and the elder Thomas no doubt looked to the day when he would have two able-bodied boys to share the work with. But those dreams were short-lived. The baby died just shy of a month old. Abe would write about it twenty years later, before he had lived to bury two of his own sons.

> As for my own grief, I do not recall. I was perhaps too young to comprehend the meaning or irrevocability of it. However, I will never forget my mother and father's torment. To describe it would be an exercise in futility. It is the sort of suffering that cannot be done justice with words. I can say only this—that I suspect it is an anguish from which one never recovers. A walking death.

It's impossible to know what killed Thomas Lincoln Jr. The common causes ranged from dehydration, to pneumonia, to low birth weight. Congenital and chromosomal abnormalities were more than a century away from being understood or diagnosed. Even under the best conditions, the infant mortality rate was 10 percent in the early 1800s.

The elder Thomas built a small coffin and buried his son near the cabin. No grave marker remains. Nancy pulled herself together and doted on her remaining children—especially Abe. She encouraged his insatiable curiosity, his innate love of learning stories, names, and facts and reciting them again and again. Over her husband's objections, she began to teach Abe how to read and write before his fifth birthday. "Father had no use for books," he recalled years later, "short of burning them when the firewood got wet." Though there is no record of her feelings, Nancy Lincoln must have sensed that her son was gifted. Certainly she was determined to see him go on to better things than she or her husband could.

The Old Cumberland Trail ran directly through Knob Creek Farm. It was a highway of sorts, the main route between Louisville and Nashville, and characters of every stripe passed in both directions daily. Five-year-old Abe would sit on a fence rail for hours at a time, laughing at the molasses wagon driver who always made a show of cursing his mules, or waving at the post rider as he galloped by on horseback. Occasionally he saw slaves being taken to auction.

> I recall seeing a horse cart pass, filled with Negroes. There were several. All women, and of varying age. They were…shackled at the wrist and chained together on the cart bed, without so much as a handful of loose hay to comfort the bumps of the road, or a blanket to relieve them from the winter air. The drivers,

> naturally, sat on the cushioned bench in front,
> each of them wrapped in wool. My eyes met
> those of the youngest Negro girl, who was close
> in age to myself. Perhaps five or six. I admit that
> I could not look at her more than a moment
> before turning away—such was the sorrow of her
> countenance.

As a Baptist, Thomas Lincoln had been raised to believe that slavery was a sin. It was one of the few lasting contributions he would make to his son's character.

Knob Creek became a place where weary travelers on the Old Cumberland Trail could spend the night. Sarah would make up a bed for each guest in one of the outbuildings (the farm consisted of a cabin, a storage shed, and a barn), and Nancy would serve a hot meal at sundown. The Lincolns never asked their overnight guests for payment, though most made contributions, either in money or, more often, in goods such as grain, sugar, and tobacco. After supper, the women would retire, and the men would pass the evening sipping whiskey and puffing pipes. Abe would lie awake in his bed in the loft above, listening to his father entertain their guests with a seemingly limitless reserve of stories, thrilling tales of the early settlers and the Revolutionary War, humorous anecdotes and allegories, and true (or partly true) stories from his own wandering days.

> Father may have been wanting in some things,
> but here he was masterful. Night upon night, I
> marveled at his power to hold listeners in rapt
> attention. He could tell a story with such detail,

such flourish, that afterwards a man would swear
that it had been his own memory, and not a
tale at all. I would...fight off sleep till well past
midnight, trying to remember every word, and
trying to fathom a way to tell the same story
to my young friends in a manner they would
understand.

Like his father, Abe had a natural gift for storytelling
and would grow to master the art. His ability to commu-
nicate—to boil complex ideas down to simple, colorful
parables—would be a powerful asset in later political life.

Travelers were expected to relay any news from the
outside world. Most simply retold stories from the newspapers of Louisville or Nashville, or repeated gossip
picked up along the road. "It was common to hear of the
same drunk falling into the same ditch three times in a
week, in three different voices." Every so often, however,
a traveler would arrive bearing stories of a different sort.
Abe recalled trembling beneath his covers one night as a
French immigrant described the madness of Paris in the
1780s.

The people had taken to calling it *la ville des
morts*, the Frenchman said. *The City of Death.*
Every night brought new screams, and every
morning, new pale, wide-eyed bodies in the
streets, or bloated victims fished from the sewers, which often ran red. They were the remains
of men, women, children. They were innocent
victims with no common bonds beyond their
poverty, and there was nary a person in France

who had any doubt as to the identity of their
murderers. "It was *les vampires!*" he said. "We
had seen them with our own eyes!" Vampires,
he told us, had been the "quiet curse" of Paris
for centuries. But now, with so much famine and
disease…so many poor beggars packed tightly in
the slums…they were growing ever bolder. Ever
hungrier. "Yet Louis did nothing! He and his
aristocrates pompeux did nothing while vampires
feasted upon his starving subjects, until finally
his subjects would tolerate no more."

Naturally, the Frenchman's story, like all vampire stories, was considered folly, a myth concocted to frighten
children. Still, Abe found them endlessly fascinating.
He spent hours dreaming up his own tales of "winged
immortals," their "white fangs stained with blood, waiting in the darkness for the next unfortunate soul to wander their way." He thrilled in testing their effectiveness on
his sister, who "frightened easier than a field mouse, but
thought it was good fun nonetheless."

Thomas, on the other hand, was quick to scold Abe if
he caught him spinning vampire yarns. Such stories were
"childish nonsense" and had no place in polite conversation.

III

In 1816, another land dispute brought an end to the Lincolns' time at Knob Creek. Ownership was a murky concept on the frontier, with multiple deeds often issued for
the same property, and records mysteriously appearing

or disappearing (depending on the nature of the bribe). Rather than face a costly legal battle, Thomas uprooted his family for the second time in Abe's seven years, leading them west across the Ohio River and into Indiana. There, having apparently learned nothing from his previous land disputes, Thomas simply helped himself to a 160-acre plot of land in a heavily wooded settlement known as Little Pigeon Creek, near present-day Gentryville. The decision to leave Kentucky was both a practical and moral one. Practical, because there was plenty of cheap land to be had after the Indians were driven out following the War of 1812. Moral, because Thomas was an abolitionist, and Indiana was a free territory.

Compared to the farms at Sinking Springs and Knob Creek, the Lincolns' new homestead was truly untamed—surrounded by an "unbroken wilderness," where bears and bobcats roamed without boundaries or fear of man. Their first months were spent in a hastily constructed lean-to barely big enough for four people and open to the elements on one side. The biting cold of that first Indiana winter must have been unbearable.

Little Pigeon Creek was remote, but hardly lonely. There were eight or nine families less than a mile from the Lincolns' home, many of them fellow Kentuckians. "More than a dozen boys my age lived within a short walk. We...formed a militia, and waged a campaign of mischief that is still spoken of in southern Indiana." But the growing community was more than a repository for boisterous children. As was often the case on the frontier, families pooled their resources and talents to increase their chances of survival, planting and harvesting crops together, trading goods and labor, and lending a hand in times of illness or hardship. Considered the best carpenter in the area, Thomas rarely wanted for work. One of his first contributions was a tiny one-room schoolhouse, which Abe would attend infrequently in the coming years. During his first presidential campaign, he would write a brief autobiography, in which he admitted that the sum of his schooling amounted to "less than a year altogether." Even so, it was obvious to at least one of those early teachers, Azel Waters Dorsey, that Abraham Lincoln was "an exceptional child."

Following Abe's fateful turkey encounter, he announced that he would no longer hunt game. As punishment, Thomas put him to work splitting wood—thinking the physical toll would force him to reconsider. Though Abe could barely lift the blade higher than his waist, he spent hour after hour clumsily splitting and stacking logs.

> It got to be that I could hardly tell where the ax stopped and my arm began. After a while, the handle would simply slip through my fingers, and my arms would hang at my sides like a pair of curtains. If Father saw me resting thus, he would cuss up a cyclone, take the ax from the ground, and split a dozen logs in a minute to shame me into working again. I kept at it, though, and with each passing day, my arms grew a little stronger.

Soon, Abe could split more logs in a minute than his father.

Two years had passed since those first months in the lean-to. The family now lived in a small, sturdy cabin

Fig.23A. - Young Abe writes in his journal by firelight, accompanied by some of his early vampire-hunting tools.

with a stone fireplace, shingled roof, and raised wooden floor that stayed warm and dry in winter. As always, Thomas worked just enough to keep them clothed and fed. Nancy's great-aunt and great-uncle Tom and Elizabeth Sparrow had come from Kentucky to live in one of the outbuildings and help out around the farm. Things were good. "I have since learned to distrust such stillness," Abe wrote in 1852, "as it is always, always prelude to some great calamity."

One September night in 1818, Abe awoke with a start. He sat straight up in his bed and shielded his face with his hands, as if someone had been standing over him, threatening to bring a club down on his head. No one did. Realizing the danger was imagined, he lowered his hands, caught his breath, and looked around. Everyone was asleep. Judging by the embers in the fireplace, it was two or three in the morning.

Abe ventured outside wearing nothing but his sleeping gown, despite the early arrival of autumn. He walked toward the silhouette of the outhouse, still half asleep, closed the door behind him, and sat. As his eyes adjusted, the moonlight coming in though the planks suddenly seemed bright enough to read by. With no book to pass the time, Abe ran his hands through the tiny shafts of light, examining the patterns they made on his fingers.

Someone was talking outside.

Abe held his breath as the footfalls of two men grew closer, then stopped. *They're in front of the cabin.* One spoke in an angry whisper. Though he couldn't make out the words, Abe knew the voice didn't belong to anyone in Little Pigeon Creek. "The accent was English, and the pitch uncommonly high." The stranger ranted for a moment, then paused, waiting for an answer. It came. This time, the voice was very familiar. It belonged to Thomas Lincoln.

> I pressed my eye to one of the spaces between
> the planks. It was indeed Father, and he was with
> someone I had never seen before. This stranger
> was a squat figure of a man, clad in finer attire
> than I had ever seen. He was missing his right
> arm below the elbow—the sleeve neatly pinned to
> his shoulder. Father, though easily the larger of
> the two, seemed to cower before this companion.

Abe struggled to make out their conversation, but they were too far away. He watched, trying his best to read their gestures, their lips, until...

Father, suddenly mindful of waking us, urged his companion away from the cabin. I held my breath as they drew closer, certain that I would be revealed by the hammering of my heart. They stopped not four yards from where I sat. It was in this manner that I overheard the last of the argument. "I cannot," said Father. The stranger stood in silence and disappointment.

Finally he gave his reply. "Then I'll take it in other ways."

IV

Tom and Elizabeth Sparrow were dying. For three days and nights, Nancy nursed her great-aunt and great-uncle through scorching fevers, delusions, and cramps so severe they made the six-foot Tom weep like a child. Abe and Sarah stuck close to their mother, helping her keep the compresses wet and the bedding clean, and praying with her for a miraculous recovery that they all knew, deep down, wouldn't come. The old folks had seen this before. They called it "the milk sick," a slow poisoning brought on by drinking tainted milk. It was untreatable and fatal. Abe had never watched someone die before, and he hoped that God would forgive him for being slightly curious to see it happen.

He hadn't dared confront his father about what he'd seen and heard a week earlier. Thomas had been especially distant (and largely absent) since that night, and seemed to want no part of the vigil taking place at Tom and Elizabeth's bedside.

They died in quick succession—he first, she a few hours later. Abe was secretly disappointed. He'd half expected a last desperate gasp for breath, or a touching soliloquy, as in the books he was now reading to himself at night. Instead, Tom and Elizabeth simply fell into a coma, lay still for several hours, and died. Thomas Lincoln, without so much as a word of condolence to his wife, set about fashioning a pair of coffins from planks and wooden pegs the next morning. The Sparrows were in the ground by supper.

> Father had never been particularly fond of Aunt and Uncle, and they were hardly the first relations he had buried. Yet I had never known him to be so quiet. He seemed lost in thought. Uneasy.

Four days later, Nancy Lincoln began to feel ill. At first, she insisted it was nothing more than a headache, no doubt brought on by the stress of Tom and Elizabeth's death. Nevertheless, Thomas sent for the nearest doctor, who lived thirty miles away. By the time he arrived, just before sunrise the next morning, Nancy was delusional with fever.

> My sister and I knelt at her side, trembling from fear and want of sleep. Father sat on a nearby chair as the doctor examined her. I knew that she was dying. I knew that God was punishing me. Punishing me for my curiosity over Aunt and Uncle's death. Punishing me for killing a creature that had shown me no malice. I alone was responsible. When the doctor was

finished, he asked for a word with Father outside. When they returned, Father could not help his tears. None of us could.

That night, Abe sat alone by his mother's side. Sarah had fallen asleep next to the fire, and Thomas had nodded off in his chair for the moment. Nancy had finally fallen into a coma. She'd been screaming for hours—first from the delusions, and then from the pain. At one point, Thomas and the doctor had restrained her while she shrieked about "looking the devil in the eyes."

Abe took the compress off her forehead and dipped it in the water bowl by his feet. He'd have to light another candle soon. The one by her bedside was beginning to flicker. As he lifted the compress and wrung it out, a hand seized his wrist.

"My baby boy," whispered Nancy.

The transformation was total. Her face was calm, her voice gentle and even. There was something of a light in her eyes again. My heart leapt. This could only be the miracle I had so earnestly prayed for. She looked at me and smiled. "My baby boy," she whispered again. "Live." Tears began to run down my cheeks. I wondered if this was just some cruel dream. "Mama?" I asked. "Live," she repeated. I wept. God had forgiven me. God had given her back to me. She smiled again. I felt her hand slip from my wrist, and I watched her eyes close. "Mama?" Once more, this time barely above a whisper, she repeated, "Live." She never opened her eyes again.

Nancy Hanks Lincoln died on October 5th, 1818, age thirty-four. Thomas buried her on a hillside behind the cabin.

Abe was alone in the world.

His mother had been his soul mate. She had shown him love and encouragement since the day he was born. She had read to him all those nights, always holding the book in her left hand and gently twirling a finger through his dark hair with the right as he fell asleep on her lap. Hers had been the first face to greet him when he entered the world. He hadn't cried. He had simply looked at her and smiled. She was love, and light. And she was gone. Abe wept for her.

No sooner was she buried than Abe resolved to run away. The thought of staying in Little Pigeon Creek with his eleven-year-old sister and grief-stricken father was more than he could bear. Before his mother was thirty-six hours dead, Abe Lincoln, nine years old, trudged through the Indiana wilderness, carrying all of his meager possessions in a wool blanket. His plan was brilliantly simple. He would walk as far as the Ohio River. There, he would beg his way onto a flatboat and float down to the lower Mississippi, then into New Orleans, where he'd be able to stow away on any number of ships. Perhaps he'd find his way to New York or Boston. Perhaps he'd sail to Europe, to see the immortal cathedrals and castles he'd often imagined.

If there was a flaw in his plan, it was his time of departure. Abe chose to leave home in the afternoon, and by the time he'd put four miles behind him, the short winter day was fading to darkness. Surrounded by untamed wilderness, with nothing more than a wool blanket and

FIG.12-B. - YOUNG ABE STANDS OVER HIS MOTHER'S GRAVE IN AN EARLY 1900'S ENGRAVING TITLED 'A PLEDGE OF VENGEANCE '.

a handful of food to his name, Abe stopped, sat against a tree, and sobbed. He was alone in the dark, and he was homesick for a place that no longer existed. He longed for his mother. He longed to feel his sister's hair against his face as he wept on her shoulder. To his surprise, he even found himself longing for his father's embrace.

There was a faint cry in the night—a long, animal cry that echoed all around me. I thought at once of the bears that our neighbor Reuben Grigsby had spotted near the creek not two days before, and felt like a rube for leaving home without so much as a knife. There was another cry, and another. They seemed to move all around me, and the more I heard, the more obvious it became that no bear, or panther, or animal was making them. They had a different sound. A human sound. All at once I realized what I was hearing. Without bothering to take my belongings, I jumped up and ran toward home as fast as my feet would carry me.

They were screams.

Two

———◆———

Two Stories

And having thus chosen our course, without guile, and with pure purpose, let us renew our trust in God, and go forward without fear, and with manly hearts.

—*Abraham Lincoln, in an address to Congress*
July 4th, 1861

I

If Thomas Lincoln ever tried to comfort his children in the wake of their mother's death—if he ever asked them how they felt, or shared his own grief—there is no record of it. He seems to have spent the months after her burial in near-total silence. Waking before dawn. Boiling his coffee. Picking at his breakfast. Working till nightfall, and (more often than not) drinking himself into a stupor. A short grace at supper was often the only time Abe and Sarah heard his voice.

Be present at our table, Lord—
Be here and everywhere adored.

> Thy mercies bless and grant that we—
> May strengthened for thy service be.

But for all his faults, Thomas Lincoln had what the old-timers called "horse sense." He knew that his situation was untenable. He knew that he couldn't keep his family going alone.

In the winter of 1819, just over a year after Nancy's death, Thomas abruptly announced that he would be leaving for "two weeks or three"—and that when he returned, the children would have a new mother.

> This took us quite by surprise, for we had
> scarcely heard him utter a word for the better of
> a year, and were unaware that he had any such
> designs. Whether he had any particular woman in
> mind, he did not say. I wondered if he meant to
> take an advertisement in the *Gazette*, or simply
> wander the streets of Louisville proposing to
> any unaccompanied lady who walked his way.
> Neither, I admit, would have surprised me much.

Unbeknownst to Abe and Sarah, Thomas did have someone particular in mind, a recently widowed acquaintance in Elizabethtown (the very place he'd first laid eyes on his Nancy some thirteen years before). He meant to show up on her doorstep unannounced, propose marriage, and bring her back to Little Pigeon Creek. That was it. That was the extent of his plan.

For Thomas, the trip marked an end to his silent grieving. For nine-year-old Abe and eleven-year-old Sarah, it marked the first time they'd ever been left alone.

At night we left a candle burning in the
center of the room, hid beneath our covers, and
barricaded the door with father's bed. I know
not what we meant to protect ourselves from,
only that we felt better for having done it. We
remained this way well into the night, listening to
the noises that came from all around us. Animal
noises. Far-off voices carried on the wind. The
cracking of twigs as something walked around the
cabin. We shivered in our beds until the candle
finally died, then fought in whispers over who
would leave the safety of their covers and light
the next. When father returned, we were each
given a good thrashing for having burned through
so many candles in such a short time.

Thomas was true to his word. When he returned, he
was accompanied by a wagon. In it were all the earthly
possessions (or at least, the ones that would fit) of the
newly minted Sarah Bush Lincoln and her three children:
Elizabeth, thirteen; Matilda, ten; and John, nine. For Abe
and his sister, the sight of a wagon brimming with furniture, clocks, and tableware was akin to beholding "the
treasures of the maharaja." For the new Mrs. Lincoln, the
sight of these barefoot, dirt-covered frontier children was
equally shocking. They were stripped down and scrubbed
thoroughly that very night.

There were no two ways about it—Sarah Bush Lincoln was a plain woman. She had sunken eyes and a narrow face, which conspired to make her look perpetually
starved. She had a high forehead made larger by the fact
that her wiry brown hair was forever pulled back in a tight

bun. She was skinny, knock-kneed, and missing two of her bottom teeth. But a widower with few prospects and nary a dollar to his name couldn't be picky. Nor could a woman with three children and debts to pay. Theirs was a union born of good old-fashioned horse sense.

Abe had been quite prepared to hate his stepmother. From the moment Thomas announced his intentions to marry, he'd busied his head with schemes to undermine her. Imagined faults to hold against her.

> It was inconvenient, therefore, that she was
> kind, encouraging, and endlessly sensitive.
> Sensitive in particular to the fact that my sister
> and I would always hold a tender place in our
> hearts for our sweet mother.

Like Nancy before her, the new Mrs. Lincoln recognized Abe's passion for books and resolved to nurture it. Among the possessions she'd carted in from Kentucky was a Webster's Speller, which proved a gold mine to the unschooled boy. Sarah (who, like her new husband, was illiterate) often asked Abe to read from her Bible after supper. He delighted in regaling his new family with passages from Corinthians and Kings; with the wisdom of Solomon and the folly of Nabal. His faith had grown since his mother's passing. He liked to imagine her looking down from heaven, running her angel fingers through his soft brown hair as he read. Protecting him from harm. Comforting him in times of need.

Abe also took a liking to his new stepsiblings, particularly John, whom he dubbed "the General" for his love of playing at war.

Where I was reluctant to stand, John was
reluctant to stand still, always concocting this
imagined battle or that and rounding up the
required number of boys to fight it. Always
urging me to leave my books and join his fun. I
would refuse, and he would harass, promising to
make me a captain or colonel. Promising to do
my chores if I joined in. Badgering me until I had
no choice but to leave the comfort of my reading
tree and run wild. At the time, I considered him
something of a simpleton. I now realize how wise
he was. For a boy needs more than books to be
a boy.

On his eleventh birthday, Sarah presented Abe with a
small, leather-bound journal (against Thomas's wishes).
She'd bought it with money earned by cleaning and mending clothes for Mr. Gregson, an elderly neighbor whose
wife had passed away years before. Books were hard
enough to come by on the frontier, but journals were truly
a luxury—particularly for little boys in poor families. One
can only imagine Abe's joy at receiving such a gift. He
wasted no time making his first entry, dutifully recorded
in his unpolished hand on the very day he received it.

This is the Journal of Abraham Lincoln.
9 February 1820—I have been given this book
as a gift for my elevnth [sic] birthday by my father
and stepmother, who is named Mrs. Sarah Bush
Lincoln. I will endevor [sic] to use it daily for the
purpose of improving my letters.
—Abraham Lincoln

II

One early spring night, not long after those words were carefully composed, Thomas called his son outside to sit by the fire. He was drunk. Abe knew this, even before being summoned to sit on a stump and warm himself. His father only made a fire outside when he felt like getting particularly plastered.

"I ever tell you about your granddaddy?"

It was one of his favorite stories to tell when he was drunk: the story of witnessing his father's brutal murder as a boy, an event that left him deeply scarred. Unfortunately the comforts of Sigmund Freud's couch were still decades away. In its absence, Thomas did what any self-respecting, emotionally crippled frontiersman did to deal with his troubles: he got blind, stinking drunk and hung them out to dry. If there was any consolation for Abe, it was this: his father was a gifted storyteller, with a knack for making every detail come alive. He would mimic accents, mime actions. Change the tenor of his voice and the rhythm of his delivery. He was a natural performer.

Unfortunately, Abe had seen this particular performance many, many times. He could recite the story word for word: how his grandfather (also named Abraham) had been plowing a field near his Kentucky home. How eight-year-old Thomas and his brothers had watched him toil in the heat of that May afternoon, turning over the soil. How they'd been startled by the yells of a Shawnee war party as it sprang out of hiding and attacked. How little Thomas took cover behind a tree and watched them beat his father's brains in with a stone hammer. Cut his throat with a tomahawk. He could describe it all—even his grandmother's face as young Thomas relayed the news after running home.

But that wasn't the version Thomas told him now.

The story began as it always had, in the heat wave of May 1786. Thomas was eight years old. He and two of his older brothers, Josiah and Mordecai, had accompanied their father to a four-acre clearing in the woods, not far from the farmhouse they'd helped him build some years before. Thomas watched his father guide the small plow as it scraped along behind Ben, an aging draft horse that had been with the family since before the war. The blistering sun had finally dipped below the horizon, leaving the Ohio River Valley in soft, blue-leaning light, but it was still "hotter than a woodstove in hell," and humid to boot. Abraham Sr. worked without his shirt, letting the air cool his long, sinewy torso. Young Thomas rode on Ben's back, working the reins while his brothers followed behind, broadcasting seed. Waiting for the welcome clang of the supper bell.

So far Abe knew every word. Next would come the part where they'd been startled by the war cries of the Shawnee. The part where the old draft horse reared up and threw Thomas to the ground. Where he ran into the woods and watched them gore his father to death. But the Shawnee never came. Not this time. This was a new story. One that Abe paraphrased in a letter to Joshua Speed more than twenty years later.

"The truth," father told me in a half whisper, "is that your granddaddy wasn't killed by any man."

The shirtless Abraham had been working the outer edge of his clearing, right up against the tree line, when there was "a great rustling and cracking of branches" from the nearby woods, no more than twenty yards from where he and his boys worked.

> "Daddy told me to pull up on the reins while he gave a listen. It was probably nothing but a few deer making their way, but we'd seen our share of black bears, too."

They'd also heard the stories. Reports of Shawnee war parties preying on unsuspecting settlers—killing white women and children without shame. Burning homes. Scalping men alive. This was still contested land. Indians were everywhere. There was no such thing as an excess of caution.

> "The rustling came from a different part of the woods now. Whatever it was, it wasn't any deer, and it wasn't alone. Daddy cussed himself for leaving his flintlock at home and started unhitching Ben. He wasn't about to let the devils have his horse. He sent my brothers off—Mordecai to fetch his gun, Josiah to get help from Hughes's Station."*

---

*It was common for early settlers to build their homes around forts, or "stations." In the event of an Indian attack, these forts offered a place to retreat. They were kept manned by a small detachment of volunteers.

The rustling changed now. The treetops began to bend, like something was jumping across them, one to the other.

> "Daddy hurried with the straps. 'Shawnee,' he whispered. My heart just about thumped a hole in my chest at the sound of it. I followed those treetops with my eyes, waiting for a pack of wild savages to run out of the woods, whooping and hollering and waving their hatchets. I could see their red faces staring at me. I could feel my hair being pulled tight…my scalp being clipped off."

Abraham was still struggling with the hitch when Thomas saw something white leap from a treetop "some fifty feet up." Something the size and shape of a man.

> "It was a ghost. The way it flew above the earth. The way its white body rippled as it moved through the air. A Shawnee ghost, come to take our souls for trespassing."

Thomas watched it soar toward them, too frightened to yell. Too frightened to warn his father that it was coming. Right above him. Right now.

> "I saw a glint of white and heard a shriek that would've woke the dead a mile off. Old Ben spooked, threw me in the dirt, and took off running wild, the plow hanging on by one strap, bouncing around behind him. I looked up where Daddy'd been standing. He was gone."

Thomas struggled to his feet with a head full of stars and (though he wouldn't realize it for hours) a broken wrist. The ghost stood fifteen or twenty feet away with its back to him. Standing over his father, patient and calm. Glaring at him like a God. Reveling in his helplessness.

> "He wasn't no ghost. No Shawnee, either. Even from the back, I could tell this stranger wasn't much more than a boy—no bigger than my brothers. His shirt looked like it'd been made for somebody twice his size. White as ivory. Half tucked into his striped gray trousers. His skin was damn near the same shade, and the back of his neck was crisscrossed with little blue lines. There he stood, with not a twitch or breath to set him apart from a statue."

Abraham Sr. was barely forty-two years old. Good genes had made him tall and broad shouldered. Honest work had made him lean and muscular. He'd never seen the losing end of a fight, and he sure as hell wouldn't see it now. He got to his feet ("slow, like his ribs were broke"), squared his body, and clenched his fists. He was hurt, but that could wait. First, he was going to knock this little son of a—

> "Daddy's jaw went slack when he got a look at the boy's face. Whatever he saw scared the hell out of him."

"What in the name of Chr—?"
The boy swung at Abraham's head. *It missed me.* Abraham took a step back and lifted his fists, but stopped short

of throwing a punch. *It missed.* He felt a stinging on the left side of his face. *Didn't it?* A tingling under his eye. He lifted the tip of his index finger to his face...the slightest touch. Blood began to run down in sheets, pouring out of the razor-thin slice that ran from his ear to his mouth.

It didn't miss.

These are the last seconds of my life.

Abraham felt his head snap backward. Felt his eye socket shatter. *Light everywhere.* He felt the blood running from his nostrils. Another blow. Another. His son screaming somewhere. *Why doesn't he run?* His jaw broken. His teeth knocked loose. The fists and the screaming growing farther away. *To sleep now...never to wake.*

It held Abraham's body by the hair, striking and striking until his forehead finally "caved in like an eggshell."

"The stranger wrapped his hands around Daddy's neck and lifted him in the air. I cried out again— sure he meant to strangle the last of him away. Instead he pushed those long thumbnails, those knives, through Daddy's Adam's apple and— *pop*—tore his neck open from the middle. He held his mouth underneath the hole, guzzling like a drunk with a whiskey bottle. Swallowing mouthfuls of blood. When it didn't come quick enough, he wrapped an arm around Daddy's chest and hugged him tight. Squeezed his heart till the last ounce was gone—then dropped him in the dirt and turned around. Looked dead at me. Now I understood. Now I knew why Daddy'd been so scared. It had eyes black as coal. Teeth as long and sharp as a wolf's. The white face of a demon, God strike me

down if I lie. My heart thumped away. My breath
abandoned me. It stood there with its face covered
in Daddy's blood and it…I swear to you it clutched
its hands to its chest and…sang to me."

It had the earnest, pitch-perfect voice of a young man.
An unmistakable English accent.

> When griping grief the heart doth wound,
> And doleful dumps the mind oppress—
> Then music, with her silver sound,
> With speedy help doth lend redress.*

That such a sound could come from something so hid-
eous—that its white face could wear such a warm smile—
it was all a cruel joke. Its song concluded, the demon gave
a long, low bow and ran into the woods. "Ran off till I
couldn't see a trace of white between the trees no more."
Eight-year-old Thomas knelt over his father's crooked,
empty corpse. Every inch of him shook.

"I knew I had to lie. I knew I could never tell a soul
what I'd seen, lest they think me a fool, or a liar
or worse. What had I seen, anyway? I might have
dreamed it for all I knew. When Mordecai came
running with the flintlock—when he demanded to
know what happened—I broke down crying and
told him the only thing I could. The only thing
he'd have believed—that it was a Shawnee war

---

*A sixteenth-century song by Richard Edwards, referenced in
Romeo and Juliet, Act IV, Scene 5.

party that killed our daddy. I couldn't tell him the truth. I couldn't tell him it was a vampire."

Abe couldn't speak. He sat across from his drunken father, letting the occasional cracks of burning wood fill the void.

I had listened to hundreds of his stories, some collected from the lives of others, some recounted from his own. But I had never known him to invent one, even in his present state. Frankly I did not think his mind capable. Nor could I think of a sensible reason to lie about such a thing. That left only one unsettling possibility.

"You think I've gone round the bend," said Thomas.

It was precisely what I thought, but I gave no answer. I had learned to keep my mouth closed on such occasions, rather than risk the angry misinterpretation of some innocent remark. I resolved to sit in silence until he sent me away or fell asleep.

"Hell, you've got every reason to."

He took a swallow of last week's work* and looked at me with a softness I had never seen

---

*Many farmers ran distilleries as a way to make extra money off their crop. Here, Abe is referring to the fact that Thomas often traded his carpentry for corn whiskey—much to the consternation of his new wife.

in him before. Putting everything else aside for the moment and seeing the two of us, not as we were, but as we might have been in some better life. Father and son. That his eyes presently filled with tears both astonished and frightened me. I felt him pleading with me to believe. Yet I could not believe something so foolish. He was a drunk telling a story. That was all.

"I'm telling you because you ought to know. Because you...deserve the truth. I'm telling you that I've seen two vampires in my life. The first was in that field. The second..."

Thomas looked away, fighting back tears again.

"The second was named Jack Barts...and I saw him just before your mama died...."

Father had spent the summer of 1817 committing the sin of envy. He'd grown tired of watching his neighbors reap kingly profits by planting wheat and corn on their land. He'd grown tired of breaking his back to build the barns they used to get rich, while sharing in none of the spoils. He felt, for the first time in his life, something like ambition. What he lacked was capital.

Jack Barts was a squat, one-armed man with a taste for expensive clothes and a thriving shipping business in Louisville. He was also one of the few Kentuckians in the business of giving private loans. Thomas had done some work for him as a young man, loading and unloading flat-boats on the Ohio River for twenty cents a day. Barts had always treated him kindly and paid him promptly, and when they'd parted company, it had been with a handshake and an open invitation to return. More than twenty years later, in the spring of 1818, Thomas Lincoln took him up on that offer. With his hat in his hands and his head hung low, Thomas sat in Jack Barts's office and asked for a loan of $75—precisely the amount he needed to buy a plow, a draft horse, seeds, and "everything else one needed to grow wheat, short of sunshine and rain."

Barts, who looked "hale and hearty as ever in his one-sleeved violet coat," agreed at once. His conditions were simple: Thomas would return with $90 (the principal plus 20 percent interest) no later than September 1st. Any profits earned above that were his to keep. Twenty percent was more than twice what any respectable bank would've charged. But seeing as Thomas didn't technically own anything (having merely helped himself to his plot at Little Pigeon Creek), he had no collateral—and nowhere else to turn.

> Father accepted the terms and went to work felling trees, pulling stumps, plowing sod, and broadcasting seeds. It was grueling labor. In all, he planted seven acres of wheat by hand. If he yielded thirty bushels an acre (a reasonable estimate), he would have enough to pay Barts back, plus a little to get us through winter. Next year he would plant more. The year after that, he would hire a hand to share the work. In five years' time, we would own the largest farm in the county. In ten years, the state. His last seed sown, father rested and waited for his future to spring from the earth.

But the summer of 1818 proved the hottest and driest in anyone's memory. When July arrived, there was nary a healthy stalk to be harvested anywhere in Indiana.

Thomas was ruined.

He had no choice but to sell the plow and horse for what little money he could. With no crops to harvest, they weren't worth much. Too ashamed to face Barts in person, Thomas sent him $28, along with a letter dated September 1st (which he'd dictated to Nancy) promising to send the rest as soon as he could. It was the best he could do. It wasn't good enough for Jack Barts.

Two weeks later, Thomas Lincoln found himself pleading in whispers, each one visible in the biting night air. He'd been roused from sleep only minutes before. Roused by something brushing against his cheek. The sleeve of a blue silk coat. A handful of banknotes, $28 in all. The shape of Jack Barts standing over his bed.

> Barts hadn't come all this way to argue, merely to warn. He liked father. He had always liked him. Therefore, he would give him three more days to find the rest of his money. It was business, you see. If word got around that Jack Barts granted special favors to delinquent borrowers, then others might think twice about paying him on time. And where would that leave him? In the poorhouse? No, no. There was nothing remotely personal about it. It was merely a matter of solvency.

They stood by the outhouse, lest their whispers wake anyone in the cabin. Barts asked him one more time:

"Can you have my money in three days?" Thomas hung his head again. "I cannot." Barts smiled and looked away. "Then…"

He turned back. His face was gone—a demon's in its place. A window into hell. Black eyes and white skin and *teeth as long and sharp as a wolf's God strike me down if I lie.*

"…I'll take it in other ways."

Abe stared at his father through the fire.

> Dread. Dread filled my stomach. My arms and legs. I was faint. Sick. I wished to hear no more of this. Not tonight. Not ever. But father could not stop. Not when he was so close to the end. The one that I had already guessed, but dared not believe.

"It was a vampire that took my daddy from me…"
"Stop…"
"Who took the Sparr—"
"Enough!"
"And it was a vampire who took your—"
"Go to hell!"
Thomas wept.

> The very sight of him awakened some heretofore unknown hatred. Hatred of my father. Of all things. He revolted me. I ran into the night for fear of what I might say; what I might do if I were in his presence a moment longer. My anger kept me away for three days and nights. I slept in the barns and outbuildings of neighbors. Stole

eggs and ears of corn. Walked until my legs shook
from exhaustion. Wept at the thought of my
mother. They had taken her from me. Father and
Jack Barts. I hated myself for being too small to
protect her. I hated my father for telling me such
impossible, unspeakable things. And yet I knew
they were the truth. I cannot explain how I knew
with such certainty, but I did. The way my father
had hushed us when we spun vampire yarns. The
screams that had carried on the wind at night.
My mother's fevered whispers about "looking
the devil in the eyes." Father was a drunk. An
indolent, loveless drunk. But he was no liar.
During those three days of anger and grief, I gave
into madness and admitted something to myself:
I believed in vampires. I believed in them, and I
hated them to the last.

When he finally came home (to a frightened stepmother and silent father), Abe didn't say a word. He made
straight for his journal and wrote down a single sentence.
One that would radically alter the course of his life, and
bring a fledgling nation to the brink of collapse.

> I hereby resolve to kill every vampire in
> America.

III

Sarah had hoped Abe would read to them after supper. It
was getting late, but there was a good fire going, and more

than enough time for a few pages of Jonah's adventures or Joseph's coat of many colors. She loved the way Abe read them. Such life. Such expression and clarity. He had a wisdom well beyond his years. Manners and sweetness seldom found in a child. He was, as she would tell William Herndon after her stepson's assassination, "the best boy I ever saw or ever hope to see."

But her Bible was nowhere to be found. Had she lent it to a neighbor and forgotten? Had she left it at Mr. Gregson's? She looked everywhere. She looked in vain. Sarah would never see her Bible again.

Abe had burned it.

It was the rash act of an angry child, one that he would live to regret (though never enough, it seems, to tell his stepmother the truth). Years later he would attempt to explain himself:

> How could I worship a God who would permit
> [vampires] to exist? A God that had allowed my
> mother to fall prey to their evil?* Either He was
> powerless to stop it, or He was complicit in it. In
> either case, He was undeserving of my praise. In
> either case, He was my enemy. Such is the mind
> of an angry eleven-year-old boy. One that sees the

---

*It's not known how Barts killed Nancy Lincoln and the Sparrows, but based on information elsewhere in the journals, he likely administered a "fool's dose" of his own blood. Pricking a finger and squeezing a few drops into a sleeping victim's mouth is the most common method. Such an amount is merely enough to produce the side effects of transformation (sickness, death) without any of its lasting benefits.

world as a choice between two disparate certain-
ties. One that believes a thing "must" be this way
or that. I am ashamed that it happened, yes. But
I would not compound that shame by pretending
that it did not.

With his faith in ruins, eleven-year-old Abe took his resolution a step further in this undated manifesto (c. August
1820):

Henceforth my life shall be one of rigerous
[sic] study and devotion. I shall become learned
in all things. I shall become a greater warrior then
[sic] Alexander. My life shall have but one purpose. That purpose is to kill* as many vampires
as I can. This journal shall be where I write about
killing vampires. No one other then [sic] me shall
read it.

His interest in books, which to date had merely been rav-
enous, became obsessive. He walked more than an hour to
the home of Aaron Stibel, a shoemaker who boasted a personal library of some 150 volumes, twice a week to return
an armful of books and borrow another armful. He accompanied his stepmother to Elizabethtown whenever she visited a relative, sequestering himself in the Village Street
home of Samuel Haycraft Sr., one of the town's founders,
and the proud owner of nearly five hundred books. Abe read

---

*It's interesting to note the repeated use of the words "kill" and
"killing" in these early entries. Abe would later use the more
accurate verbs "destroy" and "slaughter."

about the occult; found mentions of vampires in European folklore. He compiled a list of their rumored weaknesses, markings, and habits. It became common for stepmother Sarah to find him asleep at the table in the morning, his head resting on an open page.

When he wasn't improving his mind, Abe was hard at work improving his body. He doubled his daily wood chopping. He built long, winding stone walls. He practiced throwing his ax into a tree. First from ten yards. Then twenty. When stepbrother John invited him to play at war, he jumped at the chance, and fought with a new intensity that left more than one neighbor boy's lip bloodied. Based on the information he'd gathered in books, Abe whittled a dozen stakes and made a quiver to carry them in. He fashioned a small crucifix (although he had declared God his "enemy," it appears that Abe wasn't opposed to his help). He took to carrying small pouches of garlic and mustard seed. He sharpened his ax until the blade "blinded all who looked upon it." At night, he dreamed of death. Of hunting down his enemies and driving stakes through their hearts. Of taking their heads. Of glorious battle. Years later, as the clouds of Civil War loomed on the horizon, Abe looked back at his youthful bloodlust.

> There are but two types of men who desire war: those who haven't the slightest intention of fighting it themselves, and those who haven't the slightest idea what it is. Of my youth I can decidedly say that the latter was true. I ached for this "war" with vampires, knowing nothing of its consequences. Knowing nothing of holding a dying friend in my arms or burying a child. Any man

who has seen the face of death knows better than
to seek him out a second time.

But in the summer of 1821, these lessons were still
years off. Abe wanted his war with vampires, and after
months of vigorous study and exercise, he was ready to
launch the opening salvo.

He wrote a letter.

IV

Abe was uncommonly tall for a boy of twelve. He already
stood shoulder to shoulder with his father, who was himself considered tall at five-foot nine. Like his ill-fated
grandfather, good genes and years of toil had made him
exceptionally strong.

It was a Monday, "the kind of summer day one finds
only in Kentucky—shining and verdant; the breeze carrying warmth and dandelion seeds." Abe and Thomas sat
atop one of their smaller outbuildings, making repairs to
its winter-beaten roof. They worked in silence. Though
Abe's hatred had cooled, he still found it difficult to be
in his father's presence. A journal entry dated December
2nd, 1843 (not long after the birth of Abe's own son, Robert), sheds some light on the nature of his contempt.

> Age has made me temperate in many things,
> but on this point I remain steadfast. His weak-
> ness! His ineptness! He failed to protect his
> family. Thought only of his own needs, and left
> others to their cost. Had he simply gathered us

and fled to some far-off territory. Had he merely
asked our neighbors for some small advance
against future work. But he did nothing. Nothing
but sit idly. Silently. Secretly hoping that somehow, by some miracle, his troubles would simply
disappear. No, it needs no further elaboration
than this: had he been any other man, she would
be with me still. This I cannot forgive.

Thomas, to his credit, seemed to understand and accept
his condemnation. He hadn't mentioned the word "vampire" since that night. Nor had he pressed Abe to talk.

Sarah had taken the girls to help her clean Mr. Gregson's house that Monday afternoon, and John was off
fighting some imaginary war. The two Lincolns were at
work on the roof when a horse approached carrying a
child on its back. A plump child in a green coat. Either
that or a very short man. A short man with dark glasses
and...one arm.

It was Jack Barts.

Thomas put his hammer down, his heart just about
thumping a hole in his chest at the thought of what Barts
could want now. By the time he climbed down and began
walking to meet their unexpected guest, Abe was already
halfway to the cabin. Barts handed Thomas his reins and
dismounted with some difficulty, hanging on to the saddle
horn with one arm while his stout legs struggled to find
the ground. Having done so, he found the fan in his coat
pocket and put it to use, cooling his face. Thomas couldn't
help but notice that there wasn't a bead of sweat on him.

"Simply dreadful...dreadfully, miserably hot."

"Mr. Barts, I—"

"I must admit, your letter surprised me, Mr. Lincoln. A happy surprise, to be certain. But a surprise nonetheless."

"My letter, Mr. Ba—?"

"Had you written it earlier, perhaps the unpleasantness which transpired between us might have been avoided. Terrible... terrible thing..."

Thomas was too confounded to notice Abe walking toward them with a long wooden object in his arms.

"You'll forgive my haste," said Barts, "but I should like to be off at once. I have business in Louisville which must be attended to this evening."

Thomas couldn't think of a thing to say. Not a damned thing.

"Well? Do you have it, Mr. Lincoln?"

Abe joined them, cradling a long, hand-carved chest with a hinged lid. A tiny coffin for a slender corpse. He stood beside his father, facing Barts. Towering over him. Leering at him.

"Strange," said Abe, breaking the silence. "I hadn't expected you during the day."

Now it was Barts who found his brain tied in knots.

"Who is this child?"

"My son," said Thomas, petrified.

"It's here," said Abe, raising the chest. "All of it. All one hundred dollars, just like the letter said."

Thomas was sure he'd misheard. Sure this was a dream. Barts looked at Abe, suspicious. Bewildered. A smile spread over his face.

"My God!" said Barts. "For a moment I thought us all mad!"

Barts began to laugh. Abe opened the lid—just enough to slip his hand inside.

"Good boy," said Barts, laughing heartily now. "Let us have it then."

He reached his hand up and ran his thick fingers through my hair. I could think of nothing but the way my mother had done the same when she read to me. I could think of nothing but her sweet face. I glared down at this man. This creature. I joined him in laughter as my father stood helpless—a fire spreading through my chest. I felt the wooden stake in my fingers. I could do anything. I was a god.

These are the last seconds of your life.

I have no memory of driving it in—I only remember that I did. His laughter ceased and he took an awkward step. His eyes turned black in the space of a single blink, as if the inkwells in his pupils had suddenly shattered—the spill contained behind glass. His fangs descended, and I could presently make out a faint blue web beneath his skin. It was true. Until that moment there had been room for doubt. But now I saw it with my own eyes. Now I knew.

Vampires were <u>real</u>.

His arm rose, and his stout little hand instinctively grabbed the stake. There was no fear in his face yet. Merely a puzzlement, as if he was attempting to sort out just how such an object could be attached to his body. He presently lost his footing and collapsed into a seated position, where he remained for a moment before falling

the rest of the way onto his back. His hand lost
its grip on the stake, and the arm fell to his side.

I walked around him, wondering when he
would strike. Wondering when he would laugh at
the futility of what I had done and cut me down.
As I did, his eyes followed me. They were the only
things that moved now. There was fear in them.
He was dying…and he was afraid. What little
color he had left him now—and rich, dark blood
began to run from his nostrils; out the sides of his
mouth. A trickle at first…then a flood—running
over his cheeks and pooling over his eyes. More
blood than I ever thought possible. I could see
his soul (if indeed he had such a thing) depart-
ing. Bidding an unexpected, frightening farewell
to such a long, long life—one undoubtedly filled
with happiness, and agony, and struggle, and success. Filled with moments too beautiful to share.
Too painful to recall. It was all ending now, and
he was so afraid. Afraid of what nothingness
awaited him. Or worse, what punishment.

And then he was gone. I expected my eyes to
fill with tears. To feel remorse at the sight of what
I had done. I admit that I felt nothing. I only
wished he had suffered more.

Thomas stood aghast. "Look what you've done," he
said after a sickened silence. "You've killed us."

"On the contrary…I've killed him."

"More will come."

Abe had already begun to walk away.

"Then I shall need more stakes."

Three

Henry

It is the eternal struggle between these two principles—right and wrong—throughout the world.
They are the two principles that have stood face
to face from the beginning of time; and will ever
continue to struggle.

—*Abraham Lincoln, debating Stephen A. Douglas*
October 15th, 1858

I

Southeastern Indiana was in the grip of fear during the
summer of 1825. Three children had gone missing over
a six-week period beginning in early April. The first, a
seven-year-old boy named Samuel Greene, disappeared
while playing in the woods near his family's farm in Madison, a thriving town on the banks over the Ohio River.
Search parties were sent out. Ponds dredged. But no trace
of the boy was found. Less than two weeks later, before the
people of Madison had abandoned all hope of finding him

alive, six-year-old Gertrude Wilcox vanished from her bed in the middle of the night. Now alarm turned to panic. Parents refused to let their children outdoors. Neighbors leveled accusations at neighbors, all while three weeks passed without incident. Then, on May 20th, the third child was taken—not from Madison, but from the town of Jeffersonville twenty miles downriver. This time the body was found in a matter of days—along with two others. A hunter had made the gruesome discovery, following his dogs to a shallow wooded ditch where the three twisted corpses lay, hastily covered with brush. Their bodies were unnaturally decomposed—almost completely devoid of color. Each of their faces locked in an open-eyed mask of fear.

Abe Lincoln was sixteen years old that summer, and his resolution to "kill every vampire in America" was off to an inauspicious start. His father's fears had proved needless. No vampires ever came to avenge Jack Barts. In fact, in the four years since he'd staked Barts, Abe hadn't so much as seen another vampire, though not for lack of trying. He'd spent countless nights chasing distant screams on the wind and keeping watch over freshly dug graves just in case, as folklore suggested, a vampire came to feast on the corpse. But with nothing more than old books and old myths to guide him, and a father unwilling to help, Abe spent those four years in a constant state of frustration. There was little to do but keep up with his training. He'd reached his full height of six feet four inches, every square centimeter of him lean muscle. He could outwrestle and outrun most men twice his age. He could bury the head of an ax in a tree from over thirty yards. He could pull a plow every bit as fast as a draft horse, and lift a 250-pound log clean over his head.

What he couldn't do was sew. After spending weeks trying to fashion himself a long "hunting coat" only to see it fall to pieces after one or two wearings, he'd broken down and paid a seamstress to do the job (he hadn't asked his stepmother, for fear of raising the obvious question of what he needed such a coat for). The long black coat was lined with thick material over his chest and stomach, and inside pockets to store all manner of knives, cloves of garlic, and a flask of holy water, which he'd blessed himself. He wore his quiver of stakes on his back, and a thick leather collar, one that he'd commissioned from an Elizabethtown tanner, around his neck.

When word of those twisted corpses reached Little Pigeon Creek, Abe set off for the river at once.

> I told Father that I had found work on a flat-
> boat bound for New Orleans, and that I would
> return with $20 pay in six weeks' time. I did so
> in spite of having received no such offer of work,
> and despite having no idea where I would find the
> money. I could think of no other way that Father
> would have permitted such a long absence.

Contrary to his infallibly "honest" image, Abe wasn't above lying so long as it served a noble purpose. This was the chance he'd ached for those four long years. The chance to test his skills. His tools. The chance to feel the exhilaration of watching a vampire fade away at his feet. Seeing the fear in its eyes.

There were far better trackers than Abraham Lincoln. Men with far more knowledge of the Ohio River. But there was nary a human being in Kentucky or Indiana with a

more extensive knowledge of mysterious disappearances
and unsolved murders.

> When I heard a description of the bodies at
> Jeffersonville, I knew at once that a vampire
> was responsible, and I had a very good notion of
> where it was going. I remembered reading about
> a similar case in Dugre's *On the History of the*
> *Mississippi River*—one that had confounded set-
> tlers almost fifty years prior. Children had gone
> missing from their beds in small towns all along
> the river—beginning in Natchez, and continuing
> to Donaldsonville. North to south. The bodies
> had been found in groups along the river, badly
> decomposed. Unnaturally so—each with nothing
> more than small cuts on their appendages. Like
> that vampire, I was willing to bet that this one
> was heading south with the current. Furthermore,
> I was willing to bet that it was on a boat. And if
> it was on a boat, it would reach Evansville sooner
> or later.

That was where Abe lay in wait on the night of Thursday, June 30th, 1825, hiding behind brush on the wooded
banks of the Ohio.

> The moon was blessedly full, revealing every
> detail of the night…the light fog rolling over the
> river's surface, the dewdrops on the leaves of my
> hiding place, the silhouettes of sleeping birds on
> a tree branch, and the flatboat tied up not thirty
> yards from where I hid. It looked no different

from any of the small barges one saw up and
down the river: forty feet by twelve; fashioned
from rough wooden planks; all but a third of its
deck taken up by covered living quarters—yet
my eyes had been fixed on this particular boat
for hours, for I was sure that there was a vampire
inside.

Abe had spent days watching the occasional flatboat
come ashore at Evansville. He'd scrutinized every man
who had stepped onto land looking for the telltale signs
he'd read so much about: pale skin, avoidance of sunlight,
fear of crosses. He'd even followed a few "suspicious"
boatmen as they went about their business in town. But
none of this had yielded anything. In the end, it was the
flatboat that *didn't* stop that drew his suspicion.

I had been close to retiring. The sun had all but
set, and any boats upriver would be tying up for
the night. And then I saw it. The outline of a flatboat passed—barely visible in the darkness. It was
curious that a boat would pass one of the busiest
towns on this part of the river without tying up.
Even more curious that it would do so at night.

Abe ran along the river, determined to follow this strange
boat (which as far as he could see was being piloted by no
one) for as long as he could.

Heavy rains had quickened the current, and
I found it difficult to keep pace. The flatboat
continued to slip away, and when it disappeared

around a bend in the river, I feared I had lost it
for good.

But after a half hour in a near flat-out sprint, Abe
caught up. The boat had tied up on the same bank a few
miles outside of town, a small plank leading from its deck
to the shore. He set up a good distance away and began an
all-night vigil. Hungry, exhausted hours passed, but Abe
kept his post.

> I had been still for so long that I feared my
> legs might betray me when I needed them. But I
> dared not strike until I saw him. Until I saw the
> creature emerge from his sleeping place. I looked
> down at the ax in my hands to ensure that it was
> still there. I shook from the anticipation of watch-
> ing it fly into his chest. Of seeing the fear on his
> face as the last of him left this world.

There was a faint rustling of leaves and snapping of twigs
from the north. Someone approached, walking through the
woods along the bank. Abe steadied his breathing. He felt
the handle of the ax in his right hand. Imagined the sound
it would make as it tore through skin, and bone, and lung.

> I had been waiting for the creature to emerge
> these long hours. It had never occurred to me that
> the vampire might already be about. It mattered not.
> I readied my ax and waited to get a look at him.

"Him" turned out to a small woman wearing a black
dress and matching bonnet. The shape of her body sug-

gested she was quite old, though she walked along the uneven riverbank with ease.

> The possibility of it being a woman had never entered my mind, much less an old one. The madness of what I was doing suddenly rang clear. What evidence had I? What evidence beyond a suspicion that this was the boat of a vampire? Was I merely going to kill whomever it belonged to and hope that my theory proved correct? Was I prepared to take the head of this old woman without being absolutely certain?

Abe didn't have to agonize for long, for as she drew closer, he could see something in her arms. Something white.

It was a child.

> I watched as she carried him through the woods [and] toward the boat. He was no older than five years, wearing a white sleeping gown— his arms and legs hanging freely. I could see the blood on his collar. On his sleeves. I could not strike from such a distance, for fear that an errant ax blade might kill the boy (if indeed he lived).

Abe watched the vampire reach the flatboat and start up the small plank, then stop halfway up.

> Her body became rigid. She smelled the air, as I had seen animals do when they caught the scent of danger. She looked across the darkness to the opposite bank, then toward me.

Abe froze. Not a breath. Not a twitch. Satisfied there was no danger, the old woman continued up the plank and onto the flatboat.

A sickness came over me. A rage—directed more at myself than she. How dare I sit idly and let this boy be taken? How dare I allow something as petty as fear—as insignificant as my own life—keep me from what must be done? No! No, I should sooner die at her hands than die from shame! I rose from hiding and ran toward the river. Toward the boat. She heard my footfalls at once—seized on my direction and dropped the boy to the deck. Here! Here was my chance! I raised my ax and let it fly. Watched it spin toward her. Despite all appearances to the contrary, she was quite nimble—moving from the path of my ax and condemning it to the bottom of the Ohio River. I kept running, convinced that my strength and practice would win the day yet. Convinced that there was no alternative. Reaching into my coat pockets, I found a hunting knife for each hand. She waited for me, those clawed fingers outstretched. Black eyes to match her bonnet. My feet hit the plank. I leapt at her, and she swatted me away as a horse's tail swats a fly, sending me onto the deck and exorcising the air from my lungs. I rolled onto my back, every ounce of me aching, and held the knives in front of me to keep her at bay. These she grabbed by their blades and pulled from my hands—leaving me with nothing more than bare fists to defend myself. I sprang to

my feet and lunged at the wretched old demon,
my fists flying wildly. I may as well have been
blindfolded—such was the ease with which she
moved from the path of each strike. All at once I
felt a searing pain in my middle—one that nearly
knocked me from my feet and onto the sleeping
boy below.

The force of the vampire's fists had broken several of
Abe's ribs. He staggered as she hit him in the stomach
again...*again*. He coughed, sending flecks of blood flying onto her face.

Here she paused, dragging a foul finger across
her cheek and touching it to her tongue. "Rich,"
she said with a smile. I struggled to keep my feet,
knowing that if I fell again, it would be for the
last time. I thought of my grandfather—how
his face had been crushed by the fists of a vampire. How he had failed to land even one blow
in return. I refused to meet the same fate. I used
her pause to my advantage, finding the last of the
weapons in my coat, a small knife. I threw myself
at her with the last of my strength and thrust its
blade into her belly. This only improved her good
humor, for she grabbed my wrist and dragged it
along her gut, cutting herself and laughing all the
while. I felt my feet leave the deck; felt her hands
on my throat. In what seemed an instant, I was
drowning. She held my head beneath the river—
my back pressed against the side of the boat. My
feet kicking wildly. I could do nothing but look

up into her face. Her wrinkles smoothed by the
water. Then thoughts turned from struggle, and a
strange joy infected me. It would all be over soon,
and I would rest. Those black eyes changing shape
above me as the water began to calm. As I began
to calm. I would be with her soon. It was night.
    Then he came.

Abe was barely conscious when the old woman disappeared—pulled backward onto the boat. Her hands no
longer holding him down, he sank gently toward the bottom of the river.

I was pulled from the depths by the hand
of God. Placed upon the deck of the tiny boat
next to a sleeping boy in a white gown. From
this lowly vantage I watched the rest play out—
slipping in and out of sleep. I heard the woman
scream: "Traitor!" I saw the outline of a man
struggling with her. I saw her head fall to the deck
in front of where I lay. Her body was not attached
to it. And then I saw no more.

II

"And oftentimes, to win us to our harm, the instruments
of darkness tell us truths, win us with honest trifles, to
betray—"*

---

*Macbeth, Act I, Scene 3.

I woke in a windowless room to a man reading by oil light. He was perhaps five-and-twenty—slender, with dark, shoulder-length hair. Upon seeing me wake, he stopped reading and placed a marker in the pages of a thick leather volume. I asked the only question that mattered. The one that had troubled my dreams.

"The boy . . . is he—"
"Safe. Placed where he will be found."

His accent betrayed no particular origin. Was he an Englishman? An American? A Scot? He sat beside me in an intricately carved high-back chair, one leg of his dark trousers folded neatly over the other, the sleeves of his blue shirt rolled to the elbows, and a small silver cross hanging around his neck. My eyes came around, and I traced the shape of the room by the light of his oil lamp. Its walls seemed made from stones piled one on top of the other—the space between them packed with clay. Each boasted no fewer than two gold-framed paintings; some as many as six. Scenes of bare-breasted native women carrying water from a stream. Sun-soaked landscapes. A portrait of a young lady hanging beside a portrait of an old one, their features remarkably similar. I saw my belongings carefully laid out on a chest in the far corner of the room. My coat. My knives. My ax—miraculously rescued from the bottom of the Ohio. Surrounding these, some of the most elegant furnishings I had ever seen. And books!

Stacks and stacks of books of every conceivable thickness and binding.

"My name is Henry Sturges," he said. "This is my home."

"Abraham...Lincoln."

"The 'father of many.' A pleasure, indeed."

I tried to sit up, but met with such pain as to bring me to the edge of fainting. I lay on my back and looked down my chin. My chest and stomach were covered in wet bandages.

"You'll forgive the intrusion on your modesty, but you were quite injured. Don't be alarmed by the smell, either. Your dressings have been steeped in an assortment of oils—all very good for healing wounds, I assure you. Not as beneficial to the senses, I'm afraid."

"How..."

"Two days and nights. I must say, the first dozen hours were rather tenuous. I wasn't sure you would ever wake. It's a compliment to your health that you sur—"

"No...how did you kill her?"

"Ah. It wasn't difficult, really. She was quite frail, you know."

It seemed an absurd thing to say to one whose body had been shattered by her "frailty."

"And, I might add, quite preoccupied with drowning you. In that regard I suppose I owe you a debt of gratitude for distrac—may I ask you something?"

.

My silence proved a suitable substitute for "yes."

"How many vampires have you slain?"

It was shocking to hear a stranger say the word. Until that day I had heard no one other than my father speak of them as real creatures. I thought briefly of boasting, but answered him honestly.

"One," said Abe.
"Yes . . . yes, that seems about right."
"And you, sir. How many have you slain?"
"One."

I could make no sense of it. How could someone with such skill—who had so easily slain a vampire—have so little practice?

"Are you . . . not a vampire hunter?"

Henry laughed heartily at the idea.

"I can say with certainty that I am not. Though it would be an interesting choice of trade, to be sure."

In my muddled state I was slow to get his meaning. As it dawned—as I felt the truth of it sink into my skin, I was at once terrified and furious. He had killed the vampire woman. Not to save me from death, but to save me for

himself. Now there was no pain. Now there was
only the fire in my chest. I struck at him with
all my strength—all my rage. But my arms were
abruptly stopped on their way to his throat.
He had fashioned bindings around my wrists. I
screamed wildly. Pulled at the restraints until my
face turned red. A madman. Henry looked on
without so much as a blink of consternation.

"Yes," said Henry. "I thought that might be your
reaction."

III

For the next two days and nights, I refused to
say a word. Refused to eat, or sleep, or look my
host in the eye. How could I, knowing that my life
might end at any moment? Knowing that a vampire (my sworn enemy! my mother's murderer!)
was never more than a few steps away? How much
of my blood had he tasted while I slept? I heard
his shoes climb up and down a wooden staircase.
Heard the creaks and clangs of a delicate door
being opened and shut. But I heard nothing of
the outside world. No birdsong. No church bells.
I knew not when it was day or night. My only
measurement of time was the sound of the match
striking. The woodstove burning. The kettle
boiling. Every few hours, he entered the room
with a steaming bowl of broth, sat by my bed,
and offered to feed it to me. I promptly refused.

My refusal being accepted with like promptness, Henry picked up a volume of *The Selected Works of William Shakespeare* and continued reading where he'd left off. Such was our little game. For two days, I refused to eat or listen. For two days, he continued to cook and speak. As he read, I tried to occupy my mind with trivial thoughts. With songs or stories of my own creation. Anything but give this vampire the satisfaction of my attention. But on the third day, momentarily bested by my hunger, I could not help but accept when Henry came offering a spoonful of broth. I swore that I would only accept the first. Just enough to quiet the pain in my stomach, nothing more.

Abe ate three bowlfuls without stopping. When he had finally eaten his fill, he and Henry sat in silence "for what seemed an hour's time," until Abe finally spoke:

"Why haven't you killed me?"

It sickened me to look at him. I cared not for his kindness. I cared not that he had saved my life. Treated my wounds and fed me. I cared not who he was. Only <u>what</u> he was.

"And pray, what reason have I to kill you?"

"You are a vampire."

"And so the rest of me is written? Have I not the mind of a man? Have I not the same needs? To be fed and clothed and comforted? Judge us not equally, Abraham."

Now it was I who could not help but laugh.

"You speak as one who does not murder to be 'fed'! Whose 'needs' do not take mothers from their children!"

"Ah," said Henry. "And it was one of my kind who took her from you?"

> All traces of reason left me. There was some-
> thing about the ease with which he spoke of it.
> The callousness. The madman returned. I struck
> at him, knocking the soup bowl to the stone floor
> in the process. Shattering it. I would have torn his
> face off but for the bindings around my wrists.

"Never speak of her! NEVER!"

> Henry waited until my outburst had passed,
> then knelt on the floor and collected the pieces of
> the shattered bowl.

"You must forgive me," said Henry. "It has been quite a long time since I was your age. I forget the passions of youth. I shall endeavor to choose my words more carefully."

> The last of the pieces in his hands, he stood
> and made to leave, but paused in the doorway.

"Ask yourself…are we so unalike, you and I? Are we not both unwilling servants of my condition? Did we not both lose something significant to it? You a mother? I a life?"

> With this he disappeared, leaving me to my
> anger. I shouted after him: "Why haven't you
> killed me!" His answer came calmly from the

next room. "Some people, Abraham, are just too interesting to kill."

IV

Abe healed with each passing day. He took food willingly, and listened to Henry read Shakespeare with increasing interest.

> Though the sight of him still held the power to incite anger or apprehension, this power grew weaker as my body grew stronger. He loosened my bindings so that I could feed myself. Left books by my bed so that I could read alone. The more I came to know of his mind, the more I began to consider the possibility that he had no murderous designs on me. We spoke of books. Of the great cities of the world. We even spoke of my mother. Mostly, we spoke of vampires. On this subject I had more questions than words to ask them with. I wanted to know everything. For four long years, I had stumbled in the dark—relying on assumptions, and hoping that Providence alone would bring me face-to-face with a vampire. Here, at last, was my chance to learn everything: How they could live on blood alone. Whether they had a soul. How they came to exist at all.

Unfortunately, Henry didn't have the answers to any of these questions. Like most vampires, he had spent a good deal of time obsessing over his "lineage" in an attempt to uncover "the first vampire," hoping the discovery would lead to some deeper truth, perhaps even a cure. And like all before him, he had failed. Even the most resourceful vampires are only able to go back two or three generations. "This," explained Henry, "is a product of our solitary nature."

> In truth, vampires rarely socialize—and almost never with their own kind. The scarcity of easy blood breeds vicious competition, and their nomadic lifestyle makes it difficult to form lasting bonds. In rare cases, vampires might work in pairs or packs—but these alliances are usually born of desperation, and almost always temporary.

"As to our ancestry," said Henry, "I am afraid that it shall forever remain shrouded in darkness. There are some who believe that we began as a wicked spirit or demon, passed from one unfortunate soul to the next. A curse propagated through the blood. Others believe that we owe our parentage to the devil himself. And there are more still, myself among them, who have come to believe that our 'curse' never began at all—that vampires and man are merely different animals. Two species that have existed side by side since Adam and Eve were expelled from paradise. One race gifted with superior ability and length of life; the other more fragile and fleeting, but gifted with superior numbers. The only certainty is that we shall never be certain."

> When it came to the experience of being a vampire, however, Henry was endlessly

knowledgeable. He had a gift for explaining his
condition in a way that I could grasp at such a
young age. A gift for humanizing the notion of
immortality.

"Living men are bound by time," he said. "Thus, their
lives have an urgency. This gives them ambition. Makes
them choose those things that are most important; cling
more tightly to that which they hold dear. Their lives have
seasons, and rites of passage, and consequences. And ultimately, an end. But what of a life with no urgency? What
then of ambition? What then of love?

"The first hundred years are exciting ones, yes. The
world is one of infinite indulgence. We master the art of
feeding—learning where to cast our net and how best to
enjoy our catch. We travel the world, beholding the moon-
lit wonders of civilization; amassing small fortunes by
stealing valuables from our countless victims. We fulfill
every imaginable desire of the flesh...oh, it's all great fun.

"After a hundred years of conquest, our bodies are full
to the point of bursting—but our minds have been left
to starve. By now, most of us have built a resistance to
the ill effects of sunlight. The world of the living, therefore, is no longer beyond our reach—and we are free to
experience all that darkness had kept from us in our first
century. We pore through libraries, dissecting the classics; see the world's great works of art with our own eyes.
We take up music and painting, write poetry. We return
to our most beloved cities to experience them anew. Our
fortunes grow vaster. Our powers greater.

"By the third century, however, the intoxication of
eternity has worn rather thin. Every imaginable desire has

been fulfilled. The thrill of taking a life experienced again and again and again. And though we have all the comforts of the world, we find no comfort in them. It is in this century, Abraham, that most of us turn to suicide—either by starving ourselves, staking ourselves through the heart, devising some method of taking our own heads, or, in the most desperate cases, by burning ourselves alive. Only the very strongest of us—those possessing exceptional will, and driven by a timeless purpose—survive into our fourth or fifth centuries and beyond."

> That a man who had been freed from the inescapable fate of death would choose it for himself—this I did not understand, and I told Henry as much.
> "Without death," he answered, "life is meaningless. It is a story that can never be told. A song that can never be sung. For how would one finish it?"

————

Soon Abe was well enough to sit up in bed, and Henry was comfortable enough to do away with his restraints altogether. Having failed to get answers to his more general vampire questions, Abe turned to a bottomless well of specifics. On sunlight:

"When we are newly made, the slightest sunlight blisters our skin and renders us ill, much the same way an excess of sunlight can sicken a man. Over time we become resistant to these effects, and are able to walk freely during the day—so long as we stray from harsh light. Our eyes, however, never adjust."

On garlic:

"I'm afraid it merely makes you easier to perceive from a distance."

On sleeping in coffins:

"I cannot speak for others, but I am quite comfortable in a bed."

When Abe reached the question of how one becomes a vampire, Henry paused.

"I shall tell you how I came to be one."

V

Abe committed the following to his journal on August 30th, 1825, shortly after his return to Little Pigeon Creek.

> What follows is the story exactly as Henry
> related it to me. I have neither embellished, nor
> withheld, nor verified any part of it. I merely
> duplicate it here so that some record of it exists.
> "On 22nd July, in the year 1587," Henry began,
> "three ships carrying 117 English souls landed on
> northern Roanoke Island, in what is today called
> North Carolina."

Among this teeming mass of men, women, and children was a twenty-three-year-old blacksmith's apprentice named Henry O. Sturges, average in height and build, with long, dark hair to the middle of his back. He was joined by his new wife, Edeva.

> "She was but a day younger and an inch
> shorter than I, with hair of the finest flaxen and

eyes a strange shade of brown. There has never
been a more delicate, a more fetching creature in
all the annals of time."

They had just experienced a harrowing voyage, one
plagued by unseasonably bad weather and uncommonly
bad luck. While there was nothing unusual about sickness and death on an Atlantic crossing (sixteenth-century
ships were typically moldy, rat-infested breeding grounds
for any number of air- or food-borne illnesses), the acci-
dental demise of two people on two separate occasions
was ominous enough to raise alarm.

Both deaths occurred aboard the *Lyon*, the largest of
the three-vessel caravan, and the one personally cap-
tained by John White. White, a forty-seven-year-old art-
ist, was handpicked by Sir Walter Raleigh for the job of
establishing a permanent English presence in the New
World. He'd been part of the first attempt to colonize Roanoke two years earlier—an attempt that failed when the
colonists, all men, ran desperately short of supplies and
hitched a ride back to England with Sir Francis Drake,
who, as fate would have it, had decided to anchor nearby
during a break from raiding Spanish ships.

"This time 'round," Henry said, "Raleigh's plan
was more ambitious. Instead of brusque sailors, he
sent young families. Families that would put down
roots. Produce children. Build churches and school-
houses. It was his opportunity to build 'a new
England in the New World.' For Edeva and me, it
was an opportunity to leave a home that held little
in the way of happiness. All told we were ninety

men, nine children, and seventeen women, including John White's own daughter, Eleanor Dare."

Eleanor, who was eight months pregnant, was joined
by her husband, Ananias, aboard the *Lyon*. She was an
"uncommonly pretty" twenty-four-year-old, with a shock
of red hair and freckled face. One can only imagine the
discomfort she felt as the 120-ton ship pitched about in
the oppressive July heat—heat that turned the innards of
the ships into giant steam ovens.

"Even some of the surest-footed sailors found
themselves green-faced and bent over the railings
when the seas kicked up and the sun beat down
on us."

The first of the two deaths occurred on Sunday, May
24th, a little more than two weeks after the colonists set
sail from Plymouth. A ship's mate named Blum (or Bloom;
Henry never learned the correct spelling) had been in the
crow's nest at night, charged with keeping a sharp eye out
for distant silhouettes on the star-filled horizon. Spanish
carracks—with a reputation for attacking and pillaging
English ships—were a very real threat. Shortly after midnight, the ship's pilot, Simon Ferdinando (who'd already
gained fame through previous expeditions to Maine and
Virginia), recalled hearing a "crash" on the main deck.
Moments later, he found himself standing over the lifeless
body of Mr. Blum—whose neck was severely broken.

"Mr. Ferdinando thought it strange that an
experienced sailor—particularly one who'd sworn

off drink—could've taken such a fall in calm seas. But such was life on the Atlantic. Accidents happened. Other than a few prayers for the unfortunate man's soul, little was said about Mr. Blum among the passengers and crew."

Captain White recorded the matter rather succinctly and dispassionately in his log: *Man fell from crowe's nest. Deade. Throwne overboarde.*

"Had that been the only incident during our crossing, we might have counted ourselves fortunate. But our nerves were tested again on Tuesday, June 30th—when Elizabeth Barrington vanished into the night forever."

Elizabeth, an almost comically short, curly-haired girl of sixteen, had been literally dragged aboard by her father and several shipmates, kicking, screaming, and biting the whole way. To her, the *Lyon* was a prison ship.

Months earlier, she had fallen hard for a young clerk in her father's law practice. Knowing that the match would never warrant approval, the two young lovers carried on a secret affair, the discovery of which caused a minor sensation in the Inns of Court and severely damaged the reputation of her father among his fellow solicitors. Embarrassed, Mr. Barrington seized the opportunity to start a new life across the Atlantic, and dragged his insolent daughter along for good measure.

"That Tuesday, the weather grew ever violent as our caravan sailed into a wall of storm clouds.

By nightfall, all but a few deckhands had retreated
below to escape the pounding wind and rain. The
ship was tossed so severely that Captain White
ordered all candles snuffed, for fear that the waves
could knock one over and start a fire. With Edeva
in my arms, I huddled in total darkness below
deck—felt the dizzying motion of the ship; heard
the groans of wooden planks and fellow passengers being sick. I know that Elizabeth Barrington
had been there with us when the lights went out.
I had seen her myself. But she was not there in the
morning."

The storm had passed, and the sun had returned to its
oppressive perch. Because Elizabeth often kept to herself
below, it wasn't until midmorning that anyone noticed
her absence. Passengers called her name but received no
answer. A full search of the ship turned up nothing. A second search, which included bags of flour being emptied
and barrels of gunpowder sifted through, was likewise
fruitless. She was gone. Captain White made another suc-
cinct and dispassionate entry in his log: *Girle fell overboarde in a storme. Deade.*

"Privately, we all knew that the unhappy girl had
taken her own life. That she had leapt into the sea
and drowned. Prayers were said for her soul (though
we knew it to be condemned to hell—suicide
being an unforgivable sin in the eyes of God)."

The last three weeks of their voyage were free of further accidents and blessed with better weather. Even so,

the sight of dry land was an especially welcome one. The colonists set about felling trees, rebuilding abandoned shelters, planting crops, and making contact with the natives—particularly the Croatoan, who'd welcomed the English in the past. But this time their truce proved short-lived. Exactly one week after the first of John White's ships landed on Roanoke Island, one of his colonists, George Howe, was found facedown in the shallow waters of Albemarle Sound. He'd been fishing alone when a group of "savages" took him by surprise. White pieced the attack together based on the evidence at the scene. From his log:

> These Savages being secretly hidden among
> high reedes, where oftentimes they find the Deere
> asleep, and so kill them, espied our man wading
> in the water alone, almost naked, without any
> weapon, save only a smal forked sticke, catching
> Crabs therewithal, and also being strayed two
> miles from his company, and shot at him in the
> water, where they gave him sixteen wounds with
> their arrowes: and after they had slaine him with
> their wooden swords, they beat his head in pieces,
> and fled over the water.

White concluded that Howe was shot with sixteen "arrowes" because the body had sixteen small puncture wounds in it.

> "In truth, no arrows were found in or near
> Mr. Howe. Governor White also omitted an
> important detail from his record—that the body
> had already begun to decompose, even though

Mr. Howe had only been dead several hours
before being discovered."

On August 18th, the colony turned its thoughts from
the Croatoan and rejoiced at the arrival of its first baby,
Virginia Dare—John White's granddaughter. She was
the first English baby born in the New World, and like
her mother, possessed a shock of red hair. The birth was
attended by the colony's only doctor, Thomas Crowley.

"Crowley was a plump, balding man of fifty-
six. Tall in stature, he had a kind, pockmarked
face, and a well-known love of jokes. For this and
his skill as a physician he was held in high regard,
and few things gave him a greater thrill than
making a patient forget his troubles in laughter."

Satisfied that his colony was off to a strong start (the
unpleasantness of Mr. Howe's demise notwithstanding),
John White sailed back to England to report on their
progress and bring back supplies. He left behind 113 men,
women, and children—including his infant grandchild,
Virginia. If all went well, he would return in several
months with food, building materials, and goods to trade
with the natives.

"All did not go well."

A series of events conspired to keep John White in
England for the next three years.

First, his crew refused to sail back during the dangerous
winter months. The summer crossing had been dangerous

and deadly enough. Unable to find a replacement crew, White endured what must have been a maddening, worrisome winter. By the time spring finally arrived, England was at war with Spain, and Queen Elizabeth needed every worthy ship at her disposal. That included the vessels White had planned to take back to the New World. He scrambled and found a pair of smaller, older ships that Her Majesty didn't require. But shortly into the voyage, both of these were captured and plundered by Spanish pirates. With no supplies left for his colonists, White turned around and headed back to England. The war with Spain raged on for two more years, leaving John White stranded in his home country, endlessly frustrated. In 1590 (having given up on bringing back supplies), he was finally able to secure passage on a merchant ship. On August 18th, his granddaughter Virginia's third birthday, he set foot on Roanoke Island once again.

They were gone.

Every last man, woman, and child. His daughter. His baby granddaughter. The Barringtons. Gone. His colony had simply vanished into thin air. The buildings remained exactly as they had been (though weather-beaten and overgrown). Tools and supplies were exactly where they belonged. Surrounded by rich soil and abundant wildlife, how could they have starved? If there was some kind of pestilence, where were the mass graves? If there was a battle, where were signs? It didn't make any sense.

There were only two clues of any note: the word "Croatoan" carved into one of the fence posts of the perimeter wall, and the letters "CRO" carved into the bark of a nearby tree. Had the Croatoan attacked the colony? It seemed unlikely. They would have burned it to the ground, for one thing. And there would be bodies. Evidence. *Something.* White guessed (or hoped, anyway) that the cryptic carvings meant the colonists, for whatever reason, had resettled on nearby Croatoan Island. But he wouldn't get a chance to prove his theory. The weather was taking a turn for the worse, and the crew of his merchant ship refused to remain any longer. After three years spent trying to return, and only a few hours on dry land, he was given a choice: return to England and try to mount another expedition, or be left to fend for himself on a strange continent with no idea where his countrymen were—or if they were alive at all. White sailed away, never to set foot in the New World again. He spent the rest of his days haunted by grief, guilt, and above all, bewilderment over the disappearance of his 113 colonists.

> "I think," said Henry, "that it is better he never learned the truth."

––––––––––

Shortly after Governor White's first return to England, the people of Roanoke were beset by a strange illness, which produced an acute fever in its victims. This fever led to delusions, coma, and eventually death.

> "Dr. Crowley thought the disease a native one.
> He was powerless to curb its effects. In the three
> months following Governor White's departure,
> ten of us succumbed to this plague. In the three
> months after that, a dozen more. Their bodies
> were carried a distance into the woods and buried,
> lest the sickness contaminate the soil near our

> settlement. We grew ever more fearful that ours
> would be the next body carried off. A near-
> constant vigil was kept on the island's eastern
> shore, in hopes that sails would soon be spotted
> there. But none were. It is likely that things
> would have continued thus, had not the hideous
> discovery been made."

Eleanor Dare couldn't sleep. Not while her husband
fought for his life a mere fifty yards away. She dressed,
wrapped sleeping baby Virginia in a blanket, and walked
through the freezing air to Dr. Crowley's building, resigned
to spending a restless night by her husband's side in prayer.

> "Upon entering, Mrs. Dare was met with the
> ghastly sight of Crowley with his mouth around
> her husband's neck. He withdrew and presented
> his fangs, drawing screams from her. Thus alerted,
> several of our men ran into Crowley's building
> with their swords and crossbows, only to find the
> woman slaughtered, and the infant Virginia in
> the vampire's claws. Crowley warned the men to
> retreat. They refused. Having no knowledge of
> vampires, the men perished at once."

Their screams woke the rest of the colonists, including
Henry.

> "I dressed and told Edeva to do the same,
> thinking it an attack by the natives. I charged into
> the night with my pistol determined to protect my
> home to the last. But on reaching the clearing in

the center of our village, I was met with an incredible sight. A terrifying sight. Thomas Crowley—
his eyes black, a pair of white razors in his
mouth—tearing Jack Barrington in half, spilling
his innards everywhere. I saw friends scattered on
the ground. Some with limbs missing. Some with
heads missing. Crowley took notice of me and
advanced. I leveled my pistol and fired. The ball
found its mark, piercing the center of his chest.
But this failed to slow him in the least. He continued to advance. I am not ashamed to admit that
all courage left me. I could think only of escape.
Only of Edeva, and the unborn child in her belly."

Henry turned and ran the fifty yards home as fast as
he could. Edeva was already waiting in the doorway, and
he hardly slowed as he grabbed her hand and continued
toward the tree line. *The coast. Let us make haste to the
coas—*

"I could hear him running behind us. Each
step breaking the earth. Each one closer than the
last. We ran into the trees. Ran until our lungs
burned—until Edeva began to slow, and I felt his
steps behind us."

We will never see the coast.

"I remember none of it. Only that I woke on
my stomach and knew at once that my wounds
were mortal. My body lay shattered—my
limbs all but useless. Dried blood over my eyes

rendering me half blind. By the sound of Edeva's
labored breath, I knew that she was even closer
to the end than I. She lay on her side, her yellow
dress stained with blood. Her yellow hair matted
with it. I dragged myself to her with two broken
arms. Dragged my eyes close to hers—open and
distant. I ran my hand through her hair and simply looked at her. Simply watched her breathing
slow, all the while whispering, 'Don't be afraid,
love.' And then she stopped."

By sunrise, Crowley had dragged most of his fellow
settlers into the woods. He'd been left no alternative.
Explaining a plague was easy. Almost as easy as explaining a man falling from a crow's nest, or a girl jumping
overboard, or a fisherman being attacked by savages.
But screams in the night, followed by the disappearance
of four men, a woman, and an infant? That he couldn't
explain. They would question him. Discover him. And
that, he couldn't have. One by one, he dragged their battered bodies away. Of his 112 fellow settlers, only one had
been spared his wrath.

Crowley had hesitated to kill Virginia Dare. A baby
that he had personally delivered? The first English soul
born in the New World? These things had sentimental
value. Besides, she would have no memory of what had
happened here, and a young female companion might
prove useful in the lonely years to come.

"He returned from the woods with the baby
in his arms. I daresay he was surprised to see
me alive—though barely so—struggling to keep

my feet while I carved the letters 'CRO' into a tree with a knife. My dying effort to expose the identity of my murderer. Of my wife and child's murderer. His shock subsided, Crowley could not help his laughter, for I had unwittingly given him a brilliant idea. Setting the baby down and taking my knife, he carved the word "Croatoan" onto a nearby post, all the while smiling at the thought of John White massacring scores of unsuspecting natives in retaliation."

Crowley prepared to take Henry's head. But here he hesitated again.

"He was suddenly struck by the realization that he would then be the only English-speaking man for three thousand miles in any direction—a lonely prospect for one with such a love of jokes. Who, then, to laugh at them? I watched him kneel over me and cut his wrist with a fingernail, letting the blood spill over my face and into my mouth."

Crowley buried the last of the colonists and headed south toward the Spanish territories, carrying a crying baby in one arm and the half-dead body of a young Henry in the other. Soon, after the sickness and the hallucinations passed—after his bones mended themselves—his companion would open his eyes to a new life in a New World. But first, Thomas Crowley would celebrate by feasting on the first English blood born to it.

He had decided to feast on Virginia Dare.

VI

Twenty-one days after Henry carried him into the house unconscious, Abe was well enough to leave his room and take a tour.

> I was astonished to find that my windowless
> room was, in fact, part of a windowless house. A
> house dug entirely out of the earth—its walls and
> floors meticulously lined with stone and clay. A
> kitchen where he had prepared my food on the
> woodstove. A library where he had replenished
> my supply of books. A second bedchamber. All
> lit by oil light, and all decorated with elegant fur-
> nishings and gold-framed paintings, as if Henry
> thought these his windows to the outside world.

"This," said Henry, "this has been my purpose these past seven years. Building this home, one shovelful of dirt at a time."

> All four rooms centered on a small stairwell.
> Here was the only place lit in part by the sun,
> its soft light streaming down from above. Here
> were the wooden stairs that I had heard Henry
> climb up and down, up and down, countless
> times. We followed them up to a flimsy wooden
> door—sunlight squeaking through the cracks.
> Opening it and stepping through, I was surprised
> to find myself standing in a small log cabin. This
> was modestly furnished, complete with a working

woodstove, rug, and bed. Henry donned a pair of spectacles with dark lenses as we stepped into the day. Now I could see the genius of his design, for from the outside, his home looked nothing more than a modest cabin on a lonely wooded hillside. "Shall we, then?" asked Henry.

So began the only real schooling Abraham Lincoln ever had.

Every morning for the next four weeks, Abe and Henry climbed the stairs to the false cabin. Every day, Henry taught him something more about finding and fighting vampires.

Every night, theory was put into practice as Henry challenged Abe to hunt him in the dark.

> Gone were my cloves of garlic and flasks of holy water. Gone were my knives. What remained were my stakes, my ax, and my mind. It was this last weapon which Henry spent the majority of his time improving—teaching me how to hide from a vampire's animal senses. How to use its quickness to my advantage. How to drive it from hiding, and how to kill it without putting my limbs (and neck) at risk. But for all of Henry's lessons, nothing was more valuable than the time we spent trying to kill each other. At first I had been astonished by his speed and strength— convinced there was no way I would ever be its equal. Over time, however, I noticed that it took him longer and longer to subdue me. I even found myself landing the occasional strike. Soon, it was

not uncommon for me to best him three times
out of ten.

"I find myself in a curious position," said Henry after
Abe had managed to pin him one night. "I feel rather like
a rabbit that has taken a fox for its pupil."
Abe smiled.
"And I like a mouse who has taken a cat for its tutor."

———————

Early autumn came, and with it an end to Abe's stay. He
and Henry stood outside the false cabin in the morning
sun—Henry with his dark glasses, Abe carrying a few
belongings and food for his journey. He was already
weeks overdue at Little Pigeon Creek, and likely to get
a thrashing from his father for coming home without the
money he'd promised to earn.

> Henry, however, saw fit to remedy this with
> a gift of twenty-five dollars—five more than I'd
> promised my father. Naturally, pride demanded I
> refuse this gift as too generous. Naturally, Henry's
> pride demanded I accept it. I did, and thanked him
> profusely. There was much I had thought of saying
> at this moment: Thanking him for his kindness
> and hospitality. Thanking him for saving my life.
> For teaching me how to preserve it in the future.
> I thought of apologizing for the harshness with
> which I had first judged him. However, none of
> this proved necessary, for Henry quickly extended
> a hand and said, "Let us say good-bye, then say no
> more." We shook hands, and I was off. But there

was something I had forgotten to ask. Something I had wondered since we first met. I turned back to him: "Henry…what were you doing at the river that night?" He looked strangely stern upon hearing this. More so than I had seen him the whole of my stay.

"There is no honor in taking sleeping children from their beds," he said, "or feasting upon the innocent. I have given you the means of delivering punishment to those who do…in time, I shall give you their names."

With that, he turned and walked back toward the cabin.

"Judge us not equally, Abraham. We may all deserve hell, but some of us deserve it sooner than others."

Four

A Truth Too Terrible

The Autocrat of all the Russias will resign his crown, and proclaim his subjects free republicans sooner than will our American masters voluntarily give up their slaves.

—*Abraham Lincoln, in a letter to George Robertson*
August 15th, 1855

I

My dear sister is gone....

In 1826, Sarah Lincoln had married Little Pigeon Creek neighbor Aaron Grigsby, six years her senior. The couple had moved into a cabin close to both of their families, and within nine months announced that they were expecting a child. Shortly after she went into labor, on January 20th, 1828, Sarah had begun to lose an unusual amount of blood. Rather than fetch help, Aaron had tried to deliver the baby himself, too frightened to leave his wife's side.

By the time he'd realized how grave the situation was and run for a doctor, it was too late.

Sarah was twenty years old. She and the stillborn baby boy were buried together in the Little Pigeon Baptist Church Cemetery. On hearing the news, Abe sobbed uncontrollably. It was as if he'd lost his mother all over again. On hearing the details of his brother-in-law's hesitation, Abe's grief was joined by rage.

> The no-good son of a bitch let her lie there and die. For this I shall never forgive him.

"Never" turned out to be only a few short years. Aaron Grigsby died in 1831.

———

By the time he turned nineteen, Abraham Lincoln had covered nearly every inch of every page in his journal with ink (in ever-smaller lettering as he neared the end). It held seven years of remarkable records. Insights into his disdain for his father. His hatred of vampires. Accounts of his earliest battles with the walking dead.

It also held no fewer than sixteen folded letters between its pages. The first had arrived barely a month after Abe left Henry's cabin and returned to Little Pigeon Creek.

> Dear Abraham,
>   I trust this finds you well. Below is the name of someone who deserves it sooner. You will find him in the town of Rising Sun—three days upriver from Louisville. Do not construe this letter as an expectation of action. The choice

is yours, always. I merely wish to offer the
opportunity for continued study, and provide
some small measure of relief for the injustices
done you, as you will no doubt seek their redress
on your own.

Beneath this was the name Silas Williams and the
word "cobbler." The letter was signed only with an H.
Abe rode to Rising Sun a week later, telling his father that
he was off to Louisville to look for work.

I had expected to find the place plagued by a
rash of disappearances or pestilence of some sort.
However, the people seemed in excellent spirits, and their town in excellent health. I walked
among them with my weapons hidden beneath
my long coat (for it had occurred to me that the
sight of a tall stranger with an ax might engender
concern among the citizenry). I intruded upon
the kindness of a passerby, and asked where I
might find the local cobbler, for my shoes were
very badly worn. Having been directed to a
modest shop not more than fifty yards away, I
entered and found a bearded, bespectacled man
hard at work—his walls covered with worn and
dismembered shoes. He was a meek creature of
some five-and-thirty years, and he was alone.
"Silas Williams?" I asked.
    "Yes?"
    I cut his head off with my ax and left.
    When his head fell to the floor, his eyes were
as black as the shoes he had been polishing. I have

not the faintest idea what his crimes were, nor do
I care. I care only that there is one less vampire
today than there was yesterday. It is strange, I
admit, to think that I owe this fact to a vampire.
However, it has long been said that "my enemy's
enemy is my friend."

Fifteen more letters arrived in Little Pigeon Creek over
the next three years, each with nothing more than a name,
a place, and that unmistakable H.

There were times that two would arrive in as
many months. There were times that none arrived
for three months' time. Regardless of when they
came, I always set out as soon as my work would
allow. Each hunt brought new lessons. New
improvements to my skills and tools. Some were
as effortless as the beheading of Silas Williams.
Others saw me lying in wait for hours on end or
posing as prey—only to turn the tables when the
vampire attacked. Some required a day's ride or less.
Others took me as far as Fort Wayne and Nashville.

No matter how long the journey, he always carried the
same items with him.

In my bundle I carried whatever food I could,
a pan for frying pork, and a pot for boiling water.
These were wrapped in my long coat, which I
had paid a seamstress to further alter by removing
the inside pockets and sewing a thick leather lining
in their place. The whole was tied to the handle

FIG.12 – ABE STANDS AMONG HIS VAMPIRE VICTIMS IN A PAINTING
TITLED 'THE YOUNG HUNTER' BY DIEGO SWANSON (OIL ON
CANVAS, 1913).

of my ax, which I kept sharp enough to shave my whiskers. I added a crossbow to this little arsenal, too, one that I had fashioned myself using the drawings in a borrowed copy of *Weapons of the Taborites* as my guide. I continued to practice with it when time allowed, but dared not wield it in battle until my skills were much improved.

While hunting vampires offered a surplus of vengeance, it paid nothing in the way of real money. As a young man, Abe was expected to help provide for his family. And in keeping with customs of the time, any wages he earned belonged to his father until his twenty-first birthday. As one might imagine, this didn't sit well.

> The idea of handing my earnings to such a man! Of my labor rewarding his lack thereof. Of doing <u>anything</u> to benefit one so shiftless. So selfish and cowardly! It is no more than indentured servitude!

Abe was always looking for a job, whether clearing trees, hauling grain, or ferrying passengers from the banks of the Ohio to waiting steamboats on a scow of his own construction.* In early May 1828, when Abe was still reeling from his sister's death, a job came looking for him for a change. One that would change his life.

---

*Abe was amazed that passengers were willing to fork over a dollar apiece to have themselves ferried a distance of (in some cases) thirty feet. As in his days on the Old Cumberland Trail in Kentucky, he also reveled in meeting travelers and hearing their stories, many of which he would retell for the rest of his life.

James Gentry owned one of the largest and most prosperous farms around Little Pigeon Creek. He'd been an acquaintance of Thomas Lincoln for the better part of ten years and was unlike him in just about every imaginable way. Naturally, Abe had always looked up to him on account of this. For his part, Gentry had come to admire the tall, hardworking, and modest Lincoln boy. His own son Allen was a few years older than Abe, but a pinch less mature. The industrious farmer wanted to expand his reach (and his profits) by selling his corn and bacon downriver in Mississippi, where sugar and cotton were king, but where other goods were in great demand.

> Mr. Gentry asked if I would join Allen in
> building and piloting a flatboat of his goods
> downriver—stopping in Mississippi and points
> south to sell quantities of corn, pork, and other
> sundries. For this he would pay me the sum
> of eight dollars each month, and purchase my
> steamboat ticket home from New Orleans.

It's likely Abe would have accepted this job even if there'd been no promise of money. It was a chance to escape. A chance for adventure.

He put his ax (and in fairness, the carpentry skills he'd learned from his father) to work building a sturdy, forty-foot flatboat from green oak, cutting each plank and fastening it to his frame with wooden pegs. He built a shelter in the middle of the deck, which he made big enough so that he could stand inside without fear of hitting his head on the ceiling. Inside were two beds, a small stove, and a lantern as well as four small windows that could be shut "in the event of attack." Finally he coated the seams with pitch* and fashioned a steering oar.**

> At the risk of sounding proud, I must say that she turned out rather well considering that she was the first I had ever built. Even when we burdened her with ten tons of goods, she drew less than two feet of water.

Allen and Abe launched their fully loaded flatboat on May 23rd. It was to be a journey of more than a thousand miles. For Abe, it was to be his first glimpse of the Deep South.

> We battled winds and currents, and kept an ever-vigilant eye on the river ahead. On many occasions, we were forced to free our modest vessel from mud or brush after running aground on a bank. We filled our bellies with the endless reserves of corn and pork on board, and washed our clothes in the ever-present Mississippi when they grew offensive. For weeks this continued. Sometimes we covered as many as sixty miles in a day, sometimes thirty or less.

The young men would holler with excitement when they crossed paths with a steamboat, those miraculous, gleaming stern-wheelers puffing and splashing their way

---

*A tarlike resin.
**A rudder with a long handle so it could be controlled from the roof of the shelter.

against the current. Their excitement would build at the sight of distant smoke rising from the river ahead, then crescendo as they approached and passed, shouting greetings and waving to passengers, pilots, and clerks.

> The noise of engines and churning water. Black smoke rising from its chimney and white steam from its pipes. A boat that could take a man all the way from New Orleans to Louisville in under twenty-five days. Were there any limits to the ingenuity of man?

This excitement having quieted, they would float for miles with nary a sound.

> It was a sort of peace I have rarely enjoyed since. As if we were the only two souls on earth— all of nature ours to enjoy. I wondered why a creator who had dreamt such beauty would have slandered it with such evil. Such grief. Why He had not been content to leave it unspoilt. I still wonder.

When the sun dipped out of sight, Allen and Abe would start looking for a suitable place to anchor—a town, if possible. One night, not long after they'd passed through Baton Rouge, Lincoln and Gentry tied up on the Duchesne Plantation, securing the flatboat to a tree with rope. As was their routine, the young men fried their supper, checked to see if the ropes were secure, and adjourned to their shelter. Here they would read or talk until their eyes grew weary, snuff their lantern, and sleep in perfect darkness.

I woke with a start and reached for the club
that I kept near. Springing to my feet, I saw the
trace of two figures in the doorway. I daresay
they were a good deal surprised at my height—
and a good deal more surprised by the ferocity
with which I bludgeoned them about the head.
I chased them (bludgeoning my own head on a
crossbeam as I did) out onto the deck, where the
moon revealed them in full. They were Negroes—
seven in all. The other five were busily trying to
untie our boat. "Off with you devils!" I cried,
"before I brain the lot of you!" To make them
know my sincerity, I cracked another across his
ribs, and raised my club to crack another. This
proved unnecessary. The Negroes fled. As they
did, I chanced to see a broken pair of leg irons
around one of their ankles, and knew the truth at
once. These were no common thieves. They were
slaves. Likely escaped from this very plantation
and looking to throw off the scent of the dogs by
making off with our boat.

Gentry was roused by the commotion and helped Abe
chase the remaining slaves into the woods. Satisfied they
wouldn't return for the moment, they cut the flatboat loose
and took their chances navigating the Mississippi at night.

We set out, Allen holding our lantern at the
bow and squinting into the night, me working the
steering oar from atop our shelter, trying to keep
us dead down the middle. I could not help but
steal a look back at the bank, and as I did, I saw

a white figure running toward the river from the plantation. Here was the first of the overseers come to reclaim his slaves. But this man, this tiny white figure, did not stop running at the river's edge. He <u>jumped</u> to the opposite bank in one long, impossible leap. They did not run from men or dogs.

They ran from a vampire.

I thought briefly of steering us into the muddy bank. Of taking the bundle from under my bed and giving chase. I cannot say whether I thought the attempt hopeless, or the victims worthless. I can say only that I did not stop. Allen (it now dawning on him how perilously close he had come to having his throat cut) presently let forth a stream of profanity the likes of which I had never heard, and much of which I did not understand. Cursing himself for failing to bring a musket along. Condemning "those murderous sons of bitches." I remained silent—focused only on keeping us dead down the middle. I could not bring myself to hate our attackers, for it occurred to me that they were merely trying to preserve their lives. In doing so, they had thought it necessary to deprive me of mine. Allen went on. Something about "no-good black" something or others.

"Judge them not equally," I said.

II

Allen and Abe reached New Orleans at midday on June 20th, twisting round the ever-tightening bends of the

Mississippi as they neared its center, where they would be able to sell their remaining goods (and sell their boat for lumber) at any number of busy wharves. A light rain greeted them, welcome relief from the oppressive humidity that had dogged so much of their trip downriver.

> The north of the city presented itself first— sprawling and lively. Farms became houses. Houses became streets. Streets became two-story brick buildings with iron railings on their balconies. So many sailing ships! So many steamboats! Flatboats numbering in the hundreds, all clamoring for their little piece of the great river.

New Orleans was a city of 40,000, and the South's gateway to the world. Walking along its wharves, one was likely to encounter sailors from every corner of Europe and South America—even some from the Orient.

> We could not be rid of our cargo quickly enough. How we longed to explore this city of endless wonders! I was all astonishment, for I had never in my life seen such multitudes— their tongues dripping with French and Spanish phrases. Ladies fanning themselves in the latest fashions, and gentlemen clad from head to toe in suits of the highest quality. Streets filled with horses and carts; merchants selling every ware imagined. We strolled the rue de Chartres; beheld the Basilica of St. Louis in Jackson Square, so named for our president's heroic defense of the city. Here, teams of men and mules dug trenches

for gas pipes. When their months of work were
finished, one of them proudly sang, the city
would "gleam like a sparkling jewel in the night,
with nary a torch or a candle in sight."

Abe was struck by the liveliness of the city and its people. He was also struck by the age of the things around him.

I imagined myself conveyed to those places in
Europe that I had so often read about. Here, for
the first time in my life, were homes with ivy-
covered walls. Here were men of letters. Architec-
ture and art. Here were vast libraries filled with
eager students and appreciative patrons. Here
were all the things that my father would never
understand.

Marie Laveau's boardinghouse on St. Claude Street
was hardly the most impressive of the city's Spanish-style
buildings, but it was good enough for a pair of Indiana flatboatmen to rest their heads for a week.

There was a saloon not far from Mrs.
Laveau's where one could have his fill of rum
or wine or whiskey. Flush with money from
selling our goods and our boat, and flush with
the excitement of being in such a city for the
first time, I admit we indulged in these—more
even than a pair of young, foolish men should
have. The saloon was overfilled with sailors from
all parts of the world. Flatboatmen from every
point on the Mississippi, Ohio, and Sangamon.

A brawl seemed to break out every third minute. It is a wonder they did not break out more
frequently.

Surly boatmen weren't the only strange characters
Abe encountered during his first twenty-four hours in
New Orleans. The following morning, as he and Allen
stumbled through the streets in search of an inoffensive
breakfast—clutching their aching heads and shielding
their eyes from the sun—Abe spotted something incredible coming toward them on Bienville Street.

> ...a coach of lustrous white, pulled by a pair
> of white horses, and driven by a boy wearing a
> coat of the same color. Behind him sat a pair of
> gentlemen: one cherubic and red-cheeked, his suit
> an unremarkable blend of greens and grays. The
> other wore a suit of white silk, a complement to
> his fair skin and long white hair. His eyes hid-
> den behind dark glasses. He was as obvious a
> vampire as I had ever laid eyes upon, and by all
> appearances, the wealthiest. Elegant and refined.
> Unencumbered by shadows. Free to mingle as he
> pleased. And <u>laughing</u>. He and the living gentle-
> man were in the midst of what looked a very
> cheerful conversation. I could think only of stak-
> ing him through the heart as his coach neared. Of
> chopping off his head. How the blood would look
> against the white silk of his coat! Alas, I could
> only watch him—restrained by the absence of
> weapons and the presence of an aching head. The
> white-haired vampire gave me a knowing look as

he passed. And then the strangest feeling…the
feeling of invading eyes reading the pages of my
journal. The sound of a voice with no source…

Judge us not equally, Abraham.

They turned onto Dauphine Street and were
gone. But the feeling of invading eyes remained.
This time the source was plain as day. I spotted
a pale little fellow across the street, half hidden
in an alley, his eyes unquestionably fixed on me.
He was dressed entirely in black, with a mess of
hair to match, and a small mustache beneath his
dark glasses. Unmistakably a vampire. Seeing
that he had been discovered, the figure turned
and disappeared into the alley. This I could not
leave uninvestigated! Aching head be damned! I
left my friend to his own stumbling and hastened
after the stranger—chasing him down the alley to
Conti Street, then across Basin Street, where the
devil sought refuge behind the cemetery* walls. I
had been no more than ten paces behind him, but
on reaching the gates I perceived him not. He had
vanished. Lost in a maze of crypts. I wondered if
he had simply slipped into one of them; wondered
how many vampires were—

"And what mean you by chasing me so, sir?"

I spun around and raised my fists. He was
behind me—his back against the inside of the
cemetery wall, clever devil. Staring at me, his

---

*Abe is referring to what is today called St. Louis Cemetery #1.

dark glasses in his fingers. His tired eyes and high forehead.

"'Chasing' you, sir?" I said. "What meant you by running?"

"Well, sir, the manner in which you shielded your eyes from the light…the familiar glance you shared with the gentleman in the coach…I thought you a vampire."

I could scarcely believe what I had heard.

"You thought _me_ a vampire?" he asked. "But I…"

A smile grew over the little man's lips. He looked at the dark glasses in his fingers; at the look on this tall stranger's face. He began to laugh.

"I believe us both guilty of grave misjudgments."

"Forgive me, sir, but…am I to understand that you are not a vampire?"

"Regrettably, no," he said, laughing, "or I should still have my breath."

I offered my apology and extended my hand. "Abe Lincoln." The little man took it.

"Edgar Poe."

III

Abraham Lincoln and Edgar Allan Poe were born within weeks of each other. Both lost their mothers as children. Otherwise, their upbringings couldn't have been more different.

After his mother's death, Poe had been taken in by a wealthy merchant, John Allan (who dealt in slaves, among other commodities). Whisked away from his native Boston, he'd been thoroughly educated in some of England's finest schools. He'd seen the wonders of Europe that Abe could only read about in books. Around the time Abe swore his vengeance against vampires and staked Jack Barts through the heart, Edgar Allan Poe returned to America, settling with his adoptive father in Virginia and enjoying all the luxuries associated with belonging to one of its wealthiest families. Poe had everything Abe could ever want: The finest education. The finest homes. More books than he could count. A father with no want of ambition.

But he and Abe were equally miserable creatures.

As a first-year student at the University of Virginia, Poe drank and gambled away every penny his foster father sent him, until John Allan finally cut him off. Enraged and abandoned, he fled Virginia for Boston and enlisted in the army under the name Edgar A. Perry, loading artillery shells by day, and writing ever-darker stories and poems by candlelight. It was here, while stationed in the city of his birth, that Edgar Allan Poe met his first vampire.

> Using his own money, Poe published a short
> collection of poems, identifying himself only
> as "A Bostonian" on its cover (for fear of being
> mocked by his fellow enlisted men). Of the
> fifty he paid to have printed, fewer than twenty
> sold. Notwithstanding this poor reception, one
> reader saw a particular genius in Poe's collection,

and bribed its printer to learn the author's true
identity. "It was shortly [after this] that I was
visited upon by a Mr. Guy de Vere—a widower
of considerable means. He explained how he had
come to learn my name, and that he had been
much affected by my work. He then demanded
to know what a vampire was doing serving in the
army."

Guy de Vere was convinced that only a vampire could
have written poems with such an outlook on death and
grief. Poems of such darkness and beauty.

"He was surprised, then, to find a living man
their creator. I was likewise surprised to find
myself speaking to a man who was no longer
living."

Poe was endlessly fascinated by the stately, bloodsucking de Vere, and de Vere by the gloomy, brilliant Poe. The
two struck up a tenuous friendship, much as Henry and
Abe had done. But Poe wasn't interested in learning about
vampires to better hunt them—he wanted to know about
the *experience* of living in darkness, of moving beyond
death, so that he could better write about it. De Vere was
all too happy to oblige (with the understanding that Poe
would never reveal his identity in print).*
Several months after making de Vere's acquaintance,
Poe's regiment was assigned to Fort Moultrie in South

---

*An understanding Poe seemed to have forgotten by 1843,
when de Vere was used as a character in Poe's "Lenore."

Carolina. With no city to satisfy his appetite for culture, and no means of satisfying his thirst for further vampire knowledge, the army suddenly seemed a prison.

> Therefore he had decided to grant himself an "unofficial leave" and come to New Orleans for the stated purpose of "studying vampires"—for de Vere had insisted there was "not a better place in America to do so." Judging by the number of times he filled and emptied his whiskey glass, he had also come to drink himself to death. We sat that evening in the saloon near Mrs. Laveau's. Allen Gentry had gone off to "consort with ladies of a certain character," leaving us free to talk on that subject we enjoyed most, but dared not discuss freely. We spoke well into the night, sharing everything we had read, and heard, and witnessed firsthand regarding vampires.

"How then do they learn to feed?" asked Abe as the barkeep swept the empty tavern around them. "How do they know to shy away from the su—"

"How does a calf know to stand? A honeybee to…to build a hive?"

Poe took another drink.

"It is their nature, beautiful and simple. That you would destroy such beings, Mr. Lincoln, such superior creatures, seems madness to me."

"That you speak of them with such reverence, Mr. Poe, seems madness to *me*."

"Can you imagine it? Can you imagine seeing the universe through such eyes? Laughing in the face of time and death—the world your Garden of Eden? Your library? Your harem?"

"Yes. I can also imagine a want of companionship, and a want of peace."

"Well, I can imagine a want of nothing! Think of the fortune one could amass, the comforts one could afford, the wonders of the world one could see at his leisure!"

"And when this intoxication has worn away...when every desire is fulfilled and every language learned—when there are no more distant cities to explore; no classics to be studied; not another coin to be stuffed into one's coffers—what then? One can have all the comforts of the world, but what use are they if there is no comfort in them?"

Abe shared a folktale, one that he had first heard from a traveler on the Old Cumberland Road.

> There was once a man who yearned to live forever. Beginning in his youth, he prayed for God to grant him immortality. He was charitable and earnest, honest in his business dealings, true to his wife, and kind to his children. He humbled himself before God, and preached His laws to all who would listen. And yet, he continued to age with every passing year, until he finally died a frail old man. When he reached heaven, he asked, "Lord, why did You refuse to answer my prayer? Did I not live my life according to Your word? Did I not praise Your name to all who would listen?" To which God replied, "You did all of these things. And that is why I did not curse you by answering your prayer."

"You speak of eternal life. You speak of indulging the mind and body," said Abe. "But what of the soul?"

"And what use is a soul to a creature that shall never die?"

Abe couldn't help but smile. Here was a strange little man with a strange way of seeing things. Only the second living man he'd ever met who knew the truth of vampires. He drank to excess and spoke in an irritating, high-pitched voice. It was hard not to like him.

"I begin to suspect," said Abe, "that you would like to *be* one of them."

Poe laughed at the suggestion. "Is not our existence long and miserable enough?" he asked, laughing. "Who in God's name would seek to prolong it?"

IV

On the following afternoon, June 22nd, Abe wandered along St. Philip Street by himself. Allen Gentry hadn't returned from whatever depravities he'd enjoyed the night before, and Poe had staggered off to his own boarding-house at dawn. After sleeping half the day away, Abe had decided that some fresh air and a stroll were desperately needed to chase the fog from his mind and bitter taste from his mouth.

> I happened upon some great commotion in the street as I neared the river—a large crowd gathered around a platform, which had been decorated in reds and whites and blues. A yellow banner flew above this makeshift stage, upon which were

the words SLAVE AUCTION TODAY! ONE
O'CLOCK! More than a hundred men were
crowded in front of the platform. More than twice
that number of Negroes milled about nearby.
Pipe smoke choked the air as prospective buyers
mingled—the rare laugh breaking through the
din, their pencils and papers held ready as the
hour neared. The auctioneer, a man every ounce as
plump and pink as a hog, then stepped before them
and began: "Honored gentlemen, I am pleased to
present the day's first lot." Upon this, the first
Negro, a man of perhaps five-and-thirty years,
took the stage and bowed heartily, smiling and
standing tall in his ill-fitting suit (which looked
to have been purchased for the occasion). "A bull,
name of Cuff! Still in the prime of his strength! As
fine a field hand as you are ever likely to see, and
sure to sire a brood of sons with backs every bit
as sound!" That this "bull" seemed so fervent in
his hope of being bought—standing up straight,
smiling and bowing as the auctioneer described his
many uses—I could not help my pity and revul-
sion. The rest of this man's life…all the future
generations of his progeny. All of it rested on this
moment. All of it in the hands of a man he had
never met. A man willing to pay the highest price.

All told, there were more than two-hundred slaves
scheduled to be auctioned over a two-day period. For a
week leading up to the sale, they'd been held in a pair of
barns, where prospective buyers had been free to come
and inspect them.

This inspection involved all manner of invasion
and humiliation. Men, women, and children, ages
three years to five-and-seventy, were made to stand
bare before strangers. Their muscles were pulled at;
their mouths pried open and their teeth inspected.
They were made to walk and bend and lift, lest they
be concealing any lameness. They were made to list
their talents. To assist in driving up their own price.

This ran counter to their own interests, for the higher
the price,* the less likely they would ever be able to save
enough money to buy their freedom from the kind masters who allowed them to do so.

The theater of it all! Men and women! Children
and infants presented to this surly mob—this collection of so-called gentlemen! I saw a Negro girl
of three or four clinging to her mother, confused
as to why she was dressed in such clothes; why she
had been scrubbed the night before; made to stand
on this platform while men shouted numbers and
waved pieces of paper in the air. Again I wondered
why a Creator who had dreamt such beauty would
have slandered it with such evil.

If Lincoln saw any irony in the fact that he had come
downriver to sell goods to many of these same plantation
owners, he never wrote of it.

---

*A healthy man in his prime could fetch as much as $1,100 (an
impossible amount for a slave to bank), while an older woman
or those with any sort of impediment might net $100 or less.

"Gentlemen, I now ask your attention be
turned to a fine specimen of family if ever there
was! The bull by name of Israel—his teeth of the
regular sort, and his build uncommonly large.
You shall not find a better planter of rice in this
or any parish! His wife, Beatrice—with arms and
back almost as strong as that of a man's, yet hands
delicate enough to mend a lady's dress! Their
children—a boy of ten or eleven years, fated to
become as strong a worker as his father, and a girl
of four, her face as sweet as an angel's. You shall
never find four better specimens!"

Each slave followed his own sale with keen interest,
his eyes darting around as each bid was shouted out. If he
was purchased by a master with a reputation for kindness,
or one who had purchased some of his near relations, he
would leave the stage with something like contentment—
even joy on his face. But if he was sold to a man who
seemed especially cruel, or knew that he would never see
his loved ones again, the quiet anguish on his face was
indescribable.

One buyer in particular drew my interest—a
man whose pocketbook seemed bottomless, and
whose purchases seemed senseless. He arrived
at the auction after it had begun (this alone was
unusual) and snapped up a dozen slaves, with
seemingly no regard for their sex, or health, or
skills. In fact, he seemed interested only in those
Negroes described as "bargains." But his purchases were only part of the reason he drew my

suspicion. He was a slender man in a fine waist-length coat—shorter than I (though still quite tall), with a graying beard meant to conceal the scar that ran the length of his face, from his left eye, across his lips, to his chin. He held a parasol to shade himself from the sun, and wore dark glasses over his eyes. If he was not a vampire, he certainly admired their fashion. What was the meaning of it? Why had he purchased two older women of similar abilities? A boy with a lame leg? Why did he need so many slaves at all?

I resolved to follow him and find the answer.

V

Twelve slaves walked barefoot, winding their way north on a muddy road that traced the Mississippi. They were male and female, ranging from fourteen to sixty-six years of age. Some had known each other their whole lives. Some had met only an hour or two before. Each of the twelve had a rope around their waist connecting them to the others. In front of this convoy, their new gray-bearded master; behind it, a white overseer, his rifle ready to cut down any slave who dared to run. Both men rode comfortably on horseback. Abe was careful to keep his distance as they wound their way through the woods.

I walked a quarter of a mile behind the group. Close enough to hear the overseer's occasional barking, but far enough for my careful footfalls to escape the ears of a vampire.

Night had begun to fall by the time they reached a plantation eight miles north of the city, and a mile from the east bank of the river.

> It looked no different than any of the plantations I had seen up and down the Mississippi. A blacksmith's shop. A tanning yard. A grist mill. Storehouses, machinery, looms, sheds, stables, and some five-and-twenty slave quarters surrounding the planter's house. These were one-room cabins where a dozen Negroes might live together, sleeping on dirt floors or corn husk beds, their pine torches burning so the women could tend to their quilting work long into the night. By day the dark fields around me would be filled with noise and work. Gangs of a hundred men digging trenches in long rows. Women driving plows in the searing heat. The white overseers riding among them on horseback, looking for the slightest offense to punish by flogging their naked backs. In the center of it all stood the master's house. Those slaves "fortunate" enough to work here were spared the backbreaking toil of the fields, but by no means was theirs an easy existence, for they were just as likely to be flogged for the slightest transgression. Furthermore, female slaves of any age might well find themselves at the mercy of master's unspeakable whims.

Abe kept his distance as the twelve slaves were led past the *maison principale* and into a large barn, the inside lit by torches and hanging oil lamps. Hiding behind a shed some twenty yards away, he had a clear view through the open doors.

> Here they were joined by a large Negro (the
> master and overseer having adjourned to the
> house). He held a whip, which he cracked at the
> new arrivals while ordering them to form a line in
> the center of the barn. Thus arranged, they were
> made to sit—still joined at the waist by rope. A
> mulatto woman presently appeared carrying a large
> basket under her arm (this only serving to increase
> the apprehension of the newly arrived, for they had
> doubtless heard stories of slaves being branded by
> new masters). Happily, the basket was stuffed with
> food, to which the twelve slaves were instructed to
> help themselves freely. I watched their eyes shine
> at the sight of fried pork and corn cakes. Of cow's
> milk and handfuls of sugar candies. I saw such
> relief on their faces, for until this moment, they
> had been unsure of what cruelties awaited. They
> could hardly fill their starving bellies fast enough.

Abe wondered if he had been too hasty in his suspicion. Henry proved that there were vampires capable of kindness. Of restraint. Had these slaves been bought for the purpose of being freed? At the very least, would they be treated with compassion?

> This feast having gone on for what seemed a
> half hour, I watched a party of white men walk
> from the house to the barn. There were ten in all,
> including the master I had followed from New

Orleans. Each varied in age and build—though all looked to be men of some means. On their reaching the barn, the large Negro again cracked his whip and ordered the slaves to their feet, and set about removing the rope from around their waists. The mulatto woman collected her basket and made off with no want of haste.

The white men having assembled near the entrance, one of them handed something to his host (certainly papers of some sort—I suspect they were banknotes) and approached the line of slaves. I watched him pace back and forth, examining each one, until at last he stopped behind an older, thickset woman and waited. One by one, each of the eight others handed his tribute to their host, examined the remaining slaves, and picked his own to wait behind, until all nine guests were in place. The Negroes dared not turn around. Their eyes remained fixed on the ground at their feet. Nine of the slaves now being spoken for, the large Negro led the other three out of the barn and into the dark. What became of these poor souls, I cannot say. I can only speak to the anxiety I felt as they disappeared—for something was about to happen. What it was, I knew not. I knew only that it would be dreadful.

He was correct. Satisfied that the other slaves were out of earshot, the gray-bearded host gave a whistle. Upon this, nine pairs of eyes turned black, nine sets of fangs descended, and nine vampires tore into their helpless prey from behind.

The first vampire grabbed the sides of the thickset woman's head and twisted it backward so that her chin and spine met—his wretched face her dying sight. Another screamed and writhed when she felt the sting of two fangs in her shoulder. But the greater her struggle, the deeper the wound became, and the more freely her precious blood poured into the creature's mouth. I saw the head of a boy beaten until his brains poured from a hole in his skull, and another man's head taken entirely. I could do nothing to help them. Not when there were so many. Not without a weapon. The slave master calmly pulled the barn doors closed to stifle the noises of death, and I ran into the night, my face wet with tears. Disgusted with myself for being so helpless. Sickened by what I had seen. But more than anything—sickened by the truth taking shape in my mind. A truth that I had been too blind to see before.

———————

Abe purchased a black leather-bound journal on Dauphine Street the next day. His first entry, while a scant seventeen words, was a powerful statement of that truth, and one of the most important sentences he would ever write.

June 25th, 1828
So long as this country is cursed with slavery, so too will it be cursed with vampires.

— • — Part II — • —

VAMPIRE
HUNTER

Five

New Salem

The way for a young man to rise, is to improve himself every way he can, never suspecting that any body wishes to hinder him.

—*Abraham Lincoln, in a letter to William Herndon*
July 10th, 1848

I

Abe was shaking.

It was a bitter cold February night, and he'd been waiting for a man to put his clothes on for the better part of two hours. Abe paced back and forth... back and forth in the hard-packed snow, throwing the occasional glance toward the unfinished courthouse on the other side of the square, and at the second floor of the saloon across the street— where a light still burned behind the curtained window of a whore. He passed the time with thoughts of his weeks spent floating shirtless down the Mississippi in unbearable heat. "Heat a man could drown in." He thought of mornings spent splitting rails in the shade; afternoons cooling off with a swim in the creek. But those memories were all more than three years and two hundred miles away. Tonight, on his twenty-second birthday, he was freezing on the empty streets of Calhoun, Illinois.*

Thomas Lincoln had finally given up on Indiana. He'd been receiving regular reports from John Hanks, a cousin of Abe's mother, regarding the untapped wonders of Illinois.

John wrote of the "plentiful and fertile" prairies of that state. Of "flat land that needed no clearing. Free of rocks, and to be had cheap." It was all the incentive Thomas needed to leave Indiana and its bitter memories behind.

In March of 1830, the Lincolns packed their belongings into three wagons, each hitched to a team of oxen, and left Little Pigeon Creek forever. For fifteen exhausting days they navigated mud-covered roads and forded icy rivers, "until at last we reached Macon County and settled just west of Decatur," smack-dab in the center of Illinois. Abe was twenty-one then. It'd been two years since he'd witnessed the slave massacre in New Orleans. Two years of handing hard-earned wages over to his father. Now he was finally free to strike out on his own. Despite being desperate to do so, Abe stayed on an extra year, helping his father build a new cabin and helping his family settle into their new home.

But tonight he was twenty-two. And so help him, it was to be his last birthday under his father's roof.

> [My stepbrother] John was the one who
> insisted we ride to Calhoun to celebrate. I

---

* The town would be renamed Springfield the following year.

wouldn't hear of it at first, not being one to make
a fuss over the occasion. As usual, he nagged at
me until I could tolerate no more. He stated his
intentions while on our ride to town, which as I
recall was amounting to "getting blind stinking
drunk and buying you the company of a woman
friend." He knew of a saloon on Sixth Street. I do
not recall the name, or whether it had one at all.
I remember only that it had a second floor where
a man could indulge himself for a price. John's
intentions nonwithstanding [sic], I can say that
my conscience remains clear in this regard.

Lincoln may have resisted the temptations of the
saloon's perfumed ladies, but he drank its whiskey freely.
He and John shared laughs at the expense of their father;
their sisters; at each other. It was all "very good for the
soul, and a very good way to spend one's birthday." Once
again, John's nagging had paid off. Near the end of the
evening, however, while his stepbrother flirted with a
voluptuous brunette by the name of Missy ("like the
Mississippi, honey, but twice as deep, and a helluva lot
warmer"), Abe saw an average-size man walk in, wearing
clothes "hardly fit for a night so cold."

His face bore none of the redness I had
observed on the other customers as they hurried
into the light and warmth of the saloon—nor had
his breath been visible against the cold air as he
entered. He was a pale gentleman of thirty years
or less, but his hair was nonetheless a curled mix
of brown and gray, the result being something

like the color of weathered planks. He made
straight for the barkeep (it was clear the two were
acquainted) and whispered something to him,
upon which the aproned little man hurried up the
staircase. He was a vampire. He had to be—whiskey be damned. But how to know with certainty?

Abe was suddenly struck by an idea.

I barely spoke above a whisper. "Do you
see that man at the bar?" I asked John, who
had been occupied with the lady's ear. "Tell me,
can you ever recall seeing a man with such a
repulsive face?" John—who had not the slightest
idea what the man's face looked like—laughed
heartily all the same (such was his state). Upon
my whispering this, the pale gentleman spun
around and glared directly at me. I smiled back
and lifted my glass to him. No other creature
would have heard the insult over such a din,
or across such a distance! There could be no
doubt! Yet I could not take him. Not here. Not
with so many people watching. I smiled at the
thought of being dragged away and charged with
murder. What would be my defense? That my
victim had been a vampire? What's more, my
coat and weapons remained outside in my saddle
bag. No—this would not do. There must be
another way.

The barkeep returned with three women in tow and
arranged them in front of the vampire's table.

Having picked two of these, the vampire followed them up the staircase, and the barkeep rang
out his last call.

Abe's mind, half pickled with whiskey, churned until
it received "the blessings of another idea." Knowing that
his brother would never leave him to wander the streets
alone, he told John that he'd changed his mind and made
"arrangements" to spend the night with a woman.

John had hoped (fervently, I suspect) that this
would be the case, and promptly made his own
arrangements. We bade each other good night as
the barkeep snuffed out the lanterns and locked
the bottles away. Having given my brother and
his friend ample time to reach their room, I followed up the stairs, alone. Here was a single,
narrow hallway lit dimly by oil light and papered
with an elaborate pattern of reds and pinks. A
number of doors ran down both sides, all of them
closed. At the end, another closed door faced me
which, judging by the shape of the building, led
outside to a back staircase. I walked slowly down
the center, listening for clues as to which room
held my vampire. Laughter from my left. Profanity from my right. Sounds which I have not the
words to describe. Having reached the end of the
hallway with no success, I at last heard what I had
been waiting for on my right side—the voices of
two women coming from the same room. Leaving John to enjoy the warm embrace of a stranger,
I turned back, headed out into the cold, and

donned my long coat. I knew the vampire would likely finish his business and leave before sunrise. And when he did, I would be waiting for him.

But by the second hour of pacing in the street, he'd grown tired, cold, and bored.

The slaughter of sixteen vampires had left me rather audacious, I admit. Not content to wait any longer in the cold, I resolved to be done with it. I walked up the snow-covered staircase at the rear of the building, taking care to step lightly, and preparing the martyr in my hand.

"Martyr" was the name Abe had given to a new weapon of his own creation. From an earlier entry in his journal:

I have recently read of the successes of an English chemist by the name of Walker who has developed a method of creating flame using nothing more than friction. Having procured the necessary chemicals to reproduce his "congreves,"* I set about dipping a number of small sticks in this mixture. The chemicals having dried, I bundled twenty of the little sticks tightly together (the whole being roughly twice the thickness of a fountain pen) and soaked all but the tip of one end in glue. When the exposed end is struck

---

*John Walker's matches (which he called congreves) were made with a mixture of stibnite, potassium chlorate, gum, and starch. They were incredibly unstable, odiferous items.

against a rough surface, the resulting flame is brief, violent, and brighter than the sun. This has the effect of rendering my black-eyed adversaries temporarily blind, allowing me to chop them to pieces with greater ease. I have used them twice with tremendous success (though the burns on my fingers bear witness to earlier failures).

I stood before the door in question with the martyr in one hand and my ax in the other, light from beneath the door illuminating my snow-covered shoes. There were no voices coming from the other side, and I was presently struck by the thought of seeing the two girls slaughtered on the bed, their blood staining the sheets to match the patterned walls. Using the head of the ax, I knocked three times.

Nothing.

Having given them ample time to answer, I knocked again. Another moment passed with no noise from the other side. Just as I was weighing whether to knock again or not, I heard the creak-ing of the bed, followed by the creaking of some-one walking across the wooden floor. I prepared to strike. The door opened.

It was him. Curly hair, the color of weathered wood. Nothing but a long shirt between his skin and the cold.
"What in the hell is it?" he asked.
Abe struck the tip of the martyr against the wall.
Nothing.

The damned thing failed to light, it having been left in the damp pocket of my coat for so long. The vampire looked at me quizzically. His fangs did not descend, nor his eyes blacken. But on seeing the ax in my other hand, they doubled in width, and he shut the door with such force as to rattle the whole building. I stood there, looking at the door like a dog looks at a book, all the while allowing the vampire time to escape on the other side. This having occurred to me at last, I took a step back and let the door have the full force of my heel. It sailed open with a tremendous noise—a noise I mistakenley [sic] attributed to the splintering of wood. I did not recognize it as a gunshot until after the lead ball had passed my head, missing it by no more than an inch and burrowing into the wall behind me. I will admit that I was a good deal shaken by this. So much so that on seeing him drop the pistol and climb out the window headfirst (his naked backside bidding me farewell) my first thought was not to pursue, but to examine my head lest I be bleeding to death. Satisfied this was not the case, I hurried into the room after him—the two ladies quite undressed and screaming in the bed next to me. I could hear doors opening down the length of the hallway as curious customers stepped out to investigate the commotion. On reaching the window, I saw my prey pick himself off the snowy street below and run barefoot into the night, slipping and landing on his bare hide at least twice before he escaped my view, screaming for help.

This was no vampire.

I cursed aloud most of the ride home. Never in
my life had I been so embarrassed or made such
a drunken error. Never had I felt like such a fool.
If there was one comforting prospect, it was this:
soon I would finally be free.

The winter of 1831 was an especially harsh one, but
with March came the thaw, and with it the first birds in the
sky and blades of grass on the earth. For Abe, the March
thaw brought an end to twenty-two years with Thomas
Lincoln. Years that had grown increasingly cold. It's
unlikely that they parted with anything more than a handshake, if that. Abe had only this to write on the day he left
home for good.

Off to Beardstown by way of Springfield.
John, John, and I hope to make the trip in
three days.

Lincoln rode west with his stepbrother John and cousin
John Hanks. The three young men had been hired by an
acquaintance named Denton Offutt to build a flatboat and
ferry goods down the Sangamon River to New Orleans, a
round trip of about three months.

Offutt was remembered by at least one contemporary
as "a hot-tempered, strict, noisy son of a bitch." But like
most people who encountered Abe Lincoln, he'd been
impressed by the young man's hard work, intelligence,
and general disposition. On reaching Beardstown (in
three days, as they'd hoped), Abe led his team in building
the flatboat and loading it with Offutt's cargo.

> My second flatboat was twice as long and
> much improved from the first, and built with a
> great deal more speed—for not only did I have
> the experience of having done it once before,
> but I was gifted with additional hands to share
> the work. We were off about three weeks after
> we arrived, much to Mr. Offutt's surprise and
> satisfaction.

The Sangamon River twisted through 250 miles of Central Illinois. It was a far cry from the "mighty Missis-sip"—more of a stream or a creek in some places than a river, and burdened with low-hanging branches and count-less pieces of driftwood, each one at the mercy of the cur-rent. This troubled body wound its way down to the more forgiving Illinois River before reaching the Mississippi.

The quartet of flatboatmen (Offutt having elected to go along for the ride) had a terrible time getting down the Sangamon. Each day brought a new disaster—running aground; coming upon a fallen tree in the river. Legend holds that their flatboat became wedged on a dam near New Salem, Illinois, and began taking on water. As locals gathered on the shore, offering advice and laughing at the young men scrambling to save their vessel, Lincoln was again struck by one of his ideas. He bored a hole in the front of the boat (which hung over the dam) and let all the water run out of it. This raised the back of the boat enough to safely float it over. With the hole plugged, the men were on their way, and the people of New Salem were mightily impressed. Denton Offutt had been impressed, too—not so much by Abe's ingenuity, but by the booming little set-tlement of New Salem.

Regardless of the river and its obstacles, Abe managed to find something of that elusive peace again during the trip. He took the time to record drawings, lengthy remembrances, and random thoughts in his journal nearly every night after they'd tied up. In an entry dated May 4th, he begins to expand on his one-sentence statement of the connection between slavery and vampires.

> Not long after the first ships landed in this New World, I believe that vampires reached a tacit understanding with slave owners. I believe that this nation holds some special attraction for them because here, in America, they can feed on human blood without fear of discovery or reprisal. Without the inconvenience of living in darkness. I believe that this is especially true in the South, where those flamboyant gentlemen vampires have worked out a way to "grow" their prey. Where the strongest slaves are put to work growing tobacco and food for the fortunate and free, and the lesser are themselves harvested and eaten. I believe this, but I cannot yet prove it to be true.

Abe had written Henry about what he'd seen (and asking what it meant) after his first trip to New Orleans. He'd received no reply. With his departure from Little Pigeon Creek imminent, he'd decided to venture back to the false cabin and check in on his undead friend.

> I found the place deserted. The furnishings and bed were gone, leaving the cabin nothing more than an empty room. On opening the door

in the back, I found not a staircase leading down
to the rooms below, but smooth, hard-packed
dirt. Had the whole of Henry's hiding place been
filled in? Or had the whole been dreamed by me
in my delusional state?

Abe didn't stay in Indiana long enough to find out. He
wrote something in his journal, tore out the page, and
hung it on a nail over Henry's fireplace.

ABRAHAM LINCOLN
WEST OF DECATUR, ILLINOIS
CARE OF MR. JOHN HANKS

New Orleans held little of the wonder it had the first time
around, and Abe found himself eager to conclude their
business and catch a steamer north. He stayed on for a
few days to give his stepbrother and cousin a chance to
explore, but barely ventured out, not wishing to happen
upon another slave auction or wayward vampire. He did,
however, stop by the saloon near Mrs. Laveau's—not to
drink, but to indulge the slim hope that he might run into
his old friend Poe. It wasn't to be.

Denton Offutt had been so impressed with the way
Lincoln performed that he offered him another job upon
their return to Illinois. Offutt saw the Sangamon River as
a 250-mile stretch of opportunity. The frontier was booming, and towns were springing up all along its banks. Many
believed that navigation would soon be improved, and
that steamboats would soon bring passengers and goods
through their backyards. Offutt was one of the believers.

"Mark my words," he said, "the Sangamon is the next Mississippi. Today's settlement is tomorrow's town." If there was one thing Offutt knew, it was that every growing town needed a general store and a pair of men to run it. And so it happened that Abraham Lincoln and Denton Offutt returned to New Salem, Illinois, the scene of their infamous boat rescue, to stay.

New Salem sat atop a bluff on the west bank of the Sangamon, a tightly grouped collection of one- and two-room cabins, workshops, mills, and a schoolhouse that doubled as a church on Sundays. There were perhaps one hundred residents in all.

> Mr. Offutt's store being a month or more
> from opening for business, I found myself in the
> strange position of having far too much time, and
> far too little to do. I was much relieved, there-
> fore, to make the acquaintance of a Mr. William
> Mentor Graham, a young schoolteacher who
> shared my love of books and who introduced me
> to *Kirkham's Grammar*, which I studied until I
> could recite every rule and example by heart.

History remembers Abe's towering intellect but forgets that, in those days, he was more towering than intellectual. Like his father, he had a natural gift for words. But when it came to writing them down correctly, he remained a victim of his limited schooling. Mentor Graham would help to correct this, and prove a key force in Lincoln's ability to express himself eloquently later in life.

The cramped store at last stocked and ready, Abe went to work filling orders, tracking inventory, and charming

customers with his natural wit and endless facts. He and
Offutt sold cookware and lanterns, fabric and animal pelts.
They measured out sugar and flour and filled bottles of
peach brandy, molasses, and red vinegar from little barrels
on the shelves behind the counter. "Anything for anyone at
any time" as they liked to say. In addition to his meager sal-
ary, Abe received an allowance of goods and a small room
at the back of the store. Here, he would read by candlelight
and write in his journal until well after midnight.

And then, the candle having burned out, and the whole
of the settlement having gone to sleep, he would don his
coat and go out into the night in search of vampires.

II

With no Henry to guide him, and tethered to within a
few miles of New Salem (for he had to be back to open
Offutt's store every morning at seven), Abe's vampire-
killing streak ground to a halt in the summer of 1831. He
wandered the surrounding woods at night; ventured up
and down the banks of the Sangamon. But save for inves-
tigating the occasional noise, there was no excitement to
be had. It wasn't long before Abe began to put more stock
in rest than reconnaissance, and stopped venturing out
altogether.

That's not to say there weren't opportunities to fight.

About a half-hour's walk from New Salem was the
settlement of Clary's Grove, home to the rather unimagi-
natively named Clary's Grove Boys, a gang of mostly
related young men with a penchant for getting drunk and
raising hell.

They were good for no less than two brawls
a night in poor Jim Rutledge's tavern, and were
known to break up river baptisms by throwing
rocks at the parishioners from the woods. One
dared not cross them, or they might put out your
windows—even stuff you in a barrel and leave
you to the mercy of the Sangamon.

Above all, the Boys loved to "wrastle." They prided
themselves on being the "meanest, toughest, rowdiest
wrastlers around." So when word came that there was
a "big fella come to work" at the general store in New
Salem, they considered it their duty to size him up in person and, if need be, put him in his place.

Abe knew the Clary's Grove Boys would be looking
for a fight, just as they'd looked for one with every able-
bodied man who moved into their territory for years.
That's precisely why he'd avoided them at all costs, hoping they would simply grow accustomed to having him
around. He'd managed to go nearly two whole months
without a confrontation (a local record). Unfortunately,
Denton Offutt was a little man with a big mouth, and on
seeing some of the Boys about, bragged that his new clerk
was not only the smartest man in Sangamon County, but
that he was "big enough to lick the lot" of them.

They came unannounced to the store and called
me outside. On seeing ten or more gathered there,
I asked what business we had. One of them stepped
forward and said they intended to put their "best
man" on me, on account of Mr. Offutt's having
described me as "the toughest man he ever saw."

I told them that Mr. Offutt had been mistaken. That I was not tough at all, and that I had no use for such wooling around. My refusal was not taken well, for I was then surrounded and threatened by the whole of the gang. They would not permit me inside, they said, until I'd had a go. If I refused, all of New Salem would know me as a coward, and they would turn our store over from "top to bottom." I agreed, but insisted it be a fair fight. "Oh it ain't going to be much of a fight at all," said one of them, and called Jack to the front.

Jack Armstrong was a brick wall of a man, four inches shorter and twenty pounds heavier than Abe. He was the Clary's Grove Boys' unquestioned leader, and it was easy to see why.

He had a mean look about him, and kept his arms and chest taut as he moved around me, as if his whole body was a drawn bowstring that could be released at any moment. He pulled his shirt over his head and threw it to the ground, circling around me. Preferring to keep mine on, I began to roll up one of my sleeves. I had scarcely begun this when I was suddenly on my back—the air pressed from my lungs.

The Boys cheered as Jack sprang to his feet, and booed as Abe struggled to his.

Clearly, my insistence on a "fair fight" was to have no bearing. Jack came at me again, but this time I was ready—meeting his outstretched arms with mine, our backs and shoulders forming a tabletop as we leaned forward, pushing against each other. Our heads down; our feet kicking up dirt behind us. I suspect he was a good deal surprised at my strength. I was certainly surprised at his. I felt as if I had locked arms with a Russian bear.

But as mighty as Jack Armstrong was, he was nothing compared to the vampires Abe had grappled with in the past. With his lungs again full, Lincoln reached up and grabbed Jack's neck with one hand, and the waist of his pants with the other.

Holding him thus, I lifted his body clean off the ground and over my head, keeping him there as he squirmed and struggled and cussed. This spectacle produced in his friends no shortage of distress, and I was suddenly set upon by the lot of them, punching and kicking at me in a group. This was an injustice that I could not allow.

Abe's face went bright red, and he brought his full strength to bear, throwing Jack Armstrong against the side of the general store and yelling, "I'm the big buck of the lick!"

I grabbed the man nearest me by the hair and struck him in the face with my fist, rendering him insensible. The man nearest him caught another of my fists in his belly. I was quite content to

whip the lot of them, one by one, and would have
done so, had Jack not risen to his feet and called
off his men.

Now it was Lincoln's body that tensed like a drawn
bowstring, his eyes fixed on a pair of Clary's Grove Boys
just out of arm's reach.

> Jack pulled a splinter or two from his side and
> stood next to me. "Boys," he said, "I believe this
> man to be the toughest son'bitch ever to set foot
> in New Salem. Any man's got a quarrel with him's
> got a quarrel with Jack Armstrong."

It was perhaps the most important battle of Abe's early
life, for word quickly spread from one end of Sangamon
County to the other: here was a young man possessed of
strong mind and body. A man they could be proud of.
Their inauspicious introduction aside, the Clary's Grove
Boys quickly became some of Abe's staunchest supporters, and would prove invaluable political assets in
the years to come. Some of them even became his close
friends, though none so close as Jack Armstrong himself.

> I regretted losing my temper and embarrassing
> him in front of his relations. So, on the evening
> after our match, I invited him to share a drink at
> the store.

Abe and Jack shared a small bottle of peach brandy
in the store's back room, the sky still slightly blue even
though it was approaching nine o'clock. Abe sat on the

end of his bed, having offered the room's sole chair to his guest.

> I was surprised to find in this burly Armstrong
> a quiet, thoughtful man. Though four years my
> junior, he had a maturity surpassing that of many
> men twice his age, and an ease of conversation
> that one would not expect given his appearance.
> On seeing my copy of *Kirkham's Grammar*, he
> spoke of the value of reading and writing, and
> bemoaned his shortcomings in both.

"Truth is, it was more important to be rough," said Jack. "This is rough country, and it takes a rough man."

"Must you choose one or the other?" asked Abe. "I've always found time for books, and I know something of rough country."

Jack smiled. "Not Illinois rough."

Abe asked what he meant.

"You ever seen somebody you love tore up and scattered all over the ground?"

Abe had not, and was clearly surprised by the answer. Jack fidgeted a little; looked at the floor.

"I gone walkin' with a friend one night," he said. "We was both nine, and the two of us was headed home from throwin' rocks at flatboats, twistin' down a trail we knew by heart. One minute he was right there next to me, chatterin' away in the dark. Next minute he'd been pull't up by a bear's claws—pull't into a tree by his head and drug clear to the top. I couldn't see nothin' up there in the dark. I could only hear him screamin'. Feel the warm drops on my head...on my lips. I ran and fetched help, and the men came runnin' with their flintlocks. But there was nothin' for 'em to kill. We spent half the morning pickin' him up off the ground. Jared. Jared Linder was his name."

There was silence now, and Abe knew he mustn't be the first to fill it.

"Folks live 'round here know there's somethin' about these woods," said Jack. "They know a man who don't have his wits about him—a man who ain't strong enough to take all comers—well, they know that's a man liable to get himself killed walking one place to the next. People say us Boys stick close on account of our being kin. 'Cause we like raisin' a ruckus. The truth of it is, we stick close 'cause that's the only chance we got at growin' old. Truth is, we act rough 'cause a weak man's a dead man."

"And you're certain?" asked Abe. "I mean, you're absolutely certain it was a bear?"

"Well, it sure as hell weren't no tree-climbin' horse."

"I mean . . . might it have been something a bit more . . . unusual?"

"Oh," said Jack, beginning to laugh. "You mean was it somethin' like out of a story? Some kind a ghost?"

"Yes."

"Hell, those stories've been goin' up and down the river for years. Wild stories. People talking about witches, and devils, and—"

"Vampires?"

All trace of humor left Jack's face at the mention of the word.

"People talking nonsense. Just scared is all."

Maybe it was the half a bottle of peach brandy in his blood, or the feeling that he'd found a kindred spirit.

Maybe he just couldn't stand to keep all those secrets to himself anymore. Whatever the reason, Abe made a very sudden, very risky decision.

"Jack...if I tell you something incredible, will you promise to hear me fairly?"

III

Abe paced back and forth...back and forth over the soft dirt of the street, throwing the occasional glance toward the newly finished courthouse on the other side of the square and at the second floor of the saloon across the street, where a light still burned behind the curtained window of a whore. The late-summer weather was much more agreeable this time around. So was the company.

> It had taken no small amount of persuasion, but Jack had at last agreed to come to Springfield. At first, he had refused to believe a word of it—going so far as to call me a "damned liar" and threatening to "thrash" me for thinking him a fool. I begged his patience, however, and promised that I would either prove every word true, or pack my things and leave New Salem forever. I made this promise with every expectation of success, for that very morning a letter had at long last arrived.

The letter was addressed exactly as Abe had instructed above Henry's fireplace:

ABRAHAM LINCOLN
WEST OF DECATUR, ILLINOIS
CARE OF MR. JOHN HANKS

It had been delivered to his relatives two weeks earlier, and forwarded to New Salem. Abe had torn it open upon seeing the familiar handwriting, and read it a dozen times at the counter throughout the day.

> Abraham,
>   My apologies for not having written these many months. Vanishing is, I regret, a necessary part of my existence from time to time. I will write more often when I have settled into a more permanent home. In the interim, I hope you have settled into yours happily, and remain in good spirits and health. If you remain agreeable, you may visit upon the individual named below at your leisure. I believe him only a short ride from where you are now. I must warn you, however—he is quite a bit cleverer than those you have visited on in the past. You may well mistake him for one of your own kind.
> Timothy Douglas.
> The tavern near the square.
> Calhoun.
> Ever,
> —H

Abe knew the tavern well. It was, after all, the site of his greatest vampire-hunting embarrassment. *Could I have been right all along? Had the half-naked man who'd run off screaming for help been a vampire after all?*

We walked in, plainly dressed (my long coat
stored in my saddlebag outside). I took in the faces at
each table, half expecting to see the curly-haired gentleman glaring back in his snow-covered long shirt.
Would he run at the sight of me? Would his vampire
nature compel him to attack? But I saw him not. Jack
and I made to the counter, where the aproned barkeep busied himself polishing a whiskey glass.

"Pardon me, sir. My friend and I are looking for a Mr.
Douglas."

"Tim Douglas?" asked the barkeep, his eyes fixed on
his work.

"The same."

"And what business might you and Mr. Douglas have?"

"Business of an urgent and private sort. Do you know
where he is?"

The barkeep seemed amused.

"Well, sir, you needn't look far, that's for certain."

He put down the glass and stuck out his hand. "Tim
Douglas. And your name, sir?"

Jack burst out laughing. There had to be some
mistake. This inconsequential little man—a man
who spent his nights polishing dirty glasses and
playing matchmaker to whores and drunks? This
was Henry's vampire? Of course, I had no choice
but take his hand, and did so. It was as pink and
warm as my own.

"Hanks," said Abe. "Abe Hanks, and I beg your forgiveness, for I mistook you to say 'Tom' Douglas. Yes, Thomas

Douglas is the gentleman we're looking for. Do you know where we might find him?"

"Well, sir, no. I'm afraid I'm not familiar with anyone by that name."

"Then I thank you for your trouble and bid you a good night."

Abe hurried out of the tavern, Jack laughing all the while behind him.

> I resolved to wait. We had come this far, and
> Henry had never failed me in the past. At the
> very least, we would wait for this barkeep to close
> up and follow him home in the shadows.

After hours spent wandering the courthouse square, Abe (who'd since donned his long coat) and Jack (who hadn't stopped teasing him since they left the tavern) finally saw the lights go dark and the barkeep make his way into the street.

> He walked down Sixth Street toward Adams.
> We followed discreetly, Jack a good three paces
> behind; the ax ready in my hands. I darted into
> the shadows with every twitch of the barkeep's
> head—certain he meant to turn back and discover
> us (Jack could hardly contain his laughter at the
> sight of my doing so). The little man kept to the
> center of the street, hands in his pockets. Whis-
> tling. Walking as any other man would walk, and
> making me feel a fool with each step. He rounded
> Seventh Street, and we followed. He rounded
> Monroe, and we followed. But on rounding Ninth

Street, after letting him escape our sight for the
briefest of moments, we saw no trace of him.
There was no alley he could have slipped into. No
house he could have entered in so short a time.
How could it be?

"So...you're the one."

The voice came from behind us. I spun around,
prepared to strike—but could not. For here was
mighty Jack Armstrong, standing on his toes. His
back arched. His eyes wide. And here was the little
vampire standing behind him, a sharp claw pressed
to his throat. Had Jack been able to see those black
eyes and shining fangs, his terror would have been
twofold. The barkeep suggested that I lay my ax
on the ground if I did not wish to see my friend's
blood spilled. I thought his suggestion a good one,
and let the weapon fall from my hand.

"You're the one Henry spoke of. The one with a talent
for killing the dead."

Though Abe was surprised to hear Henry's name,
his face betrayed nothing. He could hear Jack's panting
quicken as the claw pressed harder against his throat.

"I'm curious," asked the barkeep. "Have you ever wondered *why*? Why a vampire takes such an interest in rid-
ding the earth of his own kind? Why he sends a man to
kill in his stead? Or have you simply done his bidding
blindly—the unquestioning, undyingly loyal servant?"

"I serve no man but myself," said Abe.

The barkeep laughed. "Avowed as only an American
could."

"Help me, Abe," said Jack.

"We are all servants," said the barkeep. "However, of the two of us, I have the fortune of knowing which master I serve."

Jack began to panic. "P-please! Let me go!" He struggled to free himself, but this only dug the barkeep's claw in deeper. A trickle of blood ran over his Adam's apple as the vampire gave a reassuring "shhhh...."

Abe used the opportunity to slip a hand into his coat pocket, unnoticed.

I must strike swiftly, lest my thoughts betray my plan.

"Your beloved Henry is no less deserving of that ax than the rest of us," said the barkeep. "He merely had the good fortune of finding you fir—"

> I pulled the martyr from my pocket and struck it against my buckle with all the quickness I possessed.
>
> It lit.
>
> Brighter than the sun—white light and sparks filling the whole of the street. The vampire retreated and shielded his eyes, and Jack pulled free. I knelt, grabbed the handle of the ax, and threw from my knees. The blade lodged in the vampire's chest with a crack of bone and rush of escaped air, and he fell, clumsily clutching at the handle with one hand, dragging himself along the ground with the other. I let the martyr slip from my fingers to burn its last upon the ground, and retrieved my ax from the creature's chest. That same familiar fear on his face. The fear of what hell or oblivion awaited. I did not care to revel in it. I raised the ax above my head and took his.

Jack was shaken to the point of being sick on his boots. Shaken by the fact that he'd been an inch away from death. By the glimpse he'd caught of those black eyes; those fangs after breaking free. He didn't say a word on the ride home. Neither man did. They reached New Salem after sunrise and were about to part company in silence when Jack, who was continuing on to Clary's Grove, pulled up his reins and turned toward the general store.

"Abe," he said. "I wanna know everything there is to know 'bout killin' vampires."

Six

—◆—

Ann

I feel how weak and fruitless must be any words of mine which should attempt to beguile you from the grief of a loss so overwhelming...I pray that our Heavenly Father may assuage the anguish of your bereavement, and leave you only the cherished memory of the loved and lost.

—*Abraham Lincoln, in a letter to Mrs. Lydia Bixby,*
mother of two sons killed in the Civil War
November 21st, 1864

I

New Salem hadn't grown as quickly as Denton Offutt hoped; in fact, it may have lost a few residents in the months after he opened the store. The Sangamon was still a long way from being "the next Mississippi." Navigation remained a treacherous affair, and all but a few steamboats remained trapped in the wider waters to the south, with all of their precious customers and cargo. It didn't help matters that New Salem had a second general store closer to the center of the settlement, siphoning off customers before they'd even had a chance to reach his front door. By the time the ice began to break on the sluggish Sangamon in the spring of 1832, Offutt's store had failed, and Abe was out of a job. His anger is evident in an entry dated March 27th.

> Bade farewell to [Offutt] this morning, the last of the goods having been sold or traded; my belongings were moved to the Herndon place until such time as I am able to make other arrangements. I care not that he has gone. I feel no sadness at his leaving, and feel not tempted in the slightest to follow his listless example. I have never known idle hands, and shall not know them now. I resolve to remain. I shall prosper yet.

As always, Abe was true to his word. He did whatever it took to make money: Splitting rails. Clearing land. Building sheds. His relationship with the Clary's Grove Boys paid its first dividends, too, in the form of the odd jobs they intimidated locals into giving him. He even found work as an "ax man" on one of the few steamboats making its way up the Sangamon, standing on its bow and chopping away any obstructions that slowed its struggle north. And through it all, he never stopped hunting.

> I have given a great deal of thought to what the barkeep said. Have I ever wondered why Henry takes such an interest in hunting vampires? Have I ever wondered why he sends me in his stead? I admit that I have spent many an hour perplexed

by these questions. Wondering if perhaps there is
some deeper truth in them. That I am the sworn
enemy of vampires doing the bidding of a vampire? There is no eluding this fact, nor the para-
dox inherent in it. That I am being used to further
the unseen ends of one vampire in particular? I
must admit the possibility. Yet after deliberating
the whole, I have come to this conclusion:

　It matters not.

　If indeed I am nothing more than Henry's servant, so be it. So long as the result is fewer vampires, I shall serve happily.

Henry's letters began to arrive more frequently, and
Abe ventured out when they did. But he didn't venture
alone.

　I have found in Jack an able and eager hunting companion, and have endevored [sic] to share
with him the whole of my knowledge with regard
to destroying vampires (I needn't teach him
anything of quickness or bravery, for he enjoys a
surplus of both). I am thankful for the help, for
Henry's letters have been coming so frequently
that I find myself running from one end of the
state to the other.

One night Abe found himself running through the
streets of Decatur with a bloodied ax in his hands, Jack
beside him with a crossbow. No more than ten paces
ahead of them, a bald man made a beeline for the Sangamon River. The right side of his shirt was soaked with

blood, and his right arm was dangling by his side, attached
to his body by nothing more than a few bits of sinew and
skin.

> We ran past a pair of gentlemen on the street.
> They watched our little procession speed by, yell-
> ing after us: "You there! Stop at once!" What a
> sight we must have made! I could not help but
> laugh.

Abe and Jack chased the one-armed man to the water's
edge.

> He dove in and disappeared beneath the black
> water. Jack would have gone in after him had I
> not grabbed him by the collar and yelled "no!"
> with what little voice I had left. Jack stood on the
> bank, gasping for breath and pointing his cross-
> bow at every bubble that surfaced.

"I told you to wait for my signal!" yelled Abe.
"We would have been waiting all damned night!"
"Well, now we've lost him!"
"Shut up and keep a sharp eye! He has to come up for
air sooner or later...."
Abe looked at Jack, his fury surrendering to a quizzi-
cal smile...then to laughter.
"Yes," laughed Abe. "I expect he shall be coming up
for air any day now."
Abe put a hand on Jack's shoulder and led him away
from the riverbank, his laughter echoing through the sleep-
ing streets.

> If [Jack] is wanting in anything, it is patience.
> He is too quick to spring from hiding—and, I fear,
> too eager to share what he knows with his compan-
> ions from Clary's Grove. I am ever reminding him
> of the need for secrecy, and of the madness that
> would overtake all of Sangamon County if word of
> our errands were to spread beyond the two of us.

He'd been in the county all of a year, but in that short
time Abe had become something of a local celebrity. A
"young man whose hands are just as skilled with an ax as
they are with a quill," as his schoolteacher friend, Mentor
Graham, put it. Abe had seen and heard enough from his
customers to know what was on their minds.

> Chief among their concerns is the river itself.
> What a state it is in! Barely more than a creek in
> some parts; choked by all manner of driftwood
> and obstructions. If we are to enjoy the bounty
> of the Mississippi, it shall need to be greatly
> improved, so that steamboats may navigate it
> freely. Such improvement, of course, will require
> a tremendous sum of money. I know of only one
> way (outside thievery) to procure it.

Abraham Lincoln decided to run for office. In
announcing his candidacy for the Illinois State Legislature in a county newspaper, he struck a populist, if somewhat defeatist, chord:

> I am young, and unknown to many of you.
> I was born, and have ever remained, in the

most humble walks of life. I have no wealthy
or popular relations or friends to recommend
me. My case is thrown exclusively upon the
independent voters of the county; and if
elected, they will have conferred a favor upon
me for which I shall be unremitting in my
labors to compensate. But if the good people
in their wisdom shall see fit to keep me in
the background, I have been too familiar with
disappointments to be very much chagrined.

———

Shortly after Abe's announcement, word of a "war with
the Indians" reached New Salem.

> A Sauk war chief named Black Hawk has
> violated a treaty and crossed [the Mississippi]
> into the village of Saukenuk to the north. He
> and his British Band* mean to kill or drive out
> every white settler they encounter and reclaim
> land believed rightfully theirs. Governor
> Reynolds has put out a call for six hundred
> able-bodied men to take up arms against
> these savages and protect the gentle people of
> Illinois.

---

*The name given to a group of some five hundred warriors and
one thousand women and children from five different tribes, all
under the command of Black Hawk. It was so named because
Black Hawk had been told he would receive assistance from the
British in any conflict with the Americans (it never materialized).

Despite his political ambitions (or because of them), Abe was among the first in Sangamon County to volunteer. He would recall his excitement years later.

> I had lusted for war since I was a boy of twelve. Here, at last, was my chance to see it firsthand! I imagined the glory of charging into battle—firing my flintlock and swinging my ax! I imagined slaughtering scores of Indians with ease, for they could be no quicker or stronger than vampires.

The volunteers gathered in Beardstown, a growing settlement on the banks of the Illinois River. Here, the men were given a crash course in the barest essentials of warfare by a handful of experienced militiamen. Before journeying north, Abe's unit—a ragtag group of volunteers that included men from New Salem and Clary's Grove—elected him to serve as their captain.

> Captain Lincoln! I will admit that tears filled my eyes. It was the first time I had felt such esteem. The first time that I had been elected to lead my fellow men, and their sacred trust gave me more satisfaction than any election I have won or any office I have held since.

Among those marching off to battle with Abe were fellow vampire hunter Jack Armstrong and a young major named John Todd Stuart. Stuart was a slender man with "a high forehead and neatly parted black hair." He had a "prominent" nose and "unkind" eyes that "did his gentle nature an injustice." Stuart would play a crucial role in

Lincoln's postwar life, as an encouraging lawyer in Springfield, as a friendly adversary in Congress, and most of all as
the cousin of a raven-haired Kentucky belle named Mary
Todd.

The realities of war proved far less exciting than Abe's
imagination had conjured. With thousands of Illinois
militiamen engaging the rebellious Indians to the north,
there was little for the volunteers to do but sit and swelter.
From an entry dated May 30th, 1832—after weeks spent
camped out miles from the fields of battle:

> My men have suffered greatly (from boredom),
> much blood has been shed (by mosquitoes), and I
> have swung my ax mightily (chopping firewood).
> Surely we have earned our place in the annals of
> history—for never has there been so little <u>war</u> in
> a war.

In early July, Abe and his men were finally discharged
and began the long journey home, not a single war story
to tell among them. Abe reached New Salem (where he
found two letters in need of his "urgent attention") less
than two weeks before the election for state legislature.
He resumed his candidacy at once, shaking hands and
knocking on doors day and night. Unfortunately the field
had ballooned to thirteen candidates while he'd been
away battling mosquitoes. With so much time lost and so
many candidates splitting votes, he didn't stand a chance.

Abe finished eighth. But there was a silver lining, one
that even the depressed and defeated Lincoln couldn't
help but see: of all three hundred votes cast in New Salem,
only twenty-three had been cast against him. Those who

knew him overwhelmingly endorsed him. "It was merely a matter of shaking more hands."

His political career had begun.

II

Lincoln needed a success in the wake of his first political defeat, and he knew just where to find it. From an entry dated March 6th, 1833:

> I shall do what Offutt could not. By God, I
> shall run a profitable store in New Salem! Berry*
> and I have today purchased the whole on $300 of
> credit, which we have every expectation of paying
> back within two years' time. In three years, we
> shall have saved enough to purchase our building!

Again, the realities proved far less exciting than Abe's imagination. There were already two general stores in New Salem by the time Lincoln/Berry opened its doors, and barely enough demand to keep those open. Historians have puzzled over why a man with Abe's intellect and his father's "horse sense" didn't foresee the problem of adding a third store to the mix. Or why he seems to have so thoroughly misjudged his partner, William Berry, who proved shiftless, unreliable, and "perpetually drunk."

The answer seems to be something more than ambition.

---

*William F. Berry, son of a local minister, and a former corporal in Lincoln's outfit.

With the store on the verge of collapse less than a year later, Abe's journal entries grow increasingly exhausted; desperate. One in particular stands out—not only for its abruptness, but for its closing reference to (we can only assume) his mother.

> I must endure.
> I must be more than I am.
> I must not fail.
> I must not fail her.

But fail he did—at least as far as the world of dry goods and ladies' hats was concerned. The Lincoln/Berry store simply "winked out" in 1834, leaving each man with debts of more than $200. In the end, the unreliable Berry couldn't even be counted on to stay alive. He died a few years later, leaving Abe saddled with the whole amount. It would take him seventeen years to pay it off.

Had the timing been different, Abe might have packed up and left New Salem forever. But as it happened, there was another election for the Illinois State Legislature just a few short months off. Having little else to do ("none of Henry's letters having arrived of late"), and encouraged by his good showing the last time around, Abe resolved to run again—and this time, he was determined to run properly. He traveled the county on horseback and on foot, stopping to speak with anyone he encountered. He shook the hands of farmhands toiling in the scorched fields and won their respect with demonstrations of his own frontier-learned skills and God-given strength. He spoke at churches and taverns, horse races and picnics, peppering his stump speech (undoubtedly written on scraps of paper in his pocket as he traveled) with self-deprecating stories of flat-boat mishaps and mosquito battles.

"I have never seen a man with a greater gift for speaking," remembered Mentor Graham after Abe's death. "He was an ungainly—some might say unpleasant-looking—fellow... tall as a tree, with pant legs that stopped a good six inches above his shoes. His hair was in a constant state of untidiness; his coat ever in need of pressing. When he took his place in front of the crowd, they studied him with furrowed brows and folded arms. But when he launched into his address, their doubts vanished, and they were inevitably moved to thunderous applause—even tears by its conclusion."

This time he shook enough hands. Abraham Lincoln was elected to the Illinois State Legislature on August 4th, 1834.

> A poor son of the frontier, with nary a dollar to his name and not a year of schooling to his credit, sent to Vandalia* to speak for his fellow man! A rail-splitter seated beside men of letters! I admit that I am intimidated at the prospect of meeting such men. Will they accept me as their collegue [sic], or shun me as the unlearned clod-hopper with holes in his shoes? In either case, I suspect that my life is forever changed, and cannot help my excitement as December nears.

Abe's feeling proved correct. His life would never be the same. He would soon count statesmen and scholars

---

*Vandalia was the state capital until 1839, when it was moved to Springfield.

among his friends; trade the backwoods folksiness of Sangamon County for the burgeoning sophistication of Vandalia. He'd taken the first step on his way to being a lawyer. His first step on the road to the White House. But it was only one of two turning points that year.

For he had also fallen madly in love.

III

Jack was giving serious thought to turning his crossbow on Abe. They'd just made a miserable 200-mile trip north to the town of Chicago, sleeping under the freezing stars of late autumn, trudging through knee-high mud and waist-high water, "and the ganglin' fool'd done nothin' but talk 'bout a girl the whole damned way."

> Her name is Ann Rutledge. I believe her twenty or one-and-twenty years, though I dare not ask. It matters not. Never has a more perfect creature graced this earth! Never has a man been more in love than I! I shall write of nothing but her beauty in these pages for as long as I live.

Armstrong and Lincoln sat with their backs against the rear of a stable stall and their bottoms on a bed of loose hay, their breath visible in the cool night air coming off of Lake Michigan. A horse's backside loomed over their heads, every twitch of its tail giving rise to the fear that something naturally foul was about to occur. They'd been waiting for their prey all night, one of them speaking in smiling whispers, the other contemplating murder.

"Have you ever been in love, Jack?"

Jack gave no answer.

"It is a strange feeling indeed. One finds oneself intoxicated with happiness for no reason at all. One's thoughts turn to the most peculiar things...."

Jack pictured a steaming pile of manure falling into Abe's mouth.

"I long for the smell of her. Do you think me strange for saying so? I long for the smell of her, and for the feeling of her delicate fingers in mine. I long to look at—"

The stable doors opened outside. Boot heels against wooden planks. Abe and Jack readied their weapons.

> The vampire could not smell us over the animal stench, nor hear us trampling hay. His footsteps ceased; the stall door opened. Before he had time enough to blink, my ax was thrown in his chest, and Jack's arrow shot through his eye and into his brain. He fell backward, shrieking and grabbing at his face as blood ran around the sides of the arrow. Upset by the noise, his horse reared up—I grabbed it by the bridle for fear that it would trample us both. As I did so, Jack pulled the ax from the vampire's chest, raised it above his head, and brought it down on the creature's face, splitting it clean in two. The vampire was still. Jack raised the ax above his head a second time, and brought it down with even greater force. He did this a third, a fourth time, striking the creature's head with the blunt side of the blade again and again until nothing more than a flattened bag of skin and hair and blood remained.

"My God, Armstrong... what's come over you?"

Jack pulled the ax blade—*crunch*—from what had formerly been the vampire's face. He looked up at Abe, out of breath.

"I pretended he was you."

Abe held his tongue on the journey home.

Ann Mayes Rutledge was the third of ten children—daughter of New Salem's cofounder, James, and his wife, Mary. She was four years Abe's junior, but every bit his equal when it came to her appetite for books. She'd been away during most of Abe's first year and a half in New Salem, tending to a sickly aunt in Decatur and reading everything she could get her hands on to pass the time. There is no record of what happened to her aunt (either she died, got better, or Ann simply grew tired of caring for her), but we know that Ann returned to New Salem before or during the summer of 1834. We know this because she and Abe first met on July 29th at the home of Mentor Graham, whose library both borrowed from, and whose tutelage both sought from time to time. Graham remembered her as a twenty-something with "large, expressive blue eyes," a "fair complexion," and auburn hair—"not flaxen as some have said." She had "a good mouth and good teeth in it. Sweet as honey and nervous as a butterfly." He also remembered the moment when Abe first made her acquaintance. "I have never seen a man's jaw hang quite so low before or since. He looked up from his book and was hit square in the heart by that ancient arrow. The two exchanged pleasantries, but I recall the conversation being one-sided, for Lincoln could hardly keep his wits about him—so struck was he by this lovely vision. So amazed was he by her love and knowledge of books."

Abe wrote about Ann that very day.

> Never has there been such a girl! Never has a
> creature so beautiful and so bright existed in one
> body! She is a good foot shorter than I, with blue
> eyes and auburn hair and a shining, perfect smile.
> She is a bit slender, though it cannot be held
> against her, for it suits her kind, delicate nature.
> How shall I ever sleep again knowing she is out
> there in the night? How shall I ever keep another
> thought in my head when she is all I care to think
> about?

Abe and Ann saw more of each other, first at Mentor Graham's, where they carried on lively discussions of Shakespeare and Byron; then on long, late summer walks, where they carried on lively discussions of life and love; then on Ann's favorite hilltop overlooking the Sangamon, where they hardly talked at all.

> I am almost ashamed to record it here, for I
> fear it may somehow cheapen the thing itself, but
> I cannot resist. Our lips met this afternoon. It
> happened as we sat upon a blanket, watching the
> occasional flatboat drift silently by below. "Abra-
> ham," said she. I turned, and was surprised to
> find her face so close to my own. "Abraham…do
> you believe what Byron says? That 'love will find
> a way through paths where wolves fear to prey'?"

I told her that I believed it with all my heart, and she pressed her mouth to mine without another word.

It is the moment that I wish to remember with my dying breath.

Three months remain before I am required in Vandalia, and I plan to fill every moment of them with Ann's company. She is the most fetching... most tender...most brilliant star in the heavens! Her only fault is that she lacks sense enough to avoid falling in love with such a fool as I!

Abe would never write with such flowery flourish again. Not of his wife; not even of his children. It was the stomach-turning, obsessive, euphoric love of youth. A first love.

December came "too quickly." He bade Ann a tearful farewell and rode to Vandalia to take his oath as a member of the legislature. The prospect of being a "rail-splitter seated beside men of letters" (which had previously given him fits of excitement) now hardly mattered at all. For two agonizing months, he sat in the Capitol thinking of Ann Rutledge and little else. When the session closed at the end of January, he was "out the door before the sound of the gavel ceased to echo," and sped home for what would be the best spring of his life.

There is no music sweeter than the sound of her voice. No painting more beautiful than her smiling face. We sat in the shade of a tree this afternoon, Ann reading *Macbeth* as I lay my head across her lap. She held the book in one hand,

and played with my hair with the fingers of the
other—gently kissing my forehead with each turn
of the page. Here, at last, is all that is right with
the world. Here is life. She is the antidote to all
the darkness that poisons this world. When she is
near I care nothing of debts or vampires. There is
only her.

I have resolved to ask her father's permission
to marry. There is but one insignificant obstacle
in the way of my doing so, and I shall see to its
removal at once.

That "insignificant obstacle" was named John Mac-
Namar—and contrary to Abe's flippant reference, he
posed a serious threat to their happiness.

That's because he and Ann were engaged to be married.

[MacNamar] is by all accounts a man of
questionable character, who pledged his love to
Ann when she was but eighteen, only to depart
for New York before such time as they could
marry. The few letters she received from him in
Decatur were hardly those of a man in love, and
it has been ages since she has received any word
from him at all. Until he releases her, however,
I shall not be satisfied. But I take heart (for the
course of true love has never run smoothly*)
and expect that all shall be swiftly and happily
resolved.

---

*Abe is either misquoting or paraphrasing *A Midsummer Night's
Dream*, Act I, Scene 2.

Abe did what he did best. He wrote John MacNamar
a letter.

IV

On the morning of August 23rd, Abe jotted ten innocuous
words in his journal:

> Note from Ann—not feeling well today. Off
> to visit.

It had been a perfect summer. Abe and Ann met nearly
every day, taking long, pointless walks along the river,
stealing kisses when they were sure no one was looking. It
didn't matter—all of New Salem and Clary's Grove knew
the two were in love, thanks in part to Jack Armstrong's
constant griping on the subject.

> Her mother met me at the door and told me
> that she wished no visitors, but on hearing our
> voices, Ann called me in. I found her lying in
> bed, an open copy of *Don Juan* on her chest.
> With Mrs. Rutledge's permission, we sat alone.
> I took her hand in mine and remarked on its
> warmth. Ann smiled at my concern. "It is merely
> a fever," she said. "It shall pass." As we talked,
> I could not help the feeling that something else
> troubled her. Something more than a summer
> cold. I pressed her, and her tears confirmed my
> suspicions. I could scarcely believe what she next
> imparted.

Ann's long-lost fiancé, John MacNamar, had returned.

> "He came to see me night before last," she
> said. "He was furious, Abe. He looked sickly;
> acted strangely. He told me of your letter, and
> demanded answer in person. 'Tell me now
> that you love this other man!' he said. 'Tell me
> that, and I shall leave this place tonight and never
> return!'"

Ann gave her answer: she loved no man but Abraham
Lincoln. True to his word, MacNamar left that night. Ann
would never see him again. Abe's fury is evident in an
entry made that evening.

> I wrote this MacNamar of our love—asking
> him to do the gentlemanly thing and release her.
> Rather than reply, he crossed a thousand miles
> of wilderness to waylay a woman he had ignored
> these three long years! To claim her as his own
> after casting her aside! Scoundrel! Had I been
> there when the coward appeared, I would have
> broken his skull and cut strops* from his back!
> Yet I rejoice, for he is gone—and with him the
> only impediment to our happiness. I shall delay
> no longer! When Ann is recovered, I shall ask her
> father's permission.

But Ann would not recover.

---

*Long, rectangular strips of leather used to sharpen shaving
razors.

By the time Abe returned on the morning of the 24th, she was too sick to speak more than a few labored words at a time. Her fever grew worse; her breathing shallow. By midday, she couldn't speak at all, and slipped in and out of consciousness. When she did wake, it was to nightmarish delusions—her body convulsing to the point that her bed rattled against the floor. The Rutledges joined Abe at her side, keeping her compresses cool, the candles burning. The doctor had been there with his sleeves rolled up since midday. At first, he'd been "certain" it was typhoid. Now he wasn't so sure. Delusions, convulsions, coma—and all in such a short time? He'd never seen anything like it.

But Abe had.

> A dread crept over me throughout the course
> of the day and evening. An old, familiar dread.
> I was a boy of nine again, watching my mother
> sweat and suffer through the same nightmares.
> Whispering the same futile prayers; feeling
> the same unbearable guilt. It was I who had
> brought this upon her. I who had written the let-
> ter demanding she be released. And who had I
> demanded this of? A man who left mysteriously
> and returned sickly and ashen…a man who had
> waited till nightfall to confront his betrothed…a
> man who would sooner see her suffer and die than
> see her in the arms of another.
>
> A vampire.
>
> This time there was no last embrace. No
> momentary reprieve. This time she merely slipped
> away. God's finest work. Defiled.
>
> Finished.

Fig.1-3. – Abe weeps as Ann Rutledge wastes away in an etching from Tom Freeman's book 'Lincoln's First Love' (1890).

Ann Rutledge died on August 25th, 1835. She was twenty-two years old.

Abe didn't take it well.

———

25th August, 1835
Mr. Henry Sturges
200 Lucas Place, St. Louis
By Express

Dear Henry,
  I thank you for your kindness these several years, and beg a parting favor of you. Below is the name of one who deserves it sooner. The only blessing in this life is the end of it.
  John MacNamar
  New York
—A

For the next two days, Jack Armstrong and the Clary's Grove Boys kept watch over him in round-the-clock shifts. They stripped him of his pocketknife and carpentry tools; took away his flintlock rifle. They even confiscated his belt for fear that he would hang himself with it. Jack saw to it that Abe's hidden stash of hunting weapons was moved well beyond his reach.

For all their care, there was one weapon they missed. None of them thought to look beneath my pillow, where I kept a [pistol] hidden. Jack having briefly left my side that second night, I retrieved it and pressed the barrel to the side of

my head—resolved to be done with it. I imagined
the ball penetrating my skull. I wondered if I
would hear the shot, or feel the pain of it tearing
through me. I wondered if I would see my brains
strike the opposite wall before I died, or if I would
see nothing but darkness—a bedside candle blown
out. I held it there, but I did not fire....

Live...

I could not....
I could not fail her. I threw the weapon on the
floor and wept, damning myself for cowardice.
Damning everything. Damning God.

Rather than kill himself that night, Abe did what he
always did in times of immense grief or unbridled joy—
he put pen to paper.

The Suicide's Soliloquy*

Yes! I've resolved the deed to do,
And this the place to do it:
This heart I'll rush a dagger through
Though I in hell should rue it!

Sweet steel! Come forth from out your sheath,
And glist'ning, speak your powers;

---

*On August 25th, 1838, the three-year anniversary of Ann's
death, *The Sangamon Journal* carried this poem on its front
page. The author chose to remain anonymous.

Rip up the organs of my breath,
And draw my blood in showers!

I strike! It quivers in that heart
Which drives me to this end;
I draw and kiss the bloody dart,
My last—my only friend!

Henry Sturges galloped into New Salem the next morning.

> He sent the others away at once, claiming to be a "close cousin." The two of us alone, I imparted the whole of Ann's murder, making no attempt to hide my grief. Henry took me in his arms as I wept. I remember this distinctly, for I was doubly surprised—both that a vampire could show such warmth, and by the sensation of his cold skin.

"It is the fortunate man who does not lose one so loved in his lifetime," said Henry, "and we are not fortunate men."

"You have lost one as beautiful as she? As kind?"

"My dear Abraham...one could fill a cemetery with the women I have wept over."

"I do not wish to live without her, Henry."

"I know."

"She is too beautiful too...too good...."

"I know..."

Abe could not help his tears.

"The more precious His gift," said Henry, "the more anxious God for its return."

"I must not be without her...."

Henry sat on the bed beside Abe, holding him in his arms...rocking him like a child...debating with himself.

"There is another way," he said at last.

Abe sat up straight on the bed; ran a sleeve over his tears.

"The older of us, we...we can wake the deceased, provided the body is whole enough, and less than a few weeks dead."

It took Abe a moment to comprehend what Henry had said.

"Swear to me you speak the truth...."

"She would live, Abraham...but I warn you—she would be cursed to live forever."

> Here was the answer to my grief! A way to
> see the smile of my beloved again—to feel her del-
> icate fingers in mine! We would sit in the shade of
> our favorite tree, reading Shakespeare and Byron
> for all time, her finger carelessly twirling my hair
> as I lay in her lap. We would walk the years away
> on the banks of the Sangamon! The thought of it
> brought such relief. Such bliss...
>
> But it was fleeting. For when I pictured her
> pale skin, her black eyes and hollow fangs, I felt
> nothing of the love we had shared. We would be
> united, yes—but it would be a cold finger gently
> twirling my hair. Not in the shade of our favorite
> tree, but in the darkness of our curtained house.
> We would walk the years away on the banks
> of the Sangamon—but it would be only I who
> grew old.

I was tempted to the point of madness, but I could not. I could not indulge the very darkness that had taken her from me. The very evil that had taken my mother.

————

Ann Rutledge was laid to rest at the Old Concord Burial Ground on Sunday, August 30th. Abe stood silently as her coffin was lowered into the earth. A coffin he'd insisted on making himself. He'd inscribed a single line on its lid:

In solitude, where we are least alone.

Henry was waiting outside my cabin upon my return from the funeral. It was not yet midday, and he held a parasol over his head to shield his skin, dark glasses over his eyes. He asked me to follow him. Not a word passed between us as we walked a half mile into the woods to a small clearing. There I saw a pale, blond-haired little man tied to a post by his arms and ankles, stripped naked and gagged. Firewood and kindling had been piled at his feet, and a large jug placed on the ground near him.

"Abraham," said Henry, "allow me to introduce Mr. John MacNamar."

He writhed at the sight of us—his skin covered in blisters and boils. "He is quite new," said Henry. "Still sensitive to light." I felt the pine torch as it was placed in my hand…felt the heat on my face as it was lit. But my eyes never left John MacNamar's. "I expect he shall be even

more sensitive to flame," said Henry. I could
think of nothing to say. I could only look at him
as I approached. He shook as I did, trying to free
himself. I could not help but pity him. His fear.
His helplessness.

This is madness.

Still, I longed to see him burn. I dropped
the torch on the woodpile. He struggled against
his bonds to no avail. Screamed until his lungs
bled with nary a sound. The flames grew waist-
high almost at once, forcing me back as his feet
and legs began to blacken and burn. So great
was the heat that his blond hair blew con-
tinually upward, as if he stood in a gale. Henry
remained close to the flames—nearer than I was
able. With the jug in hand, he repeatedly poured
water over MacNamar's head, chest, and back,
keeping him alive as his legs were burned to the
bone. Prolonging his agony. I felt tears on my
face.

I am dead.

This went on for ten, perhaps fifteen minutes
until—at my insistence—he was finally allowed
to die. Henry doused the flames and waited for
the charred corpse to cool.

Henry placed a gentle hand on Abe's shoulder. Abe
brushed it away.

"Why do you kill your own, Henry? And do me the honor of the truth, for I deserve as much."

"I have never given you otherwise."

"Then say it now and be done with it. Why do you kill your own? And why do—"

"Why do I send you in my stead, yes, yes I know. My God, I forget how young you are."

Henry ran a hand over his face. This was a conversation he had hoped to avoid.

"Why do I kill my own? I have given you my answer: because it is one thing to feed on the blood of the old and the sick and the treacherous, but quite another to take sleeping children from their beds; quite another to march men and women to their deaths in chains, as you have seen with your own eyes."

"Then why me? Why not kill them yourself?"

Henry paused to collect his thoughts.

"When I rode here from St. Louis," he said at last, "I knew that you would not be dead when I arrived. I knew it with all my heart...because I know your purpose."

Abe lifted his eyes to meet Henry's.

"Most men have no purpose but to exist, Abraham; to pass quietly through history as minor characters upon a stage they cannot even see. To be the playthings of tyrants. But you...you were born to *fight* tyranny. It is your purpose, Abraham. To free men from the tyranny of vampires. It has always been your purpose, since you first sprang from your mother's womb. And I have seen it emanating from your every pore since the night we first met. Shining from you as brightly as the sun. Do you think that it was some accident that brought us together? Do you think it was mere chance that the first vampire I sought to kill in more than a hundred years was the one who led me to you?

"I can see a man's purpose, Abraham. It is my gift. I can see it as clearly as I see you standing before me now. Your purpose is to fight tyranny...

"...and mine is to see that you win."

Seven

The Fatal First

I have now come to the conclusion never again to think of marrying, and for this reason; I can never be satisfied with anyone who would be blockhead enough to have me.

—*Abraham Lincoln, in a letter to Mrs. Orville H. Browning*
April 1st, 1838

I

Abe was on the second floor of a plantation house. He'd seen so many of them on his trips down the Mississippi—the oversize, four-columned wonders built by the hands of slaves. But he'd never been inside. Not until tonight.

> I held Jack in my arms, his innards visible
> through the slit that ran across his belly. I saw
> the color leave his face...saw the fear in his eyes.
> And then the nothingness. My brave, sturdy
> friend. The roughest man in Clary's Grove. Gone.

And yet I could not grieve him now—for I too
remained perilously close to death.

It had been another simple errand, another name on
Henry's list. But this place was different. Extraordinary.
Abe was on his knees, certain he'd stumbled into some
kind of vampire hive.

How many there were I did not know. I set
Jack's body down and entered a long second-floor
hallway, ax in hand, my long coat torn by the very
claws that had taken my friend's life. Open doors
ran the length of this corridor, and as I walked
cautiously forward, each revealed a scene more hor-
rid than the last. In one, the tiny bodies of three
children hung from ropes by their ankles—their
throats cut. Pails placed beneath them to catch
their blood. In another, the withered, white-eyed
corpse of a woman in a rocking chair. One of her
skeletal hands rested atop the head of a child in
her lap, not quite as decayed as she. Down the
corridor…the remains of a woman lying in bed.
Farther…a squat vampire with a stake through his
heart. All the while I heard the sounds of the floors
creaking around me. Above and below. I crept
down the corridor…closer to the grand staircase
at its end. On reaching its railing, I turned back to
perceive the whole of the hallway. Suddenly there
was a vampire before me—though I could not see
his face against the light. He took the ax from my
hand and threw it aside…lifted me clear off the
ground by my collar. Now I saw his face.

It was Henry.

"It is your purpose to free men from tyranny, Abraham," he said. "And to do so, you must die." Upon this, he threw me over the railing. My body fell toward the foyer's marble floor. And fell. For all time.

It was the last nightmare Abe would ever have in New Salem.

It had taken him months to emerge from the crippling depression brought on by Ann's death—and while it had renewed his hatred of vampires, he found himself without the energy and passion to hunt them. Now, when a letter from St. Louis arrived in Henry's handwriting, it might go unopened for days (and once opened, it might be weeks before Abe attended to the name inside). Sometimes, if the errand required too much travel, he sent Jack Armstrong in his stead. His despondency is clear in an entry dated November 18th, 1836.

> I have given too much of myself already.
> Henceforth, I shall hunt only when it is conve-
> nient for me to do so, and only because it honors
> the memory of my angel mother...only because
> it honors Ann's memory. I care not for the unsus-
> pecting gentleman on the darkened city street.
> I care not for the Negro sold at auction, or the
> child taken from its bed. Protecting them has
> not profited me in the least. On the contrary, it
> has left me even poorer, for the items my errands
> require are furnished at my own expense. And the
> days and weeks spent hunting are days and weeks

> without a wage. If what Henry says is the truth—
> if I am truly meant to free men from tyranny—
> then I must begin by freeing myself. There is
> nothing for me here [in New Salem]. The store
> is failed, and I fear the village is not far behind.
> Henceforth my life shall be my own.

Abe had been encouraged to pursue law by his old Blackhawk War friend John T. Stuart, who had a small practice in Springfield. After studying entirely on his own (and only in his spare time), Abe obtained a law license in the fall of 1836. Shortly thereafter, Stuart asked him to partner up. On April 12th, 1837, the two men ran an advertisement in *The Sangamon Journal* announcing their new venture, located in Springfield at "Number Four Hoffman's Row, Upstairs." Three days later, Abe rode solemnly into Springfield on a borrowed horse, carrying everything he owned in a pair of saddlebags. He was twenty-eight years old, and he was penniless—"the whole of my money going toward my debts, and the requisite books of my new profession." He tied up outside A. Y. Ellis & Co., a general store on the west side of the square, "and moseyed in with not so much as an acorn in my pocket." The clerk was a slender man named Joshua Fry Speed, twenty-four years old, with jet-black hair and a "graceful" face that framed two "unnervingly" blue eyes.

> I found him at once odd and bothersome. "Are
> you new to Springfield, sir? May I interest you in
> a hat, sir? What news from the county, sir? Must
> you routinely stoop to fit through doorways, sir?"
> Never had I been asked so many questions! Never

had I been so unwillingly dragged into conversation! I would not have dreamt of treating my customers in such a way during my own tenure as a clerk. I could not go from one shelf to the next without him buzzing about like a horsefly asking questions, when all I cared to do was conclude my business and be on my way. To this end, I handed him a list of goods—including the chemicals I required for my hunts.

"You will forgive my saying so," said Speed, "but these are strange requests indeed."

"They are what I require. I shall be glad to furnish you with the names of the—"

"Strange indeed—sir, are you certain we have not met?"

"Sir, are you able you order them or not?"

"Yes, I am sure of it! Yes…yes, I saw you give a speech July last at Salisbury! On the need for improving the Sangamon? Do you not remember, sir? Joshua Speed? A fellow Kentuckian?"

"I really must be on my—"

"A fine speech indeed! Of course, I believe you quite mistaken on the subject—every dollar spent on that miserable creek is a dollar wasted. But what a speech!"

He pledged to order the whole of my list at once, and (much to the relief of my weary ears) busied himself copying its contents. Before taking my leave, I inquired as to whether he knew of any rooms for rent—preferably cheap ones, as I had no money to pay at the moment.

"Well, sir...if you have *no* money, am I to take your meaning as 'cheap,' or 'free'?"

"On credit."

"Ah, 'credit,' yes...you will forgive my saying so, but I have learned that 'credit' is a French word meaning 'I shall never pay you.'"

"I square my debts."

"Oh, I doubt it not, I doubt it not. All the same, sir—you shall not find such a room in Springfield. People here are strangely accustomed to trading their wares for money."

"I see...well, thank you for your time. Good day."

Perhaps he pitied my circumstances or my weary countenance. Perhaps he was merely as friendless as I. In any case, he stopped me and offered to share his own room above the store "on credit—until such time as you are able to strike out on your own." I will admit that I considered refusing him. The idea of sharing a room with such a pestering fly! I should rather take my chances in a stable loft! But, having no better option, I thanked him and accepted.

"You will, of course, require time to move," said Speed.

Abe walked outside. A moment later, he returned with his saddlebags and set them on the floor.

"I am moved."

II

Springfield was booming. Wooden shacks and oxcarts were giving way to brick buildings and carriages, and there seemed to be two politicians for every farmer. It was a long way from New Salem—and even farther from the frontier hardship of Little Pigeon Creek. But for all the excitement and advantage of urban life, there also came a cruelty that Abe was unaccustomed to. His description of one incident is a window into the growing violence of a growing city, and further evidence of Lincoln's lingering melancholy.

I witnessed a woman and her husband shot and killed today—the latter being the responsible party in both deaths. I was on the street in front of our office, talking with a client, Mr. John S. Wilbourn, when I heard a scream and saw a woman of perhaps five-and-thirty years running out of Thompsons'.* A man came running after her with a pepperbox,** leveled it, and shot her square in the back. She fell face forward in the street, grabbing at her gut, then rolled onto her back and made an effort to sit upright. She could not. Wilbourn and I raced toward her at once, caring not that her husband stood over her, pistol in hand. Others came into the street, alerted by the noise, and as they did they were met with the sound of a second shot. This one left a hole in the husband's head. He, too, fell—blood pouring from the wound with every beat of his heart.

---

*A boardinghouse on the next block of Hoffman's Row.
**A small, three-barreled pistol capable of firing three shots (one from each barrel) without reloading.

It is a strange thing how quickly the body dies.
How fragile a force our presence is. In an instant
the soul is gone—leaving an empty, insignificant vessel in its stead. I have read of those sent
to the gallows and gillotines [sic] of Europe. I
have read of the great wars of ages past, and men
slaughtered by the tens of thousands. And we
give but fleeting consideration to their deaths,
for it is our nature to banish such thoughts. But
in doing so we forget that they were each as alive
as we, and that one length of rope—one bullet
or blade—took the whole of their lives in that
last, fragile instant. Took their earliest days as
swaddled infants, and their grayest unfulfilled
futures. When one thinks of how <u>many</u> souls have
suffered this fate in all of history—of the untold
murders of untold men, women, and children…it
is too much to bear.

Fortunately, Lincoln's duties as a lawyer and lawmaker
kept him too busy to dwell on death for very long. When
he wasn't required at a committee hearing or a vote, he
was likely deposing a client in his office, or filing a suit at
the Springfield courthouse (most of his cases concerned
land disputes or unpaid debts). Twice a year, Abe joined
a group of his fellow lawyers on a three-month tour of the
eighth Judicial Circuit, an area made up of fourteen counties in central and eastern Illinois. There were dozens of
settlements on the circuit, and precious few courthouses.
So when the weather permitted, the courthouse came to
them, lawyers, judge, and all. For Abe, these trips were
more than an escape from the long, candlelit hours at

his desk. They were a chance to catch up on his vampire hunts.

> Knowing that my work would take me twice yearly around the circuit, I deferred certain errands until such time as they were more suitable. By day my fellow lawyers and I tried cases, using churches or taverns as our courts. In the evenings we gathered at the supper table and discussed the business of the coming day. And at night, when all but a few were asleep in the overstuffed rooms of our boardinghouse, I ventured out with my coat and ax.

One hunt in particular stood out in Abe's memory:

> I'd received a letter from Henry bearing the instructions: "E. Schildhaus. Half mile beyond the north end of Mill Street, Athens, Illinois." Rather than set out straightaway and dispense God's justice, I chose to wait until such time as my work brought me to Athens. And so arrived the day, two months later, when our traveling mob was due in the little town to the north, and the lawyers gathered at the tavern that was to serve as our courthouse. Here they were introduced to the plaintiffs and defendants whose cases they would argue in just a few hours' time. Having been sick most of the night before, I was unable to join Stuart until midday, by which time our case was already before the judge. It was a matter of some small debt owed by our

client—an older red-haired woman named Betsy.
I recall only that we lost, and that I contributed
nothing to the effort beyond a parting, apolo-
getic handshake with her—much distracted by
my illness. That night, Stuart having turned
in along with most of our mob, I unpacked my
coat and ax and quietly made for the address on
Henry's letter. As I was feeling feverish, I had
elected to simply knock on the door and drive my
ax into whoever opened it, so that I might return
to bed with the utmost expediency. The door
swung open.

It was my client, Betsy—her red hair held in
place by an ivory comb. I closed my coat in hopes
of hiding the ax beneath it.

"May I help you, Mr. Lincoln?"

"I—I apologize for intruding at this late hour, ma'am. I
must be mistaken."

"Oh?"

"Yes, ma'am. I understood this to be the home of an E.
Schildhaus."

"Indeed it is."

A vampire and a woman under one roof?

"Mr. Lincoln, you must excuse my asking, but are you
well? You look rather pallid."

"Fine, ma'am, thank you. May I...do you think I
might speak with Mr. Schildhaus a moment?"

"Mr. Lincoln," she said, laughing, "you *are* speaking
with her."

E. Schildhaus...

Elizabeth...

Betsy.

> She caught sight of the ax in my coat. Read
> my face. My eyes. My thoughts. At once I was
> on my back fighting to keep her fangs from my
> neck, my ax knocked out of reach. I pulled at
> her red hair with my right hand and reached
> into my coat with the left. Here I found a small
> knife, which I used to stab any part of her that I
> could reach: her neck, her back, the very arms she
> pinned me with. I brought the blade down again
> and again, until at last she released me and sprang
> to her feet. I did the same, and we circled each
> other cautiously—I holding the knife in front
> of my body; she staring at me with those black
> marbles. Then, just as quickly as she had attacked,
> she stopped...and held her hands in the air as if
> to surrender.

"I must know...what quarrel have we, Mr. Lincoln?"

"Your quarrel is with God. I merely wish to offer Him
the opportunity to judge you."

"Very good," she laughed. "That is very good. Well,
for your sake, I pray you are a better combatant than you
are a lawyer."

> She struck at me, and in doing so knocked the
> knife from my hand—my strength diminished by
> fever. Her fists flew about my face and belly faster
> than I could perceive them, and I tasted the salt of
> fresh blood in my mouth. She drove me back with
> each blow, until I could no longer keep my feet

steady beneath me. For the first time since the night Henry had saved my life, I felt death looking over my shoulder.

Henry was wrong....

I collapsed, and she was on me at once—my arm shaking as I again held her by the hair. And then her fangs were in my shoulder. The pain of punctured flesh and muscle. The heat of blood rushing to the wound. The pressure in my veins. I stopped pulling at her hair and laid my hand flat upon her head, as if comforting a friend in a time of grief. All apprehension left me now. All pain. The warmth of whiskey. An unknown joy.

These are the last moments of my life.

I struck the martyr against the ivory comb in her hair. It lit—brighter than the sun, a halo behind her head. Her red hair burst into flame and I felt her fangs leave me; heard her screams as she rolled on the ground—the fire spreading to her clothes, refusing to let her go. With the last of my strength, I got to my knees, retrieved my ax, and buried it in her brain. She was no more, but I had not the strength to bury her, or walk the mile to my boardinghouse. I dragged her body inside, closed the door, and—after helping myself to a torn strip of her bedsheets to dress my wounds— helped myself to her bed.

> I do not expect I shall ever again have the opportunity of defending and murdering a client in the same day.

When Abe rode circuit, his hunts were confined to darkness. But when he worked out of Springfield, he grew increasingly fond of hunting during the day.

> One of my favorite tricks was setting a sleeping vampire's house alight when the sun was highest in the sky. This left the devil with two unsavory options: meet me in the daylight, where he would be weak and half blind, or remain inside and burn. I cared not which he chose.

By the time Abe won reelection to the State Legislature in 1838, he was becoming known around Springfield as an eloquent speaker and capable lawyer. A man with ability and ambition to match. A man worthy of esteem. He was twenty-nine years old, and in just over a year's time, he'd gone from a penniless newcomer on a borrowed horse to a man who moved with the capital's elite (though thanks to his debts, he remained penniless). He charmed dinner party guests with his backwoods folksiness and impressed fellow legislators with his easy grasp of the issues. "His table manners are a bit rough," wrote fellow Whig Ebenezer Ryan to a friend, "and his suits in need of mending. But he is possessed of the finest mind I have ever known, and has a gift for forming his thoughts into eloquent turns of phrase. I expect he could be governor someday."

Abe also thought less often of Ann Rutledge.

It is true what they say of time. I find my melancholy much improved of late, and take to my errands with renewed zeal. Mother sends news that she and my half-siblings are in good health.* I have a fine partner in Stuart, a pestilent but well-meaning friend in Speed, and the respect of the finest men in Springfield. Were it not for my debts, I should be the happiest of men. And yet I cannot escape the feeling that there is something missing.

———

John T. Stuart had a plan.

It had taken some convincing, but he'd finally managed to drag his junior partner to the cotillion at his cousin Elizabeth's.

Having much business to attend to, I did not think it a good use of my time. Yet Stuart kept at me—pestering me as [his stepbrother] John had years before. "Life is more than papers, Lincoln! Come now! It shall do our health wonders to be out among people." This continued for the better part of an hour, until I had no choice but relent. On reaching the Edwardses' house (before I'd so much as shaken the snow from my soles), Stuart whisked me through the house and introduced me to a young lady seated in the parlor. It was then that his scheme became clear.

---

*Abe had by now taken to calling Sarah Bush Lincoln "mother." It's worth noting that he doesn't mention his father.

Her name was Mary Todd—Stuart's cousin, and a new arrival to Springfield. Abe recorded his first impressions of her that very night, December 16th, 1839.

> She is a fascinating creature, just this week
> turned one-and-twenty, but so gifted in conver-
> sation—and not in the stilted, learned manner
> of excessive breeding, but rather in a natural,
> God-given way. A tiny, witty thing with a pleas-
> ing round face and dark hair. Fluent in French;
> trained in dance and music. My eye could not
> help but return to her, time and time again. More
> than once I caught her staring back, her hand
> cupped to the ear of a friend—both laughing at
> my expense. Oh, I am keen to know her more!
> When the evening was all but concluded and I
> could bear it no longer, I greeted her with a low
> bow, saying "Miss Todd, I want to dance with you
> in the worst way."

Legend has it that Mary later told friends: "And he certainly did."

She was strangely drawn to the tall, unrefined lawyer. Despite the gulf of wealth and breeding that divided them, there were a few crucial similarities that would form the basis of their relationship: Both lost their mothers at a young age, and continued to be defined by that loss. Both were decisive, emotional creatures—prone to soaring highs and abyssal lows. And both enjoyed nothing more than a good joke (especially when it came at the expense of "some deserving charlatan"). As Mary would write in her diary that winter, "He is not the handsomest suitor I have ever known, nor the most refined—but he is without question the cleverest. Yet there is a sadness that accompanies his wit. I find him quite strange...strange yet intriguing."

But as much as she was intrigued by Abe, Mary was torn, for she was already being courted by a short, stocky Democrat named Stephen A. Douglas. Douglas was a rising star in his party, and a man of considerable means, especially when compared to Lincoln. He could provide Mary with the lifestyle she'd grown accustomed to. But while he was undeniably brilliant and undeniably rich, he was also (in Mary's words) "undeniably dull."

"In the end," she recalled in a letter written years later, "I decided that it was more important to laugh than eat."

She and Abe became engaged in late 1840. But while the two were "in hearty love and a hurry to get hitched," there was still the small matter of getting permission from Mary's father. The young couple wouldn't have to wait long for his answer. Mary's parents were due in Springfield for Christmas. It was to be Abe's first encounter with his future in-laws.

Robert Smith Todd was a wealthy businessman and a fixture in Lexington, Kentucky, society. Like Abe, he was both lawyer and lawmaker. Unlike Abe, he'd amassed a great deal of wealth, some of which he'd used to purchase slaves for the mansion that he shared with his second wife and some of their fifteen children.

> I am unnerved at the prospect of being judged
> by a man of such influence and accomplishments.
> What if he should think me a fool or a peasant?

> What then of our love? I can think of nothing
> else. It has given me no shortage of worry these
> two weeks.

Abe needn't have worried. The meeting went better than he could have hoped—at least according to the poem Mary dashed off to Lexington the next day, December 31st:

> My darling Abe was at his best,
> our darling father, most impressed.
> The happy news (you might have guessed),
> is that our union has been blessed!

As one post rider carried her poem to Lexington, another delivered a letter to her newly blessed fiancé. It was addressed "urgent" in Henry's unmistakable scrawl—and carefully worded (as all the letters that passed between him and Abe were) to avoid any direct mention of vampires lest it be delivered to the wrong hands.

> Dearest Abraham,
>   Received your letter of 18th December. Please
> accept my heartiest congratulations on your
> engagement. Miss Todd seems to be possessed
> of many fine qualities, and judging by your
> lengthy description of each, you have clearly been
> possessed by them.
>   However, I must caution you, Abraham, and I
> do so only after much deliberation—for I know
> that this letter will not come as welcome news.

The woman to whom you are engaged is the
daughter of a Mr. Robert Smith Todd, known
to all of Lexington as a gentleman of means and
might. But know the truth: that his power is
built on treacherous ground. That he is more
a friend to my kind than yours. That his allies
are the very worst of us—the sort whose names
I have sent you these many years. He has been
their champion in the statehouse. Their private
bank in matters of business. He has even profited
from the sale of Negroes intended for that
cruelest of fates.

It is not my intention to discourage you from
the match, for the daughter cannot be held to
account for the sins of the father. However, being
so intimately connected with such a man could
prove dangerous. I ask only that you give the
matter serious consideration, and keep your wits
about you—whatever your decision may be.

Yours ever,

—H

————————

History would remember the next day as Lincoln's "fatal
first" of January.

Well, it is done. I have destroyed the woman
I love without so much as an explanation. I have
destroyed her happiness and my own. I am the
most miserable creature that ever lived, and I
deserve whatever sorrows are in store. I expect—
nay, I hope there will be many.

Abe had called on Mary that morning and broken off the engagement, muttering through his tears ("I recall not a word of it") before running out into the cold.

> I knew that I would never be able to shake her
> father's hand again, nor look him in the eye with-
> out betraying my rage. To think that my children
> would share his blood! A man who conspired
> against his own kind! A man who profited from
> the deaths of innocents, their color be damned!
> I could not bear it. And what was I to do? Tell
> Mary the truth? Impossible. I had but one choice.

For the second time in five years, his thoughts turned to suicide. And for the second time in five years, it was his mother's dying wish that kept him from following through.

John T. Stuart was visiting with relatives. All but a few of his fellow legislators had left to welcome the New Year in their respective districts. There was only one person in all of Springfield whom Abe could turn to.

"But you are in love with her!" said Speed. "Why in the devil would you go and do such a stupid thing?"

Abe sat on his bed in the tiny room above A. Y. Ellis & Co.—the bed he shared with the half-mad "pestering fly" buzzing about the room.

"I ache to be with her, Speed . . . but I cannot."

"On account of her father? The same man who gave you his blessing not—not six or eight days ago?"

"The same."

"You ache to be with her . . . her father has given his blessing. You must explain how courtship works here in Illinois, for I have clearly misunderstood some part of it."

"I have since learned that her father is a party to wickedness. That he keeps the worst kind of company. I can have none of it."

"If I loved a woman as you love Mary, her father could dine with the devil himself and it would not alter my affections."

"You do not understand...."

"Then make me understand! How can I be of any use if all you do is speak in riddles?"

Abe could feel it on the tip of his tongue.

"You can trust me to keep any secret, Lincoln."

"When you say 'dine with the devil,' well...you are closer to the truth than you know. I say he keeps company of the worst kind. What I mean to say is...he is a friend of evil, Speed. A friend of creatures who care not for human life. Creatures who would kill you or me and feel all the remorse of an elephant who stepped on an ant."

"Ah...you mean he is a friend of vampires."

Abe felt the blood leave his fingertips.

III

Joshua Speed had never felt at home with the other "well-bred boys" of St. Joseph's Academy. He liked to play pranks. Tell jokes. He liked to dream of life on the wild frontier, "where men were few and arrows flew." He couldn't stand the thought of suffering his father's quiet life of privilege. He yearned for something more—to strike out on his own and see the world. When he was nineteen, this yearning led him to Springfield, where he bought a stake in A. Y. Ellis. But filling orders and keeping inventory hadn't proved the "wild frontier" he was looking for.

In early 1841, not long after Abe's fatal first of January, Speed sold his interests and returned to Kentucky, leaving Lincoln to enjoy the room above the store by himself.

Arrived at Farmington. Must sleep.

It was August, and Abe had come to the Speed family's Kentucky estate, Farmington, for some much-needed time away from his troubles. He hadn't ventured out in months for fear of running into Mary or her friends, and his name was "treated as a profanity in every parlor in Springfield." Speed had written his old roommate and insisted he come for "as long as is necessary to heal your troubles."

Abe was more relaxed than he had been in years, or ever would be again. He took leisurely rides around the estate on horseback. Ventured into Lexington. Lazed afternoons away on the porch of the giant plantation house (the first he had actually set foot inside, his nightmares notwithstanding). If there was one drawback to life at Farmington, it was the inescapable sight of slaves. They were everywhere—in the house; in the fields.

> Riding on the road to town today, I saw a
> dozen Negroes chained together like so many fish
> upon a trotline. It causes me no small discomfort
> to be among them. To be surrounded by them.
> Not only because I think their servitude a sin,
> but because they remind me of all that I wish to
> forget.

Abe and Joshua Speed talked the days away. They spoke of Britain's might; of the steam engine. And they spoke of vampires.

"My own father dealt with the devils, I am ashamed to say," said Speed. "They were hardly a secret among men of his stature, and a poorly kept one in our home, my older brothers having been enlisted in his efforts to win their favor."

"So he sold Negroes to them?"

"The old and the lame, as a rule. He believed it a double blessing—a way to be rid of a useless slave and make a profit doing so. Once or twice he sold off a healthy buck, or a wench with child. Those fetched a higher price as they had more bl—"

"Enough! How can you speak of them so? Speak of men as cattle led to slaughter?"

"If I have given the impression that I take their murders lightly, I apologize. I do not, Abe. Nor have I ever. To the contrary, vampires are chief among the reasons that I never sought the warmth of my father's esteem, or mourned his passing with more than a few tears. How could I accept it, when I have heard the screams of men and women feasted upon to line his pockets? When I have seen the faces of those demons through the spaces between wooden planks? If I could banish it from my memory...if I could atone for what was done here, I would do so."

"Then atone for it."

Speed needed little convincing. He needed only be told that hunting vampires was both dangerous and thrilling, much like the wild

frontier of his imagination. As I had with Jack,*
I shared the whole of my knowledge—teaching
him how and when to strike; sparring with him
to build his poise. Like Jack, he was impatient,
too eager to run headlong into the fight. But
where Jack could rely on his strength to carry
the day, the slender Speed could not. I tried to
impress upon him the immense force and quickness possessed by vampires; how very close
he would be to death. I feared he did not fully
understand. Yet such was his eager spirit that I
found myself once again excited at the prospect
of hunting.

Abe came up with an audacious plan, one that would
put his inexperienced friend at minimal risk and kill six
birds with one stone. In late August, Joshua Speed wrote
a letter to six of his father's former associates, each a frequent buyer of unwanted slaves. Each a vampire.

The day having arrived, I found myself filled
with apprehension. How could I have been so
rash? Six vampires! And with a novice as my
partner! How I wished we had more time! How I
wished we had Jack by our side!

But it was too late to turn back. Six men joined Joshua

---

*Jack Armstrong had decided to remain in Clary's Grove
when Abe moved to Springfield, effectively ending their brief
partnership.

Speed on the shaded porch of the overseer's*—one a gray-bearded man of seventy; one boyish and barely in his twenties; the other four in between. All of them wore dark glasses and carried folded parasols.

> Speed had arranged for several Negroes to gather near the house, and instructed them to "make merry with their gospel." Such was their singing and clapping that one could hear little else while waiting on the porch outside. As we had planned, Speed invited the vampires in one by one, taking their money and leading them to the waiting feast inside.

Five can't catch me and ten can't hold me—ho, round the corn, Sally…

> But it was I who waited with my ax—and on their rounding the corner from the hall to the parlor, I swung it at their throats with the whole of my strength (which, in those days, was considerable). Of the first five vampires, all but one had his head taken on the first try. Only the third required a second effort, the blade having lodged in his face instead of his neck.

I can bank, ginny-bank, ginny-bank the weaver—ho, round the corn, Sally…

---

*A four-room house on the Farmington estate, roughly a half mile from the main residence.

The last vampire was the youngest in appearance, but elderly in spirit. He grew annoyed at being made to wait on the porch alone, and helped himself inside the house. Unfortunately he did so just as the head of his colleague rolled into the hall.

The boyish vampire ran to his waiting horse, jumped on its back without breaking stride, and galloped off.

Speed was first through the door. He jumped on the second horse, dug his heels in, and gave chase before I could even mount the third. It was an old-fashioned horse race now, and Speed rode reckless, standing on his stirrups and beating his foot against the animal's belly. The vampire saw him gaining and did the same, but his horse was a good ten years slower. Speed pulled up alongside without so much as a pocketknife to stab him with or a pebble to throw.

Speed pulled his feet from the stirrups one at a time, held the horn of his saddle with two hands, and stood. With both horses in a full gallop, he jumped, grabbing the vampire and dragging him to the ground. Both men tumbled in the dirt as their horses sped on. Speed struggled to his feet, dizzy—the sun blinding. Before he'd had time to shake the dust from his ears, a fist knocked him ten yards through the air and onto his back. He gasped for breath and brought a hand to his face, where a gash had been opened on his left cheek. The sun was suddenly eclipsed by the shape of a vampire standing over him.

"You ungrateful little cur," he said. Speed felt his innards rattle as the vampire delivered a kick to his gut.

"Who do you suppose paid for all this land?"

Another kick. Another. Speed saw flashes of color with the pain; felt his mouth fill with a strange taste. He couldn't help but be sick.

The vampire grabbed him by the collar. "Your father would be ashamed," he said.

"I...c-certainly hope s-so...," muttered Speed.

The vampire raised a clawed hand and prepared to bring it down on Speed's throat.

Fortunately the head of an ax burst through his chest before he had the chance.

As the vampire fell to his knees, grabbing helplessly at the blade, blood pouring from his mouth, Abe pulled up on his reins and dismounted. Quickly placing two hands on the handle and one foot on the vampire's back, he freed the ax, then delivered a fatal blow to the creature's skull.

"Speed," he said, rushing to his friend's side. "My God..."

"Well," said Speed, "I believe that's enough atonement for one day."

———

Abe found Springfield "lonesome and lifeless" upon his return. His time at Farmington had done wonders for his melancholy, "but with no friend to share my lonely hours, what difference if I be in the happiest or worst of moods?"

> I care not that [Mary's father] is a scoundrel,
> only that I love his daughter unconditionally.
> Speed is right—what is there in the world but

our own small happiness? I have given the matter
my serious consideration. Let Henry protest. Let
the consequences come. I have resolved to pledge
myself anew if she will have me.

"And why should I marry the man who left me to suffer
alone?" asked Mary as Abe stood in the doorway of her
cousin's house. "The man who left me without so much as
an explanation!"

Abe looked down at the hat in his hands. "I do not—"

"Who made a mockery of my name in this city!"

"My dearest Mary, I have only my humble—"

"Pray, what sort of husband would such a man make?
A man who, at any moment, might suffer a change of
heart and leave me to suffer anew? Tell me, Mr. Lincoln,
what enticement have I to pledge myself to such a man?"

Abe looked up from his hat. "Mary," he said, "if it is
my faults you wish to address, then we shall find ourselves standing here a week's time. I do not come to torment you further. I come to merely lay myself at your feet;
to beg your forgiveness. I come with a pledge to spend
my life reconciling whatever grief I have caused you these
long months. If my offer is insufficient—if the sight of me
brings you anything other than happiness—then you may
close that door knowing that my face shall never trouble
you again."

Mary stood in silence. Abe took a small step back,
expecting the door to be slammed in his face at any
moment.

"Oh, Abraham, I love you still!" she cried, and leapt
into his arms.

Their engagement resumed, Abe wasted no time. He

bought two gold wedding rings (on credit, of course) at Chatteron's in Springfield. He and Mary settled on a simple engraving to grace the inside of both.

Love is Eternal

Abraham Lincoln and Mary Todd were married on a rainy Friday evening on November 4th, 1842, in the home of Elizabeth Edwards, Mary's cousin. In all, there were fewer than thirty guests looking on as they exchanged vows.

> After the ceremony, Mary and I stole away to the parlor while dinner was served, so that we might spend our first moments as husband and wife in quiet solitude. We shared a tender kiss or two, and looked at each other with a certain perplexity—for it was a strange thing to be married. A strange and wonderful thing.
> "My darling Abraham," said Mary at last. "Do not ever leave me again."

IV

On May 11th, 1843, Abe wrote to Joshua Speed.

> What a wonder these months have been, Speed! What bliss! Mary is as devoted and loving a wife as one could want, and I am pleased, Speed—so very pleased to share the happy news that she is with child! We are both overjoyed, and Mary has already begun the task of preparing our

home for the arrival. What a fine mother she will
make! Please write me immediately, for I wish to
know how your recovery is progressing.

The evening of August 1st, 1843, was an unusually
hot one, and the open window did little to relieve the heat
in Abe and Mary's tiny second-floor room at the Globe
Tavern. Passersby looked up at that open window with
intense curiosity as sounds bled into the night air—first of
a woman's pain, and then of a shrill cry.

A son! Mother and child in the best of health!
Mary has done perfectly. It is not six hours
since the child's birth, and already she holds
little Robert in her arms, singing to him sweetly.
"Abe," she said to me as he fed, "look what we
have done." I admit that tears filled my eyes.
Oh, if only this moment could stretch on for all
eternity.

Robert Todd Lincoln (Mary insisted; Abe held his
tongue) was born a scant ten months after his parents'
wedding day.

I find myself staring at him for hours on end.
Holding him against my chest and feeling the
gentle rhythms of his breath. Running my fingers
over the smooth skin of his fat, delightful feet. I
admit that I smell his hair when he sleeps. Nibble
at his fingers when he holds them near. I am his
servant, for I shall do anything to earn his slightest smile.

Abe took to parenthood with a passion. But two decades of burying loved ones had taken their toll. As the months went on and Robert grew, Abe seemed increasingly obsessed with losing his son, whether to sickness or some imagined accident. In his journal entries, he began to do something he hadn't in years: he began to bargain with God.

> My only wish is to see him become a man. To have his own family gathered beside him at my grave. Nothing else. I shall happily trade every ounce of my own happiness for his. My own accomplishments for his. Please, Lord, let no harm come to him. Let no misfortune befall him. If ever you require one to punish, I beg you—let it be me.

In accordance with his hopes of seeing Robert reach adulthood, and in hopes of preserving the happiness he'd found in married life, Abe came to a difficult decision in the autumn of 1843.

> My dance with death must end. I cannot risk leaving Mary without a husband, nor Robert without a father. I have this very morning written Henry and told him that he should no longer count on my ax.

After twenty years of battling vampires, the time had come to hang up his long coat for good. And after eight years in the State Legislature, his moment to be recognized had come as well.

In 1846, he was nominated as the Whig candidate for the United States Congress.

Eight

———◆———

"Some Great Calamity"

The true rule, in determining to embrace, or reject
any thing, is not whether it have any evil in it; but
whether it have more of evil, than of good. There
are few things wholly evil, or wholly good.

—*Abraham Lincoln, in a speech in the House of Representatives
June 20th, 1848*

I

When Abe retired from hunting in late 1843, he left one
of Henry's errands unfinished.

> I made innocent mention of this in letters to
> Armstrong and Speed, and (as had secretly been
> my hope) both expressed interest in completing
> it. Because they remained relative strangers to the
> art of hunting vampires, I thought it best if they
> worked together.

Joshua Speed and Jack Armstrong met for the first time in St. Louis on April 11th, 1844. If Speed's letter (to Abe, written three days later) is any indication, it didn't go well.

> As your letter instructed, we met at the tav-
> ern on Market Street yesterday midday. Your
> description [of Armstrong] was precise, Abe! He
> is more bull than man! Broader than a barn and
> stronger than Samson himself! Yet you failed to
> mention that he is also a cur. As thick-skulled
> as he is thick. You must forgive my saying so,
> for I know he is your friend, but never in my
> thirty years have I encountered a more disagree-
> able, pugnacious, humorless man! It is obvious
> why you recruited him (for the same reason one
> recruits a big, dumb ox to pull a heavy cart).
> But why you—a man of the finest mind and
> temperament—would keep his company other-
> wise I shall never comprehend.

Armstrong never wrote about his impressions of Speed, but it's likely they were just as unflattering. The wealthy, dashing Kentuckian was spirited and chatty, qualities that Armstrong would have found irksome in the toughest of men. Speed, however, was soft-handed and slight, the very kind of "dandy" that the Clary's Grove Boys would have stuffed in a barrel and sent down the Sangamon.

> Out of nothing more than respect for you,
> dear friend, we agreed to forgo our grievances and
> see the errand through.

Their target was a well-known professor named Dr. Joseph Nash McDowell, dean of medicine at Kemper College.

> Henry had warned me [about McDowell]. The doctor was an "especially paranoid specimen," he'd said. Paranoid to the extent that he wore an armor breastplate beneath his clothes at all times, lest some assassin try to stake him through the heart. I related this to Armstrong and Speed, and added my own warning: because McDowell's "death" would likely cause a stir in St. Louis, they must take care to remain unseen during the errand, and avoid making inquiries as to the doctor's where-abouts. To do either would be disastrous.

Armstrong and Speed did both.

The reluctant duo stood at the corner of Ninth and Cerre Streets that April afternoon, each in a conspicuous, bulging long coat, asking every man who entered the four-story medical building: "Sir, do you know where we might find Dr. Joseph McDowell?"

> At last we were directed to a steep, circular lecture hall. A miniature coliseum of ever-expanding rows and railings, upon which curious gentlemen rested their hands, their faces illuminated by the hissing gaslights of the surgical table below, their eager eyes trained on the wild-haired, pale figure cutting into the flesh of a male corpse. We took our places on the uppermost level and watched Dr. McDowell remove the heart and hold it up for all to see.

"Banish all poetic notions from your minds," he said. "What I hold here knows nothing of love or courage. It knows only rhythmic contraction." McDowell squeezed the heart in his hand several times. "A single, beautiful purpose…to keep fresh, rich blood flowing to every corner of the flesh."

A vampire teaching anatomy to men! Can you imagine it, Abe? (I must say, I rather liked the fellow's cheek.)

He cut further into the corpse as his demonstration continued, removing and discussing organs until at last the dead man resembled a gutted fish. (Armstrong was rendered weak-kneed for the whole—I, on the other hand, found it all quite fascinating.)

The lecture ended "to the polite tapping of canes against railings," and McDowell's students filed out. All but two. After hurriedly gathering his instruments and papers, the doctor "made haste to a small door at the rear of his stage and disappeared." Armstrong and Speed followed.

We wound down a narrow stone stairway in complete darkness, feeling our way along the rough, wet walls until at last our hands met something smooth. I struck a match against my heel, and a black door appeared before us—the words J. N. McDowell, M.D. Private in gold paint. Out came my pistol and Armstrong's crossbow. Out went the match. My heart presently took to its "single, beautiful" purpose with great enthusiasm—for we knew that a vampire waited on the other side of the dark.

FIG.12.2 – IN AN UNDATED PHOTOGRAPH (CIRCA 1850), A GROUP OF SURGEONS EXAMINE THE HEART AND LUNGS OF AN UNIDENTIFIED MAN. THE FACT THAT HE'S WEARING RESTRAINTS SUGGESTS THAT HE'S STILL CONSCIOUS – AND THE FACT THAT HE'S WEARING DARK GLASSES SUGGESTS THAT HE'S A VAMPIRE.

Speed felt his way to the knob and pulled it quietly, quietly open...

Sunlight.

> Here was a long, tall room with smooth walls. High above our heads, a row of small windows let in the soft light of late day, and framed the feet of passersby. To our right, a long table of caged rats, glass vessels, and silver instruments. Ahead, what appeared to be a body on a stone slab, covered by a white sheet. And to our left, Abe...to our left... naked corpses ran the length of the room, each on a narrow shelf, stacked one atop the other to a height of seven or eight feet.

We were in a morgue.

I'd expected to find the doctor waiting for us. To be attacked at once. But there was no trace of him. Armstrong and I moved slowly toward the slab, our weapons at the ready. Only now did I see the dark glass tubes running over our heads, running from the bodies on our left to the vessels on our right. Only now did I see the blood running into those vessels, kept warm by a row of tiny gas flames beneath.

Only now did I see the chests of these "corpses" moving with each shallow breath.

And here the whole horror of it struck me, Abe. For now I realized that these were all <u>living</u> men. Packed onto shelves as books in a library. Each given barely enough room for his chest to rise. Each kept fed through holes in their stomachs…drained. Too weak to move, too nourished to die. Each imprisoned by the creature whose whistling we suddenly heard from an adjoining room. Whistling…washing his hands in a water basin. Preparing, no doubt, to butcher the poor soul whose chest still rose and fell beneath that white sheet.

And at once our plan became clear.

———

McDowell returned wearing an apron and carrying his surgical instruments on a tray. He set these down, whistling all the while, and peeled back the white sheet.

This isn't the man I remember.

Armstrong sat bolt upright and fired his crossbow into the bastard's heart—his <u>heart</u>, Abe! I
needn't tell you that the arrow merely bounced
off with a *clang*, for the big, dumb ox had forgotten about the breastplate!

It was a costly mistake, Abe, for McDowell
now revealed his true self and struck with his
claws. Jack heard something clang against the
stone floor. He looked down at where his crossbow had been a moment before. Neither it nor
his right hand remained. His face went pale at the
sight of blood running from his wrist—and his
severed hand upon the floor.

Jack's cries were loud enough to wake some of the
barely living on the opposite shelves.

I had no choice but to remove from hiding
and fire my pistol at the vampire's head. But my
shaking hands could not be trusted. The bullet
sailed past him and into his precious glass vessels!
Imagine the noise, Abe! Imagine the volume of
blood that ran onto the stone floor! One might
have drowned! Such was the delicacy of his creation that <u>all</u> of the overhead tubes now shattered
in unison, the effect being a shower of blood from
above.

"No!" screamed McDowell. "You've ruined
it!"

I do not remember being struck. I only know
that I was thrown into the shelves of bodies with
enough force to break the bones of my right leg.

The pain was more severe than any I had ever
known—more severe even than the thrashing I'd
received at Farmington. The whole of my body
felt suddenly cold. I remember McDowell (a pair
of him, actually, for I had been rendered rather
senseless by the blow) coming toward me as I lay
helpless, the entire floor covered by an inch or
more of blood. I remember the strange, amusing
thought that a mortuary was as good a place to
die as any…the warmth pouring down on all of
us…the taste of it. And I remember McDowell
suddenly grabbing at his face.

The tip of an arrow had broken through the
flesh beneath his right eye! The rest protruded from
the back of his skull. Behind him, the big, dumb ox
held a shaking crossbow in his remaining hand.

With an unnatural volume of blood rushing down his
face (adding to the already grizzly scene), the paranoid
McDowell panicked and fled.*

God be praised, we were but steps from the
finest hospital in St. Louis. Armstrong and I

---

*This brush would only deepen McDowell's paranoia. He left
Kemper and founded his own college of medicine at Ninth and
Gratiot Streets, outfitting the building with rooftop cannons
and keeping a store of muskets on hand to ward off attack. He
would go on to serve in the Confederate Army before disappearing from history altogether. The St. Louis building that
housed his school is said to be haunted by his ghost, though no
record of his death has ever surfaced.

helped each other up the stairs (I struggling along on my good leg, and carrying his severed hand in one of mine), both of us soaked from head to toe in the blood of two dozen men.

The surgeons were able to save Jack's life. His hand is gone forever, Abe. He was quite close to death. Closer than he will likely admit. It was his strength that saw him through. His strength, and the prayers you doubtless said for our safety. I shall stay on long enough to see him well (though he refuses to speak to me). I am just now told that my leg shall heal, and that I shall walk with only the slightest limp, if any. Grieve not for your dear Speed, friend—for he counts himself the most fortunate fool alive.

II

On August 3rd, 1846, Abe was elected to the United States House of Representatives. In December of 1847, well over a year after his election, Abe arrived in Washington with his family for the beginning of his term. They took a small room at Mrs. Sprigg's boardinghouse*— a room made all the more cramped by the addition of a fourth family member.

We are doubly blessed with another boy, Edward Baker, born this 10th of March [1846]. He

---

*A modest two-story home that stood on the present-day site of the Library of Congress.

is every bit the laughing rascal Bob is, though I
suspect he has a sweeter disposition. My love is
not diminished slightly at his being the second.
I am every bit the servant of Eddy's smile—
nibbling at his toes to make him laugh…smelling
his hair when he sleeps…holding his sleeping
chest to mine. What a simpleton these boys make
of their father!

This time there was no fear of Edward falling ill or
dying. No bargaining with God (at least none that Abe
saw fit to record in his journal). Perhaps he'd grown more
confident as a parent. Perhaps he was simply too busy to
obsess over it. Busy keeping tabs on his thriving law practice back in Springfield. Busy adjusting to a new city and
a new level of political intensity. Busy with everything but
hunting vampires.

[Henry's] letters arrive monthly. He begs I
reconsider. Insists that it is crucial I take up my
errands again. I answer each one with the same
simple truths: that I will not risk leaving my wife
a widow, or my children fatherless. If I am <u>truly</u>
meant to free men from tyranny, I tell him, then I
must do so in the spirit of that old adage concerning the pen and the sword. My sword has done its
part. My pen must take me the rest of the way.

Washington turned out to be a disappointment on
nearly every level. Abe had come expecting a gleaming metropolis filled with men of the "finest minds, and
dedicated to the service of their constituents." What he

found were "a few brilliant beacons in a fog of fools." As for his dreams of life in a big city, Washington, D.C., felt more like Louisville or Lexington—albeit with a handful of gleaming architectural wonders. "A few palaces on a prairie," as Abe liked to say. The cornerstone of the Washington Monument had yet to be laid. Neither it nor the Capitol would be completed in his lifetime.

One of Washington's greatest disappointments was its abundance of slaves. They worked at Mrs. Sprigg's boardinghouse where Abe stayed with his family. They were auctioned off on the streets he took to work. They were kept caged on the future site of the National Mall, where Abe's giant likeness would one day keep watch for all eternity.

> [There is] in view from the windows of the
> Capitol a sort of livery stable, where droves of
> Negroes are collected, temporarily kept, and
> finally taken to Southern markets, precisely
> like droves of horses. Men—chained together
> and sold! Here, in the shadow of an institution
> founded on the promise that "All men are created
> equal"! Founded with cries of "give me liberty,
> or give me death!" It is more than any honorable
> man can bear.

In one of the few highlights of his congressional career, Abe introduced a bill to outlaw slavery in the District of Columbia. He'd been careful to write it in such a way that "it seemed neither severe to slave owners, nor feeble to abolitionists." But there was only so much a first-term Congressman could do, brilliant or not. The bill never came to a vote.

His legislative failures notwithstanding, Abraham Lincoln made quite an impression in the halls of Congress—and not just because of his towering height. His contemporaries described him as "awkward and gangly," with pantaloons that "scarcely came to within six inches of his ankles." Though he was not yet forty, many Democrats (and a few of his fellow Whigs) took to calling him "Old Abe" on account of his "rough, ragged appearance and tired eyes."

> I related this to Mary one night while she bathed our boys, and confessed that it annoyed me. "Abe," she said with nary an upward glance or moment's hesitation, "one might find men in Congress who possess twice your good looks, but not one who possesses half your good sense."
> I am a fortunate man.

But unflattering nicknames were the least of his concerns, as he wrote only days after taking office:

> A man cannot walk from one end of the chamber to the other without hearing talk of vampires! Never have I heard the subject so often discussed, and by so many! These long years I have thought myself privy to some dark secret—a secret I have kept hidden from my wife and kin. Yet here, in the halls of power, it is the secret everyone seems to know. Many in our delegation are rife with whispers about "those damned Southerners" and their "black-eyed" friends. Jokes are told over meals. Even [Senator Henry]

Clay* participates! "Why does Jeff Davis wear his collar so high? To hide the bite marks on his neck." There must be some truth in their jests, however, for I have yet to hear of a South- ern congressman who isn't beholden to vampire interests, sympathetic to their cause, or fearful of their reprisal. As to my own experiences with [vampires], I shall remain silent. It is a part of my life that I do not wish to visit again—whether in practice or conversation.

Abe was startled awake by shattering glass.

A pair of men had broken through the win- dows of our second-floor room. There was no pis- tol under my pillow. No ax beside my bed. Before I had time enough to stand, one of them struck my face with such force that the back of my skull splintered our headboard.

Vampires.

I struggled to regain my senses as one of the devils grabbed Mary, covering her mouth to stifle the screams. The other took Bob from his small bed, and the creatures made off the way they came—out the windows and onto the street below. I willed myself upright and gave chase,

---

*The seventy-year-old founder of the Whig Party, elder states- man, and idol of Lincoln's.

leaping from the window without hesitation, tearing my flesh on shards of glass as I did. On the dark, scarcely peopled streets of Washington now. I could hear Bob's screams ahead of me in the dark. I ran after them with a panic I had never known. A rage.

I'll tear you to goddamned pieces when I catch you....

The tears in my eyes...the uncontrollable grunts...the torn muscles of my legs. Block after block, turning onto this street, that street, as Bob's voice changed direction. But his screams grew ever fainter on the wind, and my legs ever weaker. I collapsed...weeping at the thought of my son—my helpless little boy carried off into that darkness—that darkness where not even his daddy could reach him.

Abe lifted his trembling head, astonished to find himself in front of Mrs. Sprigg's boardinghouse.

And now...now a terrible thought came over me, and the panic returned.

Eddy...

I bounded up the stairs and into our room. Silence...empty beds...broken windows... curtains fluttering—and Eddy's crib against the far wall. I could not see its contents from here. I could not bear to look. What if he was gone?

I beg you, Lord….

How could I have left him? How could I have abandoned my ax? No…no, I could not look—I could only stand in the doorway, weeping—for I knew in my heart he was dead like the others.

And then his cries rang out, thank God, and I hurried across the room, eager to feel his warmth in my arms. But upon reaching his crib and looking down into it, I saw his white sheets awash in blood. Not Eddy's blood—no, for there was a demon lying there in his place. Lying atop those soaked sheets with a stake through his heart and a hole in the back of his skull. Lying motionless in the crib, the blood pouring from his familiar body…at once a child and a man. His weary eyes open, yet empty. Staring into mine. I knew him.

It was me.

Abe woke—his heart pounding. He turned to his left and saw Mary sleeping peacefully beside him. Checked his sleeping boys and found them unharmed.

He scribbled four words in his journal that night before trying (unsuccessfully) to go back to sleep.

This city is death.

III

Abe shared the warmth of Mrs. Sprigg's fireplace with an old acquaintance on a February night in 1849.

Edgar Allan] Poe has been in Baltimore these
few weeks, and with Mary and the boys departed
for Lexington, I thought it time for a reunion.

They'd kept up a sporadic correspondence over the
years: occasional praise for Poe's stories and poems; congratulations on Lincoln's election victories. But tonight,
face-to-face for the first time in twenty years, they spoke
only of vampires.

I told Poe of Henry; of my hunts and the terrible truths they have led me to. He told me of
his abiding obsession with vampires—that he has
befriended an immortal named Reynolds, and is
close to uncovering a "sinister plot" of some sort.
He speaks with great enthusiasm and assuredness,
yet it is difficult to believe most of what he says,
for it is said through the mask of drunkenness.
He looks weary. Aged by whiskey and bad luck.
The years since our last meeting have not been
kind. His dear wife has departed this earth, and
success has not rewarded him with riches.

"Men kept on the edge of death!" said Lincoln. "Stored
as living barrels in a cellar—their precious blood kept
warm by gas flames. Are there no limits to a vampire's
evil?"

Poe smiled and took another drink.

"You have heard of the Blood Countess, I presume?"
he asked.

Abe's face made it clear that he hadn't.

"You?" asked Poe. "With all of your gallivanting around

chasing vampires? Then I beg you indulge me a moment, for she is a favorite of mine—and an important piece of our country's history.

"Elizabeth Báthory was the jewel of Hungarian nobility," said Poe. "Beautiful; wealthy beyond compare. Her only burden was sharing a bed with a man she did not love—a man to whom she had been promised since her twelfth year: Count Ferenc Nádasdy. He was a generous husband, however, and allowed Elizabeth to indulge her every whim. Unbeknownst to him, her favorite indulgence was a dark-haired, fair-skinned woman named Anna Darvulia. The two became lovers. It is unclear when—"

"Two women...lovers?"

"A trivial detail. It is unclear when Elizabeth learned that Anna was a vampire, or when she became one herself, but the pair were nonetheless eager to begin eternity together. Upon the count's mysterious death in 1604, the lovers began to lure young peasant girls to Čachtice Castle* with promises of employment; with money for their starving families. In truth, these girls were meant to be the playthings of lesser gods...to be robbed of their blood and their lives. In all, Elizabeth and Anna would kill more than *six hundred* girls in three years' time."

"My God..."

"Ah, but it is worse, for the pair seemed to pride themselves on crafting the most gruesome, the most degrading, the most painful methods of murder. Girls were tortured. Ravaged. Consumed for days at a time. Some were suspended above the floor by hooks through their arms and legs. Elizabeth and Anna would lie beneath,

---

*In present-day western Slovakia.

using knives to make tiny cuts in the girl's skin, letting her blood drip slowly over their bodies as they made love below. Some girls were partially crucified, their hands nailed to wooden—"

"I beg you be done with this, Poe. It is too much."

"At last, the peasants would tolerate no more, and the castle was stormed. Inside, the mob found a dungeon filled with iron cages. Half-dead victims with bites taken from their arms and stomachs. Girls whose hands and faces had been held over flames until they were blackened to the bone. But no trace of the vampires. A trial was staged, and a pair of innocent women cast into a pit of fire to appease the peasantry. But the real Elizabeth Báthory and Anna Darvulia had escaped.

"The horrors, Lincoln...the horrors that these women were able to inflict in such a short time...the efficiency and imagination with which they murdered...there is a beauty in it. One cannot help but admire them."

"It is vile," said Lincoln.

"Surely life has taught you that a thing can be both beautiful and vile."

"I was promised 'an important piece of our country's history.' Pray, is there some lesson in this unpleasantness, or do you merely take pleasure in tormenting an old friend?"

"The lesson, old friend, is this: Elizabeth Báthory is, in some measure, to blame for the many vampires we enjoy here in America."

Now Poe had Abe's attention.

"Word of her atrocities spread through Europe," he said. "Rumors of a vampire Blood Countess and the hundreds of girls she slaughtered. In the space of ten years, centuries of whispered superstitions turned to open hatred. Never had a story caused such fervor! Gone forever were the days of accepting vampires as a cost of life, and gone was the fear of challenging them. Vampire hunters began to appear from England to Croatia, learning from one another, chasing the undead across the continent. Chasing them into the stinking sewers and diseased slums of Paris. Chasing them down the dark alleys of London. Vampires, reduced to sleeping in crypts. Reduced to drinking the blood of stray dogs. Lions hunted by sheep! It had become intolerable to be a vampire in Europe. They wanted freedom. Freedom from persecution. From fear. And where could such freedoms be found?"

"In America."

"In America, Lincoln! America was a paradise where vampires could exist without fierce competition over blood. A place where it was common for families to have five, or eight, or a dozen children. They loved its lawlessness. Its vastness. They loved its remote villages and its ports brimming with the newly arrived. But more than anything, Lincoln, they loved its *slaves*. For here, unlike any other country fit for civilized men—here was a place they could feed on the intoxicating blood of man without fear of reprisal!

"When the English came to our shores, charged with bringing us back under the control of the Old World, America's vampires took up the fight. They were there at Lexington and Concord. They were there at Ticonderoga and Moore's Creek. Some returned to their native France, where they persuaded King Louis to lend us his navy. They are as American as you or I, Lincoln. True patriots—for America's survival is their survival."

"I have heard them discussed in the Capitol," Abe whispered. "Even there, one sees their influence."

"It is everywhere, Lincoln! And it shall only deepen, as it did for so many centuries in Europe. How long can it endure? How many vampires can cross our shores before the common man takes note of them? And what then? Do you think the good people of Boston or New York would be content to live with vampires for their neighbors? Do you believe that all vampires possess the same agreeable disposition as your Henry or my Reynolds?

"Imagine, Lincoln. Imagine what might have happened in Europe had there been no America for vampires to flee to. How long would the lions have allowed the sheep to hunt them? How long before they began to behave like lions again?"

Abe didn't like the picture forming in his mind.

"I tell you," said Poe, "some great calamity awaits us."

———

For Poe, at least, it proved an ominous prediction.

On October 3rd, 1849, less than eight months after his reunion with Abe, Poe was discovered wandering the streets of Baltimore, half dead, confused, and wearing clothes that weren't his own. He was hurried to the Washington College Hospital, where doctors tried to diagnose his worsening illness.

> Patient suffers from high fever and delusions.
> Calls out for a "Reynolds" when he is conscious.
> Symptoms similar to typhoid, though the rapid
> progression suggests some other underlying cause.
> His case is hopeless.

FIG. 7-C - EDGAR ALLAN POE POSES WITH ABRAHAM LINCOLN IN
MATHEW BRADY'S WASHINGTON, D.C. STUDIO - FEBRUARY 4TH, 1849.

On Sunday, October 7th, at five o'clock in the morning, Poe woke with a start. He uttered the words "Lord help my poor soul" and passed away.

IV

March 5th, 1849, brought an end to Abe's brief, unmemorable congressional career. He'd chosen not to run for a second term.

> Being elected to Congress…has not pleased
> me as much as I expected. I have neglected my
> dear wife and rascals terribly these two years, and
> there is nothing in Washington to tempt me from
> returning to Illinois.

He returned to Springfield and dove headfirst into his law practice, apprenticed by a thirty-year-old lawyer named William H. Herndon (who would go on to write a comprehensive, controversial biography of Lincoln after his assassination). Abe took great care to keep the truth of his dark past away from his young partner.

He wrote letters of recommendation for friends seeking appointments. He argued cases across Illinois. He wrestled with his boys and took long walks with his wife.

He lived.

> No more talk of men with fangs,
> Or lives that never cease.
> I only long for simple things,
> I only long for peace.

He wouldn't get it.

———————

Eddy Lincoln was three years, ten months, and eighteen days old when he died.

From an entry dated February 1st, 1850, only hours after his son's passing:

> I lost my little boy...I miss him very much.
> There is no joy in this life....

There's no reason to suspect that Eddy's death had anything to do with vampires. He'd been sick since December (probably with tuberculosis) and wasted away gradually, his mother keeping a vigil by his bed, rubbing balm on his little chest to no avail.

> Mary could not bear to let Eddy die in his bed
> alone. She held his unconscious body to her own,
> cradling our little boy against her chest, rocking
> him through the night...until he was gone.

Mary would never be the same. Though she would bury two more sons, nothing would ever match the grief of losing her beloved "Angel Boy." Three days after his death, she hadn't eaten, or slept, or stopped crying.

> [Mary] is inconsolable. It is just as well, for
> I am of no mind to console. Sent word to Speed
> and Armstrong requesting they come. Received
> a letter from Henry expressing his condolences,
> and his promise to arrive [in Springfield] no later

than tomorrow midday. How he learned of Eddy's passing, I do not know.

Eddy was laid to rest in Hutchinson's Cemetery, just a few blocks away from Abe and Mary's house.

> I held on to Bob and Mary for the whole of the service, the three of us weeping. Armstrong and Speed stood at our side, as did many friends and well-wishers. Henry watched from a distance, not wanting to cause me any added grief by raising Mary's suspicions.* However, he saw to it that I received a note before the service. In it were his further condolences…and a reminder that there was another way.
> A way to see my boy again.

Despite what must have been a maddening temptation to see his little boy again, Abe surrendered to reason.

> He would be small forever. An angelic murderer. I could not bear the thought of keeping him locked away in the dark. Of teaching him to kill so that he might live. I could not condemn my son to hell.

Mary wrote a poem (possibly with Abe's assistance), which was published in the *Illinois State Journal* around

---

*Mary had no idea who Henry Sturges was, or that such a thing as vampires existed.

the time of Eddy's burial. The final line is engraved on his tombstone.

Those midnight stars are sadly dimmed,
That late so brilliantly shone,
And the crimson tinge from cheek and lip,
With the heart's warm life has flown—
The angel of Death was hovering nigh,
And the lovely boy was called to die.
The silken waves of his glossy hair
Lie still over his marble brow,
And the pallid lip and pearly cheek
The presence of Death avow.
Pure little bud in kindness given,
In mercy taken to bloom in heaven.
Happier far is the angel child
With the harp and the crown of gold,
Who warbles now at the Savior's feet
The glories to us untold.
Eddy, meet blossom of heavenly love,
Dwells in the spirit-world above.
Angel Boy—fare thee well, farewell
Sweet Eddy,
We bid thee adieu!
Affection's wail cannot reach thee now
Deep though it be, and true.
Bright is the home to him now given…
Of such is the Kingdom of Heaven.

Nine

———◆———

At Last, Peace

We have been the recipients of the choicest bounties of Heaven. We have been preserved, these many years, in peace and prosperity. We have grown in numbers, wealth and power, as no other nation has ever grown. But we have forgotten God. We have forgotten the gracious hand which preserved us in peace, and multiplied and enriched and strengthened us.

—Abraham Lincoln, proclaiming a National Fast Day
March 30th, 1863

I

From the *New York Tribune*, Monday, July 6th, 1857:

VIOLENT CLASHES TERRORIZE CITY
Curious Sightings in Gang Brawl
by H. Greeley

The savage clashes which laid siege to much of Manhattan these two days and nights have at last been quieted. By order of the Governor, militiamen entered the Five Points late Sunday and engaged the remaining combatants with volley upon volley of musket fire. Untold numbers of dead could this morning be seen lining Baxter, Mulberry and Elizabeth Streets—victims of the worst rioting this or any city has seen in memory. The violence seems to have begun when those notorious Five Points gangs, the Plug Uglies and Dead Rabbits, sprung an attack against their shared enemy, the Bowery Boys. It is the opinion of the [police] that the killings began on Bayard Street around Saturday midday, before spreading through the Five Points with all the rapidity and ferocity of a fire.

The innocent were forced to barricade their doors as rival thugs stabbed, shot and bludgeoned one another to death in the streets. Merchants saw their shops destroyed; their wares brazenly stolen in the chaos. Eleven passersby—a woman and child among them—were mauled for no cause but their straying too close to the fight.

CURIOUS SIGHTINGS IN GANG BRAWL

The *Tribune* was inundated with testimonies of "strange" and "impossible" feats throughout Saturday evening and Sunday morning. Men were said to leap across rooftops "as if carried by the air" in pursuit of one another; climb the sides of buildings "as effortlessly as a cat climbs a tree."

One witness, a merchant by the name of Jasper Rubes, claims to have seen a Dead Rabbit "lift a Bowery Boy above his head and throw him against the second story of [a Baxter Street factory] hard enough to leave a hole in the bricks." Incredibly, the victim "landed on his feet," said the witness, "and kept up the fight as if nothing had happened."

"His eyes," said Rubes, "were black as soot."

Hunting vampires was the furthest thing from Abraham Lincoln's mind in the early 1850s.

Ten months after burying their son, Abe and Mary welcomed another. They named him William "Willy" Wallace Lincoln in honor of the physician who'd stayed at Eddy's side until the end. In 1853, they welcomed one more boy, Thomas "Tad" Lincoln, born April 4th. Along with ten-year-old Robert, the three formed a "boisterous brood."

"Bob howls in the next room as I write this," Abe said in an 1853 letter to Speed. "Mary has whopped him for running off and disappearing. I suspect that by the time I finish this letter he will have run off and disappeared again."

Abe made very few journal entries in the wake of Eddy's death. Those six and a half little leather-bound books had become a record of his life with vampires—a record of weapons and vengeance; of death and loss. But those days were behind him now. That life was over. After his entries had resumed in 1865, Abe looked back on that "last, peaceful, wonderful spell."

They were good years, to be sure. Quiet years.
I wanted nothing more of vampires or politics.
To think of all that I had missed whiling away
the hours in Washington! How much of Eddy's
brief, beautiful life had escaped my notice! No…
never again. Simplicity! That was the oath I swore
now. Family! That was my errand. When I could
not be with my boys at home, I let them run
about the office (much to Lamon's* consternation, I suspect). Mary and I took lingering walks,
regardless of the season or weather. We spoke of
our dear boys…of our friends and futures…of
the speed with which the whole of our lives had
passed.

There were no letters from Henry. No visits or
hints of his whereabouts. At times I wondered if
he had finally come to accept that I would hunt
no more—or if he himself had fallen prey to the
ax. Whatever the reason behind his absence, I was
glad for it. For while I had come to regard him
with tremendous affection, I loathed every memory the mere mention of his name conjured up.

Abe's long coat, riddled with the rips and scars of battle, was unceremoniously burned. His pistols and knives
were locked in a trunk and forgotten in the cellar. The
blade of his ax was allowed to rust. The specter of death,

---

*In 1852, Abe started a law practice with Ward Hill Lamon, an
imposing figure of a man who would later serve as his presidential bodyguard. As he had with his former partner, Abe kept
Lamon in the dark about vampires.

which had hung over the old vampire hunter since his ninth year, seemed at last to be lifting.

It returned briefly in 1854, when Abe received word from a friend in Clary's Grove that Jack Armstrong was dead. From a letter to Joshua Speed:

> The damned fool's gotten himself killed by a horse, Speed.
>
> Old Jack stood in an early winter [downpour], trying to drag the stubborn beast by its lead. For nearly an hour they tugged against each other. Jack (ever the Clary's Grove Boy) didn't think to fetch his coat or holler for help, despite his being one-handed and soaked to the bone. By the time he got the animal out of the rain, Jack had caught his death. He burned a fever for a week, slipped away, and died. It seems an ignoble end to such a sturdy man, does it not? A man who survived so many brushes with death? Who saw the terrible things you and I have seen?

In the same letter, Abe admitted to being "unnerved" by his "lack of anguish" over Armstrong's passing. He grieved, sure. But this was a "different sort of grief," unlike the crippling depression that had followed his mother's death, Ann's, and Eddy's.

> I fear that a life of death has made me numb to both.

Four years later, Abe would defend Jack's son, "Duff" Armstrong, when he stood trial for murder. Abe refused payment. He worked tirelessly, litigated passionately, and (with a stroke of legal brilliance) won Duff his freedom,* a final thank-you to a brave friend.

II

The same year that saw Abe mourn the loss of an old friend saw him dragged back into politics by an old rival.

Abe had known Senator Stephen A. Douglas since they were both young Illinois state legislators (and eager suitors of Mary Todd). Though a Democrat, Douglas had long been opposed to allowing slavery into territories where it didn't already exist. But in 1854, he suddenly reversed himself and championed the Kansas-Nebraska Act, a bill that repealed the federal ban on the spread of slavery. President Franklin Pierce signed it into law on May 30th, enraging millions of Northerners and stirring up long-simmering tensions on both sides of the issue.

> Try as I might, I could not ignore my anger.
> It seeped into my mind as water is drawn into
> the roots of a tree, until at last it permeated the
> whole of my being. Sleep provided no refuge, for
> I was nightly visited by a sea of black faces, each
> the nameless victim of a vampire. Each of them

---

*A witness claimed that he saw Duff commit the murder from a distance of 150 feet "by the light of a full moon." Abe produced an almanac, which proved that the night in question had been a moonless one.

crying out to me. "Justice!" they cried. "Justice, Mr. Lincoln!"

That [slavery] existed at all was insult enough. That I knew the institution to be <u>doubly</u> evil made it all the worse. But this! The idea of slavery's diseased fingers reaching farther north and west! Reaching into my own Illinois! It would not stand. I had retreated from politics, but when asked to debate [Douglas] on the issue, I could not refuse. Those ghostly faces would not permit me to.

On October 16th, 1854, Lincoln and Douglas squared off in front of a large Peoria, Illinois, crowd. A reporter with the *Chicago Evening Journal* described his amazement at witnessing Abe speak.

His face [began] to light up with the rays of genius and his body to move in unison with his thoughts. His speaking went to the heart because it came from the heart.

"I cannot but hate it!" said Mr. Lincoln of the proposal. "I hate it because of the monstrous injustice of slavery itself!"

I have heard celebrated orators who could start thunders of applause without changing any man's opinion. Mr. Lincoln's eloquence was of the higher type, which produced conviction in others because of the conviction of the speaker himself.

"I hate it because it deprives our republican example of its just influence in the world!" he continued. "Enables the enemies of free institutions, with plausibility, to taunt us as hypocrites!"

His listeners felt that he believed every word he said, and that, like Martin Luther, he would go to the stake rather than abate one jot of it. In such transfigured moments as these he was the type of the ancient Hebrew prophet as I learned that character at Sunday school in my childhood.

Though it failed to sway Douglas or his allies in Congress, the speech would nonetheless prove a turning point in Abe's political life. His anger over the slavery issue (and by extension, the vampire issue) had nudged him back into the political arena. His genius and eloquence that night in Peoria would ensure that he never left it again. The speech was transcribed and reprinted across the North. The name Abraham Lincoln began to take on national significance among the opponents of slavery. In the years to come, one of its passages would prove eerily prophetic.

> "Is it not probable that the contest will come to blows, and bloodshed? Could there be a more apt invention to bring about collision and violence, on the slavery question, than this?"

Senator Charles Sumner lay unconscious on the Senate floor, facedown in a pool of his own blood.

The abolitionist had been attacked by a thirty-seven-year-old congressman named Preston Smith Brooks, a proslavery South Carolinian who'd taken offense at the

Massachusetts senator's mocking of his uncle in an anti-slavery speech two days earlier. On May 22nd, 1856, Brooks entered the Senate chamber accompanied by a fellow South Carolina congressman named Laurence Keitt and approached Sumner at his writing desk. "Mr. Sumner," said Brooks, "I have read your speech twice over carefully. It is a libel on South Carolina, and Mr. Butler, who is a relative of mine." Before Sumner had a chance to reply, Brooks began to beat his head with his gold-tipped cane, opening new gashes with each blow. Blinded by his own blood, Sumner staggered to his feet before collapsing. His victim now unconscious and bleeding, Brooks continued to strike until his cane broke in two. As horrified senators rushed to Sumner's aid, they were held back by Keitt, who brandished a pistol and yelled, "Let them be!"

The blows fractured Sumner's skull and vertebrae. He would live but wouldn't be able to return to his Senate duties for three years. When South Carolinians heard of the attack, they sent Brooks new canes by the dozen.*

> I am more assured than ever of my being wise
> to leave Washington, and more certain than ever
> that it is a repository of idiots—just as I am cer-
> tain that we are now on a course for the "great
> calamity" Poe warned of those long years ago.
> One can see the masts of an angry fleet on the
> horizon, and every week seems to bring them
> a mile closer. If, as many think, it is the winds
> of war that fill their sails, then it is a war I am
> content to let others fight. My boys are healthy.

---

*Brooks died eight months after the attack.

My wife is in good spirits. And we are a long,
long way from Washington. I am happy to make
a speech or two; happy to lend my pen where it
is needed. But I am happy. And happiness, I have
decided, is a noble ambition. I have lost too much
already, and have been a slave to vampires these
thirty years. Let me now be free. Let me now seek
the enjoyment of whatever time God may grant
me. And if this peace be merely prelude to some
peril or other, so be it. I shall enjoy the peace.

There was no shortage of passion or violence on either
side of the slavery issue. Infuriated by the attack on
Charles Sumner, a radical abolitionist named John Brown
led an attack on a settlement at Pottawatomie Creek, in
the Kansas Territory. On the night of May 24th, 1856 (just
two days after Sumner was beaten), Brown and his men
brutally murdered five proslavery settlers, dragging each
man from his home, running him through with a sword,
and firing a bullet into his skull for good measure. It was
the first in a series of reprisals that would be dubbed
Bleeding Kansas. The violence would continue for three
years and claim over fifty lives.

On March 6th, 1857, the Supreme Court pushed the
country closer to the brink.

Dred Scott was a sixty-year-old slave who'd been
trying to win his freedom in the courts for more than a
decade. Between 1832 and 1842, he'd traveled with his
master (U.S. Army Major John Emerson) through the free
territories of the North, acting as a personal valet. During
these travels, Scott married and had a child (all on free

soil), and upon the major's death in 1843, tried to buy his freedom. But the major's widow refused, continuing to hire him out and pocketing the wages for herself. Advised by abolitionist friends, Scott sued for his freedom in 1846, on the grounds that he'd ceased to be property the moment he'd set foot in free territory. The case worked its way through the courts, attracting national attention before finally reaching Washington in 1857.

In a 7–2 decision, the Supreme Court ruled against Scott, arguing that the Founding Fathers had considered Negroes "beings of an inferior order, and altogether unfit to associate with the white race" when they drafted the Constitution. Consequently, Negroes couldn't be citizens of the United States, and couldn't bring suit in federal court to begin with. They had no more right to due process than the plows they drove.

It was a devastating outcome for Scott, but it had implications far beyond his personal freedom. In issuing its ruling, the Court declared that:

- Congress had exceeded its authority when it banned slavery from spreading to certain territories—and that these territories had no power to ban slavery on their own.
- Slaves and their descendants (whether free or not) were not protected by the Constitution, and could never be United States citizens.
- Escaped slaves who reached free soil were still the legal property of their masters.

In the wake of the Dred Scott ruling, the *Albany Evening Journal* accused the Supreme Court, Senate, and newly inaugurated President James Buchanan of being part of a "conspiracy" to spread slavery, while the *New York Tribune* ran an editorial that captured the fury of many Northerners:

> Now, wherever the stars and stripes wave, they protect slavery and represent slavery.... This, then, is the final fruit. In this, all the labors of our statesmen, the blood of our heroes, the life-long cares and toils of our forefathers, the aspirations of our scholars, the prayers of good men, have finally ended! America the slave breeder and slaveholder!

Southern Democrats were more emboldened than ever, some boasting that the ruling would lead to "slave auctions on Boston Common." Republicans and abolitionists had never been more electrified in their opposition. America was beginning to tear itself apart.

But few Americans knew just how much danger they were *really* in.

III

On June 3rd, 1857, Abe received a letter addressed in a familiar scrawl. It contained no inquiries after his health or happiness; no regards to his family.

> Abraham,
> I beg you forgive my failure to write these five years. You must also forgive my abruptness, for matters here require my urgent attention.

I must ask another sacrifice of you, Abraham. I realize how presumptuous a request it must seem given all that you have suffered, and what little enticement I can offer against the contentment of home and family. Trust that I would not burden you unless the situation was dire, or if there were any other man capable of what I ask.

I have enclosed everything necessary to your swift passage to New York. If you are willing, then I beg you come no later than 1st August. Further instructions will be delivered upon your arrival. However, if your answer is no, I shall not bother you again. I ask only that you write at once with your refusal, so that we may consider a new strategy. Otherwise I look forward to our reunion, old friend—and to giving you the explanation you have long deserved.

It is time, Abraham.

Ever,

—H

Enclosed were various train and steamboat schedules, $500, and the name of a boardinghouse in New York City where a room had been rented under the name A. Rutledge.

Oh, how [the letter] annoyed me! Henry was clever indeed—for though he claimed to have little enticement to offer, <u>every</u> <u>word</u> was designed to entice: the self-censure; the flattery; the promise of an explanation—even the name left at the boardinghouse! That he would have me abandon my affairs, my family, and cross a

thousand miles without so much as an intimation
of the purpose!

And yet I could not refuse.

And this was more annoying than the letter
itself, for Henry was right. It was <u>time</u>. Time
for what, I knew not. Only that the whole of my
life...the suffering, the errands, the death...that
it had all been leading to something more. I had
felt this, even as a child—the sense that I had
been placed on a long, straight stretch of river
from which there could be no deviation. Carried
ever faster by the current...surrounded by wilderness on both sides...destined to collide with
some unseen object far, far downstream. I had
never spoken of this feeling, of course, for fear
of being thought vain (or worse, being proven
wrong—for if every young man who was assured
of his future greatness was proven correct, the
world would be brimming with Napoleons). Now,
however, the object was beginning to take shape,
though I could not yet make out its features. If a
thousand miles was the price of seeing it clearly at
last, then so be it. I had traveled farther for less.

———————

Abe arrived in New York City on July 29th. Not wanting
to raise suspicion (or leave his family unattended), he'd
decided to take Mary and the boys along for a "spontane-
ous" trip to experience the wonders of New York City.

They couldn't have picked a worse time to visit.

The city was in the midst of a violent summer. Two
rival police forces had been locked in a bloody battle for

legitimacy since May, leaving crime largely unchecked—
a field day for muggers and murderers alike. The Lincolns
reached New York just three weeks after the worst gang
rioting in the city's history, rioting in which witnesses
described seeing men perform "impossible feats." Abe had
seen New York only once before, briefly passing through
on his way north. Now he was able to appreciate the
largest, most energetic of all American cities for the first
time.

> The drawings do it no justice—it is a city with-
> out end or equal! Each street gives way to another
> more grand and bustling than the last. Buildings
> of such size! Never have I seen so many carriages
> crowded together. The air rings with the clop-
> ping of horseshoes against cobblestones and the
> murmur of a hundred conversations. There are
> so many ladies carrying so many black parasols,
> that if a man were to look down from a rooftop,
> he would scarcely see the sidewalk. One imagines
> Rome at its height. London and its grandeur.*
> Mary insists we stay a month at least! For how else
> can we ever hope to appreciate such a place?

On the night of Sunday, August 2nd, Abe rose from
bed, dressed in the dark, and tiptoed out of the room where
his family slept. At precisely eleven-thirty, he crossed
Washington Square and walked north, just as the note
slipped under his door that morning had instructed. He

---

*As big as New York City was, it was still only a quarter of
London's size in 1857.

was to meet Henry two miles up Fifth Avenue, in front of the orphanage at the corner of Forty-fourth Street.

> With each passing block the streets grew emptier. Darker. Here, the grand buildings and murmuring sidewalks melted into rows of two-story homes, nary a candle alight in any window. Nary a gentleman about. Passing though Madison Square Park, I marveled at the unfinished skeleton of some immense, unknown structure.* Marveled at the absolute quiet. The barren streets. I began to imagine myself the only soul in New York, until the sound of heels against cobblestones caught my ear.

Abe glanced over his shoulder. The silhouettes of three men followed close behind.

> How had they escaped my notice until now? In light of the city's recent troubles, I thought it best to double back and head south to Washington Square, back to the safety of gaslight and crowded streets. Henry could wait. Oh, what a damned fool I was! I had ventured out unarmed, knowing too well that many a gentleman had been robbed (or worse) on these streets of late—and that the police could hardly be counted on to intervene. Silently cursing myself, I turned left down Thirty-fourth Street. My heart sank as I heard their footsteps follow me around the bend—for now there could be no question of their intent.

---

*Likely the Fifth Avenue Hotel, completed in 1859.

My pace quickened. Theirs quickened. "If only I
could reach Broadway," I thought.

He wouldn't. His pursuers broke into a sprint. Abe did
the same, making another left and running between two
lots in hopes of eluding them.

My speed could still be trusted—but as fast as
I was, [they] were faster. All hope of escape lost, I
turned and met them with my fists.

Abe was nearly fifty years old. He hadn't wielded a
weapon or been in a fight for fifteen years. Even so, he
managed to land a few blows on each of his assailants
before one of them landed his own, knocking him out
cold.

I woke in absolute darkness, the faint rumble
of a coach's wheels beneath me.
"Put him out again," said the unfamiliar voice.
A sharp, oh so brief pain on the top of my
head…the universe before me in all of its color
and majesty…and then…nothing.

———————

"I am deeply sorry," said the familiar voice, "but we can
trust no living man with our whereabouts."

It was Henry.
My hood was presently removed, and I found
myself in the center of a grand, two-tiered ballroom, its intricate ceiling thirty feet above my

aching head; its long, dark red curtains drawn;
the whole lit dimly by chandeliers. Gold upon
gold. Marble upon marble. The finest carvings
and furnishings, and a floor of wood so dark and
polished it might have been black glass. It was the
most splendid room I had ever seen or, for that
matter, ever thought possible.

Three men of varying age and build stood
behind Henry, each leaning against the hearth of
a kingly marble fireplace. Each with contempt in
his eyes. These, I assumed, were my assailants. A
pair of long sofas faced each other in front of the
fireplace, with a low table in between. Upon this,
a silver tea service reflected the light of the fire,
casting strange, intoxicating patterns on the walls
and ceiling. A diminutive, graying gentleman sat
on the left sofa, teacup in hand. I had seen him
before…I was sure of it…but in my confused
state I could not place him.

My senses returning, I noticed perhaps twenty
more gentlemen scattered about the room, some
standing behind me, some seated in high-backed
chairs against the walls. Another twenty loomed
above, looking down from the shadowy mezzanines on each side of the room. It was clear [they]
meant to keep their faces hidden.

"Please," said Henry. He motioned for Abe to sit across
from the diminutive gentleman.

I hesitated to come any closer until Henry
(sensing the reason behind my reluctance)

motioned to my assailants, and they removed
from the fireplace. "I give you my word," he
said as they went, "no further harm shall befall
you tonight." Believing him sincere, I took a
seat across from the gentleman whom I could
not yet place, clutching the back of my head
with my left hand and steadying myself with
the other.

"Vampires," said Henry—tilting his head toward the
three men who now took their seats along the wall.

"Yes," said Abe. "I'd worked that out on my own,
thank you."

Henry smiled. "Vampires," he said, motioning around
the ballroom. "The cursed, bloodsucking lot of us. The
exceptions being yourself... and Mr. Seward here."

Seward...

Senator William Seward was the former governor of
New York, one of the leading antislavery voices in Congress, and the man widely expected to be the Republican
presidential nominee in 1860. He and Abe had met nine
years earlier while campaigning for General Zachary
"Old Rough and Ready" Taylor in New England.

"A pleasure to see you again, Mr. Lincoln," he said,
extending his hand.

Abe shook it. "Likewise, Mr. Seward, likewise."

"You are doubtless aware of Mr. Seward's reputation?"
asked Henry.

"I am."

"Then you must know that he is a favorite to be nominated this time around."

"Of course."

"Of course," said Henry. "But tell me...did you know that Seward here has hunted and destroyed nearly as many vampires as you have?"

Abe had to bite his lip to keep his jaw from dropping. *Bookish, privileged little Seward—a vampire hunter? Impossible.*

"Revelations," said Henry. "Revelations are what bring us together tonight." Henry paced in front of the hearth.

"I have brought you here," he said, "because my colleagues wished to see for themselves the purpose that I have seen in you. To see this Abraham Lincoln I have spoken of these many years. I have brought you here because they wanted proof that you were capable of what we ask; to judge you directly before going any further."

And how shall I be judged? By the expediency with which I behead them?

A man's voice rang out of the darkness: "I am sure we can find a more agreeable method than that, Mr. Lincoln."

A few scattered laughs echoed through the room. Henry silenced them with a wave of his hand.

"It is already done," he said. "From the moment you were carried into this room, they saw your past and your pain; peered into your soul—just as I have. Had you been deemed unworthy, you would not have been permitted to wake among us."

"'Us...'" said Abe. "I have long believed that vampires form no alliances."

"Desperate times. Our enemies have allied themselves—so must we. They have recruited living men to their cause—so have we."

Henry stopped pacing.

"There is a war coming, Abraham," he said. "It is not a

war of man, but it is man who shall spill his blood fighting it—for it concerns his very right to be free.

"A war...," he continued. "And you of all men must win it."

There was nothing else now—no vampires in the mezzanines, no Seward or silver tea service...there was only Henry.

"There are those of my kind," he said, "who choose to remain in the shadows. Who cling to that last piece of themselves that is human. We are content to feed and be forgotten. To go about our cursed existence in relative peace, killing only when our hunger becomes unbearable. But there are others of my kind...those who see themselves as lions among sheep. As kings—superior to man in every way. Why, then, should they be confined to darkness? Why should they fear man?

"It is a conflict that began long before there was an America. A conflict between two groups of vampires: those who seek to coexist with man, and those who would see all of mankind in chains—bred, raised, and corralled as cattle."

Judge us not equally, Abraham...

"These fifty years," said Henry, "we have done everything in our power to prevent this war. Each of the errands I have sent you on—each has been with the aim of destroying those who would see it hastened, and your efforts— those of Seward and others—have indeed slowed its progress. But we can no longer hope to prevent it. Indeed, not four weeks ago we saw the first battle fought here on the streets of New York."

Strange sightings...impossible feats...

"Our enemies are shrewd," said Henry. "They have

made their cause the cause of the South. Allied themselves with living men who defend slavery as fervently as they. But these men have been deceived into quickening their own doom, for Negroes are only the first of the living to be enslaved. If we lose, Abraham, then it is only a matter of time before every living man, woman, and child in America is a slave."

Abe felt as if he might be sick.

"*That*, old friend, is why we must not lose. *That* is why we have allied ourselves. We are vampires who believe in the rights of man," said Henry. "We are the Union . . . and we have plans for you, old friend."

Part III

PRESIDENT

Ten

A House Divided

"A house divided against itself cannot stand." I believe this government cannot endure, permanently half slave and half free. I do not expect the Union to be *dissolved*—I do not expect the house to *fall*—but I *do* expect it will cease to be divided. It will become *all* one thing or *all* the other.

—*Abraham Lincoln, accepting the Republican Party's nomination for senator June 16th, 1858*

I

In the predawn hours of February 23rd, 1861, a tall, cloaked figure was rushed onto the platform of the Baltimore & Ohio Railroad Depot before his train had even come to a stop, ten hours before anyone expected him to arrive. His feet seldom touched the ground as a mass of armed men hurried him into a waiting coach, which sped off as soon as its reinforced door had clicked shut. Inside, two bodyguards joined him behind the black curtains, their revolvers at the ready as if they expected the night to be shattered by gunfire at any moment. Outside, a third man sat next to the driver, his black eyes peering into the dark streets of Washington, D.C., looking for any sign of danger ahead. There were more of his kind waiting at the hotel, making sure no one entered without their knowledge and blessing; making sure their precious cargo was delivered safely to his bed. There was even a man stationed on the roof of the building across the way, looking for anyone who might try to crawl down the facade and enter through a window.

Henry Sturges had insisted on this unprecedented level of security—and his insistence had proven wise....

For President Elect Abraham Lincoln had just survived his first assassination attempt.

————

In late 1857, not long after his return from that fateful meeting in New York, Abe announced that he would run against Stephen Douglas for the Senate. Unbeknownst to his supporters, this announcement had been preceded by the arrival of a letter:

> Abraham,
>   As you guessed in your letter of September 13th, we must ask you to oppose Mr. Douglas. The Senator, as you no doubt suspect, is one of the many living men who have fallen prey to our enemy's influence. Do not concern yourself with the outcome of this election—rather, use your particular passion and oratory skill to combat

slavery at every turn. We will see to it that the
results are favorable to our cause. Trust in yourself,
Abraham. Never forget that this is your purpose.

Ever,

—H

P.S. Matthew 12:25*

Abe accepted the Republican Party's nomination for
Senate on June 16th, 1858, with what would be known
as his "House Divided" speech. In it, he accused Senator Douglas of being part of the "machinery" designed
to spread slavery to all of America. Without any mention
of vampires, Abe alluded to the "strange, discordant, and
even hostile elements" that had come together to fight a
"proud and pampered enemy" to the south.

Between August 21st and October 15th, he and Douglas held a series of seven debates throughout Illinois, some
attended by as many as 10,000 onlookers. They became
an instant sensation, thrusting both men onto the national
stage as transcripts of their battle appeared in newspapers
throughout the country. For his part, Douglas tried to
paint Abe as a radical abolitionist. He excelled at whip-
ping the crowd into a frenzy with images of freed slaves
flocking to Illinois; of black settlements springing up in
white backyards; of black men marrying white women.

If you desire [blacks] to vote on an equality with
yourselves, and to make them eligible to office, to

---

*Every kingdom divided against itself will be ruined, and every
city or household divided against itself will not stand.

FIG.29 - A MAN AND WOMAN (LIKELY VAMPIRES) POSE OUTSIDE A SLAVE AUCTION COMPANY IN ATLANTA, GEORGIA SHORTLY BEFORE THE CIVIL WAR.

serve on juries, and to adjudge your rights, then support Mr. Lincoln and the Black Republican party, who are in favor of the citizenship of the Negro!

Abe struck back at Douglas's doom and gloom with a simple moral truth—one that he owed (whether he would admit it or not) to his father's Baptist upbringing.

I agree with Judge Douglas—[the black man] is not my equal in many respects—certainly not in color, perhaps not in moral or intellectual endowment. But in the right to eat the bread, without the leave of anybody else, which his own hand

earns, he is my equal and the equal of Judge
Douglas, and the equal of every living man.

Still, Abe was frustrated by his inability to get at the
real issue—the fact that Douglas was the servant of creatures who would see *all* of mankind in chains.* Following
a debate in Charleston, Illinois, Abe vented this frustration in his journal.

> More signs in the crowd today. "Negro Equal-
> ity Is Immoral!" "America for Whites!" I look out
> at these crowds…at these fools. These fools who
> haven't the <u>slightest</u> idea how to live the morals
> they espouse. These fools who proclaim them-
> selves men of God, yet show not the <u>slightest</u>
> reverence to His word. Christians preaching
> slavery! Slaveholders preaching morality! Is it
> any different from a drunkard preaching temper-
> ance? A whore preaching modesty? I look at these
> fools campaigning for their own doom, and I am
> tempted to tell them the <u>whole truth</u> of what they
> face. Imagine their reaction! Imagine their panic!
> Oh, if I could but say the word once! "Vampire!"
> Oh, if only I could point at that portly runt** and
> shame him before all of creation! Expose him
> for the traitor that he is! The traitor to his own
> kind! If only I could see men like Douglas and

---

*There is no evidence that Douglas knew about these plans,
only that he was in league with several of its vampire architects.
**Abe is referring to Douglas here.

Buchanan in chains—victims of the very institution they champion!

His frustration (or his desire to throw Douglas off guard), led Abe to insert several thinly veiled references to the vampire threat during the final debate on October 15th.

> That is the issue that will continue in this country when these poor tongues of Judge Douglas and myself shall be silent. It is the eternal struggle between these two principles—right and wrong—throughout the world. They are the two principles that have stood face-to-face from the beginning of time; and will ever continue to struggle. *The one is the common right of humanity and the other the divine right of kings.*

Abe had electrified antislavery forces across Illinois and the North. Unfortunately senators were still elected by their state legislatures in 1858. The Democratic majority (or more accurately, its vampire backers) in Springfield sent Stephen Douglas back to Washington for another six years. "Another six years," as Abe wrote in his journal, "of doing the bidding of Southern vampires." For the first time in years, he found himself struggling with a bout of depression.

> I have failed the oppressed…the helpless faces crying out for justice. I have failed to meet the expectations of freedom-loving people everywhere. Is this the "purpose" which Henry so often speaks of? To fail?

His melancholy wouldn't last long. Three days after his defeat, Abe received a letter from Henry consisting of three short sentences.

> We are pleased to hear of your loss. Our plans continue unabated. Await further instructions.

II

The theater had become one of Abe's favorite escapes over the years. Perhaps it was his love of storytelling that drew him in; the theatrical flourishes he added to his carefully scripted performances that allowed him to relate. Perhaps the nervous thrill he felt when speaking before thousands gave him an appreciation for the performers. Abe enjoyed musicals and operas, but he was particularly fond of plays (whether they were comedies or tragedies didn't seem to matter). More than anything, he enjoyed seeing his beloved Shakespeare brought to life.

> And so it was with particular delight that Mary and I took in a performance of *Julius Caesar* on a blustery February evening—the recent troubles of the election behind us at last. Our dear friend Mayor [William] Jayne had been kind enough to lend us his box and its four seats.

The Lincolns were joined that evening by Abe's law partner Ward Hill Lamon and his thirty-four-year-old wife, Angelina. The production was, in Abe's words, "a splendid spectacle of ancient dress and painted scenery"—with the exception of a misspoken line in the first act.

> I nearly broke out laughing when the wretched soothsayer warned Caesar: "Beware the Ides of April."* I thought it a miracle (and a relief) that no one in the audience had snickered or yelled out a correction. How could such an error be made by an actor? Had my ears deceived me?

In Act III, Scene 2, Marc Antony stood over Caesar's slain, betrayed body and began the play's most iconic speech:

> Friends, Romans, countrymen, lend me your ears;
> I come to bury Caesar, not to praise him;
> The evil that men do lives after them,
> The good is oft interred with their bones…

Abe's eyes welled up at the young actor's impassioned delivery.

> I had read those words countless times; marveled at the genius of their construction. Only now, though, in the hands of this gifted young man did they ring true. Only now did I comprehend the whole of their meaning. "You all did love him once, not without cause," he said. "What cause withholds you then, to mourn for

---

*The line is "Beware the Ides of March" (March 15th). *Julius Caesar*, Act I, Scene 2.

him now?" Upon this, however, his speech came to a stop. He leapt from the stage and into the audience.

What strange interpretation was this? We watched him, bemused yet fascinated, as he bounded toward our side of the theater and disappeared through the door which led to our box. Apprehension suddenly filled the whole of my body, for I was sure that he meant to make a spectacle of my being in attendance. I had reason to worry, for this had happened several times in the past. Such exhibitions were one of the perils of being a public figure, and [they] always produced in me no small measure of embarrassment.

Just as Abe feared, the young actor entered the box with a flourish, drawing light laughter and applause from the audience. Every eye in the theater was trained on him as he stood behind the Lincolns and their guests. Abe smiled nervously, sure of what was coming next. But (to his surprise and relief) the actor simply continued his speech:

"Oh judgment!" he cried. "Thou art fled to brutish beasts and men have lost their reason!" Upon this, he produced a revolver from his costume, leveled it at the back of [Angelina's] head, and fired. The noise quite frightened me, and I laughed, momentarily certain that this was all part of the play. But when I saw her dress covered with pieces of brain; when I saw her slump forward in her chair—the blood running not only

from her wounds, but from her ears and nostrils
as water from a well—I knew.

Mary's screams set off a panic below, the audience trampling each other to reach the rear of
the hall. I drew the knife from my coat (I had
taken to carrying one since my meeting with the
Union) and rose to meet the bastard as Lamon
attended to his wife, lifting her head and calling
to her in vain as her blood poured over his hands.
I reached the actor just as he leveled his pistol at
Mary. I brought my blade down on him, sinking
the whole of it into the muscle where his neck and
shoulder met, causing him to drop the gun before
he fired. I pulled my blade out and made to bury
it again. Before I could, the world turned on its
side.

The young actor kicked Abe's legs out from under him,
sending him to the floor and sending the knife flying from
his hands. Abe looked down the length of his body—
toward the strange, pulsing pain coming from his left leg.
It had been twisted at the knee so that it bent neither forward nor backward, but grotesquely to the side.

At once I felt terribly sick. Seeing me in this
state, Lamon left his wife and joined the fight. He
turned to meet the devil with his own revolver,
but before he could level it, the actor drove a fist
into his mouth with such force as to push his
teeth inward and loose his jaw from its hinge.

A goddamned vampire…

Mary could bear the scene no longer and
fainted dead away, falling to the ground near her
chair. Lamon stumbled backward and steadied
himself against the railing—clutching at his jaw,
instinctively trying to force it back into place. The
vampire retrieved his weapon, leveled it at Lamon's
head, and fired, sending pieces of skull flying over
the railing and onto the empty seats below. He was
gone. The vampire next turned the gun on Mary,
and despite my screams of protest, shot her through
the chest as she slept. She would never wake.

He came for me next, standing over me as I lay
helpless. He aimed the barrel of his revolver at my
head. Our eyes met.

They were <u>Henry's</u> eyes.

"Sic semper tyrann—"
The last word was cut off by the sound of the shot.
Abe awoke with a start.

He sat straight up in his bed and shielded his face with
his hands, just as he had all those years ago, on the night
he saw his father dealing with the devil. The night Jack
Barts had condemned his mother to death.

Mary slept peacefully by his side. His boys
were safely in their beds. A thorough check of
the house turned up no evidence of trespassers—
living or otherwise. Still, Abe would sleep no more
that February night. There'd been something so
familiar about the dream. So *real*. He could see
every detail of the theater in his mind; every detail
of the costumes and scenery. He could feel the

nauseating pain of his leg, and hear Angelina's
blood running onto the floor. But try as he might,
Abe couldn't remember those three damned words
that his murderer uttered just before he woke.*

———————

Shortly after Abe's dream, William Seward, still the
heavy favorite to be the Republican presidential nominee
in 1860, made a strange tactical decision:

> Seward has abruptly left for a tour of Europe,
> and shall be gone these next six months at least.
> What can it mean on the eve of so crucial an elec-
> tion? How can such an absence be to his advan-
> tage? There are many who have criticized [the trip]
> as proof of his arrogance; his aloofness. I, however,
> am reluctant to levy such condemnation—for I
> suspect that he has been sent at the Union's behest.

Abe's suspicion was confirmed by Henry's next letter.

> Abraham,
>   Our friend S has been sent on an errand—one
> which we hope will shore up support for our cause
> in the coming months and years. We now ask that
> you turn your whole heart toward that greatest of
> political contests.
> —H

———————————————————————

*Angelina Lamon actually did die two months after Abe's
dream. Her cause of death remains unknown. It's doubtful that
vampires were involved.

In Seward's absence, Abe's political allies worked to shore up support for a presidential run, while Abe worked on raising his national awareness. On the evening of February 27th, 1860, at New York's Cooper Institute, he delivered what some historians consider to be the greatest political speech of all time to an audience of more than a thousand.

"Neither let us be slandered from our duty by false accusations against us," Abe shouted, "nor frightened from it by menaces of destruction to the Government nor of dungeons to ourselves. Let us have faith that right makes might, and in that faith, let us, to the end, dare to do our duty as we understand it."

The full text ran in every major New York newspaper the next day, and within a couple of weeks, pamphlets containing "Lincoln's Cooper Speech" were available throughout the North. Abe was emerging as the intellectual leader of the Republican Party, and its most gifted speaker.

The Democratic Party, meanwhile, had been split in two.

Northern Democrats nominated Abe's old rival Stephen Douglas for president, while Southerners picked the incumbent vice president, John C. Breckenridge. The fracture was no accident. Rather, it was the result of a decades-long effort by the Union. Since the early nineteenth century, Henry and his allies had worked to undermine their enemies at every turn: ferrying slaves to the North on the Underground Railroad, dispatching spies across the South, and more recently, discouraging secessionist talk in state legislatures. But their greatest achievement came on May 18th, 1860, on the third ballot of the Republican National Convention in Chicago.

Abe was in Springfield when he learned that he, not Seward, had been nominated for president.

> I can scarcely comprehend that such an honor has been bestowed upon me, and yet (and there is no hope of putting this modestly, so I shall not attempt to) it comes as no surprise. There is a war coming. It shall not be a war of man—but it is man who shall spill his blood fighting it—for it concerns his very right to be free. And I, of all men, must win it.

III

In 1860, presidential candidates weren't expected to campaign on their own behalf. The speechmaking and handshaking were traditionally left to political allies and subordinates, while the candidates themselves remained behind the scenes, quietly writing letters and greeting well-wishers. Abe saw no reason to break with tradition. While his supporters (including Seward who, despite losing the nomination, threw his full weight behind Abe) tirelessly traveled the country on his behalf, candidate Lincoln remained with his family in Springfield. From an entry dated April 16th:

> I walk to and from my office each morning, greeting friends as I pass; thanking strangers for their good wishes. When my business is concluded, I gambol about with my two youngest at home before seeing them off to bed, and when the

Fig. 13-2. – Abe poses in front of his family's abandoned cabin at Little Pigeon Creek in 1860 -- leaning on his trusty old axe. The image was meant to bolster his reputation as a candidate with humble roots, and was conceived by Henry Sturges himself.

> weather is suitable, I join Mary for a [walk]. Life is much as it ever was, with three exceptions— those being the three vampires who have come to keep watch over us.

Abe's swift-footed assailants had been reassigned by Henry and the Union. They were now his personal body-guards, sworn to protect him at all costs.

> I suspect they are somewhat embittered for being thus assigned (though it is impossible to know, for they rarely speak). I have several times referred to them as my "unholy trinity" in jest, but this has yet to produce in them a single smile.

> They are a deadly serious lot. Which, I suppose,
> makes them well suited to the task of keeping me
> alive.

Mary and the children were told that the men were "campaign volunteers" who'd come to ward off "over-eager supporters." It was a plausible explanation. Abe had become quite famous, and the Lincolns' home was beset by well-wishers and favor seekers at all hours. But vampire bodyguards were only one of the secrets "Honest Old Abe" kept from his wife and adoring public that summer.

He'd also scraped the rust off his ax.

And for the first time, his target was a living man.

> Abraham,
>   I must ask one more errand of you. He is one
> of your kind—but is looked after by two of mine
> at all times. Take every caution.

Abe nearly gasped when he saw the name below...

> Jefferson Davis.

There was hardly a more accomplished Southern politician in America. Davis had graduated from West Point, fought valiantly in the Mexican-American War, served as governor of Mississippi, served in Franklin Pierce's cabinet, and been twice elected to the Senate. He was an outspoken proslavery advocate, and, as a former Secretary of War, the man best suited to lead the South against the better-armed, more populous North.

This time, Abe refused to go.

Henry,

I am an old man with three sons and a wife who has wept over too many graves already. I will cause her no further grief by getting myself killed. Surely there are a hundred, or a <u>thousand</u> among your kind better suited to the task. Why must you prevail upon me when I am years removed from my best?

Send someone else.

Yours,

—Abraham

Henry's reply came by express a mere four days after Abe sent his refusal off to New York.

Abraham,

It is a difficult thing to know the future. We see it reflected as in ripples of water—distorted and ever moving. There are moments, however, when the ripples subside and the reflection becomes clear. The Union saw one of those moments in your future that night in New York: you are destined to defeat Jefferson Davis, Abraham. You alone. Further, I do not believe that it is your destiny to die on this errand. I feel this with my whole self. I would not send you otherwise. It must be you, Abraham. I beg you reconsider.

Ever,

—H

Abe was fifty-two years old. And while he remained remarkably agile for his age, he was a far cry from the young hunter who could split a log from fifty yards. He needed backup.

> I have sent word to Speed to meet me in
> Springfield at once, and—after a great deal of
> consideration—I have brought Lamon to the
> truth, as well. He thought me either "round
> the bend or a damned, lying fool" when first
> I revealed the story of vampires and their evil
> designs on man, and very nearly lost his tem-
> per—until I prevailed upon one of the trin-
> ity to confirm my story—which he did in
> dramatic fashion. There are few men who can
> be trusted in this war, and though [Lamon]
> and I disagree on a great many things (slav-
> ery being not the least of them), he has proven
> himself a loyal friend. With Jack gone, enlisting
> a man of his size seems prudent—particularly
> when Speed is so slight, and I am getting on in
> years.
> My God…I feel rather like [King] Henry at
> Harfleur.*

In July, the three hunters traveled by train to Bolivar County, Mississippi, where, Abe had been told, Jefferson Davis was recovering after undergoing eye surgery. Concealed in their luggage was a traveling armory of revolv-

---

*A reference to Shakespeare's *Henry V*. In Act III, Scene 1, King Henry delivers a rousing speech to his troops, beginning with the famous "Once more unto the breach, dear friends, once more!"

ers, knives, crossbows, and Abe's ax—newly sharpened, glistening once again. Candidate Lincoln had spent days secretly whittling new stakes for his quiver and fashioning a new chest plate to wear beneath his coat. He'd retreated to the woods with his ax and practiced throwing it into tree trunks ten, then twenty yards distant. He'd even dusted off his old martyr recipe and prepared a new batch.

> I insisted that the trinity remain in Springfield to look after my family. It was a simple errand, I told them. Our target was merely a living man, after all—one rendered infirm and half-blind by surgery. Speed, Lamon, and I were more than capable of dispensing with Davis and his vampire minders.

The hunters tied up their horses on the edge of Davis's property just after one o'clock in the morning on Monday, July 30th. They kept their distance from the main house, lying in the surrounding woods for a watchful half hour, whispering occasionally, waiting in the faint light of a cloud-covered moon.

Abe had received a second letter from Henry before they'd departed Springfield, a letter bearing new intelligence. The Union's spies had learned that Davis was confined to a bedroom on the west side of the second floor. Intent on giving him peace while he healed, his wife, Varina, had taken to sleeping in an adjacent room with their two infant sons and five-year-old daughter. At night, Davis's two minders took turns patrolling the grounds while the other remained in the house.

I thought it strange, therefore, that we saw no sign of such patrols, or lights burning in any of the windows. Henry's instructions, however, were precise, and we had traveled a long way. There could be no thoughts of turning back. Satisfied that we had waited long enough, we readied our weapons and crept into the clearing around the two-story house. It was white (or yellow, I could not tell in the dark), with a raised front porch and first story, as these parts were often deluged when the Mississippi swelled beyond its banks. I half expected to see a vampire waiting at the front door, long since alerted to our presence by the distant whinnying of our horses, the scent of the martyrs in my coat. But there was nothing. Only stillness. Doubts flooded my mind as we climbed the steps to the porch. Did I still possess the strength to best a vampire? Had I prepared Lamon to face an opponent of such speed and strength? Was Speed still equal to the task at hand? Indeed, the ax in my hands felt heavier than it had since I was a child.

Abe slowly nudged the front door as Lamon took aim, ready to shoot the vampire that was almost certainly going to leap out of the shadows the moment it was opened. None did.

We entered—I with my ax held high; Speed looking down the barrel of his .44 caliber [rifle]; Lamon with a revolver in each hand. We searched the dark, sparsely furnished first floor, our every

step announced by creaking floorboards as we
went. If indeed there was a vampire guarding
Davis above, he knew we were here now. Finding
no sign of the dead (or living) below, we returned
to the front of the house and its narrow staircase.

Abe led the way up. There were vampires here—he
could *feel* it.

I could see the next several moments unfold
in my mind as I climbed the stairs. Upon reaching the top, one of the vampires would spring
from hiding and strike from my right side. I
would turn my ax in his direction and lodge it
in his chest as we met, but in doing so, I would
be knocked backward—and the two of us would
be sent tumbling down the stairs. As we wrestled,
the second vampire would strike Speed and
Lamon above. Lamon would panic (this being
his first hunt) and empty his revolvers wildly,
but his bullets would miss the mark. It would
therefore fall to Speed and his rifle to silence
the creature, which he would do by shooting it
cleanly through the heart and head. The noise
would rouse Mrs. Davis and the children from
sleep, and they would scurry into the hall at precisely the moment I freed my ax from the first
vampire's chest and took his head at the base of
the staircase. Their screams would bring the frail,
half-blind Jefferson Davis stumbling out of his
own bedroom, upon which Speed and Lamon
would shoot him to death. With our sincere

apologies to his family, we would then run off
into the night.

But on reaching the top of the stairs, Abe found nothing. Every door was open. Every room empty.

> Could we be in the wrong place? Could Davis
> have suddenly and inexplicably risen from his bed
> and departed for Washington? No—no, Henry's
> instructions had been meticulous. This was the
> house. This was the intended date and time of our
> strike. It was all wrong.

There are vampires here... I can feel *it.*

> The truth now formed in my mind. Oh, that
> I had ignored my instincts! That I had come at
> all! Damn Henry's rippling water! How could I
> have been so reckless? How could I have ventured
> my life with three sons at home? A wife who was
> already fragile from grief? No... I would not die
> tonight. I refused.

"Out," whispered Abe. "Out at once—and make ready
your weapons... we are betrayed."

> We bounded down the stairs toward the
> front door, but on reaching it found it locked
> from the outside. The clapping of wood against
> wood now surrounded us as storm shutters were
> slammed shut over every window, and a chorus of
> hammers pounded nails into the house, ensuring

they could not be opened. "Upstairs!" I cried.
But here, too, the shutters had been closed and
fastened.

"They've trapped us!" said Lamon.

"Yes," said Speed. "However, all things being equal,
I'd rather be in here with us than out there with *them*."

Abe said nothing. He knew it wouldn't be long before
they smelled the smoke; before they felt the heat of the
fire as it ate through the walls and floorboards. As if
answering this thought, Lamon exclaimed, "Look!" and
pointed to the flickering orange light coming through the
crack beneath the front door.

They had no choice.

Whatever horrors waited outside, they couldn't be
worse than certain death by burning. The flames were
now visible all around them through the slats in the storm
shutters.

I had a plan. Once through the door, we would
remain shoulder to shoulder, three across, and
charge straight ahead until we reached the tree
line. I would take the center, using my ax to cut
down whatever came at us from the front. Speed
and Lamon would be on my right and left, shooting whatever came at us from the sides. It was a
plan almost certain to fail (based on how quickly
the shutters had closed around us, there were at
least a dozen men, vampires, or some combination
of the two outside), but it was the only one we
had. I lifted my ax and steadied myself. "Gentlemen," I said.

The front door flew open with a single blow of Abe's ax, sending smoke and hot ash flying away from the porch.

> The heat was immediate. It drove us back at
> first, blistering our skin and very nearly setting
> our clothes alight. When my eyes adjusted to the
> flames on the front porch (by now fully engulfed),
> I saw that the fallen door had provided a narrow
> path across. I held my breath and led the way,
> hurrying over the door, down the front steps
> and onto the grass below. No sooner had my feet
> touched the ground than I realized the hopeless-
> ness of our effort. For in the light of the burn-
> ing house behind us, I discerned no fewer than
> twenty figures ahead—some aiming rifles, others
> wearing dark glasses to shield their eyes from the
> flames. Living men and vampires—conspiring to
> cut off all hope of escape. One of the living, an
> older gentleman, stepped forward and stood but
> ten feet from me.

"Mr. Lincoln, I presume," he said.

"Mr. Davis," said Abe.

"I'd be much obliged," said Davis, "if your compan-ions would put those irons down. I'd hate for one of my men to startle and fill the three of you with holes."

Abe turned to Speed and Lamon and gave a nod. Both dropped their guns.

"The big one is concealing another pistol," said one of the vampires behind Davis. "He's thinking about reach-ing for it right now."

"Well, if he does," said Davis, "then I suggest you kill him." Davis turned back to Abe. "Your ax as well, if you please."

"If it's all the same, Mr. Davis," said Abe, "I don't expect to live but a few moments longer, and I would very much like to die holding the ax my daddy gave me as a boy. Surely one of your men will shoot me if I raise it in anger."

Davis smiled. "I like you, Mr. Lincoln—I do. Kentucky born, same as me. Self-made. As fine an orator as ever lived—and dedicated, my Lord! Coming all the way down here just to kill a man! Leaving your family alone and unprotected in Springfield...no, sir, let no man speak ill of your convictions. I could sing your praises till morning, sir—but some of my associates are rather sensitive to sunlight, and...well, I'm afraid we just don't have that long.

"Tell me," said Davis, "with your many fine qualities and famous mind, how is it that you've arrived on the wrong side of this fight?"

"I?" asked Abe. "I must have misheard you, sir—for of the two of us, only one is conspiring against his fellow man."

"Mr. Lincoln, vampires are superior to man, just as man is superior to the Negro. It's the natural order of things, you see. Surely we agree on this much, at least?"

"I agree that *some* vampires are superior to *some* men."

"Am I wrong, therefore, to recognize the inevitability of their rule? Am I wrong to side with the greater power in the coming war? Sir, it brings me no pleasure to think of white men in cages. But if it must come to pass—if vampires are to be the kings of men—then let us work with them while time remains. Let us regulate the thing—limit it to the Negro, and to the undesirables of our own race."

"Ah," said Abe. "And when the blood of Negroes is no longer sufficient; when the 'undesirables' of our race have been exhausted—tell me, Mr. Davis...who then shall your 'kings' feed upon?"

Davis said nothing.

"America," Abe continued, "was forged in the blood of those who opposed tyranny. You and your allies...would you not see it delivered into the hands of tyrants?"

"America is thataway, Mr. Lincoln," laughed Davis, pointing north. "You're in Mississippi now." He stepped forward, to the very edge of where Abe's ax could reach if he chose to swing it. "And let us speak plainly, sir. We're *both* the servants of vampires. But when these hostilities are at an end, I will be left to enjoy the peace of my remaining years in comfort and wealth, and you will be dead. And there it is."

Davis paused a moment, offered a slight
bow, and retreated. Three of the living men now
stepped to the front of the group—each with a
rifle aimed at us. Each waiting for Davis to give
the order.

"Damn it, Abe," said Lamon. "Are we just gonna stand here and do nothing?"

"I'm wearing a watch," Speed told the executioners, his voice cracking. "It belonged to my grandfather, I—I ask only that someone see it back to my wife in Louisville."

These are the last seconds of my life.

"Well, if I'm dying," said Lamon, "I'm dying with a gun in my hand." He reached for his coat.

"Boys," said Abe to his friends, "I'm sorry for dragging you into th—"

The crack of rifles filled the night before he could finish.

> In that instant I saw the faces of all those loved ones departed from this earth: my dear, sweet little boy; my sturdy Armstrong and beloved Ann. I saw my sister, and my angel mother. But when this instant passed, and my eyes remembered themselves, my executioners remained in the light of the burning house, shock on their faces. Speed and Lamon remained standing on either side of me.
>
> We still lived. Our executioners, however, were not as fortunate. All three fell in unison, bullets having torn though their skulls.
>
> It was a <u>miracle</u>.

That miracle was Henry Sturges.

> He charged out of the dark with eleven Union vampires on his heels. Some held rifles, others revolvers, firing as they came. The Southern vampires nearest Davis hurried him off, while the others prepared to meet their Northern counterparts. One of them, however, remembered that the job of my execution remained unfinished. He leapt at me from twenty yards distant, fangs and claws extended, eyes black behind his dark

glasses. I let my ax fly, and the blade found its target—but my strength not being what it once was,
it failed to sink more than an inch or two into
his middle. He fell back briefly and looked at the
dark ribbons pouring from the gash in his belly.
They were of no concern. He picked my ax off the
ground and came at me again. I thrust a hand into
my coat, looking for a knife that had not been
there in twenty years…helpless. With the vampire not four feet from me, Lamon aimed over my
shoulder and fired, forever diminishing the hearing in my left ear, but silencing the creature with
a bullet through the face.

As the smoke from Lamon's revolver hung in the air
around his head, Abe became aware of a sharp pain coming from his chin.

I pressed my hand to it. [The vampire] had
come close enough to open a gash with the tip
of my ax. Blood dripped from the wound and
down the front of my shirt as vampires clashed
before us in the light of the flames—jumping
impossible distances, crashing into each other
with enough force to shake the ground beneath
our feet.
Here, for the first time, I saw Henry Sturges in battle. I watched him run headlong into
a Southern vampire and drive the devil into a
tree—the result being that its trunk split in two.
Yet Henry's opponent was hardly affected, for
he pushed back and began to swing wildly with

his hands, as if holding a sword in each. Henry
defended each of these strikes with his own
clawed hands, until, being the better swords-
man of the two, he saw an opportunity and ran
his opponent through the middle—forcing five
straightened fingers into the vampire's belly and
out his back, snapping his spine in the process.
Henry withdrew his hand, and his opponent fell
to the ground, unable to move. I watched him
twist the vampire's head backward and rip it from
his shoulders.

The living men unfortunate enough to find
themselves in the middle of this melee were
torn apart, their limbs taken by errant claws,
their bones crushed by the force of the vampires colliding around them. Realizing that
the numbers were not in their favor, the remaining Southern vampires made a hasty retreat.
Several Union vampires gave chase—the others,
including Henry, hurried to meet us where we
stood.

"Abraham," he said. "I'm pleased to see you alive, old
friend."

"And I to see you dead."

Henry smiled. He tore a sleeve from his shirt and held
it to Abe's chin to slow the bleeding, while his compan-
ions attended to Lamon and Speed (who were shaken up
but otherwise unharmed).

The Union had been given false information by
a traitorous spy—information meant to lure me

to my death. Henry and his allies did not learn
of this treachery until after we left Springfield.
With no means of getting word to us (for we traveled under false names), they rode for two days
and nights to head us off, while sending word to
the trinity to have Mary and the boys placed in
hiding.

"And you're sure they're safe?" asked Abe.

"I'm sure they're in hiding, and protected by three of
my most cunning, most vicious allies," said Henry.

It would suffice. Abe knew that the trinity took their
work seriously.

"Henry," he said after a long pause, "I was certain that
I was going to—"

"I told you, Abraham…it wasn't your time."

It would be the last hunt of Abe's life.

———————

On November 6th, 1860, Abe sat in a cramped telegraph
office in Springfield.

The tide of well-wishers and appointment
seekers had risen to unbearable levels as the election approached. When the 6th came at last, I
declared that I wished to see no one until all
the votes were in. My only company was to be
the young [telegraph] operator. If the outcome
was the one I and my supporters expected, there
would be few peaceful days in the coming years.

He'd grown a beard for the first time in his life to conceal the scar on his chin.* It gave his face a fuller, healthier appearance. "More distinguished," as Mary said. "A face befitting the next president."

> Mary was, at first, quite opposed to my running—having not enjoyed her previous time in Washington, and being all too aware of the time such an endeavor would require of me. As my campaign met with increasing success, however, her position began to change. I suspect that she rather enjoyed the well-wishers who came to our door at all hours; the wealthy couples who invited us to their homes for dinner; and the lavish events thrown in my honor. I suspect that she began to see the many social possibilities of being married to the president of the United States.

As the returns began to trickle in over the telegraph wires that Tuesday evening, it seemed more and more certain that Abe would be just that.

> I admit it came as little surprise, for I believed that the Union would see to my victory—whether earned or not.** I could therefore feel none of the

---

*It's widely believed that Abe got the idea to grow a beard from eleven-year-old Grace Bedell. While it's true that Bedell wrote with the suggestion (insisting that "ladies like whiskers" and would therefore urge their husbands to vote for him), he'd already begun to grow it by the time her famous letter arrived.
**There was no cause for the Union to intervene—Abe comfortably won the election on his own merits.

honor that had accompanied my being elected
captain by my fellow soldiers. The weight of the
thing was immense. The challenges and miseries
ahead unknowable and numerous.

Henry's telegram had been one of the first to arrive that
morning—long before a single vote had been counted.

CONGRATULATIONS MR PRESIDENT
EVER H

IV

President Elect Abraham Lincoln's journey to the White
House began in Springfield on February 11th, 1861. A private train was ordered to shepherd Abe, his family, his
close associates, and his private security detail to Washington, D.C.

It hadn't been an easy transition.

Just over a month after the election, South Carolina's
legislature voted to secede from the Union. One by one,
more Southern states followed—seven in all by Inauguration Day: Louisiana, Mississippi, Alabama, Florida,
Georgia, South Carolina, and Texas. Abe could only
watch as President Buchanan did nothing to stem the
crisis.

[Buchanan] continues to rest on his rump as
the country comes apart. As the ships of our navy
and forts are daily surrendered to the South, and
the Union dissolves before our eyes. His weakness

astonishes. It seems clear that he has decided to
kick this crisis down the road. I, on the other
hand, am very much looking forward to kicking
him onto Pennsylvania Avenue.

Three days before Abe's train left Springfield, the
self-proclaimed "Leaders of the Southern People" met in
Montgomery, Alabama, to formally adopt a constitution
and announce the Confederate States of America.

They chose Jefferson Davis as their president.

———————

Abe's trinity patrolled the train day and night. Officially,
they were "detectives" from Springfield who'd volunteered to look after the new president. His security detail
also included a pair of humans—a detective named Allan
Pinkerton and his old friend Ward Hill Lamon. Lamon had
volunteered to be Abe's bodyguard out of nothing more
than friendly concern for his safety. He was one of the
few around the new president who knew the gravity of the
threats he faced. In the coming years, White House staff
would grow used to seeing Lamon patrol the White House
grounds after dark, or sleeping in front of the door to the
president's bedroom. He was big, tough, handy with a gun,
and fiercely loyal—and his help was desperately needed.

Abe's train was scheduled to stop in at least ten major
cities on the way to Washington. In each one, thousands
(if not tens of thousands) of locals came in hopes of seeing
the new president with their own eyes. Abe would often
make an impromptu speech from the rear car—sometimes
only inches from those who'd packed in to hear him speak.
He would then leave the stations by coach to meet with

local leaders, attend banquets, or watch parades in his honor. It was a security nightmare.

> It has been an overwhelming several days. The boys are in fine spirits, though—running about the train, watching the country roll by through its windows. Bob finds it "all so very exciting," while Willie and Tad seem not the least bit affected by the crowds, or by the presence of so many new faces. Mary, too, seems to be taking it all in stride, though her head has been especially bothersome this trip.*

For all the excitement, there was a conspicuous tension hanging over the train. Everyone on board felt it, though no one spoke of it openly.

> There are some who have sworn that I shall never live to see the White House. Such talk breeds grave concern (an appropriate kind given the subject) on the faces of my protectors. I, however, can honestly say that it costs me not one nickel of sleep—for I have known death my entire life, and have come to regard him as something of an old friend. Of course, Mary is roused to great anxiety by these rumors (but then, she is roused to great anxiety by a great many things).

---

*Mary suffered from debilitating headaches (possibly migraines) throughout her adult life. Many historians suggest they were related to her famous bouts of depression. Some even suggest that she was schizophrenic, though it is impossible to know.

So long as our boys hear nothing of it, I am
content.

The trip continued without incident for ten days,
through Indiana, Ohio, New York, New Jersey, and
Pennsylvania—and it began to seem that all the talk
of assassination was just that. But on February 22nd in
Philadelphia, Abe received an urgent visit from William
Seward's son, Frederick. He came bearing a sealed letter.

Dear Mr. President Elect,
Our mutual acquaintance wishes it known that
a plot has been discovered in Baltimore. Four men
will stab and shoot you to death when you change
trains at the Calvert Street Station. He thought it
best you should be aware of this, so that you may
take every precaution against it.
Yours,
—Wm. Seward

It was decided that Abe, accompanied by Pinkerton
and Lamon, and wearing a hat and cloak to conceal his
identity from the other passengers, would take a separate
train through Baltimore directly to Washington. Pinkerton and Lamon would be armed, Abe wouldn't.

This caused quite a squabble, I recall. Lamon
(who knew me to be proficient with such weapons) insisted I be given a revolver and a long
knife. Pinkerton refused. "I will not have it said
that the future president of the United States
entered the capital armed!" The two nearly came

to blows over the matter, until I offered a compromise: Lamon would carry two of each weapon, and would give them over only if we came under attack. It was agreed to, and we prepared to be off.

But their plans changed when Pinkerton realized that the trinity was gone.

[They] had simply vanished somewhere between Philadelphia and Harrisburg—giving no reason for their absence. As I refused to leave Mary and the boys without an armed escort, it was quickly decided that Pinkerton would stay behind and look after them while Lamon accompanied me on the other train. The telegraph lines between Pennsylvania and Maryland were then cut, so that any conspirators would be unable to relay word of our departure from Harrisburg.

Just after midnight on the 23rd, Abe's "secret" train passed through Baltimore on its way to Washington.

There were anxious moments as we passed through the heart of the city (more slowly, it seemed, than any train I had ever ridden on). Could these assassins have discovered our trick? Were they, at this very moment, preparing to bombard our train with cannon fire?

Abe needn't have worried. By the time his train rolled through the station, three of his would-be assassins were already dead—and the fourth was dying beneath his feet.

—————

The partial bodies of four men were found near Calvert Street Station the next morning. From the February 23rd edition of the *Baltimore Sun*:

> Two gentlemen have had [their] heads taken. Another has been viciously beaten, to the extent that police are as yet unable to determine his age or race. The fourth, it seems, was halved beneath the wheels of a passing locomotive. Incredibly, a witness claims that the gentleman survived for several minutes thereafter—his spine being severed in such a way that he was still able to move his head and arms. He was seen faintly crying out and attempting to drag his remaining body from the tracks before dying.

Though they never spoke a word about the incident, Abe never doubted that his three vampire protectors had been responsible for the carnage.

V

On March 4th, 1861, Abraham Lincoln—exceptional boy of Sinking Springs Farm, apple of his departed mother's eye, survivor of the trials of Job, and one of the nation's most accomplished vampire hunters—was sworn in as the sixteenth president of the United States.

> We are not enemies, but friends. We must not
> be enemies. Though passion may have strained it
> must not break our bonds of affection. The mystic
> chords of memory, stretching from every battle-
> field and patriot grave to every living heart and
> hearthstone all over this broad land, will yet swell
> the chorus of the Union, when again touched, as
> surely they will be, by the better angels of our
> nature.

Tens of thousands gathered in front of a covered wooden platform on the Capitol steps to hear him speak. Little did they know that they were witnessing the largest security operation in history. Troops were stationed around the city, ready to put down any violent protests or large-scale attacks. Police (both uniformed and not) stood guard beneath the podium where Abe spoke, keeping an eye out for anyone who might raise a revolver or long rifle. Closer to the president elect, Ward Hill Lamon hovered on the platform with two revolvers in his coat and a long knife on his belt. The vampires of the trinity were stationed at different points, but they were never far from Abe.

> Only later would I learn that the hearts of two
> armed men had been discreetly run through dur-
> ing my speech. Unlike the assassins in Baltimore,
> these had been vampires.

———

Five weeks into Abe's young presidency the country's strained "bonds of affection" finally broke.

Fort Sumter, a federal stronghold in Charleston Harbor, South Carolina, had been under siege by Confederates since January. The Southerners demanded that the Union troops (commanded by Major Robert Anderson) surrender the fort, as it was in South Carolina, and therefore not the property of the federal government. Abe had done everything in his power to prevent hostilities from breaking out, but Anderson's men were running desperately short of food, and the only way to resupply them was by sending warships into Confederate territory.

> I am now forced to choose between two evils. Either I must allow a few soldiers to starve, or provoke a war that will undoubtedly kill <u>scores</u> of soldiers. Struggle as I might, I can see no third option.

Abe sent the ships.

The first of them reached Charleston Harbor on April 11th. The next morning, before sunrise, Confederate Colonel James Chestnut Jr. gave the order to fire on the fort.

It was the first shot of the Civil War.

Eleven

——◆——

Casualties

Fellow-citizens, we cannot escape history. We of this
Congress and this administration, will be remembered in spite of ourselves. No personal significance,
or insignificance, can spare one or another of us. The
fiery trial through which we pass, will light us down,
in honor or dishonor, to the latest generation.

—*Abraham Lincoln, in a message to Congress December 1st, 1862*

I

On June 3rd, 1861, Stephen A. Douglas was found dead
in a stairwell of his Chicago home.

> I have just this hour heard the shocking news.
> Though the full facts have not yet come to light, I
> have <u>no</u> <u>doubt</u> that it is the work of vampires—and
> that <u>I</u> bear some of the responsibility for his murder.

Publicly, the cause of death was reported as typhoid
fever, even though none of Douglas's friends remembered

him feeling unwell the night before he was discovered. The body was taken by coach to Mercy Hospital, where it was examined by a young Chicago physician, Dr. Bradley Milliner. From the autopsy report:

- Four small, circular puncture wounds on deceased's body—two on left shoulder directly over axillary [artery]; two the neck directly over right common carotid [artery].
- Both sets surrounded by significant bruising; uniformly spaced one and one-half inches apart.
- Whole of deceased's body badly decayed and gray-blue in color; face is sunken; skin brittle, suggesting death occurred weeks or months before examination.
- Stomach contains brightly colored, whole pieces of undigested food, suggesting deceased ate shortly before death, and that death occurred less than twenty-four hours before examination.

Along with his observations, Dr. Milliner scribbled a single word in the report's margin:

"Incredible."

The report itself was deemed "inconclusive" and suppressed by Milliner's superiors, who thought that releasing such information would only add to the "climate of conjecture and suspicion" surrounding the senator's death.*

---

*The report was thought lost in the Great Chicago Fire of 1871, until it was discovered during a renovation of Mercy Hospital in 1967. On the day the news went public, Mercy received an anonymous donation of a million dollars. The day after that, the report was declared a hoax by hospital officials.

———

Lincoln and Douglas had been the most famous rivals in America. For two decades, they'd competed over everything from a woman's love to the highest office in the land. But for all their political antipathy, the two had grown to respect, even like, each other over the years. Douglas was, after all, one of Abe's "brilliant beacons" in Washington's "fog of fools." And while the so-called Little Giant spent years appealing to Southern passions, he was, in his heart, no son of the South. In fact, Douglas loathed the idea of disunion, going so far as to call secessionists "criminals," and declaring: "We must fight for our country and forget our differences. There can be but two parties: the party of patriots and the party of traitors. We belong to the first."

When the Union began to tear itself apart in the wake of his failed 1860 campaign, it was Stephen Douglas who first reached out to his old rival—the new president elect.

> He wishes to join me in the cause of opposing secession. To that end I have asked him to make a speaking tour of the Border States and the Northwest (those places where the flame of unity might yet be fanned by our efforts, or snuffed out by a lack of them). I can think of no better messenger, no ally more symbolic of the need for unity. I will admit that his offer took me quite by surprise. I suppose it possible that he has come to regret his association with the vampire South, and is looking for some means of redemption. Whatever his reasons, I welcome his help.

Douglas made pro-Union speeches in three states before returning to Washington. At Abe's inauguration, with the threat of assassination hanging in the air, he placed himself near the podium and declared, "If any man attacks Lincoln, he attacks me!" And on Sunday, April 14th, 1861, as Fort Sumter was being surrendered to the Confederates, Stephen Douglas was among the first to race to the White House.

> He came today with no appointment, only to find that I was meeting with the Cabinet, and would be thus engaged for quite some time. [Presidential secretary John] Nicolay asked him to call again, but Judge Douglas flatly refused. When I had grown weary of hearing his familiar baritone shouting profanities in the hall, I swung my office door open and exclaimed, "By God, let the man in or we shall have <u>two</u> wars to fight!"
>
> We met privately for an hour or more. I had never seen him in such a panicked state! "They will march headlong into Washington and kill me!" he cried. "Kill the lot of us! I demand to know what plans you have to combat this menace, sir!" I told him, in the calmest voice I could muster, the truth—that I was to call for 75,000 militia the next morning; that I was to suppress this rebellion with every power of my office and weapon in my arsenal. These reassurances, however, only seemed to deepen his panic. He urged me to call for <u>three times</u> that number. "Mr. President," he said, "you do not know the dishonest purposes of those men as I do. You do not, and

I say this with the deepest respect, sir, know the
<u>real</u> enemy you face."

"Oh, but I assure you, Mr. Douglas—I know
them too well."

Thanks to Henry, Abe had known about Douglas's
connection to Southern vampires since their Senate race
three years earlier. Douglas, however, never suspected
that the gangly, graying man before him had once been
the mightiest vampire hunter on the Mississippi.

I can scarcely describe his astonishment at
hearing the word "vampires" pass my lips. Now,
with the truth out at last, each of us told the
other his story: I of my mother's death; of my
years spent hunting vampires. Douglas of the
fateful day when—as a young, ambitious Democrat in the Illinois State Legislature—he was
approached by a pair of "sallow" men from the
South. "It was then that I first learned of [vam-
pires]," he said. "It was then that I first became
intoxicated by their money and influence."

Douglas repaid their support by railing against abolitionists in the Senate and by using his natural talent for
speechmaking to rally proslavery forces across the country. But he'd begun to question his vampire patrons in
recent years.

"Why do they reject compromise with the
North?" he asked. "Why do they seem intent on
war at any cost? And why, by God, do they care

so fervently for the institution [of slavery] at all? I could see no logic in it, and I could not, in good conscience, continue down the path to disunion."

It became clear that Douglas did not know the whole truth; clear that—while guilty of some small treachery—he could not be judged with the likes of the traitorous [Jefferson] Davis. Moved by his remorse, I determined to tell him all: the marriage of slavery and Southern vampires. Their plan to enslave all but the fortunate few of our kind; to keep us in cages and chains as we had kept the Negro. I told him of their plan to create a <u>new</u> America; a nation of vampires—free from oppression, free from darkness, and blessed with an abundance of living men to feast upon.

By the time I finished speaking, Douglas wept.

———

That night, Abe sat at the head of a long table in his office, with Secretary of State William Seward to his left. They were joined by the rest of the Cabinet, all of them anxious to hear why they'd been summoned from their supper tables and rushed back to the White House.

"Gentlemen," I said at last, "I wish to speak to you this evening about vampires."

Abe had met with his Cabinet on a near daily basis since the inauguration. They'd discussed every detail of the coming war: uniforms, supply lines, commanders, horses, provisions—everything but the truth of what they were really fighting for, and who they were really fighting against.

And yet I had asked these men to plan me a
war! Was it not akin to asking a group of blind
men to pilot a steamboat?

The encounter with Douglas had changed Abe's mind.
When they parted company that evening, he had ordered
Nicolay to reconvene the Cabinet at once.

I thought it crucial that these men—these
men who were to be my counsel through untold
miseries—knew <u>exactly</u> what they faced. There
would be no more revelations in this office. No
more half-truths or omissions. Now, just as I
had with Douglas, I would tell them the <u>whole</u>
truth—with Seward there to endorse every
word of it. My history. My hunting. My alli-
ance with a small band of vampires called the
Union, and the unthinkable consequences of the
coming war.
Some were shocked to hear vampires spoken
of at all. [Secretary of the Navy Gideon] Wells
and [Secretary of the Treasury Salmon] Chase,
it seemed, had managed to go the whole of their
lives thinking them nothing more than myth.
Wells sat in ashen silence. Chase, however, grew
indignant. "I will not stand for folly in the face of
war!" he declared. "I will not be summoned from
my home to be made a fool for the president's
amusement!" Seward rose to my defense, insisting
that every word was true, and admitting his own
complicity in keeping it from the rest of the Cabinet. Chase remained unconvinced.

He was not alone in his doubts. [Secretary of War Edwin] Stanton—who had long believed vampires real, but confined to the shadows—was the next to speak. "What sense can it make?" he asked. "Why would [Jefferson] Davis…why would <u>any</u> man conspire against himself? Why would any man hasten his own enslavement?"

"Davis has only his own survival in mind," I said. "He and his allies are pilot fish—cleaning the teeth of sharks to avoid being themselves bitten. Perhaps they have been promised power and riches in this new America, exemption from chains. But know this—whatever they have been promised is a lie."

Chase could bear it no longer. He rose from his seat and left the room. I waited for others to join him. Satisfied that none would, I continued.

"Even now," I said, "there is a part of me that finds it all impossible to believe. A part of me that expects to wake from a half-century's dream. Even after all these years, and all of the things I have witnessed. And why not? After all, to believe in vampires is to reject reason! To acknowledge a darkness that is not supposed to exist anymore. Not here, in this great age, where science has illuminated all but a few mysteries. No…no, that darkness belongs in the Old Testament; in the tragedies of Shakespeare. But not here.

"That, gentlemen…that is why they thrive. That belief—that we live <u>beyond</u> the reach of darkness—is one that vampires have worked tirelessly to instill through the centuries. I submit

to you that it is nothing less than the greatest lie
ever sold to mankind."

II

Three days after the fall of Fort Sumter, Virginia seceded
from the Union, and the Confederate capital was relo-
cated to its industrial heart, Richmond. Over the next
few weeks, Arkansas, Tennessee, and North Carolina followed. There were now eleven states in the Confederacy,
with a combined population of nine million people (four
million of which were slaves). Even so, most Northerners
were convinced that the war would be a short one, and
that the "sechers" (secessionists) would be stamped out
by summer's end.

They had reason to be confident. The North, after
all, had more than twice the population of the South. It
had railroads that could speed troops and provisions to
the battlefield in a fraction of the time; superior factories
to supply boots and ammunition; warships to blockade
ports and pound coastal cities. Pro-Union newspapers
urged the president to bring about a "swift end to this
unpleasantness." Cries of "Forward to Richmond!"
were heard across the North. Henry Sturges agreed. In a
telegram dated July 15th, he used a quote from Shakespeare to send Abe a coded message*: strike Richmond
now.

---

*For fear of spies, all of Henry's wartime messages to Abe
were coded in one way or another.

Abraham,
   "In God's name, cheerly on, courageous
friends, to reap the harvest of perpetual peace, by
this one bloody trial of sharp war."*
—H

Abe followed the advice. The day after receiving the letter, he ordered the largest fighting force ever assembled on North American soil—35,000 men—to march from Washington to Richmond under the command of Brigadier General Irvin McDowell. Most of McDowell's soldiers came from the 75,000 militiamen hurriedly called up in the wake of Fort Sumter. They were, for the most part, farmers and tradesmen. Baby-faced teenagers and frail old men. Some had never fired a shot in their lives.

McDowell complains that his men are inexperienced. "You are green," I told him, "but [the Confederates] are green also. You are all green alike! We must not wait for the enemy to come marching into Washington. We must meet him where he lives! To Richmond, by God!"

To get there, McDowell and his men would have to march twenty-five miles south into Virginia, where General Pierre Beauregard and 20,000 Confederates were waiting for them. In the sweltering heat of Monday, July 21st, 1861, the two armies met near the town of Manassas.

---

*Spoken by the character Richmond in *Richard III*, Act V, Scene 2.

It would be remembered as the First Battle of Bull Run—
so named for the little creek that would soon run red.

Two days after the battle, a Union private named
Andrew Merrow wrote home to his new bride in Massachusetts.* His letter paints a gruesome picture of the day's
events, and offers some of the earliest evidence that the
Confederate Army had vampires in its ranks.

> We had [the Confederates] whipped at the
> start. Blessed with greater numbers, we drove
> the devils south up Henry House Hill, and
> into a group of trees at its peak. What a sight
> to see them scatter like mice! To see our ranks
> spread half a mile wide! To hear the cracking of
> gunpowder from all directions! "Let us chase
> them all the way to Georgia!" cried Colonel
> Hunter, to the delight of the men.
>
> As we neared the top of the hill, the rebels
> covered their retreat by firing on us. The gun
> smoke grew so thick that one could scarcely see
> ten yards into the trees where they hid. From
> behind this curtain of smoke suddenly came a
> chorus of wild yells. The voices of twenty or
> thirty men, growing louder by the moment. "First
> ranks! Fix bayonets!" ordered the colonel. As
> they did, a small band of Confederates emerged
> from the smoke, running toward us as fast as any
> men have ever run. Even from a distance, I could

---

*Merrow's letter, housed in the Harvard University Archives,
has long been mistaken for a work of epistolary fiction.

see their strange, wild eyes. There was not a rifle,
or a pistol, or a sword among them.

Our first ranks began to fire, yet their rifles
seemed to have no effect. Melissa, I shall swear
until my grave that I saw bullets strike these
men in their chests. In their limbs and faces. Yet
they continued to charge as if they had not been
hit at all! The rebels smashed into our ranks
and tore men apart in front of my eyes. I do not
mean to suggest that they ran them through
with bayonets, or fired on them with revolvers.
I mean to say that these rebels—these thirty
unarmed men—tore one hundred men to pieces
with nothing more than their bare hands. I saw
arms pulled off. Heads twisted backward. I saw
blood pour from the throats and bellies of men
gutted by mere fingertips; a boy grasping at the
holes where his eyes had been a moment before.
A private three yards in front of me had his rifle
plucked away. I was close enough to feel his blood
on my face as its stock was used to smash his skull
in. Close enough to taste his death on my tongue.

Our lines broke. I am not ashamed to say
that I dropped my rifle and ran with the others,
Melissa. The rebels gave chase, overtaking and
savaging men on either side of me as we retreated.
Their screams following me down the hill.

Reports of similar "rebel charges" poured in from
McDowell's commanders. "Well," he is rumored to have
said (on learning that the Union was in full retreat), "we
brought the superior army, but it seems they brought the

superior men." McDowell had no idea that those "superior men" weren't men at all.

The fighting lasted a matter of hours. When the gun smoke gave way, more than a thousand men were dead, another three thousand severely or mortally wounded. From the diary of Union Major General Ambrose Burnside:

> I rode past a small pond at dusk and saw men washing their wounds in it. The water had turned quite red as a result—but this did not deter the desperate from drinking it when they crawled to its edge. Near this, I saw the body of a rebel boy who had been hit by a shell. Only his arms, shoulders and head remained—his eyes open and face expressionless. A group of buzzards was gathered around him, picking at his entrails. Pecking at the bits of his brain that had spilled onto the ground. It is a sight that shall never leave me.
>
> And yet I have seen a hundred such horrors this day. A man could walk a mile in any direction without his feet touching the ground—such are the number of bodies. Even as I write this, I hear the screams of the wounded on the air. Begging for help. For water. In some cases, begging for death.
>
> I have no more fear of hell, for I have this day seen it with my own eyes.

———

The North was in a state of shock and mourning after Bull Run.

Had I only listened to Douglas! To McDowell!
Had I only called for more men and given them
more time to train—this war might be over, and
the suffering and death of thousands avoided. It
is clear, now, that the South means to compensate
for her smaller numbers by sending vampires to
the fields of battle. So be it. I have spent a lifetime
hunting vampires with my ax. I shall now spend a
little while longer hunting them with my army. If
this is to be a long and costly struggle, then let us
redouble our resolve to win it.

Once its shock subsided, the North took a cue from its
president and dug its heels in. Men turned out in droves to
enlist, and states pledged new regiments and provisions.
On July 22nd, 1861, the day he signed a bill calling for
500,000 new troops, Abraham Lincoln scribbled a pre-
scient thought in his journal.

Let us pray now for the future dead. Though
we do not yet know their names, we know that
there shall be far too many of them.

III

It had been a bitter, frustrating winter for the president
and his Cabinet. With rivers frozen and roads covered
with mud and snow, there was little either army could do
but tend its fires and wait for the thaw. On February 9th,
1862, his 53rd birthday, Abe was in his office when the
first sign of spring came at last.

I have just received word of [General Ulysses S.] Grant's success at Fort Henry in Tennessee. It is a crucial victory for us in the west, and a welcome change from these long months of waiting. Together with the sound of my rascals playing outside, it is a fine Sunday indeed!

"Rascals" Tad and Willie Lincoln—seven and ten years old, respectively—were the unquestioned life (some would say scourge) of the White House. The boys spent countless hours running rampant over the mansion and its grounds during the first year of their father's presidency, a fact that aggravated some of Abe's associates to no end, but offered the president a much-needed distraction from the stresses of running a country and a war.

The sound of my boys at play is (too often, I confess) the only joy between sunrise and sleep. I am therefore too happy to wrestle and chase them about whenever the opportunity presents itself— and regardless of who looks on. Not one week ago, [Iowa Senator James W.] Grimes walked into my office for an appointment, only to find me pinned to the floor by four boys: Tad and Willie holding my legs, Bud and Holly* my arms. "Senator," I

---

*Horatio "Bud" Nelson Taft Jr. and Halsey "Holly" Cook Taft were Willie and Tad's best friends. They were often accompanied by their teenage sister, Julia, whom Abe affectionately called a "flibbertigibbet." Fifty-nine years later, she would write about her memories of Abe and his boys in *Tad Lincoln's Father*.

said, "if you would be kind enough to negotiate the terms of my surrender." Mary thinks it beneath the dignity of a president to gambol so, but were it not for these moments—these tender little pieces of life—I should go mad in a month's time.

Abe was a doting, loving father to all three of his boys, but with Robert off at Harvard (where he was guarded by a handful of local men and vampires) and Tad "too young and wild to be still," he grew especially fond of Willie.

He has an insatiable appetite for books; a love of solving riddles. If there is a fight, he can be counted on to step in and make the peace. Some are eager to point to the similarities between us, but I do not see us as so very similar—for Willie has a kinder heart than I, and a quicker mind.

As he celebrated the good news that Sunday afternoon, Abe happened to catch a glimpse of his boys playing on the frost-covered South Lawn below his office window.

Tad and Willie were busy holding a court-martial for Jack* as they often did—accusing him

---

*A small soldier doll that had been given to Tad as a gift. He and his brother enjoyed putting the doll through mock court-martials for treason or dereliction of duty, sentencing him to death, burying him—and then repeating the whole process. Abe was once implored by his boys to write a pardon for their toy, which he did happily: "The Doll Jack is pardoned by order of the President. A. Lincoln."

of this offense or that. Not ten yards from where
they played, two young soldiers (not much more
than boys themselves) looked after them—both
of them shivering, no doubt wondering what they
had done to deserve such an assignment.

They were just two of the dozen living guards who
patrolled the White House and its grounds around the
clock. At Abe's insistence, his wife and children were
accompanied by no fewer than two men (or one vampire)
whenever they ventured outdoors. There were no fences
between the street and the mansion in 1862. The public
was free to roam the grounds—even enter the mansion's
first floor. As journalist Noah Brooks wrote, "the multitude, washed or unwashed, always has free egress and
ingress." The multitude was not, however, permitted to
carry firearms onto the property.

At half-past three o'clock, a small, bearded man with a
rifle was spotted approaching the White House from the
direction of Lafayette Square. The sentry assigned to the
North Entrance leveled his weapon and ordered the man
to stop—yelling at the top of his lungs.

The commotion drew me to the north windows, where I watched the little man continue
his approach, a rifle held across his body. Guards
came running now from every corner of the
grounds, alerted, as we had been, by the repeated
shouts of "stop at once or be shot!"

Three of these guards came running quite a
bit faster than the others, and made straight for
the intruder with no fear of being shot. At the

FIG. 3A-1. - SOUTH LAWN OF THE WHITE HOUSE UNDER HEAVY GUARD, CIRCA 1862. THE MAN ON THE PORTICO IS BELIEVED TO BE A MEMBER OF ABE'S TRINITY.

sight of their advance (and, I suspect, their fangs), the little man at last dropped his rifle and raised his hands in the air. He was nonetheless brought violently to the ground, and his pockets searched by Lamon while the trinity held his limbs. I was later told that he seemed frightened; confused. "He gave me ten dollars," he supposedly said with tears in his eyes. "He gave me ten dollars."

Only now, with the immediate danger passed, did my eyes find two of the several soldiers now forming a circle around the intruder.

Abe's heart stopped. They were the same young soldiers who'd been looking after Willie and Tad.

His children were alone.

The boys had been too engrossed to pay any mind to the shouting, or notice their shivering guards running off to investigate it. In this vulnerable moment, they were set upon by a stranger.

He, too, might have escaped their notice, had the heel of his boot not come down on their doll and brought an end to their game. Willie and Tad looked up to see a man of average height and build standing over them, wearing a long black coat, with a scarf and top hat to match. His eyes were obscured by dark glasses, and his lip obscured by a thick brown mustache. "Hello, Willie," he said. "I have a message for your father. I would very much like you to give it to him."

Now it was Tad's screams that brought the guards running.

The vampires were the first to arrive, with Lamon and several soldiers on their heels. I came bounding down the steps of the South Portico next, and found Tad frightened and crying, but seemingly unharmed. Willie, however, was rubbing his tongue with his coat sleeve and spitting repeatedly. I took him in my arms and looked him over—turning his face and neck this way, that way—all the while praying there were no wounds on his body.

"There!" Lamon cried, pointing to a figure running south. He and the trinity gave chase, while the others hastened us into the house. "Alive!" I cried after them. "Alive!"

Lamon and the trinity chased the figure across Pennsylvania Avenue and through the Ellipse.* When it became clear that he couldn't keep pace, the breathless Lamon drew his revolver and, with no regard for the innocent bystanders he might have hit, fired at the distant figure until his cartridges were spent.

The trinity was gaining on its target. The four vampires ran south toward the unfinished Washington Monument, into the field of grazing cattle that surrounded it. Construction of the massive marble obelisk (at 150 feet, it was only one-third its eventual height) had been halted, and a temporary slaughterhouse erected in its shadow to help meet the needs of a hungry army. It was into this long, wooden building that the stranger now disappeared, desperate to lose the killers who were only fifty yards behind him. Perhaps there would be knives to fight with inside...blood to throw them off his scent...*anything*.

But there were no carcasses in the slaughterhouse that Sunday afternoon. No workers cutting the throats of cattle. Only dozens of metal hooks hanging from rafters overhead, each reflecting the late-day sun that squeezed through the open doors at both ends of the long building. The stranger ran across the bloodstained wooden floor looking for a place to hide, a weapon to wield. He found neither.

The river...I can lose them in the river...

He sprinted toward an open door at the far end, determined to head south to the Potomac. Once there, he would

---

*A circular fifty-two-acre park often used as campgrounds for Union troops.

dive beneath its surface and slip away. But his exit was blocked by the silhouette of a man.

The other door . . .

The stranger stopped and turned back—there were two more silhouettes behind him.

There would be no escape.

He stood near the center of the long building as his pursuers advanced from either end, slowly, cautiously. They meant to capture him. Torture him. Demand to know who'd sent him, and what he'd done to the boy. And, if captured, chances were that he would tell them everything. This he could not allow.

The stranger smiled as his pursuers neared. "Know this," he said. "That you are the slaves of slaves." He took a breath, closed his eyes, and leapt onto one of the hanging hooks, stabbing himself through the heart.

> I like to think that in his final moments, as his
> body convulsed and blood poured from his nose
> and mouth—joining that of the animals' below—
> that he saw the flames of hell beneath his feet, and
> felt the first of an eternity's agony. I like to think
> that he was afraid.

———

As guards sealed the White House and searched the grounds, Willie sat in his father's office, calmly relating what had happened, while a doctor looked him over.

> The stranger had grabbed his face, he said,
> pried his mouth open, and poured something
> "bitter" into it. My thoughts turned at once to

my mother's death from a fool's dose of vampire
blood, and I fell into silent despair at the thought
of seeing my beloved little boy suffer her fate.
The doctor found no signs of injury or symptoms
of poisoning, but made Willie swallow several
spoonfuls of powdered charcoal* as a precaution
(an experience he found far worse than the assault
itself).

    That night, as Mary tended to Tad (who had
been quite shaken by the day's events), I sat by
Willie's bedside, watching him sleep; watching
him for the slightest sign of sickness. To my great
relief, he seemed well the next morning, and I
began to entertain the faint hope that it had all
been nothing more than a scare.

But as Monday wore on, Willie grew increasingly
tired and sore—and by the second night, he was running a
fever. All business ground to a halt as Willie grew worse,
and the best doctors in Washington were summoned to
treat him.

    They did all they could to treat his symptoms,
but could find no cure for them. For three days
and nights, Mary and I kept a vigil at his bedside,
praying for his recovery, fervent in our belief that
youth and Providence would see him through. I
read him passages from his favorite books as he

---

*Activated charcoal has long been used a treatment for poison-
ing. It works by absorbing toxins in the intestines before they
can reach the bloodstream.

slept; ran my fingers though his soft brown hair
and wiped the sweat from his brow. On the fourth
day, our prayers seemed answered. Willie began
to mend on his own, and my faint hopes returned.
It could not be a fool's dose, I told myself—for he
would surely be dead by now.

But after a few hours' reprieve, Willie's health began to
worsen again. He couldn't eat or drink without being sick
to his stomach. His body withered and weakened, and his
fever refused to subside. On the ninth day, he could not
be roused from sleep. And on the tenth, despite the best
efforts of the best physicians available, it became clear
that Willie was going to die.

Mary could not bring herself to hold another
of our little boys as he left this earth. It fell to me
to cradle our sleeping son against my chest and
gently rock him through the night…through the
next morning…and through the day that followed. I refused to let him go; refused to let go of
that faintest hope that God would not be so cruel.

On Thursday, February 20th, 1862, at five p.m., Willie
Lincoln died in his father's arms.

Elizabeth Keckley was a freed slave who worked
mainly as Mary Lincoln's dressmaker. Years later, she
recalled the sight of Lincoln weeping openly, his tall
frame convulsing with emotion. "Genius and greatness,"
she said, "weeping over love's idol lost." John Nicolay
remembered the tough, towering president walking to
his office door "as if in some trance." "Well, Nicolay," he

FIG.19-1. - MARY TODD LINCOLN POSES WITH TWO OF THE THREE SONS SHE WOULD LIVE TO BURY - WILLIE (LEFT) AND TAD (RIGHT).

said, staring off into space, "my boy is gone...he is actually gone." Abe barely made it into his office before bursting into tears.

For the next four days, Abe conducted little government business. He did, however, fill nearly two dozen pages in his journal. Some of them with lamentations...

[Willie] will never know the tender touch of a woman, or experience those particular joys of a

first love. He will never know the complete peace
of holding his <u>own</u> tiny son in his arms. He will
never read the great works of literature, or see the
great cities of the world. He will never see another
sunrise, or feel another drop of rain against his
sweet face...

Others with thoughts of suicide...

I have come to believe that the only peace in
this life is the end of it. Let me wake at last from
this nightmare...this brief, meaningless nightmare of loss and struggle. Of endless sacrifice. All
that I love waits on the other side of death. Let
me find the courage to open my eyes at last.

And sometimes, with blind rage...

I wish to see the face of the cowardly God who
delights in these miseries! Who delights in striking down children! In stealing innocent sons from
their mothers and fathers! Oh, let me see his face
and rip out his black heart! Let me strike him
down as I have so many of his demons!

———————

Arrangements were made to transport Willie's body to
Springfield, where it would be buried near the Lincolns'
permanent home. But Abe couldn't bear the idea of having his little boy so far away, and at the last minute it was
decided that Willie would lie in a Washington crypt until
the end of his father's presidency. Two days after the funeral

(which Mary, overcome with grief, could not attend), Abe returned to the crypt and ordered his son's casket opened.

> I sat beside him, as I had on so many nights during his brief life; half expecting him to wake and embrace me—for such was the skill of his embalmer, that he seemed merely asleep. I stayed with him an hour or more, speaking to him tenderly. Laughing as I told him stories of his earliest mischief...his first steps...his peculiar laugh. Telling him how very loved he would always be. When our time was through, and the lid again affixed to his coffin, I began to weep. I could not bear the thought of his being alone in that cold, dark box. Alone where I could not comfort him.

With Mary confined to bed, Abe sought refuge behind his closed office door in the week after Willie's death. Fearing for his health, Nicolay and Hay canceled all of his meetings indefinitely, and Lamon and the trinity guarded his door at all hours. Dozens of well-wishers came to offer the president their sympathies that week. All were thanked and politely turned away—until the night of February 28th, when one man was ushered directly into his office.

He'd given the name that could never be refused.

IV

"I cannot imagine the burden you bear," said Henry. "The weight of a nation on your shoulders...of a war. And now, the weight of another son buried."

Abe sat in the light of the fireplace, his old ax hanging above its mantel. "Is this why you come, Henry? To remind me of my miseries? If that be the case, then I assure you—I am too aware of them already."

"I come to offer my sympathies to an old friend...and to offer you a choi—"

"No!" Abe choked up at once. "I will not hear it! I will not be tormented with this again!"

"It is not my wish to torment."

"Then what is it, Henry? Tell me—what is your wish? To see me suffer? To see the tears run freely down my cheeks? Here—does this face satisfy you?"

"Abraham..."

Abe rose from his chair. "The whole of my life has been spent on your errands, Henry! The whole of my life! And to what end? To what happiness of my own? All that I have ever loved has fallen prey to your kind! I have given you everything. What have you given me in return?"

"I have given you my everlasting loyalty; my protection from the—"

"Death!" said Abe. "You have given me death!"

Abe looked at the ax over his mantel.

All that I have ever loved...

"Abraham...do not give in to this despair. Remember your mother—remember what she whispered with her dying breath."

"Do not try to manipulate me, Henry! And do not pretend to care that I suffer! You care only for your own gains! For your war! You know nothing of loss!"

Now Henry rose to his feet. "I have spent these three hundred years mourning a wife and child, Abraham! Mourning the life that was stolen from me; a thousand loves lost to time! You know nothing of the lengths I have gone to protect you! Nothing of that which I have suff—"

Henry composed himself.

"No," he said. "No...it mustn't be this way. We have come too far for this." He grabbed his coat and hat. "You have my respects, and you have my offer. If you choose to leave Willie buried, so be it."

The sound of Willie's name roused such wild-ness in me—Henry's callous tone such rage that I grabbed the ax from its perch and swung at his head with a scream, missing him by less than an inch, and shattering the clock on the mantel. I recovered and swung again, but Henry leapt over my blade. The office door now flew open behind us, and two of the trinity rushed in. On seeing us, they froze—unsure of where their loyalties lay. Lamon, however, was plagued by no such uncer-tainty. On entering, he drew his revolver and aimed it at Henry—only to have it taken by one of the vampires before he could fire.

Henry stood in the center of the room, arms at his sides. I charged again—raising my ax as I ran. Henry didn't so much as blink as I came. Rather, he grabbed the handle as I brought it down on his head, took it from me, and snapped it in two, throwing the pieces on the floor. I came at him with my fists, but these he caught as well, twisting them around and forcing me to my knees. Holding me thus, he knelt behind me and brought his fangs to my neck. "No!" cried Lamon, rushing forward. The others held him

back. I felt the tips of those twin razors against
my flesh.

"Do it!" I cried.

The only peace in this life is the end of it…

"Do it, I beg you!"

I felt the tiny trickles of blood run down my
neck as his fangs broke through my skin. I closed
my eyes and prepared to meet the unknown; to
see my beloved boys once more…but it was not
to be.

Henry withdrew his fangs and let me go.

"Some people are just too interesting to kill,
Abraham," he said, rising to his feet. He gathered
his coat and hat again and walked to the door,
toward the three anxious guards whose hearts
were racing faster than my own.

"Henry…"

He turned back.

"I will see this war to its end…but I do not care to see
another vampire so long as I live."

Henry offered a slight bow. "Mr. President…"

With that, he disappeared.

Abe wouldn't see him for the rest of his life.

Twelve

"Starve the Devils"

Fondly do we hope, fervently do we pray, that this mighty scourge of war may speedily pass away. Yet, if God wills that it continue...until every drop of blood drawn with the lash shall be paid by another drawn with the sword, as was said three thousand years ago, so still it must be said "the judgments of the Lord are true and righteous altogether."

—*Abraham Lincoln's Second Inaugural Address*
March 4th, 1865

I

Washington, D.C., was under attack, and Abe wasn't about to miss his chance to see the fighting up close.

On July 11th, 1864, ignoring the pleas of his personal guard, he rode alone on horseback to Fort Stevens,* where

---

*The Battle of Fort Stevens marks the only occasion in American history a sitting president was under fire in combat.

Confederate General Jubal A. Early was leading 17,000 rebels in a brazen assault on Washington's northern defenses. The president was greeted by Union officers and whisked directly into the fort, where he would be able to relax and enjoy a cool drink behind the safety of its thick stone walls.

> I hadn't come to be coddled or hear the battle described to me—I'd come to see the horrors of war for myself. To see what others had suffered these three long years, while I had remained behind the walls of warmth and plenty. Try as they might, the officers couldn't discourage me from peeking over the parapet to watch boys line up and ceremoniously shoot one another—to see them blown apart by [cannon fire] and run through by bayonets.

The sight of Abraham Lincoln towering over the battlefield in his stovepipe hat must have seemed a godsend for the rebel sharpshooters at Fort Stevens that day. Abe had three bullets zip past him in as many minutes, each one giving his minders terrible fits of anxiety. Finally, when a Union officer standing next to him was struck in the head and killed, the president felt a tug at the bottom of his coat, and heard First Lieutenant (and future Supreme Court Justice) Oliver Wendell Holmes yell: "Get down, you damned fool!"

But he didn't.

He'd completely lost his fear of death.

———

There were no more vampires at the White House. Abe had banished them in the wake of Willie's death and his confrontation with Henry. Even the trinity—his most capable and ferocious protectors—had been sent back to New York.

> I shall save this Union because it merits saving.
> I shall save it to honor the men who built it with
> their blood and genius, and the future generations
> who deserve its liberty. I shall give every miser-
> able hour to the cause of victory and peace—but I
> shall be damned if I lay eyes on another vampire.

The first family was now guarded exclusively by living men, and the president guarded less and less at his own insistence. Each day brought new restrictions on his guards; each day fewer rooms he welcomed them in. Over Ward Hill Lamon's objections, Abe insisted on riding out in an open carriage when the weather was agreeable, and on walking between the mansion and the War Department alone after dark. As Lamon recalled in his memoirs years later: "I believe that it was more than an absence of fear. I believe that it was an invitation of death."

A journal entry from April 20th, 1862, sums up Abe's growing fatalism.

> In the course of a week, I greet a thousand
> strange faces in the White House. Should I treat
> each as the face of my assassin? Indeed, any man
> willing to give his life to take mine would have
> little trouble doing it. Am I therefore to lock
> myself in an iron box and wait for this war to
> end? If God wants my soul, He knows where He
> may collect it—and He may do so at the hour and
> in the manner of His choosing.

In time, through sheer force of will, he would pull himself out of this depression, just as he had all the ones before it. Not long after Willie's death, when his long-time friend William McCullough was killed fighting for the Union, Abe sent a letter to the grieving daughter McCullough had left behind. The comfort and advice he offered was meant as much for himself as for the girl.

> Perfect relief is not possible, except with time. You cannot now realize that you will ever feel better. Is not this so? And yet it is a mistake. You are sure to be happy again. To know this, which is certainly true, will make you some less miser-able now. I have had experience enough to know what I say; and you need only to believe it, to feel better at once. The memory of your dear Father, instead of an agony, will yet be a sad sweet feeling in your heart, of a purer and holier sort than you have known before.

But while Abe was picking himself up and soldiering on, Mary was only getting worse.

> She cannot bring herself to leave her bed for more than an hour's time. Nor can she attend to Tad, who grieves not only for a brother, but a mother as well. I am ashamed to admit that there are moments when the very sight of her angers me. Ashamed because it is no fault of hers that she suffers fits of rage, or believes the charlatans who "commune" with our beloved sons for money. She has borne more than any mother ought to bear.

I fear that her mind has gone, and that it shall
never return.

II

Though Abe refused to have any direct contact with
Henry or the Union, he was pragmatic enough to accept
their help in winning the war. In New York, the grand
ballroom (where Abe first learned of the Union and its
plans for him) had been transformed into a war room,
complete with maps, chalkboards, and a telegraph. They
acted as envoys to the sympathetic vampires of Europe.
They fought where they were able, and supplemented the
White House's intelligence with that collected by their
own spies. This intelligence was delivered to Seward,
who—after reading and burning the messages—related
their contents to the president. From an entry dated June
10th, 1862:

> Today comes word that the Confederates are
> handing Union prisoners over to Southern vam-
> pires for the purpose of torture and execution.
> "We hear of men," said Seward, "hung upside
> down and stretched between posts. Using a log-
> ger's saw, two vampires slowly cut the prisoner
> in half beginning at his [groin]. As they do, a
> third vampire lies on his back beneath the poor
> wretch—catching the blood that runs down his
> body. Because the prisoner's head is nearest the
> ground, his brain remains nourished, and he
> remains conscious until the blade tears slowly

> back and forth through his stomach, then chest.
> The other prisoners are made to watch this before
> being made to suffer it themselves."

Rumors of Confederate "ghosts" and "demons" snatching men from their tents and drinking their blood spread through the Union ranks during the war's second summer. Soldiers could be heard singing a popular song around their campfires at night.

> From Flor'da to Virginny you can hear him revel,
> for ol' Johnny Reb's made a deal with the devil.
> Sent him up north, that snake-eyed liar,
> to drag us boys off to the lake of fire…

In at least one case, these rumors led a group of Union soldiers to turn on one of their own. On July 5th, 1862, Private Morgan Sloss was murdered by five of his fellow soldiers while encamped near Berkley Plantation in Virginia.

> They pulled him from his tent in the dead
> of night and beat him, all the while accusing
> him of being a "blood-drinkin' demon." (Had
> the boy actually <u>been</u> a vampire, he would have
> made a better show of defending himself.) They
> tied him to a hitching post, and set on him with
> sticks and shovels—demanding he confess. "Tell
> us yer a blood-drinkin' demon and we'll let ya
> go!" they cried, all the while thrashing him till
> he wept and begged for mercy. After a quarter of
> an hour of this, the mumbled confession at last

came from his bloodied lips. I suspect the boy
would have confessed to being Christ Himself if
it had meant an end to his agony. His confession
noted, he was then doused in lamp oil and burned
alive. The fear he must have felt…the confusion
and the fear…I cannot think of it without my
fists clenching in anger. If only by some miracle
of time and heaven I could have been there to
intervene.

Abe found the incident deeply troubling—not only for
its cruelty, but because it meant that the Confederate strategy was working.

How can we hope to win this war when our
men have begun killing each other? How can we
hope to prevail when they will soon be too frightened to fight? For every vampire sympathetic to
our cause, there are ten fighting for the enemy.
How am I to contest them?

As it often did for Abe, the answer came in a dream.
From an entry dated July 21st, 1862:

I was a boy again…sitting atop a familiar fence
rail in the cool of a cloudy day, watching travelers
pass on the Old Cumberland Trail. I remember
seeing a horse cart filled with Negroes, each of
them shackled at the wrist, without so much as a
handful of loose hay to comfort the bumps of the
road, or a blanket to relieve them from the winter
air. My eyes met those of the youngest, a Negro

girl of perhaps five or six, as they passed. I wanted
to turn away (such was the sorrow of her countenance), yet I could not...for I knew where she was
being taken.

Night had fallen. I had followed the Negro
girl (I know not how) to a large barn—the inside
lit by torches and hanging oil lamps. I watched
from the darkness as she and the others were
made to stand in a line, their eyes firmly fixed on
the ground. I watched as a vampire took its place
behind each of the slaves. Her eyes found mine as
a pair of fangs descended behind her, and a pair of
clawed hands grabbed her tiny neck.

"Justice...," she said, staring at me.

The fangs tore into her.

Her screams joined my own as I woke.

———————

Abe convened his Cabinet the next morning.

"Gentlemen," I began, "we have spoken a great
deal about the <u>true</u> nature of this war; about our
<u>true</u> enemy. We have argued—always in the spirit
of friendship—over the wisest way to meet such
an enemy, and bemoaned his power to strike fear
into the hearts of our men. I daresay that we have
even come to share in that fear ourselves. This
will not do.

"Gentlemen...let our enemy fear us.

"Let us deny him the laborers who tend the
farms of his living allies; who build his garrisons
and carry his gunpowder. Let us deny him the

poor wretches who are themselves grown as crops
to be consumed by darkness. Now, gentlemen, let
us starve the devils into defeat by declaring every
slave in the South free."

Cheers went up around the table. Even Salmon Chase
(who still refused to believe that vampires were real) saw
the strategic genius of attacking the engine of the South.
Seward, while joining the others in his approval, offered a
piece of humble advice:

> [He] suggested that such a proclamation be
> given to the country on the heels of a victory, so
> as not to appear an act of desperation.
> "Well," I said, "then I suppose we need a vic-
> tory."

III

On September 17th, 1862, the Union and Confederate armies collided at Antietam Creek, near the town
of Sharpsburg, Maryland. The Confederate forces were
commanded by General Robert E. Lee, who'd enjoyed a
warm relationship with the president before the war. The
Union forces were commanded by General George B.
McClellan, a Democrat who despised Abraham Lincoln
with every fiber of his being. Abe writes:

> [McClellan] thinks me a buffoon—unfit to
> command a man of his superior breeding and

intellect. This would not bother me in the least
if only he won more battles! Instead he sits in
his camp, using the Army of the Potomac as his
personal bodyguard! He suffers from an excess of
caution: observing when he should attack, retreat-
ing when he should stand his ground and fight.
This is a sin that I cannot forgive in a general.

Lee and McClellan's armies waited quietly in the predawn hours of that Wednesday, September 17th, unaware
that they were about to embark on the bloodiest day in
American military history. At first light, both sides
unleashed their artillery. For nearly an hour the shells
flew one after the other, many with fuses timed to make
them explode over their targets, sending burning pieces
of shrapnel through the bodies of any soldier unfortunate
enough to be nearby. From the diary of Union soldier
Christoph Niederer,* 20th New York Infantry, 6th Corps:

> I had just got myself pretty comfortable when
> a bomb burst over me and completely deaf-
> ened me. I felt a blow on my right shoulder and
> my jacket was covered with white stuff. I felt
> mechanically whether I still had my arm and
> thank God it was still whole. At the same time I
> felt something damp on my face; I wiped it off.
> It was bloody. Now I first saw that the man next
> to me, Kessler, lacked the upper part of his head,
> and almost all his brains had gone into the face
> of the man next to him, Merkel, so that he could

---

*Civil War Misc. Collection, USAMHI.

scarcely see. Since any moment the same could
happen to anyone, no one thought much about it.

When the cannons fell quiet, Union troops were given
orders to fix bayonets and charge across an open cornfield
toward the entrenched Confederates. But an artillery bat-
tery was waiting for them in the tall stalks, and when they
neared, the rebel cannons unleashed round after round of
grapeshot,* taking heads off and scattering body parts
across the field. From a letter by Lieutenant Sebastian
Duncan Jr.,** 13th New Jersey Infantry, 12th Corps:

> Stray shot and shell began to whiz over our
> heads and burst around us…lying just in front
> of our lines was a great number of dead and
> wounded. One poor fellow lay just before us with
> one leg shot off; the other shattered and other-
> wise badly wounded; fairly shrieking with pain.

When the charge was over, the cornfield was a bare,
smoldering ruin covered with the dead and the dying
from one end to the other. The wounded were left to suffer alone as shells continued to fall—taking fresh limbs,
and scattering the ones that had been taken already. The
battle was barely two hours old.

---

*Grapeshot is a type of cannon ammunition similar to a shot-
gun shell. Small metal balls are packed tightly together in a
projectile. When fired, the balls spread out to cause a greater
damage. Grapeshot was packed into canisters and used for
close-range engagement.

**Duncan Papers, New Jersey Historical Society.

More than 6,000 men would lose their lives at Antietam that day, and another 20,000 would be wounded, many of them mortally.

Lee would eventually be forced into retreat. But after using only two-thirds of his available forces to fight the battle (a fact that continues to baffle military historians), General George B. McClellan simply watched as the battered Confederate Army limped into Virginia to regroup. Had he chased them down, he could have dealt a crippling blow to the South and brought the war to a speedy end.

Abe was furious.

"Damn it!" he cried to Stanton on learning that McClellan had failed to follow the enemy's retreat. "He has done more to cause me grief than any Confederate!"

He left for McClellan's camp at Sharpsburg at once.

———————

There's a famous photograph of Abraham Lincoln and George B. McClellan sitting across from each other in the general's tent at Sharpsburg. Both look stiff and uncomfortable. History knows that Abe flippantly told McClellan: "If you do not want to use the army, I would very much like to borrow it." What history has never known, however, is what happened shortly before that uncomfortable picture was taken.

> Upon greeting [McClellan] in his tent and shaking the hands of his officers, I asked that we be given a moment alone. Closing the flap of his tent, I placed my hat upon a small table, straightened my coat, and stood before him. "General," I said, "I must ask you a question."

Fig. 8-47. - Abe sits with a nervous General George McClellan immediately after their confrontation at Sharpsburg. Note the axe leaning against the President's chair -- brought just in case his hunch about McClellan had proven right.

"Anything," said he.

I grabbed him by the collar and pulled him close—so close that our faces were only inches apart. "May I see them?"

"What in God's name are you talking about?"

I pulled him closer still. "Your fangs, General! Let me have a look at them!" McClellan began to struggle against me, but his feet were no longer touching the ground. "Surely they must be in there," I said, prying his mouth open with one hand. "For how could <u>any</u> living man seek to prolong the agony of war? Come! Show me those black eyes! Show me those razors and let us face each other!" I shook him violently. "Show me!"

"I—I do not understand," he said at last.

His confusion was genuine. His fear palpable.

I released him, suddenly ashamed that I had allowed my temper to run wild. "No," I said. "No, I can see that you do not." I straightened my coat again and reached for the tent flap.

"Come," I said. "Let us give Gardner* his photograph and be done with each other."

Abe relieved McClellan of his command a month later.

————

After leaving the camp at Sharpsburg, Abe surveyed the aftermath of the battle for himself. The sight of mangled, rigid bodies strewn across Antietam Creek was enough to bring the emotionally weary president to tears.

I wept, for each of these boys was Willie. Each of them had left a father cursed as I am cursed; a mother weeping as Mary weeps.

————

*Alexander Gardner, the Washington, D.C., photographer who would also take Abe's last portrait.

Fig. 27-c — A group of freed slaves collects Confederate bodies in Cold Harbor, Virginia after the War in 1865. Note the fangs visible in the skull to the kneeling man's left.

Abe sat on the ground beside the corpse of one Union soldier for nearly an hour. He was told that the boy had been struck in the head by cannon fire.

> His head was split open at the back, and most of his skull and brains were gone—the result being that his face and scalp lay flat on the ground like an empty bag of grain. The sight of him repulsed me, yet I could not avert my eyes. This boy—this nameless boy—had risen that September morning, unaware that he would never see another. He had dressed and eaten. He had run bravely into battle. And then he had been gone—every moment of his life reduced to a

single misfortune. All of his experiences, past and future, emptied onto some strange field far from home.

I weep for his mother and father; for his brothers and sisters. But I do not weep for him—for I have come to believe that old saying with all my heart...

"Only the dead have seen the end of war."

IV

As horrible as Antietam was, it was the victory that Abe had been waiting for. On September 22nd, 1862, he issued the first Emancipation Proclamation, declaring all slaves in rebel states "forever free."

Reaction was swift. Abolitionists argued that by freeing *only* the slaves in Southern states, Abe hadn't gone far enough. Moderates feared that the measure would only make the South fight with more determination. Some Northern soldiers threatened mutiny, arguing that they were fighting to preserve the Union, not "[Negro] freedom."

Abe didn't care.

The only reaction that concerned him was that of the slaves themselves. And judging by the reports that began trickling in during the last months of 1862, it was precisely the one he'd hoped for.

I received today a remarkable account from
our allies in New York (related by Seward) of a
recent uprising on a plantation near Vicksburg,

FIG. 11.2 - ABE'S HOPES WERE REALIZED WHEN SLAVES BEGAN REVOLTING AGAINST THEIR VAMPIRE CAPTORS IN THE WAKE OF THE EMANCIPATION PROCLAMATION.

Mississippi. I am assured that no part of it has been embellished, the account having been conveyed by a runaway Negro boy who witnessed the events firsthand. "The happy news of [the Emancipation Proclamation] having reached their quarters that morning," said Seward, "the Negroes rejoiced with spirited songs. Their revels, however, were met with the angry whips of their masters, and a wench collected and chained at the ankles—this being the common manner of taking away those who were never to be seen again. Rather than allow this sorry fate to befall her, as they had allowed it to befall so many before, the Negroes formed a mob and encircled the fattening pen into which she had been taken. When they burst in, carrying sickles and scythes, they were met with a sight which made even the bravest of them cry out in horror. A pair of wild-eyed gentlemen knelt over the shackled wench, each of their bloodstained mouths affixed to one of her naked breasts. She was insensible, most of the color having left her by this time. Composing themselves, several of the Negro men raised their weapons and charged at the devils—thinking them mortals. The vampires, however, moved with such speed as to confound them. They leapt about the pen, clinging to the walls with the ease of insects, as blades swung violently about them. Those who led the charge were slain—their throats opened by pointed claws; their heads struck with such force as to render them dead before they fell. But such were their numbers, that the mob was able to overwhelm the gentlemen. Though it took no fewer than six men to restrain each of them, the vampires were finally dragged from the fattening pen, held over a watering trough, and beheaded."

Word was spreading. The days of America's vampires were numbered.

On November 19th, 1863, Abe rose before a crowd of 15,000. He pulled a small piece of paper from his pocket, unfolded it, cleared his throat, and began to speak:

Fourscore and seven years ago our fathers brought forth on this continent a new nation, conceived in

liberty, and dedicated to the proposition that all
men are created equal…

He'd come to Gettysburg to dedicate a memorial to
the 8,000 men who had given their lives in the three-
day Union victory. As he spoke, Ward Hill Lamon (who
can be seen sitting next to Abe in one of the few surviving photos of the event) scanned the crowd anxiously—
his hand on the revolver inside his coat; his stomach in
knots—for he was the only man protecting the president
that day.

> For three hours we sat upon that stage. Three
> hours of ceaseless worry—for I was certain that
> an assassin would strike. Every face seemed to
> wear an expression of hatred for the president.
> Every movement seemed prelude to an attempt on
> his life.

At first, Abe had insisted on going to Gettysburg without any guard, worried that the sight of armed men would
be "inappropriate" at an event honoring those who'd died
for their country. Only after Lamon half-jokingly threatened to sabotage the president's train to prevent the trip
did Abe agree to bring him along.

> …that we here highly resolve that these
> dead shall not have died in vain—that this
> nation, under God, shall have a new birth of
> freedom and that government of the people, by
> the people, for the people, shall not perish from
> the earth.

FIG.14C-3. – WARD HILL LAMON SITS IMMEDIATELY TO ABE'S RIGHT IN THE MOMENTS AFTER THE GETTYSBURG ADDRESS, NERVOUSLY SCANNING THE CROWD FOR VAMPIRE ASSASSINS. A CLOSER LOOK AT THE EDGE OF THE PHOTO SUGGESTS THAT HIS FEARS MAY HAVE BEEN JUSTIFIED.

Abe folded the paper and took his seat to moderate applause. He'd spoken for all of two minutes. In that short time, he'd given perhaps the greatest speech of the nineteenth century, one that would be forever ingrained in America's consciousness. And in that short time, Ward Hill Lamon, Abraham Lincoln's most devoted human bodyguard, had reached a decision that would forever alter the course of America's history.

The anxiety at Gettysburg had been more than he could bear. As they rode back to Washington, Lamon respectfully told the president that he could no longer guard him.

V

On the night of November 8th, 1864, Abe walked though driving wind and rain, alone.

> I resolved to sit in the telegraph office alone
> and await the returns, just as I had in Spring-
> field four long years ago. If I lost, I did not wish
> to be consoled. If I won, I did not wish to be
> congratulated. For there were many reasons
> to welcome the first outcome, and mourn the
> second.

The war had claimed nearly 500,000 lives by Election Day. Despite these unimaginable losses, growing war-weariness, and deep divides over emancipation in the North, Abe and his new vice president, Democrat Andrew Johnson of Tennessee, won in a landslide against George B. McClellan (the same McClellan Abe had confronted after Antietam). Eighty percent of the Union Army voted to reelect its commander in chief, an astonishing number given the fact that Abe had run against a former Union general, and given the miserable conditions they'd endured for years. On hearing the election results, Union troops outside the Confederate capital of Richmond gave such a cheer that its beleaguered citizens were sure the South had just surrendered.

They had reason to expect defeat. Richmond had been surrounded for months. Atlanta (the heart of Southern manufacturing) had been captured. Across the South, emancipated slaves continued to escape to Northern lines by the tens of thousands—crippling Southern agriculture, and forcing Confederate vampires to scavenge for easy blood. As a result, the dreaded "ghost soldiers" who had slaughtered and terrorized Union troops became increasingly scarce. By the time Abe was inaugurated for the second time on March 4th, 1865, the war was all but over.

> With malice toward none, with charity for all, with firmness in the right as God gives us to see the right, let us strive on to finish the work we are in, to bind up the nation's wounds, to care for him who shall have borne the battle and for his widow and his orphan, to do all which may achieve and cherish a just and lasting peace among ourselves and with all nations.

During the procession that followed his address, a battalion of Negro soldiers joined the others marching past the president's reviewing stand.

> I was moved to tears as they passed, saluting me—for in each of their faces I saw the face of a nameless victim crying out for justice; of a little girl passing by on the Old Cumberland Trail all those many years ago. On each of their faces I saw the anguish of the past, and the promise of the future.

General Robert E. Lee surrendered his army on April 9th, 1865, effectively ending the Civil War. The following day, Abe received a letter in a familiar scrawl.

Abraham,

I beg you put enmity aside long enough to read a few words of congratulations.

It brings me joy to report that our enemy has begun its exodus—many back to Europe, others to South America and the Orient, where they are less likely to be hunted. They have looked to the future, Abraham—and they have seen that America is now, and shall forever be, a nation of living men. Like your namesake, you have been a "father to many" these four long years. And like your namesake, God has asked impossible sacrifices of you. Yet you have endured it all as brilliantly as any man could have hoped. You have blessed the futures of those who share this time on earth, and those who have yet to live.

She would be proud.

Ever,

—H

As a boy, Abe had vowed to "kill every vampire in America." While that had proven impossible, he'd done the next best thing: he'd driven the worst of them out of America. There was one vampire, however, who refused to leave...who believed that the dream of a nation of immortals was still within reach—so long as Abraham Lincoln was dead.

His name was John Wilkes Booth.

FIG. 3E – JOHN WILKES BOOTH (SEATED) POSES FOR A PORTRAIT WITH CONFEDERATE PRESIDENT JEFFERSON DAVIS IN RICHMOND, CIRCA 1863. IT IS THE ONLY KNOWN PICTURE OF BOOTH IN HIS TRUE VAMPIRE FORM.

Thirteen

Thus Always to Tyrants

I leave you, hoping that the lamp of liberty will burn in your bosoms until there shall no longer be a doubt that all men are created free and equal.

—Abraham Lincoln, in a speech at Chicago, Illinois
July 10th, 1858

I

On April 12th, 1865, a lone man walked across the White House lawn toward the towering columns of the South Portico—where, on clear spring afternoons such as this, the president himself could often be seen on the third-floor balcony. The man walked briskly, carrying a small leather attaché. The legislation that would create the Secret Service was sitting on Abraham Lincoln's desk that Wednesday evening, and would remain there for the rest of his life.

At three minutes before four o'clock, the man entered the building and gave his name to one of the butlers.

"Joshua Speed, to see the president."

A lifetime of war had finally taken its toll on Abe. He'd felt increasingly weak since Willie's death. Clouded and unsure. The lines in his face were deeper, and the skin beneath his eyes sagged so as to make him appear forever exhausted. Mary was nearly always depressed, and her rare moments of levity were spent on frenzied fits of decorating and redecorating, or on séances to "commune" with her beloved Eddy and Willie. She and Abe hardly spoke beyond simple civilities. Sometime between April 3rd and April 5th, during his journey downriver to inspect the fallen city of Richmond, the president scribbled the following poem in the margins of his journal.

> Melancholy,
> my old friend,
> visits frequent,
> once again.

Desperate for distraction and companionship, Abe invited his old friend and fellow vampire hunter to spend a night at the White House. Upon being notified of Speed's arrival, Abe politely excused himself from a meeting and hurried into the reception room. Speed recalled Abe's entrance in a letter to fellow hunter William Seward after the president's death.

> Placing his right hand upon my shoulder, the
> president paused momentarily as our faces met.
> I daresay he found mine surprised and saddened,
> for when I studied him, I saw a frailty that I
> had never encountered before. Gone was the

broad-shouldered giant who could drive an ax
clean through a vampire's middle. Gone were the
smiling eyes and confident air. In their place was
a hunched, gaunt gentleman whose skin had taken
on a sickly pallor, and whose features belonged to
a man twenty years his senior. "My dear Speed,"
he said, and took me into his arms.

The two hunters dined alone, Mary having confined
herself to bed with a headache. After dinner, they retired
to Abe's office, where they remained well into the early
morning hours, laughing and reminiscing as if they were
above the store in Springfield again. They spoke of their
hunting days; of the war; of the rumors that vampires
were fleeing America in droves. But most of all, they
talked of nothing: their families; their businesses; the
miracle of photography.

It was precisely as I had hoped. My troubles
were distant, my thoughts quieted, and I felt
something like my old self again—if only for
those ephemeral hours.

Sometime well after midnight, after Abe had kept his
friend laughing with his bottomless well of anecdotes, he
told him about a dream. A dream that had been troubling
him for days. In one of his final journal entries, Lincoln
recorded it for posterity.

There seemed to be a death-like stillness about
me. Then I heard subdued sobs, as if a number of
people were weeping. I left my bed and wandered

downstairs. There the silence was broken by the
same pitiful sobbing, but the mourners were
invisible. I went from room to room; no living person was in sight, but the same mournful
sounds of distress met me as I passed along...
I was puzzled and alarmed. What could be the
meaning of all this? I kept on until I arrived at
the East Room, which I entered. There I met with
a sickening surprise. Before me was a catafalque,
on which rested a corpse wrapped in funeral vest-
ments. Around it were stationed soldiers who
were acting as guards; and there was a throng
of people, gazing mournfully upon the corpse,
whose face was covered, others weeping pitifully.
"Who is dead in the White House?" I demanded
of one of the soldiers, "The president," was his
answer; "he was killed by an assassin." Then came
a loud burst of grief from the crowd, which woke
me from my dream. I slept no more that night.

II

John Wilkes Booth loathed sunlight. It irritated his skin;
overwhelmed his eyes. It made the fat, pink faces of boast-
ful Northerners blinding as they passed him on the street,
crowing about Union victories, celebrating the end of the
"rebellion." *You have no idea what this war is about.* The
twenty-six-year-old had always preferred the darkness—
even before he became its servant. His home had always
been the stage. Its braided ropes and velvet curtains. Its
warm, gaslight glow. Theater had been the center of his

life, and it was a theater he entered just before noon to collect his mail. There would no doubt be letters from admiring fans—perhaps someone who had witnessed his legendary Marc Antony in New York, or thrilled to his more recent Pescara in *The Apostate*, performed on the very boards now beneath his boots.

The backstage loading door had been opened to allow daylight in, as had the exits in the rear of the house, but Ford's Theater remained mostly dark. The first and second balconies were draped in shadow, and every time Booth's heel landed on the stage, the resulting echoes filled the emptiness. There was no place more pleasing—more natural to him than this. Booth would often pass the daylight hours in darkened theaters, sleeping on a catwalk, reading in an upper balcony by candlelight, or rehearsing for an audience of ghosts. *An empty theater is a promise.* Isn't that what they said? *An empty theater is a promise unfulfilled.* In a few hours, everything around him would be light and noise. Laughter and applause. Colorful people packed together in their colorful finery. Tonight, the promise would be fulfilled. And then, after the curtain came down and the gaslights were snuffed out, there would be darkness again. That was the beauty of it. That was theater.

Booth noticed a pair of men working in the stage left boxes, about ten feet above his head. They were removing the partition between two smaller boxes in order to make a single large one, no doubt for a person of some import. He recognized one of the stagehands as Edmund Spangler, a callused, red-faced old acquaintance and frequent employee. "And who are to be your honored guests, Spangler?" Booth asked. "The president and first lady, sir—accompanied by General and Mrs. Grant."

Booth hurried out of the theater without another word. He never collected his mail.

———————

There were friends to be contacted, plans to be drawn up, weapons to be readied—and so little time to do it all. *So little time, but such an opportunity!* He made straight for Mary Surratt's boardinghouse.

Mary, a plain, plump, dark-haired widow, was Booth's former lover and an ardent Southern sympathizer. She'd met him years before, when he'd been a guest at her family's tavern in Maryland. Though fourteen years his senior, she'd fallen passionately in love with the young actor, and the two had carried on an affair. After her husband died, Mary sold the tavern and moved to Washington, where she opened a small boardinghouse on H Street. Booth was a frequent guest—but in recent years, he'd seemed less interested in "matters of the flesh." Mary's feelings for him, however, remained unchanged. So when Booth asked her to ride out to the old tavern and tell its current owner, John Lloyd, to "make ready the shooting irons," she didn't hesitate. Booth had left a cache of weapons with Lloyd weeks before, in preparation for a failed plot to kidnap Lincoln and exchange him for Confederate prisoners. Now he would use the same weapons to take a more direct approach.

Mary's love for Booth would prove her undoing. For delivering his message, she would hang three months later.

While Mary was on her fatal errand, Booth visited the homes of Lewis Powell and George Atzerodt in quick succession. Both had been involved in his failed kid-

napping plot, and both would be needed to carry out the
audacious plan that was still taking shape in his head.
Atzerodt, an older, rough-looking German immigrant and
carriage repairman, was an old acquaintance of Booth's.
The boyishly handsome Powell, not yet twenty-two years
old, was a former rebel soldier, member of the Confederate Secret Service, and friend of the Surratts. A meeting
was arranged for seven that evening. Booth gave no reason for it.

He merely told the men to be on time, and to bring
their nerve.

III

Abe was in fine spirits.

"Laughter shook his office door all morning," wrote
Nicolay years later. "At first I mistook the sound for something else—so accustomed had I grown to the president's
cheerlessness." Hugh McCullough, Treasury Secretary,
remembered "I never saw Mr. Lincoln so merry." Abe had
been buoyed by the reunion with his hunters, and by the
telegrams flying out of the war office on an almost hourly
basis. Lee had surrendered to Ulysses Grant five days
earlier at the Appomattox Courthouse in Virginia, effectively bringing the war to a close. Jefferson Davis and his
government were on the run.

In order to personally congratulate Ulysses Grant on
his brilliant defeat of Robert E. Lee, the Lincolns had
invited him and his wife to the theater that evening. There
was a new comedy at Ford's, and a few hours of carefree
laughter was exactly what the president and Mrs. Lincoln

needed. However, the general had respectfully declined, as he and Julia were to leave Washington by train that evening. This set off a flurry of replacement invitations, all of which were promptly (and respectfully) declined for one reason or another. "One would think that we were inviting them to an execution," Mary is reported to have remarked during the course of the day. It mattered little to Abe. No amount of rejection—respectful or otherwise— could sully his mood that warm Good Friday afternoon.

> I am strangely buoyant. [Speaker of the House Schuyler] Colfax called this morning to discuss reconstruction, and upon observing me for a quarter hour, paused and asked if I had eschewed my coffee for a Scotch—such was my disposition. Neither the Cabinet nor [Vice President Andrew] Johnson were successful in their efforts to dampen my spirits today (though both tried mightily to do so). However, I dare not speak of this happiness aloud, for Mary would surely see such boastfulness as a bad omen. It has long been her nature—and mine—to distrust these moments of quiet as prelude to some unforeseen disaster. And yet the trees bloom beautifully today, and I cannot help but take note.

The journal entry was dated April 14th, 1865. It was the last Abe would ever make.

By late afternoon, with the day's official business done, the president prepared to take a late afternoon carriage ride with his wife. Though not as jovial as her husband, Mary also seemed to be in unusually good spirits, and she'd asked Abe to join her for a "brief turn about the yard." As the president stepped out of the North Portico, a one-armed Union soldier (who'd been waiting there most of the day in hopes of such an encounter) shouted, "I would almost give my other hand if I could shake that of Abraham Lincoln!" Abe approached the young man and extended his hand. "You shall do that, and it shall cost you nothing."

IV

Booth arrived in Lewis Powell's rented room at seven o'clock sharp, accompanied by a short, nervous twenty-two-year-old pharmacist named David Herold, whom he'd met through Mary Surratt. Atzerodt was already there. Booth wasted no time.

In a few hours, the four of them would bring the Union to its knees.

At precisely ten o'clock, Lewis Powell was to kill Secretary of State William Seward, who was currently bedridden after falling from a carriage. Powell, who was unfamiliar with Washington, would be led to Seward's house by the nervous pharmacist. After the secretary was dead, the two conspirators would ride across the Navy Yard Bridge and into Maryland, where they would meet up with Booth. At the same time, Atzerodt was to shoot Vice President Andrew Johnson in his room at the Kirkwood House, before joining the others in Maryland. As for Booth, he would return to Ford's Theater. There, he would kill the president with a single-shot derringer pistol before plunging a knife into General Grant's heart.

With the Union government decapitated, Jefferson Davis and his Cabinet would have time to reorganize. Confederate generals like Joseph E. Johnston, Meriwether Thompson, and Stand Watie, whose armies were fighting valiantly against the Yankee devils even now, would be able to rearm. From Maryland, Booth and his three companions would continue south, relying on the kindness of their fellow sympathizers for food and shelter while the Union pursued them. As news of their deeds spread, a chorus of joyful voices would ring from Texas to the Carolinas. The tide would turn. They would all be hailed as heroes, and John Wilkes Booth would be called "the Savior of the South."

Atzerodt protested, insisting that he'd agreed to a kidnapping, not a murder. Booth launched into a stirring speech. There is no record of what he said—only that it was soaring and thoroughly convincing. Probably it contained references to Shakespeare. Certainly it had been rehearsed for this very occasion. Whatever Booth's words, they worked. Atzerodt reluctantly agreed to go forward. But what the apprehensive German didn't know—what none of the living conspirators would ever know, even as they climbed the thirteen steps to their deaths—was the truth behind the young actor's hatred of Lincoln.

On the surface, it made no sense. John Wilkes Booth had been called the "handsomest man in America." Audiences packed theaters all over the country to watch him perform. Women trampled one another to catch a glimpse of him. He'd been born into the nation's preeminent acting family, and made his professional debut as a teenager.

Unlike his famous older brothers Edwin and Junius, who were actors in the classic sense, John was raw and instinctive—leaping about the stage, screaming at the top of his lungs. "Every word, no matter how innocuous, seems spoken in anger," wrote a reviewer for the *Brooklyn Daily Eagle*, "and yet one cannot help but be captivated by it. There is an almost ethereal quality to the gentleman."

One night, following a performance of *Macbeth* at the Richmond Theater, Booth reportedly took six young ladies back to his boardinghouse and wasn't seen for three days. He was rich. He was adored. He was doing what he loved. John Wilkes Booth should have been the happiest man alive.

But he wasn't alive.

> Life's but a walking shadow, a poor player
> That struts and frets his hour upon the stage,
> And then is heard no more. It is a tale
> Told by an idiot, full of sound and fury,
> Signifying nothing.*

When he was thirteen years old, Johnny Booth paid an old gypsy woman to read his palm. He'd always been obsessed with fate, particularly his own—due in large part to a story often told by his eccentric mother. "On the night you were born," she'd say, "I asked God for a sign of what awaited my newborn son. And God saw fit to answer." For the rest of her life, Mary Ann Booth would swear that flames had suddenly leapt from the hearth of their fireplace and formed the word "country."

**Macbeth, Act V, Scene 5.

Johnny spent countless hours pondering the meaning of it. He knew that something special awaited him. He could feel it.

"Oh...a bad hand," the gypsy said at once, recoiling slightly. "Sorrow and trouble...sorrow and trouble, wherever I look." Booth had come expecting a glimpse of his future greatness. What he got were forecasts of doom. "You'll die young," said the gypsy, "but not before amassing a thundering crowd of enemies." Booth protested. She was wrong! She had to be wrong! The gypsy shook her head. Nothing could prevent it....

John Wilkes Booth would "make a bad end."

Seven years later, the first part of her grim fortune came true.

———————

Of the six young women Booth took back to his Richmond boardinghouse that night, only one remained by morning. He'd sent the others scurrying out the door before sunrise, their hair a mess, clothing bundled in their arms. After the fog of whiskey had lifted, he'd found them to be nothing more than the same silly, chatty, opportunistic girls who greeted him at every stage door in every city. He had no use for them beyond what had already transpired.

The girl in bed with him, however, was something entirely different. She was a small, dark-haired, ivory-skinned beauty of twenty or so, but carried herself with the calm confidence of a much older woman. There was a slyness to her, and though she seldom spoke, when she did it was with humor and wisdom. They made love for hours at a time. No woman—not Mary Surratt or his countless stage door conquests—had ever made Booth feel like this. He was drawn to her in a way he'd only been drawn to the theater.

Every woman before her has been a promise unfulfilled.

In moments of rest, Booth filled the silences with stories of his youth: the word "country" in the fire…the gypsy…the inescapable feeling that he was destined for greatness—something more than fame or money could provide. The ivory-skinned girl placed her lips against his ear and told him of a way that he could achieve that greatness. Perhaps he believed her; perhaps he was merely humoring his young lover—but at some point during that second night, John Wilkes Booth willingly drank her blood.

For the next two days, he suffered through the worst, and last, sickness of his life. He drenched his sheets in sweat; suffered horrific visions; convulsed so violently that the legs of his bed clattered against the floor.

Three days after he'd last been seen in public, Booth awoke. He rose and stood in the center of the room—alone. The ivory-skinned girl was gone. He would never learn her name; never see her again. He didn't care. He'd never felt more alive than he did at this moment; never seen or heard with such clarity.

She spoke the truth.

Booth had craved immortality since he was a child. Now it was his. He'd always known that some special fate awaited him. Here it was. He would be the greatest actor of his generation…of every generation. His name would be renowned in ways that Edwin and Junius could only imagine. He would grace the theaters of the world; watch empires crumble to dust; commit every word of Shakespeare to memory.

He was the master of time and space. Booth couldn't help but smile as another thought crossed his mind. *The old gypsy was right.* He'd died young, just as she said he would. And now he would live forever.

I am a vampire, he thought. *God be praised.*

———————

Immortality, however, proved somewhat disappointing at first. Like so many vampires, Booth had been left to learn the hard lessons of death on his own. There was no mentor to explain the thousand whispers that now filled his head when he faced an audience. No shopkeeper to suggest the right pair of dark glasses, or the proper means of removing blood from the sleeve of an overcoat. When his first cravings came, crashing against his mind in waves, he'd wandered the dark streets of Richmond for hours, following endless wobbling drunks down endless winding alleys, never quite working up the nerve to strike.

When the cravings became so severe that he felt himself slipping into madness, Booth found his nerve—but not in Richmond. Twenty days after being made immortal, he mounted his horse after dark and set off for a plantation in nearby Charles City. A wealthy tobacco farmer named Harrison had been to see his *Hamlet* and invited the actor to dine the following week. Booth meant to take him up on that offer a bit earlier.

He tied his horse to a tree in an orchard about eighty yards from the slave quarters—comprised of ten uniformly built, tightly packed brick shelters. Their chimneys were smokeless. Their tiny windows dark. Booth settled on the building nearest him (merely a matter of convenience) and peered through one of its windows. No fire burned inside, and there was hardly any moon in the sky above—yet he saw everything as if it had been illuminated by the gas footlights that blinded him nightly.

A dozen Negroes of varying sex and age slept soundly inside, some on beds, others on woven floor mats. Nearest him, directly below the window, a little girl of seven or eight slept on her stomach in a tattered white nightgown.

Minutes later, Booth was in the orchard, sobbing, her lifeless body in his arms, her blood running down his fangs and chin. He dropped to his knees and held her tightly against his chest.

He was the devil.

Booth felt his fangs puncture the thick muscle of her throat. He began to drink again.

V

After a full day of respectful rejections, the Lincolns finally had a couple willing to accompany them to the theater. Major Henry Rathbone and his fiancé, Clara Harris, daughter of New York senator Ira Harris, rode backward facing Abe and Mary as the president's carriage cut through a light mist. Mary could feel the cool air in her black silk dress and matching bonnet. Abe was perfectly warm in his black wool overcoat and white gloves. The party pulled up to Ford's Theater just before eight-thirty, by which time the play, *Our American Cousin*, was already underway. Abe, who detested being late, gave his apologies to the doorman and greeted his relief body-guard, John F. Parker.

Parker, a Washington policeman, had shown up for his

shift at the White House three hours late with no explanation. William H. Crook, Lincoln's daytime bodyguard, angrily sent him ahead to Ford's and told him to wait for the president's party. In time, the nation would learn that Parker was a notorious drinker who'd been disciplined for falling asleep on duty more than once.

Tonight, he was solely responsible for protecting Abraham Lincoln's life.

The Lincolns and their guests were led up a narrow staircase to the double box, where four seats had been arranged. Farthest left was a black walnut rocking chair for the president. Mary was seated beside him, followed by Clara and the major at the far end. No sooner had the four of them taken their seats than the play was halted and the president's arrival announced. Abe stood, somewhat embarrassed, as the orchestra played "Hail to the Chief," and the audience of more than a thousand rose to its feet in polite applause. As the play resumed, John Parker took his seat outside the door. Here, he'd be able to see anyone approaching the president's seats.

Backstage, no one paid much attention to John Wilkes Booth when he arrived an hour after Abe's party. He was a regular at Ford's, free to come and go as he pleased, and he often took in performances from the wings. But Booth had no interest in the play tonight; no time for small talk with impressionable young actresses. Using his knowledge of the theater's layout, he wound his way through a labyrinth of hallways and crawl spaces until he reached the staircase that led to the stage left boxes. Here, he was shocked to discover that there were no guards posted. Booth had expected at least one, and had planned on using his fame to gain access to the president. *A great actor paying his respects to a great man.* He was carrying a calling card in his coat pocket for this very purpose.

There was nothing but an empty chair.

―――――――

John Parker had grown frustrated by the fact that he couldn't see the stage. Incredibly, during the second act, he'd simply left his post to find another seat. By the beginning of Act III, Parker had left the theater altogether, going for a drink at the Star Saloon next door. Now, all that stood between Booth and Lincoln was a narrow staircase.

Upstairs, Mary Lincoln held her husband's hand. She stole a glance at Clara Harris, whose hands were resting modestly in her lap, and whispered in Abe's ear, "What will Ms. Harris think of my hanging on to you so?"

"She won't think anything of it."

Most historians agree that these are Abraham Lincoln's last words.

Booth quietly climbed the staircase and stood outside the box, waiting for the one line that he knew would get a huge laugh.

A laugh big enough to muffle the sound of a pistol.

Onstage, Harry Hawk stood alone, delivering a spirited soliloquy to the crowd. Booth held steady, waiting, as Hawk's voice boomed through the theater. He crept forward, leveled the pistol at the back of Lincoln's head, and carefully . . . carefully pulled the hammer back. If Abe had been ten years younger, he might have heard the *click*— might've reacted with the speed and strength that had saved his life so many times before. But he was old. Tired. All he felt was Mary's hand upon his. All he heard was Harry Hawk's booming voice: "Don't know the manners of good society, eh? Well, I guess I know enough to turn you inside out, old gal; you sockdologizing old man-trap!"

The audience roared. Booth fired.

The ball entered Abe's skull, and he slumped forward in his rocking chair, unconscious. Mary's screams joined the deafening laughter as Booth produced a hunting knife and turned to his next target—but instead of General Grant, he was met by the young Major Rathbone, who leapt from his chair and came at him. Booth plunged the knife into Rathbone's bicep and made for the railing. Clara's screams joined Mary's as laughter gave way to murmuring and people turned their heads toward the commotion. Rathbone grabbed Booth's coat with his good arm, but couldn't hold on. Booth leapt over the railing. But as he did, one of his riding spurs snagged the Treasury flag that Edmund Spangler had put up earlier in the day. Booth fell awkwardly to the stage, breaking his left leg, twisting it grotesquely at the knee.

Fig. 6e. - A black-eyed John Wilkes Booth fires the fatal shot as Major Henry Rathbone reacts.

Though injured, the consummate actor couldn't resist a flourish. He pulled himself to his feet, faced the audience, which had begun to panic, and yelled, "Sic semper tyrannis!" The state motto of Virginia. *Thus always to tyrants!* With that, John Wilkes Booth left the stage for the last time.

Like the speech to his conspirators, it was a moment he'd probably rehearsed.

VI

At roughly the same moment, Lewis Powell ran out of Secretary Seward's front door, screaming, "I'm mad! I'm mad!" Although he didn't know it yet, his mission had been a failure.

Herold, the nervous pharmacist, had done his part. He'd led Powell to Seward's mansion. Now he watched from a safe distance as Powell knocked on the front door just after ten o'clock. When a butler answered, Powell delivered his own carefully rehearsed line: "Good evening. I have medicine for the secretary. I alone am to administer it." Moments later, he was on the second floor, only a few yards from where his ailing target slept. But before he could slip into Seward's room alone, the secretary's son Frederick approached.

"What cause have you to see my father?"

Powell repeated his carefully rehearsed line, word for word. But the younger Seward wasn't convinced. Something was amiss. He told Powell that his father was asleep, and to call again in the morning.

Lewis Powell had no choice. He drew his revolver, pointed it at Frederick's head, and squeezed the trigger. Nothing. The gun had misfired.

I'm mad! I'm mad!

There was no time. Powell bashed Frederick's skull with the gun instead, sending him to the floor, blood pouring from his nose and ears. Powell then ran into his target's room, where he encountered a screaming Fanny Seward, the secretary's daughter. Ignoring her for the moment, he drew his knife and brought it down on the old man's face and neck, again and again and again, until he rolled onto the floor—dead.

Or so Powell thought. Seward was wearing a metal neck brace as a result of his carriage accident. Despite deep gashes to his face, the blade failed to find his jugular.

Powell stabbed Fanny Seward in the hands and arms as he ran past her and into the hallway. Continuing down the staircase, another of the secretary's children, Augustus, and an overnight guest, Sergeant Robinson, tried to stop him. Both were stabbed for their efforts, as was Emerick Hansell, a telegram messenger who'd had the misfortune to arrive at the front door just as Powell was running out of it.

Incredibly, none of the victims died.

Outside, the nervous pharmacist was nowhere to be found. The sound of Fanny Seward's screams had frightened him off. Powell, who knew little of the area, was left to fend for himself. He threw the bloody knife into a nearby gutter, untied his horse, and galloped off into the night.

As disastrous as the attack on Seward had been, Powell could have consoled himself in the knowledge that he'd fared far better than George Atzerodt. The reluctant German had lost his nerve, gotten drunk in the bar at the vice president's boardinghouse, and then wandered the streets of Washington until sunrise.

VII

Charles Leale, twenty-three, helped his fellow soldiers lower the president onto a bed on the first floor of Petersen's Boarding House—directly across the street from Ford's Theater. They were forced to lay him diagonally, as he was too tall to lie straight. Leale, an army surgeon who'd been in the audience, had been the first to attend to the president. He'd shoved his way through the crowd, up the narrow stairs, and into the box, where he'd found Lincoln slumped over in his chair. Upon lowering the president and examining him, he'd detected no pulse; no breath. Moving quickly, the young doctor had felt around the back of Lincoln's head until he'd found a hole just behind the left ear. After a blood clot was removed from the wound, Lincoln had begun to breathe again.

Leale was young, but he wasn't naive. He'd seen enough of these injuries in the field to know the outcome. Minutes after the president had been shot, he'd delivered his bleak, accurate medical opinion: "His wound is mortal. It is impossible for him to recover."

Mary couldn't bear to be in the room with her dying husband. She remained in the parlor of Petersen's Boarding House all night, weeping. Robert and Tad arrived sometime after midnight and took their place at Abe's bedside, just as Abe had knelt at his dying mother's side almost fifty years earlier. They were joined by Gideon Welles, Edwin Stanton, and an endless parade of Washington's best doctors, all of whom came to offer their advice. But nothing could be done. Dr. Robert King Stone, the Lincolns' family physician, examined the president during the night and concluded that his case was "hopeless."

It was only a matter of time.

By sunrise, a large crowd had gathered outside. The president's breathing had become increasingly faint through the night, his heartbeat erratic. He was cool to the touch. Many of the doctors remarked that a wound of this type would have killed most men in two hours; maybe less. Abe had lasted nine. But then, Abe Lincoln had always been different. Abe Lincoln had always lived.

> The infant a mother attended and loved;
> The mother that infant's affection who proved;
> The husband that mother and infant who blessed,
> Each, all, are away to their dwellings of rest.*

Abraham Lincoln died at 7:22 in the morning, on the Ides of April 1865.

The men at his bedside lowered their heads in prayer. When they were finished, Edwin Stanton declared, "Now he belongs to the ages." With that, he returned to his telegrams. John Wilkes Booth was on the run, and Stanton meant to catch him.

VIII

Booth and Herold had managed to elude the Union Army for eleven days, escaping first to Maryland, then to Virginia. They'd hidden in swamps for days on end; slept on

---

*From Abe's favorite poem by Scotsman William Knox.

beds of cold earth. Booth had expected to be embraced as a hero, the Savior of the South. Instead, he'd been cast out into the cold. "Ya gone too far," they'd said. "The Yanks'll burn every farm from Baltimore to Birmingham lookin' fer ya."

The second of the gypsy's predictions had come true. Booth had amassed a "thundering crowd of enemies."

On April 26th, Booth woke to shouting, and knew at once.

Goddamned double-crossing son of a bitch...

Richard Garrett had been one of the few Virginians who hadn't turned them away. He'd given them food to eat and a warm tobacco barn to sleep in. Judging by the Union soldiers outside, he'd sold them out for the reward money, too.

Herold was nowhere to be found. *The coward gave himself up.* It didn't matter. He would be faster on his own, anyway. Night had fallen, and the night belonged to Booth's kind. *Let them wait*, he thought. *Let them wait and see what I am.* His leg had long since healed, and even though he was weak with hunger, they would be no match for him. Not in the dark.

"Give yerself up, Booth! We ain't gonna warn ya again!"

Booth stayed put. True to their word, the Union soldiers issued no further warnings. They simply set fire to the barn. Boards were set alight; torches thrown onto the roof. The dry old barn was engulfed in a matter of seconds. The blinding flames made the barn's dark corners seem deeper. Booth put his dark glasses on as ancient beams began to creak overhead, and fingers of gray smoke crawled up the walls. He stood center stage and tugged on the bottom of his coat—an old actor's habit. He wanted to look his best for this. He wanted the Yankee devils to see exactly who it was before they ...

Someone is in here with me ... someone who means me harm....

Booth turned in circles, ready for an attack that might come from any direction, at any moment. His fangs descended; his pupils swelled until his eyes were nothing more than black marbles. He was ready for anything....

But there was nothing. Nothing but smoke, and flame, and shadow.

What sort of trickery is this? Why could I not sense him until ...

"Because you are weak ..."

Booth spun in the direction of the man's voice.

Henry Sturges stepped out of the darkest corner of the barn. "... and you think too much."

He means to destroy me....

Somehow, Booth understood everything. Perhaps this stranger wanted him to understand—forced him to understand.

"You would destroy me over a living man?" Booth backed up as Henry advanced.

"OVER A LIVING MAN?"

Henry said nothing. There was a time and a place for words. His fangs descended; his eyes turned.

These are the last seconds of my life.

Booth couldn't help but smile.

The old gypsy was right....

John Wilkes Booth was about to make a bad end.

Fourteen

———◆———

Home

I have a dream that one day this nation will rise
up and live out the true meaning of its creed: "We
hold these truths to be self-evident: that all men are
created equal."

> —*Dr. Martin Luther King Jr.*
> *August 28th, 1963*

I

Abraham Lincoln had a dream.

He watched his prey move among the men below;
watched how confidently it circled them. Choosing. Glaring at them like a god. Mocking them; reveling in their
helplessness. *But you*, he thought. *You're the helpless one
tonight.*

Just a moment now. Just another moment and it would
begin. A series of rehearsed movements. A performance
refined with each passing night. Perfected. Just a moment,
and then the force and commotion and speed. He would

stare into the blackness of its eyes and watch the life leave them forever. And then it would be over. For tonight.

He was twenty-five again, and strong. He was so strong. All of the sorrows in his life—all of the doubts and deaths and disappointments—all of them had been for this. They were the fires that burned in his chest. They were his strength. They were *her*. There was a prayer that came to mind in these moments. Before the screaming. Before the bargaining and the blood. He wasn't much for prayers, but he liked this one:

> If my enemies be quick, grant me speed. If they
> be strong, Lord, then grant me the strength to see
> them defeated. For mine has always been the side
> of righteousness. The side of justice. The side of
> light.

His ax blade had been sharpened and resharpened. *If I swung it hard enough, I could make the air bleed.* Over the years, the handle had been worn into the perfect companion for his massive hands. Each furrow a welcoming friend. It was hard to know where he ended and the ax began. Impossible to know how much . . .

Now.

He leapt from the barn roof and soared over his prey. The creature looked up. Its eyes went black from lid to lid. Its fangs descended, hollow and hungry. He swung the ax with all of that strength and felt the handle leave his hands, his body still high above the earth. As he fell, he caught one of their faces in the corner of his eye. The face of a helpless man, frightened and bewildered. Not yet aware that his life had just been saved. *I'm not doing this for you,* he thought. *I'm doing it for her.* He watched his old friend somersault through the air... *wood metal wood metal wood metal.* He *knew.* From the moment he let it go, he *knew* the blade would find its target. Knew the sound it would make when it broke through the skull of that false god, splitting its confident smile in two... tearing through its brain... denying it everlasting life. He knew because this was his purpose.

It had always been his purpose....

———————

Abe woke in his White House office.

He dressed and sat at a small desk by one of the windows overlooking the South Lawn. It was a perfect late August morning.

> It's good to be in Washington. It feels strange to write those words, but then—I suppose I've been swept up in the excitement of the day. It promises to be a historic one. I only pray that it's remembered for the right reasons, and not for the violence that some have predicted (and others hoped for). It's not yet eight o'clock, but I can already see the crowds marching across the Ellipse toward the Monument. How many will there be? Who will speak, and how will their speeches be received? We will know in a few short hours. I only wish they had chosen a different venue. I admit that it causes me no small discomfort to be near that thing. I was surprised, however, at what little discomfort I felt sleeping in my office. It is fitting, I suppose. For it was

here, in this very room, that I signed my name to the ancestor of this day. I must remember to send President Kennedy a note of thanks for having me as his guest.

II

On the morning of April 21st, 1865, Abraham Lincoln's funeral train left Washington and began the journey home to Springfield.

Thousands lined the tracks as the "Lincoln Special" pulled away from the Baltimore & Ohio Railroad Depot at five minutes past eight o'clock, its nine cars draped in black garlands, a framed portrait of the late president hanging over the steam engine's cowcatcher. Tearful men stood with their hats in their hands; ladies with their heads bowed. Soldiers, some of whom had left their beds at St. Elizabeths Hospital to see the train off, stood up arrow straight, saluting their fallen commander in chief.

Two of Abe's sons were aboard with him, Robert, now a twenty-one-year-old army captain, and Willie, whose coffin had been removed from its temporary crypt and placed beside his father's. Tad remained in Washington with Mary, who was too grief stricken to leave the White House. For thirteen days and nearly 1,700 miles, the train wound its way through the North, stopping in designated cities to lie in state. In Philadelphia, 300,000 people pushed and shoved to catch a glimpse of the slain president's body. In New York, 500,000 stood in line to lay eyes on Abe, and a six-year-old Theodore Roosevelt watched his funeral procession go by. In Chicago, hundreds of thousands gathered around an outdoor viewing stand engraved with the words "Faithful to Right—Martyr to Justice."

In all, more than twelve million people stood by the tracks to watch the funeral train pass, and more than a million waited in line to view the president's open casket.

On Thursday, May 4th, 1865, a sea of black umbrellas shielded thousands of mourners from the scorching sun as Abe's casket, sealed for all eternity, was carried into Oak Ridge Cemetery on a hearse pulled by six white horses.

As Bishop Matthew Simpson gave a stirring eulogy for the "Savior of the Union," one particularly ashen mourner looked on from behind a pair of dark glasses, a black parasol in his gloved hands. Though his eyes were incapable of tears, he felt the loss of Abraham Lincoln more deeply than any living person in Springfield that day.

Henry remained by the closed gates of the receiving vault (where Abe and Willie's caskets would remain until a permanent tomb could be built) long after the sun had set and the crowds dispersed, standing guard over his friend of forty years. Standing guard over the man who'd saved a nation from enslavement and driven darkness back into the shadows. He remained there most of the night, sometimes sitting in silent contemplation, sometimes reading the little slips of paper that people had left along with flowers and keepsakes at the foot of the iron bars. Henry found one of them particularly moving. It read simply:

"I am a foe to tyrants, and my country's friend."*

Julius Caesar, Act V, Scene 4.

In 1871, Tad Lincoln—then living with his mother in Chicago—was stricken with tuberculosis. He died on July 15th at the age of eighteen. His body was taken to Springfield and placed in his father's tomb beside brothers Willie and Eddy. Again, it was Robert who accompanied the funeral train, as Mary was too distraught to attend.

Of all Abe's children, only Robert survived to see the new century. He would marry and father three children of his own, and in later life, he would serve two presidents, James Garfield and Chester A. Arthur, as secretary of war. He died peacefully at his estate in Vermont in 1926, at the age of eighty-two.

Tad's death had been the final, irreparable blow to Mary Lincoln's mental health. In the years that followed, she became increasingly erratic, often swearing that she saw her late husband's face staring at her from the darkness on nighttime walks. She suffered from paranoia, insisting that strangers were trying to poison her or steal from her. She once had $56,000 worth of government bonds sewn into the linings of her petticoats for safekeeping. After Mary attempted suicide, Robert had no choice but to commit his mother to a psychiatric hospital. After her release, Mary moved back to Springfield, where she died in 1882, at the age of sixty-three. She was laid to rest beside the three young sons she'd wept for in life.

There would be several attempts to steal Abraham Lincoln's body following the Civil War—until, at Robert Lincoln's request, the casket was covered with cement in 1901, never to be seen again. None of the would-be grave robbers had had much success. In fact, none had even managed to pry the president's heavy casket lid open.

If they had, they would have been shocked by what they found.

III

On August 28th, 1963, Henry Sturges stood in front of the Lincoln Memorial, his clothing and hair in keeping with the times, a black umbrella protecting his skin and dark glasses covering his eyes. He was accompanied by an uncommonly tall friend, his eyes behind a pair of Ray-Bans; his shoulder-length brown hair beneath a floppy brimmed hat. A bushy beard obscured his angular face, the same one staring down at him from its marble throne (and causing him no shortage of discomfort). Both listened intently, proudly, as a young black preacher looked out on more than 250,000 faces.

"Five score years ago," the preacher began, "a great American, in whose symbolic shadow we stand, signed the Emancipation Proclamation. This momentous decree came as a great beacon light of hope to millions of Negro slaves who had been seared in the flames of withering injustice. It came as a joyous daybreak to end the long night of captivity. But one hundred years later, we must face the tragic fact that the Negro is still not free."

Abe and Henry had come to help finish the work begun a century before. They'd been there during Reconstruction, driving out the vampires who continued to terrorize emancipated slaves....

"I have a dream that one day on the red hills of Georgia,

the sons of former slaves and the sons of former slave owners will be able to sit down together at a table of brotherhood."

They'd been there in Mississippi, dragging white-hooded devils to their deaths by the light of burning crosses....

"Now is the time to make justice a reality for all of God's children."

And they'd been there in Europe, where millions gave their lives defeating the second vampire uprising between 1939 and 1945.

But there was still work to be done.

"Free at last! Free at last! Thank God Almighty, we are free at last!"

The crowd cheered wildly, and the preacher took his seat. It was a perfect late-summer day. A defining day in man's struggle for freedom. Not unlike the day Abraham Lincoln was laid to rest, ninety-eight years before.

The day Henry made a choice...

...that some men are just too interesting to die.

ACKNOWLEDGMENTS

Thanks go to Ben Greenberg, Jamie Raab, and all my new friends at Grand Central for being excited by the idea and seeing it through brilliantly; to Claudia Ballard for making it all happen, Alicia Gordon for making more things happen, and everyone at William Morris Endeavor; to the wonderfully terrifying Gregg Gellman; to the Internet (without which this book would not have been possible), particularly Google, Wikipedia, and the Lincoln Log—invaluable resources, all; to Starbucks—you complete me; to Stephanie Isaacson for her Photoshop genius; to David and everyone at MTV for bearing with me as I bit off more than I could chew; and to my fearless research assistant, Sam.

A special thanks to Erin and Josh for letting me sit out most of 2009.

And finally, to Abe—for living a life that hardly needed vampires to make it incredible—and to Henry Sturges—wherever you are . . . .

The three Wise Men have been
celebrated since they first appeared in
the New Testament. Countless works of
art have been made in their image.
But almost nothing is actually
known about them.

Now acclaimed author
Seth Grahame-Smith reenvisions
the legendary magi in a
thrilling new novel...

Please turn this page
for a sneak preview of

UNHOLY NIGHT

The magic of Old Testament times is coming to an end.

Great floods, mystical beasts, and parting seas have given way to the empires of man. Many believe that God has abandoned the world—most of which is ruled by Rome and its new emperor, Augustus Caesar.

One of many Roman provinces, Judea (in modern Israel), is ruled by a cruel puppet king named Herod the Great, who—although sickly and dying—fiercely clings to power through murder and intimidation. And he has reason to be paranoid, for the Old Prophesies tell of the imminent birth of a messiah—a *King of the Jews*—who will topple all the other kingdoms of the world...

1

Last Stand of the Antioch Ghost

"No king is saved by the size of his army; no warrior escapes by his great strength."

—*Psalm 33:16*

I

A herd of ibex grazed on a cliff high above the Judean Desert—each of their tiny, antelope-like bodies dwarfed by a pair of giant, curved horns. A welcome breeze blew across their backs as they searched for what little shrubbery there was here in the great big nothing, each of them pushing their hot, cracked noses across the hot, cracked earth, gnawing at whatever succulent bits of green had managed to push their way through.

One ibex grazed apart from the others, closer to the bone-shattering drop than even they dared go. It had been tempted by the sight of a few lonely blades of grass on the cliff's edge. Blades it now pulled at oh so carefully with its teeth. Its cloven hooves clacked against the loose rocks of its perch as it shifted its weight, sending the occasional pebble tumbling hundreds of feet into the valley below. Ten million years of geological aspirations undone in seconds.

Miles to the north of where it chewed this hard-earned cud, a carpenter was making his way toward Jerusalem in the blistering heat of midday—his head swimming through stories of plagues and floods to keep the thirst from driving him mad, his young, very pregnant wife asleep on the donkey behind him. And though the ibex would never know this—though its life, like the lives of all ibexes, would go completely unnoticed and unappreciated in the annals of history—it was about to become the sole living witness to a truly extraordinary sight.

Something's wrong . . .

Perhaps it was a glint in the corner of its eye, a tiny, almost imperceptible vibration beneath its hooves. Whatever the reason, the ibex was suddenly compelled to lift its head and take in the sight of the vast desert below. There, off in the distance, it spotted a small cloud of dust moving steadily across the twisted beiges and browns. This in and of itself was hardly unusual. Dust clouds sprung up all the time, dancing randomly across the desert like swirling spirits. But two things made this cloud unique: one, it was moving in a perfectly straight line, from right to left. Two, it was being followed by a second, much larger cloud.

At least it looked that way. The ibex had no idea if clouds of dust could, in fact, chase each other. It only knew that they were to be avoided if at all possible, since they were murder on the eyes. Still chewing, it turned back to see if the others had spotted it. They hadn't. They were all grazing away without a care in the world, noses to the ground. The ibex turned back and considered this strange phenomenon a moment longer. Then, convinced there was no danger to itself or the herd, it went back to its meal. The two clouds moving silently, steadily in the distance.

By the time it yanked another blade of grass out of the rock with its teeth, the ibex had forgotten they'd ever existed.

Balthazar couldn't see a damned thing.

He rode his camel across the desert valley, kicking its sides like mad, his eyes the only things visible through the shemagh he wore to fight off the sun and the odor of the beast beneath him. Two overstuffed saddlebags hung off either side of his animal, and a saber hung from his belt, swinging wildly as they galloped along, kicking up the desert behind them. Balthazar turned back to see how close his pursuers were, but all he saw was the Cloud. The same, massive, relentless cloud that had been chasing him since Tel Arad. The cloud that made it impossible to tell how many men were after him. Dozens? Hundreds? There was no way to know. It was, at present, a cloud of undetermined wrath.

From the direction of that cloud there came a faint whistling, almost like the movement of wind through a ravine. At first it was just a single note, its pitch bending steadily lower and growing louder with each second. This note was joined by another and another, until the air behind Balthazar's head was a chorus of faint whistles— each of them starting soprano and tilting tenor as they grew louder, closer. Just as Balthazar realized what they were, the arrows began to strike the earth behind him.

They're shooting from horseback, he thought.

None of the arrows had come close enough to cause

concern. Balthazar wasn't surprised. Any experienced archer knew that firing an arrow from a galloping horse was akin to saying a prayer with a bow. Even at twenty yards, you had little chance of hitting your target. From this distance, it was hopeless—a sign of either desperation or anger. Balthazar didn't think the Judeans were desperate. They were furious, and they were going to take that fury out on his skull if they caught up to him. After all, the untold legions in that cloud weren't just chasing the thief who'd made off with a fortune of stolen goods, and they weren't after the murderer who'd killed a handful of their comrades...

They were trying to catch "the Antioch Ghost."

It was a nickname born of the only two things the Romans knew about him: that he was Syrian by birth, in which case it was a good bet that he'd grown up in Antioch, and that he had a knack for slipping into the homes of the wealthy and making off with their riches without being seen or heard. Other than those scant facts and a rough physical description, the Romans had nothing—not his age, not even his real name. And while "the Antioch Ghost" wasn't particularly inspired as nicknames went, it wasn't all that bad, either. Balthazar had to admit, he enjoyed seeing it among the "known criminals" painted on the side of public buildings—always in red, always in Latin: *Reward! The Antioch Ghost—Enemy of Rome! Thief of the Eastern Empire!* Sure, he hadn't achieved the infamy of a Hannibal or a Spartacus, but he was something of a minor celebrity in his little corner of the world.

There was a second chorus of whistling, followed by a second strike of arrows behind him. Balthazar turned and watched the last of them fall. While still too far away to cause concern, this volley hadn't been quite as hopeless as the last. *They're getting closer*, he thought.

"Faster, stupid!" he yelled at the stubborn beast, kicking its sides with his heels.

If only he could get out of their sight for a minute or two, change direction. Even now, with an indeterminate number of Judean soldiers chasing him through the middle of nowhere, with only a tired, pungent camel and a dull sword to protect him, and even though his pursuers were only two minutes behind him at best, Balthazar still had a chance. He'd spent years memorizing a network of hidden caves to hide out in, shortcuts across barren lands, the best places to scrounge up food and water on the run. He'd trained himself how to survive. How to carry on in times when the whole world seemed hell-bent on snuffing him out. Times like now.

He sensed his camel slowing down and gave it another swift kick in its side.

C'mon...just a little longer...

The beast had struggled to keep pace with the weight of all that treasure on its back, and Balthazar had been forced to toss some of his heavier spoils overboard as they'd fled Tel Arad. The sight of all that wealth skipping across the sand had nearly made him sick to his stomach. The thought of some lucky shepherd stumbling upon his spoils made his jaw clench and his teeth grind. There was nothing more enraging, more unjust than denying a man the hard-earned fruits of his labor, especially when those fruits were made of solid gold. Balthazar had briefly considered cutting off one of his own limbs to shed an equal amount of weight. But the long-term prospects of a one-armed marauder were limited.

"Faster!" he cried again, as if this would spur on the camel any more than the thousand sharp kicks he'd delivered to its sides. It was still losing steam, and once again, Balthazar was forced to consider the unthinkable: jettisoning more of his hard-earned treasure.

He reached into one of the large saddlebags and fished around until his hands found something that felt heavy. He almost couldn't bear to look as he pulled it out into the sunlight. There, in his hand, was a solid silver drinking cup—nearly the size of a bowl. Intricately carved and adorned with precious stones. It was a stunning piece, made from the finest materials with the finest artistry. It was also incredibly heavy. Balthazar held the chalice out to his side. Then, with his eyes averted and his stomach churning, he let it slip from his fingers. He turned away to spare himself the sight of it rolling across the desert floor and gave the camel another swift kick in retaliation.

C'mon, stupid...just a little longer...

It *couldn't* be thirsty. A camel could drink forty gallons in one go, and its body could cling to that water for weeks. Its piss came out as a thick syrup of pure waste. Its shit was dry enough to use as firewood, for the love of God. No...it wasn't thirsty. Not a chance. Tired? Unlikely. Camels had been known to live fifty years or more. And while Balthazar had gotten only a brief look at the face of this particular beast in the process of stealing it from a *very* unhappy Bedouin, he guessed that it was no more than fifteen years old. Twenty, tops. Still in the prime of its wretched life.

Just a little longer, you son of a bitch...

No, this camel was just being stubborn. And stubbornness could be corrected with a firm kick or two. Balthazar reckoned the beast could flat-out gallop for another hour. Maybe two. And if that estimate held up—if this camel could be coaxed through its stubbornness—then he had a real shot at making Jerusalem. And if he made Jerusalem, he was home free. There, he'd be able to blend in with the masses that were no doubt choking the streets for the census. He'd be able to disappear. Trade his stolen goods for coins, clothes, food—certainly a new camel.

Balthazar may have been a thief, but he deplored risk. Risk got men killed. Risk was unnecessary. When a man was prepared, when he was in control, things usually went according to plan. But the minute he left something to chance? The minute he trusted in partners, or instinct, or luck? That's when everything went to hell. That's why he was being chased across the desert by a giant cloud atop a stinking, unmotivated beast. Because he'd taken a risk. Because he'd committed the unforgivable sin of trusting his instincts.

As much as it irked him, as much as it went against everything in his nature, Balthazar had to accept that the outcome of his current predicament was beyond his control. He could kick and curse all he wanted...

It was up to the camel now.

II

It had all seemed so perfect. All the enticements had been there: a loosely guarded stash of expensive items, a corrupt nobleman, a populace being taken advantage of by the Romans. A more direct route to Balthazar's heart couldn't have been charted by a mapmaker.

Location had been another enticement. The city of Tel Arad was more than fifty miles south of Jerusalem. And the farther you were from Jerusalem, the less likely you were to encounter troops, whether they were King Herod's Judean troops or Rome's elite soldiers. And while Tel Arad still paled in comparison to Judea's great city, it was home to a new, impressive temple of its own. To the noncriminal, that may have seemed like a trivial detail. But to Balthazar, it was everything. Temples meant travelers and money changers. They meant that a man with a strange appearance or accent was less likely to draw attention and that someone looking to trade stolen goods for gold and silver coins could do so with ease. Temples were a thief's best friend.

Tel Arad had been settled thousands of years earlier, destroyed and rebuilt more times than any of the locals cared to remember. And for thousands of years, it had never grown beyond the rank of "desolate village." But times had changed. Empires had sprung up on either side of the once-forgotten village and transformed it into a thriving center of trade. Suddenly Ted Arad was the central point between Roman goods heading east and Arabian goods heading west toward Israel, the Mediterranean, and, ultimately, Rome—and its status had been steadily upgraded to "small city."

The strongest sign of its growing importance had come only a year earlier, when Rome had decided to dispatch a governor—Decimus Petronius Verres—to look after the little city. Officially, Decimus was there to make sure Tel Arad adhered to the traditions and upheld the virtues of Roman life. Unofficially, and more importantly, he was there to put troublemakers to death and make sure the locals paid their taxes on time.

Decimus, for his part, had been crushed when he learned of the assignment. It had been presented as an "honor," of course. He'd been "handpicked by Augustus *himself* to represent the empire in the East." But Decimus knew what it really was: a castration. A punishment for taking sides against the emperor one too many times in the senate.

He'd privately sobbed when he'd heard the news. How could they do this to him? For one thing, the desert was no place for a Roman, especially one of his considerable weight and fair complexion. For another, he had been perfectly happy where he was: safely, quietly ensconced in the suburbs of Rome, surrounded by the trappings of reasonable, if not exorbitant wealth. He was in his fifties—far too old to be picking up his entire life and traipsing around in the heat. Rome was the center of the world. Home to all the entertainment and enticement a man could want. The desert, by contrast, was a death sentence. But the emperor had spoken. And castration or not, Decimus had no choice but to go.

Even the exiled members of Roman nobility weren't expected to travel without the comforts of home. Shortly after his arrival in Tel Arad, Decimus ordered a walled compound built to his exact specifications—a scaled-up, fortified replica of the villa he owned in Rome. The same painter was brought in to re-create his favorite frescos, the same artisans to lay the mosaics on his floors tile by tile. The same formal garden and fountains dominated the courtyard at its center. The same slaves had made the journey to serve Decimus by day and the same concubines to serve him by night.

The finished compound was an impressive sight. A gleaming symbol of Roman superiority hidden from the public behind ten-foot walls. It sat atop a hill overlooking the northwest quarter of the little city, looking down on the temple and the bazaar below, where, as Decimus said, "the *braying* of animals, *paying* of merchants, and *praying* of men join together in a relentless chorus that deprives me of even a moment's peace."

But it wasn't all bad in Tel Arad. It had taken some time, but Decimus had warmed to his new city. Not because of its cultural riches or natural beauty—it had neither. Not because of the local women—he'd imported his own. No, he'd taken a shine to his new home because it was, politely speaking, a garbage heap.

In Rome, there was always someone more powerful, someone who had to be placated or paid off. Things like treason and treachery bore very real, very severe consequences. Rome was a city of laws. But the desert was lawless. In Tel Arad, Decimus was the only one who had to be placated. His pocket was the only one that needed to be lined. *He* was the law. It was a role he'd never had the opportunity to play in Rome, and it was one he found himself relishing more by the day.

As the governor of this godforsaken little sandpit, he had the power—indeed, the responsibility—to make sure the Arabian goods on their way to the West were up to "Roman standards," a term that had a very loose and ever-changing definition but that could be more or less summed up as: "things Decimus didn't feel like keeping for himself."

He deputized a group of local men to serve as his "inspectors," then turned them loose on the bazaar, where they conducted so-called quality checks at will. These inspectors targeted everything from jewelry to pottery to fabric to food. And if an item appeared to be of "lesser quality" or was "suspected of being a forgery"? It was confiscated and brought back to the governor's compound for further inspection. There, Decimus had the final say on whether the item would be returned or whether it would be held indefinitely, in a room he'd specially built for the purpose. In the six months since the inspections had begun, not a single merchant could recall having an item returned. And if they complained? If they caused even the slightest trouble? Decimus made sure they never set foot in his bazaar again.

Now *he* was the one with the power to exile.

With that many stolen valuables stockpiled in one place, it hadn't been long before Balthazar had caught wind of it. The rumors had reached him through the usual channels, and they'd been conveyed with the usual hyperbolic flair:

"Never has there been such a thieving Roman! He sits atop a pile of riches that would make the gods envious!"

And while these rumors usually amounted to nothing, even the remote possibility of stealing a little stolen treasure, and embarrassing a Roman governor in the process, warranted a firsthand look. And so Balthazar had set out from Damascus, where he'd been chasing another rumor. The one he'd been chasing for years. *The only one that really matters.* He'd ridden south through Bosra, avoiding the roads as much as possible. And on the fifth night of his journey, he'd seen the torches of Tel Arad burning in the distance and the grand white walls of the governor's compound above them.

The next day, he'd asked around the bazaar, hoping to verify some of the stories that had reached him up north. To his surprise, not only did they check out, but also the value of the confiscated goods was far greater than he'd imagined. Gold chalices, silver bracelets, rare perfumes and spices—all of it taken by this "Decimus." All of it locked away behind his walls.

It seemed that this was one of those rare instances where the truth was even bigger than the legend.

Balthazar had his motive. Now all he needed was an opportunity. He surveyed the governor's compound from afar, taking note of how many guards there were, when and how they patrolled the grounds, what kind of weapons they carried. Although Tel Arad was a Roman province, and its locals paid Roman taxes, the Roman Army couldn't be bothered to come this far east—not to babysit a governor who'd fallen out of the emperor's favor, anyway. Decimus had been forced to settle for a handful of soldiers from the less-impressive Judean Army, on loan from Herod the Great, to guard his compound. The Judean troops may not have been as professional or well equipped as their Roman counterparts, but they were nothing to take lightly. Storming the compound alone was out of the question.

Balthazar needed a way in. A way through its defenses. Two days after arriving in Tel Arad, he found one.

Her name was Flavia.

———

At seventeen, she should have been in Rome, enjoying the trappings of wealth and youth in the world's great city, living it up with the other sons and daughters of the ruling class. Instead, her father had dragged her to the desert of the Eastern Empire and left her to wither in the heat. With nothing to do. No one to talk to but concubines and slaves.

Balthazar had watched her for three days. Every morning, she walked down the hill from her father's compound, accompanied by a pair of Judean soldiers. For the next few hours, she wandered up and down the network of crowded streets that made up the bazaar, buying everything from silks to harps to figs, either unaware or undeterred by the fact that *any* of these goods could be had for free back at her father's compound. Then, at midday, she climbed the hill and disappeared behind the compound's walls, not to be seen again until the following day.

When Balthazar finally made his move, he'd done so using the oldest, easiest trick in the book. So easy, that he was almost ashamed of himself.

"Excuse me," he said.

Flavia turned, as did the soldiers at her side. She was a curly haired blonde—a rarity in this part of the world—with a full figure, a pretty face, and a lightly freckled nose, also a rarity. Not his type, but not bad at all.

"I believe you dropped this."

He offered his closed hand, which was promptly grabbed by one of the bodyguards. Balthazar smiled and opened his fingers, revealing a beaded bracelet inside. The bracelet Flavia's mother had given to her before she died.

The bracelet that Balthazar had stolen off of her wrist moments before.

Flavia studied it in disbelief. *They always do.* She wondered how on earth she could've dropped something so dear to her. Shooing her guards aside, she thanked Balthazar profusely and introduced herself with an extended hand. "Flavia," she said.

"Sargon," Balthazar replied, taking it.

"Sargon...would you care to join me for a walk around the bazaar?"

Now I hesitate...my face flushed with modesty. Yes, I'll join you for a walk around the bazaar. But I'm going to make you believe it was the furthest thing from my mind...

"Come," she said, sensing his hesitation. "Let me buy you something. A reward for your good deed."

"Oh, well...I don't know..."

Of course I do. But now I hesitate some more. Not too long—not long enough for you to lose interest. Just long enough for you to believe I'd say no. And then, the instant I see that belief in your eyes, I answer—

"I guess I can, but...your company is the only reward I need."

And you silently swoon...as I prepare to win you over with a lifetime's worth of lies.

Flavia and "Sargon" walked for hours, telling each other everything. Two lonely spirits who'd finally— *miraculously*—found kinship in this faraway land. And though her bodyguards eyed this Sargon with suspicion, though they would've liked to rough him up and warn him off, they knew better than to cross the only daughter of Decimus Petronius Verres.

Three nights and three trips around the bazaar later, Flavia snuck Balthazar into the compound and into her bedchamber...just as he'd known she would.

———

The next two weeks had been fun. More importantly, they'd been fruitful.

Each night as Flavia slept, Balthazar rose silently from her bed and went to work—slowly, methodically sneaking his way through the slumbering compound. Mapping it in his mind until he knew its every corner by heart. Until he knew the sleeping habits of every slave and the position of every guard. Until he knew how to walk from one side to the other without setting foot in the glow of the torches. And most of all, until he had examined every confiscated item in the governor's fabled storeroom, which he'd found on the first night, and which, like everything in Tel Arad, had exceeded his expectations.

And on the night that Balthazar felt he could know no more, he'd filled two large saddlebags—the most he could reasonably carry and still move quickly if he had to—with predetermined items chosen for their value-to-weight ratios. Bags stuffed, he'd snuck back along his carefully rehearsed route toward the compound's rear gate. The one that was always unmanned for a ten-minute window at this time of night, thanks to a guard with a *phenomenally* regular constitution.

He crept along in the dark, through the garden—*twenty-seven steps*—past the fountain—*another ten but veering slightly left*—then a sharp right turn at the sundial. After that, it was just thirty steps in a straight line to the gate. *Thirty steps to free—*

"Sargon?"

Balthazar nearly let out a yelp as he spun in the direction of the voice. At first, he thought he'd come face-to-face with a ghost. A translucent white being seemed to float toward him out of the darkness, barely perceivable in the light of the moon. He stood, frozen, as it moved closer...until Balthazar saw what it *really* was: a white sleeping gown, fluttering in the warm night air.

"Flavia...," he whispered.

"You're...you're a thief," she said.

What gave you that idea? Is it the two huge bags of stolen treasure I'm carrying out here in the middle of the night?

"No—"

"You used me."

Yes, I used you, and I'd use you again. And who are you to feel used, anyway? You're a Roman. *All your kind does is use. All you do is rape, and burn, and steal, and murder.*

"No," said Balthazar. "Flavia, listen to m—"

"Shut up!"

All she had to do was scream and the guards would come running. And when that happened, the exciting trouble currently making Balthazar's heart pound against the back of his ribs would become real trouble—*blood trouble*—in a hurry.

On the other hand, she could just as easily let him slip away into the night. No one would ever suspect her unwitting part in the robbery. Her chastity would never be called into question, and Balthazar would be halfway to anywhere by morning, with a promise to return and "take you away, Flavia—when the time is right, take you away from all of this so we can be together." A promise he would have no intention of keeping.

"Flavia," he said. "Listen to me, okay? Yes...yes, I was taking these. Taking them from your father's storeroom. But you have to believe me—I have good reason to take them! Your father stole these things from the people of Tel Arad! Poor people! Honest men! I couldn't stand by and watch them suffer. The truth is, I was stealing them, yes. Stealing them from the man who stole them first. Stealing them back so that I could return them to their rightful owners! Aren't you always talking about how cruel and selfish your father is? Well *here*, Flavia! Here's the proof!"

I'm getting through to her. Now make it personal...turn her mind away from the theft.

"And...and yes," he continued, "I know I should have told you first. But I didn't want to get you involved. What if something had gone wrong? What if you'd gotten in trouble? I wouldn't have been able to live with myself, Flavia. You're too good for this."

"I...I don't know..."

Yes, you do.

"Flavia, I swear on our love...on my *soul*—every-thing I say is true."

She stood there for a moment, conflicted and confused. A victim of youth and inexperience and a deep desire—a *need*—to believe that everything he was saying was, in fact, true.

"Please, Flavia, there isn't much time..."

I could always give her a knock on the head. If it came down to it, just a little knock on the head. Not enough to really hurt her, but enough to let me get the hell out of here.

But Balthazar didn't think that would be necessary. His instincts were beginning to tell him this was going to be okay—and he decided to trust them.

She's not going to scream. She hates her father. Yes, she hates her father, hates the fact that he brought her here. Besides…we've shared everything. Our deepest secrets. Our deepest love. And yes, that's all bullshit— but not to her. There's no way she'd give me up. She loves me. No…I'm a man with a knack for knowing things, and I know she's not going to scream. I've never been more certain of anything in my life.

She screamed.

III

It was clear he wasn't going to make Jerusalem. The camel had been gradually slowing down over the past hour. And as much as Balthazar kicked and cursed, it wouldn't pick up the pace. This wasn't stubbornness…he'd stolen a dud.

Balthazar knew of a good-sized village just north of Jerusalem—Bethel, if he remembered correctly. Or Beit El. Or whatever the hell they called it. *The one that sounds like "Bethlehem" but isn't.* It didn't matter. He knew it was there, some eight miles ahead, and it would have to do. With his camel fading fast, he pointed its nose in the village's direction. There was still a chance. He could still get away, as long as the beast held up.

What's that story the Jews tell? The one about the menorah that had enough oil for only one night but burned for eight? That's my camel…only enough fuel left for one mile. If it lasts eight, it'll be a miracle.

Miracle or not, the camel made it, and Balthazar gal-loped into Bethel (he'd been right the first time) only a minute or so ahead of the untold menace behind him. It was one of the nicer satellite villages that orbited Jeru-salem. A small village of less than 2,000 people where many Jewish noblemen chose to escape the noise and bustle of the city with their families. There were no inns to accommodate travelers, no massive temple spewing sacrificial smoke or bazaar spewing noise and fragrances. And while the census was currently packing the streets of Jerusalem only eight miles to the south, you'd hardly know there *was* a census looking at Bethel. Fewer than ten people took note of him as he galloped into the village's small central square.

Balthazar brought the camel to a stop, which it was all too happy to do, and leapt to the ground. He pulled the half-empty saddlebags off its back, threw both of them over his left shoulder, and gave the camel a firm smack on its hindquarters. He couldn't have it standing around. God knows how many soldiers were about to come riding into the village with orders to find and kill him at all costs. If they saw the camel, they'd have a pretty good idea where to start looking.

"Go! Get outta here!"

It didn't budge. He smacked it again.

"GO!"

It groaned deeply, knelt forward on its spindly legs, then fell over on its side with a ground-shaking thud—all 1,200 pounds of it.

Dead.

Balthazar took a moment to consider this. In retrospect, maybe he *had* ridden it a bit too hard. And now that he got a better look, it wasn't nearly as young as he'd thought. Not even close to fifteen or twenty. In fact, it was one of the oldest camels he'd ever seen. Come to think of it…it *was* a miracle they'd made it this far.

Balthazar didn't know what to say. Partly because he

was pressed for time, but mostly because sincerity wasn't his strong suit, he settled on, "Sorry."

Then, the grieving period over, he ran like hell.

He knew the villagers would keep him safe. They hated the Romans just as much as he did. *Okay, so these aren't actual Roman troops chasing me—they're Judeans. But really, when you get right down to it, is there a difference? They all take their orders from Rome, just like Herod the Great, that lying, festering, murderous puppet.* If there was one thing the Jews hated more than Augustus Caesar, it was the client king he'd sent to rule Israel. And while Balthazar wasn't a Jew per se, he was certainly no friend of Herod. That had to count for something, right? The enemy of my enemy?

He was the Antioch Ghost, and people loved a celebrity. Even a minor one.

No, the villagers would take pity on him. They would keep him safe and hidden when the army came kicking down their doors any minute now. And if pity wasn't enough, then bribing them with a share of his remaining treasure would make up the difference.

Balthazar ran across the square, his bags half full of twice-stolen gold and silver, frankincense and silk, his face still covered by the shemagh. He was headed for the largest building in sight—the only one with a second story and one of the few made from brick. The building had an arched roof and small, glass-paned windows along its eastern and western faces, an extravagance rarely seen outside of Rome. And though Balthazar couldn't see the source, a column of white smoke rose from behind the building. There wasn't much strategy behind his choosing it. A bigger building offered more hiding places. And more hiding places meant a greater chance of survival.

But as soon as he crossed the threshold, Balthazar knew he was a dead man.

He *had* to be dead…for this was surely heaven. There were wet, naked women everywhere. Beautiful. Bare. Steam rising off of their glistening bodies, the vapors glowing in the rays of sunlight that streamed through the glass above.

A bathhouse.

An arched ceiling peaked twenty feet overhead, its smooth surface painted to resemble olive trees reaching toward a cloudy sky. The bath itself, which took up most of the room, was lined with mosaic tiles. Mosaic tiles and the naked bodies of fifteen women. Women who were currently staring at the dusty man with a covered face and large bags over his shoulder. The man who had no business being in the women's bath.

This was no Flavia situation. There was no question in Balthazar's mind that *these* women were about to start screaming unless he acted quickly. Shaking himself back into focus, he brought a finger to his lips—*shhhh*—and in as nonthreatening a voice as he could manage, said, "A thousand pardons…"

He pulled the shemagh down, revealing his face—a handsome mix of sunburn and stubble, a prominent scar on his right cheek in the shape of an *X*. He gave them a smile. Charming, reassuring. Even a bit dashing, he suspected. It was a smile he'd spent hours practicing in the reflective waters of the Orontes River, and it was, if he didn't mind saying so, one of his stronger assets.

"I," he continued, "am the Antioch Ghost."

Was that the twinkle of recognition in some of their eyes?

"I'm just looking for a place to hide from Herod's men. Once they're gone, I'll be on my way without another word. You have nothing to fear, my sisters—I promise you."

They didn't scream.

People love a celebrity.

Short of his remaining treasure, Balthazar would've given anything in the world to stay and soak in this sight a little longer, but he could hear the rumble of horses' hooves growing near outside. *Time to disappear.* Certain that he and the women had reached an understanding, he proceeded as rapidly and respectfully as possible across the room, toward a row of hanging women's robes on the opposite wall. Enough of them to hide a man and a pair of saddlebags behind, no problem.

It was perfect. The soldiers wouldn't dare intrude on the privacy of bathing women. Nor would the women likely run into the streets and tattle without their clothes. Balthazar could hear the muffled sounds of orders being shouted outside, the clanging of swords and armor as men fanned out. Seconds later, three Judean soldiers entered. Balthazar watched as the men had the same sequence of reactions he'd had: shock, followed immediately by embarrassment, followed immediately by enticement.

One of the soldiers regained his composure enough to speak: "Pardon us . . ."

Go ahead, you dog. Go ahead and ask them if they've seen a man come through here. My sisters won't say a word. If anything, they'll tell you to go to hell.

"Have you seen—"

Balthazar's heart sank as every last woman pointed toward his hiding place in unison.

They didn't even let him finish the question…

So here it was. After a day in the desert, a dead camel, and a fortune in abandoned spoils, it would come to this.

Balthazar was an exceptional thief. An excellent aggravator and proven survivor. But what he excelled at, what he was truly gifted at, was taking human lives with his sword. This wasn't a point of pride. *Well, maybe just a little.* But in general, he measured success in treasure, not blood. "Success," he was fond of saying, "is stealing a fortune without drawing your sword. Failure is a pile of bodies and no profit."

The three soldiers drew their swords and started across the room, toward the row of hanging robes the women had pointed to.

None of them had more than a few seconds to live.

———

Peter could almost taste his victory. As a captain in Herod's army, there were few priorities higher than catching the Antioch Ghost. And now it seemed he was within moments of doing just that. Such an honor would mean a promotion, of course. Money. Land. Maybe even a slave to farm it for him. Best of all, it would mean a ticket out of Tel Arad and an end to dealing with that fat, corrupt Roman, Decimus Petronius Verres.

His men were kicking in every door, searching every house in the area. The Ghost couldn't have gone far. They'd reached the square less than a minute after he'd reached it, and he'd stupidly left a dead camel as a starting point for their search. The fact that he'd taken the time to kill it for no reason showed just how vile their fugitive really was.

Of course, some of his men doubted that their target really *was* the Antioch Ghost. But Peter knew. He'd been around long enough to recognize his methods. His choice of prey. Even before Flavia had described the man she'd seen robbing her father's compound—*tall and olive-skinned, with a strong build, dark hair to his shoulders, and an X-shaped scar across his right cheek*—he'd known. He also knew enough to suspect that she'd left out the part about inviting him into her bed, but that wasn't important. So when reports of a similar-looking man stealing a Bedouin's camel came in, Peter had gathered as many soldiers as he could and given chase across the Judean Desert—choking on dust and praying that the Ghost didn't beat him to Jerusalem, where he would've disappeared in seconds.

Captain Peter had asked God for a miracle, and God had answered. Here he was in Bethel. The last place he'd expected to be when he'd woken up this morning. The place he would always remember as the home of his great victory... assuming God would help him just a little more. Once again, Peter appealed to the Lord....

Give me a sign, Heavenly Father. Help me bring this murderous thief to justice. Help me to protect the children of Israel and uphold your law, O God.

Of course, he left out the part about being rewarded with money and land and slaves, but that wasn't important. Once again, God delivered. For no sooner had Peter finished his prayer than a sound reached his ears. A beautiful sound that meant glory was at hand:

Muffled screams coming from the bathhouse.

The head landed in the water, its eyes still blinking as it sank to the bottom, and the women finally released their pent-up screams. They climbed over each other, trying to get out of the bath as a dark red cloud spread through it.

Balthazar had waited until the advancing soldiers were within arm's length before jumping out from behind the robes and swinging at the closest man. It'd been one of those lucky swings—one in a hundred, really—where the blade had hit the neck *just* right, between the vertebrae, and gone clean through. Before the first soldier's head had even splashed down, Balthazar had kicked the second in the chest, knocking him onto his back. Then, just as the first screams began to echo through the room, he'd run the third soldier through the belly and out the back. He'd held the soldier—who wasn't much more than a boy—up with his blade, watching his face drain from pink to ash white, then yanked it out, spilling his blood and entrails onto the tiled floor.

By this point, the second soldier had managed to get back to his feet. But it was only a brief stay. Balthazar swung again and cut his throat. The soldier dropped his sword and clutched at the wound—the blood pouring through his fingers in sheets. His face turned that same shade of white, wore that same mask of fear as he came to that same old, dreadful realization. The one Balthazar had seen so many other men come to: *This can't be happening. This can't be the day I die.* And then it was done. The soldier fell face-first into the bath, his blood mixing with the other's. Naturally, this only served to elicit more screams from the already-screaming women.

Those screams will bring more soldiers any second now. Time to go.

He stood for a moment, mourning the days and weeks he'd spent working to fill those saddlebags. Mourning the lost fruits of his labor. Then, another brief grieving period over, he ran like hell again.

Failure is a pile of bodies and no profit…and this is shaping up to be a dismal failure.

Balthazar ran out the rear of the building and into the small, dirt-lined courtyard, enclosed by a six-foot wall and a wooden gate that led into the street. It was empty, save for a massive brick furnace that abutted the bathhouse. This furnace, Balthazar knew at once, was the source of the white smoke he'd seen earlier. A male slave stood beside the furnace's open iron door, stoking the raging fire inside. Its hot air channeled into a system of ducts under the bathhouse floor, keeping the water nice and warm for the nude elite. Even where Balthazar stood, ten feet away from the flames, the heat was almost too much to bear, and the noise of crackling wood and rushing air was almost deafening. As such, the slave had been oblivious to the screams coming from the bathhouse and the shouts of Judean soldiers swarming outside. But now, as he looked up from his work and found himself face-to-face with a blood-spattered, sword-wielding Syrian, he abandoned his post and ran for his life—out the open wooden gates and into the streets. Balthazar was about to do the same thing when a disembodied voice cried, "Stop where you are!"

He turned and saw a lone, boyish Judean soldier standing in the bathhouse's rear doorway, his sword trembling in his hands.

"OVER HERE!" he shouted to his comrades. "OVER HERE! I'VE FOUND HIM!"

Balthazar wasn't about to be held prisoner by a lone soldier with a trembling sword. And he certainly wasn't going to wait around for others to arrive. He started toward the wooden gate.

"Stop!"

The soldier lifted his sword and held it out in front of his body, exactly as he'd been trained to hold it. He charged at Balthazar, exactly as he'd been trained to charge. But as he prepared to run his enemy through, just as he'd been trained to do, the soldier experienced something he was entirely unequipped and unprepared to handle: Balthazar rolled onto his back and used his legs to launch him into the air—

—and into the open furnace.

The soldier heard the clang of the iron door slam behind him. He heard the latch close. He tried to stand, but there wasn't enough room to do more than crouch. Instinct grabbed a hold of him, and he tried to push the flames away with his hands, but they were already burning. He could see his flesh blistering and blackening, sliding off of his bones like wax down the side of a candle. He could feel his clothes burning against his body, becoming one with his skin, his hair melting against his scalp.

Balthazar could hear his screams through the iron door. He closed his eyes and turned away as the pounding of fists rattled it from the other side. When he opened them, there were ten soldiers standing in front of him.

"Drop your sword!" one of them yelled.

Faced with the idea of taking them all on, Balthazar placed the sword in his mouth—its blade still dripping with blood—turned back, and climbed the brick wall of the bathhouse. He could always fight his way across the rooftops, jumping from building to building until he found a horse, or a camel, or anything better than fighting ten men at once.

But when he pulled himself onto the arched roof and got to his feet, he felt the hope run out of his body like blood from a severed head. There were nearly a hundred men in the square below, plus the corpse of his miraculous camel. The Cloud of Undetermined Wrath had become a crowd of *very* determined soldiers, and Balthazar had to face the fact that he was completely, hopelessly surrounded.

His options were thus: He could fight to the death and take as many of these emperor-worshipping bastards with him. Result? One hundred percent chance of death. Or, he could surrender and be all but certainly executed. Result? Ninety-nine percent chance of death.

It was a no-brainer.

———————

Balthazar's wrists had been bound firmly behind his back, his clothes meticulously searched for contraband. With a soldier holding his arms on either side, he was marched across the square to where Peter waited with a deeply satisfied smirk on his face. The victorious captain hesitated a moment, taking it all in. Relishing it. He was face-to-face with the end to all his troubles.

"The Antioch Ghost," he said at last. "Scourge of Rome."

"You forgot 'plunderer of the Eastern Empire,'" said Balthazar.

Here it comes . . .

Sure enough, Balthazar was rewarded with a jaw-rattling punch for daring to speak. But snide remarks were just about all he had left in his arsenal. For the first time he could remember, Balthazar couldn't see a way out. There was no hidden weapon to pull at the last second. No well-timed distraction on the way. His fate was completely out of his hands now. He'd risked everything on a 1 percent chance of survival.

"On your knees," said Peter, drawing his sword.

Oh well… it was worth a try.

Balthazar didn't budge, so the soldiers helped him, pushing down on his shoulders and making him kneel in the dirt. He braced himself, wondering if he would feel his spine break or feel the blade tear through his neck and throat. He wondered if he would still be able to see as his head fell to the ground and rolled across the sand. *What a strange sight that would be… rolling along with no breath or body, fading to nothing as the blood ran out of me…*

Balthazar examined the faces of the Judean soldiers closest to him, felt the binds on his wrists with the tips of his fingers, smelled the desert air. He looked at the sand beneath his feet and the sky above his head, taking it all in. Relishing it. Here it was, the sum of his twenty-six years. He would die on his knees in Bethel—or "Beit El." Or whatever the hell they called it. His blood would run into the dirt. The soldiers would spit on his corpse, hack it to pieces, and leave it to the dogs. And that would be that.

Lesser men would've prayed at a moment like this. Would've begged God's forgiveness as they were confronted by his imminent judgment. Balthazar took comfort in the fact that even now, he felt no such compulsion. Even now, in the final seconds of his life, he stood firm. And while he couldn't help the fact that his heart was pounding harder than it ever had—*which will make the blood shoot higher from my headless neck and hopefully right into this captain's face*—he refused to give his executioners the satisfaction of seeing him squirm.

What's this?

Balthazar was suddenly confronted by a vision. A sea of stars dancing before him.

It had already happened.

Here he'd been, wondering about what it would be like when his head was cut off, and he'd missed the actual moment. The world narrowing, darkening into a single, distant point. Somewhere, far away—where the winds blew cool and the naked women bathed—he felt a sharp pain wash over him. And he could see something in that distant light, something moving. It was hard to make out, but yes, there was definitely something there. A man. A man leading an animal through the desert…a woman on its back…

So…this is what it's like to die. Funny…men spend so much effort, so much anxiety trying to avoid this moment. But really, when it's all said and done, dying isn't so bad. In fact, it's kind of…

The soldiers watched Balthazar slump forward, then fall to the ground, his blood running into the dirt. Peter examined the blunt handle of the sword he'd bludgeoned him with, making sure it hadn't been soiled by flecks of blood or tufts of hair, then returned it to its sheath. He'd given the Antioch Ghost a ferocious whack on the skull, and it'd done the trick.

Balthazar was out cold.

Decimus had ordered the thief executed on the spot, his head brought back to Tel Arad to be displayed as a warning. And as much as Peter would've enjoyed that—

as much as he would've liked to behead this piece of filth for slaughtering his men and making him spend an entire day in the desert—he had orders to take the Antioch Ghost alive.

And those orders came from a power higher than a Roman governor.